REBELS:
CITY OF INDRA

KENDALL JENNER
KYLIE JENNER
AND
ELIZABETH KILLMOND-ROMAN
with MAYA SLOAN

REBELS:
CITY OF INDRA

THE STORY OF LEX AND LIVIA

HUNTER

Gallery Books   Karen Hunter Publishing

New York   London   Toronto   Sydney   New Delhi

G

Gallery Books
An Imprint of Simon & Schuster, Inc.
1230 Avenue of the Americas
New York, NY 10020

HUNTER

Karen Hunter Publishing,
A Division of Suitt-Hunter Enterprises, LLC
P.O. Box 692
South Orange, NJ 07079

Copyright © 2014 by Kendall N. Jenner and Kylie K. Jenner and Elizabeth Killmond-Roman

First Karen Hunter Publishing/Gallery Books trade paperback edition November 2016

GALLERY BOOKS and colophon are registered trademarks of Simon & Schuster, Inc.

For information about special discounts for bulk purchases, please contact Simon & Schuster Special Sales at 1-866-506-1949 or business@simonandschuster.com.

The Simon & Schuster Speakers Bureau can bring authors to your live event. For more information or to book an event contact the Simon & Schuster Speakers Bureau at 1-866-248-3049 or visit our website at www.simonspeakers.com.

Interior design by Akasha Archer

Manufactured in the United States of America

10 9 8 7 6 5 4 3 2 1

The Library of Congress has cataloged the hardcover edition as follows:

Jenner, Kendall Nicole.
 Rebels, city of Indra : the story of Lex and Livia / Kendall Jenner, Kylie Jenner ; with Elizabeth Killmond-Roman and Maya Sloan.
    pages cm.— (City of Indra ; 1)
 I. Jenner, Kylie. II. Elizabeth Killmond-Roman. III. Maya Sloan. IV. Title.
 PS3610.E557R43 2014
 813'.6—dc23
                    2014014071

ISBN 978-1-4516-9442-0
ISBN 978-1-4516-9455-0 (pbk)
ISBN 978-1-4516-9454-3 (ebook)

"To our fans, your support means the world to us! You are the best!"

PROLOGUE

The light broke through the surface.

Twenty feet tall and armed with bits the size of a man, the drill engines had been running continuously. Andru read the depth sensors and knew that the end was nearly in sight. Already his crew had broken two more drill bits as they clawed their way upward, covered in dirt and ash and dust and clay. The last two engines carried on, alternating running times to stave off overheating. Even this close, closer than any had been in the thousand years since the world went dark, the heat pooled and sweltered. Andru oversaw the engines' running when his team needed rest. He found that he had no need for sleep. It had been five days since he last laid his head down, and it remained that way no more than an hour. He'd been woken by a breeze, fresh air traveling through an unseen vent. The first taste of fresh air in his life. He'd lived beneath the Earth for too long. He would wait no longer.

His crew were loyalists, committed men who'd left their families to give them better lives. None of them had ever met anyone who'd survived the Great Catastrophe, and they were no longer sure just how long they were supposed to live beneath the crust, without questioning the world that could be reclaimed above. Generations and generations had carved out communities beneath the Earth and grown pale and weak-sighted. Generations upon generations had inherited the conditions wrought by the Great Catastrophe and the evils it had created. Humanity had been left behind, and there was no longer hope. Even the tales of former Earth lost their wonder. Andru was not like the rest.

Once he'd salvaged and repaired the engines for his expedition, Andru petitioned the council to arm and feed his men. They gave him enough to gamble on the dream he sold, but not nearly enough to truly believe in it. Even his brother had tried warning him off his journey, but Andru couldn't quit his stubbornness. And that is why he also left his wife and son and daughter behind, promising to come back when he finally had sky overhead. He wrapped them in his arms and kissed them all good-bye, then left to assemble his men. Most thought his pursuit of the overworld mortally foolish, but Andru thought the same of their willingness to war with each other, splintered factions fighting over dwindling supplies and inhabitable caverns. They would continue killing each other down below until none were left.

The drill engine pounded at the stone, and Andru persisted through its unrelenting assault. The light overhead was no more than the size of a fist and yet it was glorious, though it hurt his eyes. He pulled his goggles on and watched to his satisfaction as it grew larger.

Many of his men had died along the way. From cave-ins and blasting explosions. From toxic exposure to unknown elements and collapsing lungs and vicious attacks from what had once been their own people. Andru was not without blood on his hands.

Sacrifice.

Each man had agreed to his part, knowing that their pilgrimage to the world beyond afforded a better life than what below could ever give. Sacrifice themselves and reclaim the ruined land for a new future.

He heard the rock fracture and crack and his men yell as it fell upon the drill engine. Its operator was killed instantly. The light grew brighter. He couldn't allow his men's faith in him to falter.

He stepped up and manned the last remaining engine himself. If more were to die, then he would be next.

He had taken but a mere moment's rest, still seated in the running engine. He wiped the sleep from his eyes, touching the beard that had grown so wildly that his own wife wouldn't recognize him. Thoughts of her and his children kept him sane. Had it been a year since he last saw them? No. Not that much. It couldn't have been. . . .

He drank enough to wet his mouth and wash the grit from it when one of the spotters came running.

For him to have deserted his post . . . something was terribly wrong.

As the spotter came closer, Andru could see blood streaming from his face, and even worse, an eye missing. His shouts were unintelligible and panicked.

Andru hopped down, the engine still firing into the world above. He waved one of his men in to replace him, even as wild calls rose from the darkness beyond the camp.

"Gear up!" Andru shouted. They'd escaped being attacked since the surface had been broken, and he'd hoped . . .

His hope was foolish. He could show them only through action that testing his might was immensely foolish.

There were almost two dozen of his crew remaining, minus the spotter with the savaged eye. In their hands they held metal bars and pikes. Andru hefted his sledge in two hands. It was still stained with the blood of the last pack who'd thought his men would be easily broken.

Did they not know that his men had broken Earth itself?

And yet, they weren't prepared for the force of men who flooded their camp, perhaps three, even four times the size of his crew. It just meant more for his sledge, which he swung now with unmatched resolve and felt a man's skull give way.

Yet these men who attacked were not savages, or mutants, marred by pollution and interbreeding.

"Atros?"

He saw the man who he once called brother knife a grunt of no more than sixteen cycles. More of his men died around him, as Andru continued to swing his sledge, breaking bone whenever it landed. His arms cried through the strain. The drill engine hammered away.

By the time Atros and his men took the camp, they'd left only three men alive, but wounded. All three would surely die. None could remain to remember the truth of the attack. Andru was forced to kneel at Atros's feet. The drill engine was now silent, its operator killed in his chair.

"Why?" Andru asked, his mind reeling, betrayed by his own people. His own brother.

"The world will not be yours," Atros said. "It will be greater than that. Know that your journey was not in vain. Your plans will continue, but you will not see them through."

And then, looking into his brother's eyes, Andru was killed, a knife passed across his throat, and he slumped over as the life left his body and soaked into the earth. He cast his eyes upward with the last of his energy at the broken ground, a gust passing through it to cool his face, and finally he saw the sky and the hard-won heavens above.

CHAPTER 1

Countdown to Emergence Ball: Day Before

Livia

I'm breaking the rules, and I absolutely refuse to care.

Veda gallops through the floating gardens and whinnies ecstatically as we pass the last of the designated security posts. Each gallop takes us farther and farther away from the main quarters, and closer to where the island ends and the clouds begin.

For a moment, I forget I'm virtually a prisoner. I can leave this island, but not unsupervised. And even then, there is little I'm allowed to see, especially what lies below.

Back in the main quarters, Governess will go to wake me from my rest. She'll be displeased at my unexpected absence, to say the least, with so many tasks yet to be done: final gown mods, vitamin injections, rosebud cheek infusions, last-minute blemish inspection and evulsion.

Then there is practice. There is *always* practice.

The curtsy: low, but not unladylike. The conversation: pleasant, but not probing.

There are fan drills to rehearse. The art of fan communication is delicate, this I've been endlessly taught. An incorrect flick of the wrist, a hereafter with a man I despise.

Expand the fan wide to indicate interest. Tap his shoulder to flirt. Right hand: *I am available.* Smack closed: *I daresay we are incompatible.*

I plan on using that last one a great deal.

The guest list must be memorized, ranked in order of importance. There are more insults to perfect, not to mention an inhuman amount of grooming.

Tomorrow is the most important day of my life, after all. I've been told it so much I'm starting to believe it and fear it.

"Keep going," I tell Veda. The rhythmic thumps of her hooves grow faster. A frenzied, unrestrained drumbeat.

My mother loved music just as I do. She spent entire days on her air harp, her fingers dancing along its cords, weaving songs while painting her studio with colorful beams of light.

My mother, according to Governess, was a charming conversationalist and graceful dancer. Governess tells me all about my mother, and she often repeats herself. There is only so much to tell. Only so many stories. I know that she designed her own formal wear, and enjoyed berries and chocolate after dining. That she favored the color blue, and wore one long braid down her back unless the occasion dictated a more formal updo.

I know a great deal about my mother, and yet nothing at all.

A sudden rush of cold smacks me across the face, the air off the clouds growing stronger. "Faster," I tell Veda. I pass the hedge maze and Tranquillity Pastures. Roar underneath the welcoming gate.

Not that anyone is really welcome. Not to Helix Island.

I want to go faster than I ever have. Farther than I ever thought possible.

Now, Governess will have gone from displeased to frantic. This is worse than skipping penmanship, worse than rolling my eyes when one of the debutees expresses her unfortunate opinion during Etiquette Training.

"Why can't you just try?" asks Governess when I'm reported for impropriety. "Can't you put forth the tiniest bit of effort?"

What she will never understand: *not* saying those things takes *a lot* of effort.

This is the farthest I have gone without a chaperone. Beneath me, Veda snorts with elation, and fear. "Don't be afraid, girl," I say. I hold my own fear tight, letting it surge through my body and push me farther.

When I'm found, Waslo will be informed. He is sure to engage me in a Discussion. Waslo Souture was my father's protégé. My father had friends as well, though I haven't met any. They have good reason to keep their distance from the legacy he left behind.

I can't imagine Waslo was ever a friend to my father. A most talented student, I can't deny, for his ascent into the Independent High Council is praiseworthy. *If* that's the sort of thing you'd like to do with your life.

Waslo has been around for as long as I can remember. There have also been Discussions as long as I remember.

Perhaps he will choose "Respect for the Family Name" or "Appropriate Behavior as a Reflection of Upbringing." Those *classics* I have committed to memory. Waslo grows especially passionate nearing the end of "Appropriate Behavior"; sometimes even a little spittle catches on his bottom lip.

No, those are not suitable enough. Not for an offense this bold. For this, he will choose "Being a Proper Young Woman."

"A Proper Young Woman would never dishonor her legacy in such an inappropriate manner," he will say. "And on the eve of your Emergence Ball, at that! What would your father think?"

I wish I knew, I will think but never dream of saying. Instead, I will stay silent, head bowed in shame, waiting for him to finish. Hoping his spit doesn't find purchase farther than his thin lips.

I will feel inadequate, just as he intended. Perhaps this is why

Waslo is so important: he has a gift for making others feel unsatisfactory.

This will be our last Discussion, I suppose. In a few hours, I will reach my seventeenth year of life. Tomorrow is my Emergence Ball; within the week I will have a cohabitant. Shortly after, I will be relocated to my cohabitant's island or, as is done in some cases, he will come to live on Helix. And then we will officially, as *The Book of Indra* tells us, "embark upon the journey of becoming Proper Cohabitated Citizens of Indrithian Society."

Waslo shouldn't fret so much; soon I will be someone else's problem.

Strangely enough, the thought makes me laugh, hard enough to shift across Veda's bare back. I can't help but regard my laughter as highly unbecoming. But I do it anyway. I shake the pins from my head, letting my hair fall against my shoulders, allowing the wind to whip it into tangles, and surge forward.

Proper Young Women of the New Indrithian Society are happy to practice elocution and become versed in etiquette. They will memorize flower sonnets, never questioning that real flowers have not existed for centuries. Once flowers even had a scent, like perfume. There were more strains than we have selected to synth.

I'm sure grass must have smelled wonderful as well, not like the synth-fields Veda tramples with each stride. Synth is as close to the former Earth as Indra's finest scientists can replicate, but it will never be truly real. I often wonder if anything is in Indra.

Proper Young Women of the New Indrithian Society understand that penetrating questions are unnecessary. Curiosity is rude. Proper Young Women need not think beyond the gift of each magical Indrithian day: the lovely blooming of the synth-trees, the filtered air, and purified water. "Best not dwell below," the old saying goes. Or as written in *The Book of Indra*, "Unpleasant topics bring about un-pleasant feelings, so why ever broach such subjects?"

I cannot help myself. I want to question everything.

I want to rip off my sashes and shriek like a hellion. I want to roll in the grass and soil my spotless white frock. Nothing is more point-less than a white gown. It's like telling the world you are incapable of interaction.

I'm not normal, I think. *Or, at least, I'm not like anyone else.*

When they find me, Governess will sputter and cry, "Your happiness is my sole reason for existence." Needless to say, I will apologize pro-fusely. I will play at embarrassment, put the fault on my nervousness, willingly submit myself to her itinerary of torture.

Even better? I will pin the blame on heartbreak. "My impending cohabitation means leaving you, dear Governess. You are the closest I have ever had to a mother."

That should quiet her quickly.

Strangely enough, the sentiment is true.

I often wonder how she felt, after all those years of training, for the High Council to assign her to an orphan. An impossibly strange one at that. An odd little girl who, when choosing her leisure pastime as a child, insisted on swordsmanship. Not social dancing or needle-point, as practiced by the highest ranks. I would wager Governess has regretted her assignment every day since.

But doesn't she see the respect with which I hold my zinger? With every slash it *barks*. In the hands of a skilled swordsman, it would weave dangerous melodies. The more adept, the more sophisticated the song. The dissonant chorus of my practice must haunt her wak-ing moments. Can't she imagine the songs it will one day sing?

Raising me cannot have been an easy task, but tomorrow is the day Governess has been planning since my infancy. My birth into the social stratosphere, my official welcome into the realm of Indrithian Citizens of Importance . . . and I am off riding Veda.

My Emergence Ball will be spectacular, and that is all that matters. As for me? I'm more of a gilded centerpiece to be admired. I'm Livia Cosmo, the Orphan Airess. Living, breathing memorial to the great Armand Cosmo. My father was a true Indrithian of Importance.

Before he died. The dead are never as important.

My mother is at his side. I'm the only one who remembers them. And yet, I have no memories of them.

I'm not sad. I never knew them. You cannot miss something you never had in the first place.

Orphans are rare in Upper Indra. In fact, I believe I'm the only one. Life expectancy is long here. Citizens are limited to a single progeny per cohabitation. This is how it has always been: father, mother, and child.

A child on their own? An orphan? Who would look out for such a thing? Who would show it care?

Veda is an anomaly, too. Horses have not existed for centuries, but my father successfully bred them in his labs. The colts were pitch-black, and none survived very long. Only a solitary mare.

Most refer to Veda as white, but they're mistaken. Veda is ivory. And that is altogether different.

No one knows how long she will live, but I do not worry. No one knows what to expect from me either. Veda belonged to my mother, and now she is mine.

And she has never run faster.

What I know: my father was the most famous geneticist of Indra. He worked in the City of Indra, where the Middler population is trained from birth to serve those of us on the Islands. My father had Middlers at his beck and call, perhaps even wiping his backside after a visit to the privy if he so demanded, which I very much hope he did not.

My father was that important.

According to Governess, I'm an Indrithian of Importance as well. I inherited the Armand Cosmo legacy.

Too bad I won't understand a word of it. Life Guide refuses to instruct me in genetics. I excel at every other subject, especially mathematics. I solved proofs and deciphered evolutionary patterns before Life Guide even taught me how. But still, genetics are too advanced, he says.

"But what about the test?" I ask him. "The one the High Council administered when I was little? The results said I have an aptitude for genetics. A gift."

Life Guide pretends not to have heard me. If I persist, he claims that I'm remembering incorrectly.

I have a flawless memory.

"Just like her father!" That is what Waslo exclaimed when he heard the results, my memory is clear. "She is like him," he said, looking down at me with shiny eyes half filled with wonder, half with fear.

I wish to understand the secrets in our cells, the mysteries of the blood that beats within our flesh. We all exist as one, but forever apart. Did my father even know this? I want to know all that he knew, and more.

Instead, Life Guide and I study Indrithian history, to marvel at our great society and its innovations and advancements.

Mostly we study *The Book of Indra*.

"Best not dwell below," Life Guide cites when I ask a question he wishes not to answer.

What he means: learn what you are told to learn. Close your mouth and memorize a flower sonnet.

Sometimes I think he doesn't know the answers himself.

Sometimes I think "the answers" are all he knows.

◊   ◊   ◊

In my father's time, genetics research was of the utmost importance. Population control, ensuring sufficient air and water supply for every Indrithian. The EX2 pill was his creation. I have taken my daily supplement since I turned twelve, as has every other Proper Young Woman. When I am cohabitated, I will discontinue my daily dosage, conceive my single offspring, and resume my daily EX2 pill after the birth. Except for the small human creature growing within me for nine months, everything will remain exactly the same.

Perhaps it's good we're only allowed one. I can barely manage myself.

Due to my father and the EX2 pill, the population is suitably controlled. Indra thrives. Now genetic research and implementation have evolved into something else entirely. Geneticists specialize in enhancements: dimple insertions, skin replenishment, skeletal adjustment. Nothing that changes the world, just your appearance.

Governess begged me to get a chest alteration before the party season. "No need to inflate for the whole evening," she confided. "Only your debut entrance. And perhaps for the formal dinner."

I refused again and again, and she would sigh dramatically, whole body crumpling as though I had stabbed her with my zinger. Governess believes in enhancements with the same intensity she believes in perfectly tied waist sashes. Her own face ceased changing when she began her yearly visits to the Rejuvenation Island Clinic. You could not discern her age unless you noticed the dullness in her eyes. She has yet to have the sparkle put back in, which is a very painful procedure.

Up here in the upmost of Upper Levels, we have everything we could possibly want for, according to Governess, who never fails to want for an opinion. Unfortunately, this doesn't include an actual person with whom I can have an actual conversation.

Life Guide doesn't count. Master comes once a week to oversee my swordsmanship, and he doesn't count either.

I have never visited the City of Indra, and the only Middlers I know are the maids appointed to scour the endless white surfaces of the main quarters, and the garden crew that reprograms the synth-trees to bloom for new seasons. Their leaves are gold and red and orange now.

Last year Governess chose white blossoms. I thought much the same of them as of my white dress. This year they grew apples. They look far better than they taste.

Veda neighs nervously. I'm getting closer to the edge. "Keep going, girl," I tell her.

My Emergence Ball will be the biggest of the season. Everyone will be there, desperate to see Helix Island up close. Desperate to see my inadequacy up close as well.

And the Proper Young Men of Indrithian Society? They will line up to cohabitate with the Cosmo Airess. I will be forced to pick one of them—that's how it's done. That's how it's always been done.

The air grows chilly. The clouds draw closer.

Veda comes to a sudden halt. We've reached the edge. Nowhere else to go.

I gaze up at the dome that keeps us all protected. It is far above and faint, but I'm always aware of it. It is what keeps us from burning with radiation.

I gaze down. The floating islands glide through the clouds beneath me, caught in their predictable orbits. They're beautiful from afar—you can almost imagine each is a slice of paradise, but must paradise feel so limited? For a moment, in the space between, I see the bottomless City of Indra, the twin towers of the High Council rising above all others. There is so much glass that it's hard to look at directly, the way it refracts the sun's light. It all looks as if it could be broken so easily, yet it has stood for centuries.

Behold Indra: city of impossible architecture, her beauty timeless, her secrets dark. Whose mind dreamed her to life?

For a split second, I imagine leaping into the sky and falling into the endless, unknown Indrithian void. Past one of the construction rigs, the crew of Hubbers astonished at my falling form, distracting them from island maintenance for a mere moment. . . .

The feeling I get is exactly like experiencing an Emergence Ball. Falling into an endless, unknown social void. . . .

Veda senses something. She backs us up. I shift her so we face Helix Island. My home, though not for much longer, if everything, unfortunately, goes according to the very well thought out and endlessly practiced plan.

I will return to the main quarters and apologize to Governess. Tomorrow I will open my fan wide and curtsy low but not too low. I shall smile at each of the Proper Young Indrithian Men as though they are the most fascinating Young Men in existence, and then I will choose one with which to spend the rest of my life. At least it's my choice, right?

In that moment, I feel something boiling to the surface of my skin. This part of me I cannot control. This part is not only improper but something far worse. Dangerous.

I give Veda a squeeze with my heels, and we gallop toward an enormous tree. On its branches hang the last of the apples. We're going faster now, the wind blowing through my hair. When we're practically flying, I draw the zinger from the sheath on my back.

I swing as we race, cutting through the air, and the blade releases a few notes.

The sound rises, growing angrier and more distorted. I hold the blade steady, the feedback disrupting the island's well-preserved harmony. I pull myself to standing, balanced upright on Veda as she races forward, just as a burst of melody emerges from my zinger.

Not a song, but closer than I've ever gotten.

In the split second, we race under the tree and I launch into mid-air. I land where I started: sitting safely on Veda's back. Veda halts. As I'm catching my breath, she turns.

Beneath the tree looms a tall figure in white.

Master.

I don't have swordsmanship today. Why's he here?

Is he constantly watching?

Are others?

He bends down, picking up an apple from the ground. He holds it out to me in his open palm, gives it a slight twist. The apple falls into two perfectly cut halves.

"Livia," he says. "We do not damage nature. We do not kill what grows."

"But it isn't real, Master. Nothing here is real."

Excerpted from The Book of Indra, *Chapter VII:*
"The Archives: A Universe of Wonderment"

The Archives are a gift to Indrithian Society. Accessed via wrist implant, entering the Archives can be easily mastered by both child and adult. A fully immersive environment, these Archive experiences range in nature and are entered via access chips.

As for your memory Archives, they are stored on an individualized chip assigned to each Indrithian citizen by the High Council at childhood.

From replications of historical events pre–Great Catastrophe and educational training programs ("simulations") to reduplication of your personal memories, the Archives serve to Educate, Entertain, and Enlighten.

To Access Archives:

- Find a calm, quiet location that is free of distraction. The Archives can be accessed from any location, though many prefer to do so in the comfort of an Archive access center. Archive access centers are located throughout Upper Indra, the City of Indra, and the HCP Hub. (For a complete listing of locations, see appendix LXIV.)
- Administer two quick, firm taps to the wrist to circulate the blood. Insert Archive access chip into left wrist slot.
- Quickly place thumb tip to pulse point.
- Once thumbprint has been matched, DNA activation will be immediate.*
- The length of the simulation is dependent on the Archive accessed. Memories provide the briefest duration, while historical archives can be looped to ensure the most satisfaction with your experience.
- To end an Archive, within the memory or simulation tap your wrist twice to remove the access chip. Upon removal, you will immediately regain consciousness within the safety of your Archive access location.

The Archives: just another example of Indra's greatness!

The Archives: offering a wealth of knowledge, a virtual preservation of your personal history, and hours of fun!**

The Archives: a universe of delight at your fingertip!***

* Your Archive access is monitored by the High Council via thumbprint DNA matching. Your individual Archive access is restricted at their discretion.

** If you attempt to access an Archive the Indra High Council has not made available to you, you will face immediate dismissal from the Archives. This process, also referred to as "flinging," is both shameful and illegal. Repeat offenders will face punishment as dictated by the High Council. In extreme cases, the High Council Archive Commission may choose to give the offending citizen permanent "shadow" status. Shadowed citizens are rendered voiceless and sentenced to wander the Archives for the remainder of their lives. You will know them due to their blank stares and hooded cloaks. Do not interact with them. Shadowed citizens serve as living reminders of the great gifts bestowed on the citizens of Indra, the Archives being among them, and the severe penalty for taking advantage of them.

*** Archive areas and experiences are restricted by and provided at the sole discretion of the High Council. The High Council has the power to alter, modify, and adjust archival simulations. All further matters regarding Archive operations and "shadow" status are restricted by High Council command.

CHAPTER 2

The Orphanage

Lex

There is a story that everyone in the Orphanage knows. It is not about family, hope, or love. It's about genetics. Mutations.

The ones that lurk beneath the Earth, that are cloaked in shadows and hidden within the eaves of the cavernous mantle. Though I have never seen one, they have made orphans of many.

If you listen closely while nestled in your too-small sleeper, you can hear their breathing beyond the security gates. Their bloodcurdling cries, their savage grunts. Each night, at lights-out, we feel we are at their mercy.

That is why twice a year the caretakers round up orphans, no one knows how they choose, in the middle of the night while everyone is asleep. They are forced to walk outside in their bare feet, their slippers left bedside to be reused by someone else. They are taken to a junction and there they wait. How long they wait depends on how hungry the mutations are.

The mutations . . . they can look like anything. The one I imagine has fused eyes and twin mouths that feed into the same throat. Its spine arcs so much it almost breaks through the skin of its back.

Its pupils are the color of mother's milk, and its jaws are powerful enough to snap through bone.

When you're brought to the junction, you're left in the pitch-black. You cry, and every noise frightens you. You don't know yet how to be strong. When they come for you, if they don't eat you immediately, they will take you back to their tribe, far below, to be raised among them. They will put you to work, and your own body will betray you. It will become like theirs. Your legs will crack as they grow into new forms, and if you are pretty, you will lose that, too.

Twice a year the mutations take orphans, gifted to continue our sanctuary here in the bowels of the Earth. At the point where the City of Indra doesn't care what goes on—we are *that* far beneath. There are greater worries.

After all, who's going to miss an orphan?

All I had was my own hyper-crib at the Orphanage, and sometimes even that I had to share. A tiny box on tall legs, stuffed with two hungry babies. It was but one of a dozen in my unit, and but one unit among a dozen others.

The Independent High Council sent Recruiter to the Orphanage twice a year to inspect the new babies born without names. He wandered the rows of identical cribs, serving Indra in its "moral obligation" to its underprivileged. Recruiter came, he looked, and he left. He didn't expect to find anything worthwhile. In fact, he was pretty confident he wouldn't.

If you made it past the crib stage, you were assigned to Infant Surveillance. That wasn't so bad. You're so little, you don't know any different. If you made it a few more years, you got a cot in the Inter-mediate Dormitory.

Now *that* was something else entirely.

During processing, I got a way-too-big uniform. "Room to grow," said Caretaker.

If you got the chance, that is. At the time I didn't know that not all of us do.

Caretaker leaned over and looked at me. She hated me, I could tell. All the caretakers did. Even as an infant, I didn't play by the rules. Made too much noise, used the playthings incorrectly. Led the group in building entire cities with the polyblox, then gleefully clomped the whole structure to pieces. The other kids didn't do things like that. They liked watching me do them, though. Giggled and clapped their hands.

"Destructive tendencies," muttered the caretakers, powerless to punish me, at least not when Recruiter was hanging around.

His uniform wasn't like theirs. It was impeccably clean, his boots unsullied by grime, his collar unyellowed. I thought he was supposed to be special. He could've been my champion.

Recruiter walked the rows, inspecting the quiet babies, the ones whose parents never smiled at them, never sang or bounced them on their knee. All they got were the Caretakers, who didn't hug or kiss or hold your hand. So these babies never learned to emote, their faces completely made of stone. Orphan babies never cry. They rarely make noise at all.

When Recruiter got to me, he stared down into my hyper-crib. His face was enormous and implacable. "There's nothing here," he said, as he had probably said on every inspection at every crib.

I reached out for him and I grabbed the rail instead. I fumbled forward as he walked away. I grabbed the rail with both hands, pull-ing myself up, my doughy legs barely able to support my plump weight. He didn't linger over each crib for too long. I watched him as he worked. There are orphanages all over. I'm sure we looked like nothing more than underdeveloped meat. He finished my row and moved on to the next. Still I watched him, a string of sounds starting to fall out of my mouth. He looked up.

He looked at *me*.

He inspected more cribs. I pushed my body over the lip of the crib and let gravity do the rest. I pushed to a wobbly stand and edged around the crib, guiding myself by the rails. More sounds that this time he ignored. I slapped the rail with one hand of pudgy fingers. He looked up again, annoyed. I returned his gaze with equal force. He looked around, as if unsure that this was really happening. He cut back to my crib and stared at me standing there. Then he pushed me down. A slight touch and he sent me back on my bottom. Perhaps he expected me to cry. When I didn't, he walked away.

I fell onto my side and rolled onto my belly. As he continued his rounds, I stood again. I slapped the rail until I got his attention. He tried to ignore me, shooting glances across the room, but couldn't. He removed his cap and ran a hand through his hair. He sighed.

He came over, and just as he was about to push me again, I spoke. "No," I said.

And he didn't.

I've been telling people "no" ever since.

My memory's good, but not good enough to penetrate the infant haze. Something to do with underdeveloped brains prevents us from remembering those years. But I did manage to snatch my holofile off Recruiter's desk one visit—he's been cursed with a small bladder and doesn't have the influence to get it modded, so his trips to the receptacle were frequent during testing. Recruiter would have taken it with him, but how did he know I could read? I didn't even know myself.

I was only three. He hadn't administered that test yet.

The holofile seemed to be no more than a toy. A toy that burst with sculpted light as soon as I opened it, casting forth images of me turning in circles. My tiny body, my little-kid legs. Is that what I looked like?

Watching myself during an activity unit, where I was made to hit targets with zip balls. They monitored my heartbeat with sensors all over my body and asked me questions like, "Do you enjoy pain?"

"No."

"What do you dream about?"

"I don't know."

"Why do you hate the polyblox?"

"I love them," I said excitedly. "Especially the part where I smash them!"

Recruiter's assessment of me trailed beneath: "Early rebellious tendencies. Accelerated, aggressive reflexes. Correctly channeled, SUBJECT could prove Useful to Society. Unheard of development considering her status as Offspring Waste."

Reading this, I'm surprised I hadn't been thrown out the gates to mutants.

The Caretaker looked at her holofile, then back at me. "You already have a name," she said, surprised. "How very *odd*. I've never seen one of you already having a name. Who gave it to you?"

"I don't know," I said.

Later, I'd find out they didn't assign names until we'd assimilated from Infant Surveillance to Intermediate Dorm. Never knew how we'd react to the dorm transition. Some didn't make it through the first night, so why waste a good name on a defective orphan?

"Well, you always were . . . different," she said, like I had an extra foot or something. "Now you are Lexie. Say it after me. Lex-ie."

"Lex," I said. That sounded better.

"No. Lex-*ie*. That's what it says right here."

"Lex," I said again.

She sighed, knew it was pointless to argue. She practically shoved me down the corridor to be issued my thermasheets. Relieved to see me go, I could tell. Now I'd be someone else's problem.

Lex or Lexie, it didn't matter. No one learned names in the Intermediate Dorm. The closest you got to existing was your cot number.

My real new name? 242.

The dorm was enormous. Cots as far as you could see. Lots of kids, all bigger than us new transfers. All wearing the same gray uniforms on their skinny bodies, their skin colorless from lack of exposure.

No one noticed our arrival.

Even with all those kids, the dorm was dead quiet. We were still little, didn't know orphan rule #1: *Don't draw attention*. Not that I followed rules. But still, I could tell this place wasn't like Infant Surveillance. Not at all.

Orphan rule #2: *Don't ask questions*. I could never get that one either.

It was the first week and 241 had been right next to me at evening cot confinement. I'd heard her snoring. Come morning, every trace of her was gone, even her thermasheets. "Where'd she go?" I yelled.

No one answered me. Just looked away. "New transfer," someone whispered.

"Where'd she go?" I said louder. Sharp stares. Pale faces pinched in worry.

That just made me want to scream. I raised my voice. "Where'd she—"

"Shhhhhhhh." Someone placed a hand on my shoulder. An older girl was leaning over, smiling at me. I'd noticed her before because, unlike the rest of us, she had some color. Like she was glowing from the inside.

The older girl looked down at me. I shut up. Her smile was what did it. You didn't see those very often.

"I like you," she said softly. "You say what you think. But right now, you should know when that becomes dangerous."

"But where did—"

My stomach growled.

"You're hungry?" she asked.

I nodded. Little kids, I quickly learned, got pummeled in the rush to the ration line. As hard as I'd pushed through the crowd, the food was gone when I got there. With so few caretakers, no one seemed to notice. Or maybe they just didn't care.

Sometimes little kids starved to death. It happened once in my first year there, a little boy who didn't wake up in the morning, and caretakers just carted away the husk of his weightless body.

So that morning the older girl took my hand and led me right to the front of the line, other kids stepping aside for her. I was starving and by then completely forgot about my neighbor's empty cot. Kids are dumb like that. Easily distracted. Maybe she did it on purpose. Maybe she didn't want to tell me about 241 just yet. The older girl was eleven, a year shy of graduating. When you made it to eleven, other orphans respected you because you were a survivor. You might actually make it out. You could teach them how to do the same.

The older girl's name, she told me later, was Samantha. "But don't tell anyone I told you, Lex," she whispered. "That'll be our secret. You call me 374 and I'll call you 242 and only we will know the truth."

Samantha, I'd thought, grinning. I loved having a secret, and I kept it. I never said her real name aloud, not once.

374 watched out for me. I never knew why she chose me, but she did. In exchange, she got little 242 shadowing her every move. She didn't seem to mind taking care of me. Those first weeks were scary, and she'd

sneak to my cot and hold my hand and keep me from slipping away in the dark. No polyblox empires here, no other kids clapping at my antics. Without 374, I'd have disappeared. Maybe even to the mutants.

She made sure I got fed. Made sure I washed my face at grooming. Even showed me how to sleep with my sanibrush and day uniform lodged under my body so no one would steal them in the night.

No one ever bothered me with 374 around. "Just do everything like you mean it," she told me. "And no one will ask questions."

She should have picked another kid. I was always doing everything wrong. Just stay quiet, that's all that was required of me. I couldn't keep my mouth shut.

"She's gonna bottom out," the others whispered, staring at me.

I got written up again and again.

One night 374 was braiding my hair before evening confinement. "You're the only one who can make my hair listen," I told her. She smiled at that. Unlike me, she kept silent until recreation.

"What's 'bottom out'?" I asked.

Her hands stopped moving in my hair. She sighed before braiding again. "Bottoming out is when you go away and never come back," she said quietly.

"Like turning twelve?"

"Not exactly."

"Like 241?"

"Yes," she said. "Like 241. When you bottom out, that means the Orphanage decides to kick you out."

"Where do they take you?"

"I'm not sure," she said. She was working my hair more quickly now and pulling harder.

"But why . . . *ow!*"

"Sorry," she said, easing up. She turned me around so I was facing her and leaned in close. "I won't lie to you, 242. I already know you can keep a secret."

I nodded. *Lex and Samantha*, I thought.

"No one knows exactly where they take you, but probably the Lower Levels. The lowest, to be exact. Rock Bottom."

"Like the stories. Of the mutations."

"Don't listen to the stories. Rock Bottom's where they find most of us, you know. Bring us here to see if we're worth anything. And if we aren't, they just send us back." This was a big secret, I could tell. Bigger even than our real names. "Rock Bottom isn't a nice place, either. I can still remember it. Orphans sent back there won't last long. They don't have the skills or strength."

"That isn't right!" I squealed, horrified. "That doesn't make any—"

She put her hand over my mouth. "Of course it isn't," she said calmly. "But you can't change it by complaining."

"Then how?"

She smiled at me. "Someday we'll talk about that, but not today. I'm afraid your hair needs to listen more."

Gently, she turned me back around to finish my hair. I had a million questions, but I knew not to ask. There was a long silence. The repetitive motion of her hands calmed me. At least for a few minutes. In the end, I couldn't help myself.

"Why do they take some of us and not others?" I said, trying to keep my voice as calm and quiet as hers.

"Lots of reasons."

"What about 241?"

"The freckles, maybe. Those spots on her face. They didn't like them."

I didn't understand, but I nodded anyway. I liked the spots. No one else had them. I'd thought 241 had gotten lucky to be so different.

Genetic flaw was a term I wouldn't know the meaning of until I was much older.

"You have the most amazing eyes," Samantha said then. "Like none I've ever seen."

I had never noticed. Though I would spend time later on searching out just what had made her say that.

"But what if they take me?" I asked.

"They won't," she said firmly. "I promise."

"How do you know?"

"Because, 242, you're special."

I smiled to myself. "And they'll never take you either," I said. "'Cause you're special too."

I really believed that. There was no one else like 374. She could cut the ration line and braid hair and everyone respected her. She and I would be fine.

She didn't say anything, just finished braiding.

But being special doesn't mean you aren't a dumb kid sometimes.

Sometimes 374 would disappear for hours. When I asked where she'd been, she just smiled. "You know I can keep a secret," I told her.

"But if I gave them all to you, you'd burst."

"Nuh-uh."

"Someday I'll tell you. I promise."

It was a promise she wouldn't keep.

My eyes popped open right before the official arise sensor. At wake-up, I liked to run over and stare at her until her eyes flickered open. "Oh, hi, 242," she'd say sleepily. She'd yawn and tell me my hair looked crazy.

But on one morning, her cot was empty. In her place, a cleansing machine hummed, blowing the cot with a steady stream of antisepticizer. No matter how many times she reminded me that when she turned twelve she'd be gone, I was still shocked. I could barely move from her bedside. An orphan with stringy blond hair tapped me on the shoulder.

"I know where she went," she said, even though she'd never spoken to me before. None of them had.

"She graduated," I said.

"No, she didn't."

"She was twelve," I said, fighting back a sob. "She graduated."

"No, she was still eleven," she spit back. "She was bottomed out."

"That's a lie!"

"No, it's not. We came in the same day. She wouldn't leave before me. Everyone knows it."

I looked around. Kids were pretending not to listen to us. "Well?" I said to them. No one answered, of course. "Is that true?" I said louder. Pale faces pinched even tighter. One girl looked up and gave me a tiny nod before just as quickly looking away.

"Liar."

"Believe what you want," said the one with stringy hair. "But I heard Caretaker say it. Probably happened 'cause of you. 'Cause she spent time with you. And you're bad. Probably happened 'cause you get written up so much, and they figured she was the same." Then she smugly smiles at me.

I knew another write-up wouldn't matter, so I finished our conversation with my fists.

She lost a tooth, and I won another write-up. But I was right: it didn't matter. I was still alone.

My own turning twelve was so far away, and 374—Samantha— created an absence I couldn't replace.

That night I cried, feeling more alone in my cot than I had ever been, fighting to stay silent so no one could hear my shame. I was still here, stuck, and I cried for the first and last time, overwhelmed by years of abuse for no reason other than being born into misfortune, and blessed with the knowledge that it was on me to make my life better. To become what I wanted to be. I made a promise to myself, one that I would die before breaking: *I won't need anyone else. Not ever.*

Not ever, ever, ever.

CHAPTER 3

Countdown to Emergence Ball: 10 Years

Livia

"She must be initiated into society," Waslo said, as though I couldn't hear him. As though I wasn't right across from him, lifting spoonfuls of pudding from the bowl in front of me, catching every word.

He had yet to realize the extent of my capabilities, I suppose. To Waslo, I appeared to be a normal child. However, I understood more than he could possibly know, and my memory was sharp enough to recall the smallest incidents.

I had yet to understand this could be used in my favor.

Though as much as I disliked Waslo, without him, there would be no Marius.

She is perhaps the loveliest woman I have ever seen. Most others agree she is fetching, though are quick to add a hushed "despite the obvious misfortune."

Marius is a mere five foot two, a burden for which most In-drithian women would be utterly devastated. Had they not reached five foot eight by age thirteen, they would have already partaken of every alteration available. They would have sought out Rejuvenation Island for stretching treatments, subsisted on genetic cocktails, and willingly traded a finger for a few added inches. Though I am tall,

Marius has taught me that height is not everything. Even Governess, who by comparison is gargantuan, once told me Marius is rather brave. Marius needs not her pitying admiration, or anyone else's, to accept her genetics. Perhaps she sees things differently from such a low perspective.

Marius is beloved by all, myself included. I often wish Marius lived with me and not on another island.

When I was little, I once asked her if she might relocate to Helix. "Please!" I whined. "We have plenty of room!"

To this, she simply laughed. "Well, in that case, I would have to bring Waslo with me."

I didn't ask again.

Unlike with Veda or Governess or even Marius, though, I was incapable of reading Waslo's feelings. I found this especially frustrating: my ability to read others filled me with confidence. Though I didn't speak much, I could feel what the people around me were going through. The boredom of a maid as she scrubbed down a corridor, the excitement of a gardener as he programmed new flowers in the orchard. In this way, I was never truly alone.

Yet despite my best efforts, Waslo emoted less than a synth-tree. For this reason, I scrutinized his every last gesture.

"Soon she must enter the rest of Indra," he continued.

"But it is rather early for all this, dear," responded Marius. "She is very young." She moved toward me and gently pushed the hair off my forehead. I smiled up at her. I loved Marius. She was little, just as I was, and always kind to me.

"Perhaps not young enough," said Waslo. "She is seven now. People wonder."

"Let them wonder," said Marius, though I felt her hesitation.

"That is not an adequate solution, my dear. At some point, she must know Indra as we do. I must speak to Governess first, of course. Affirm the necessity of proper discipline. The child has been given too much freedom here, which will make the transition even more trying. I find it worrying how she will appear to others."

"I, on the other hand, worry about *her*," said Marius. I took another mouthful of pudding. Waslo put a hand to her chin and gently turned her face toward his own.

"I know you worry, dear," he said softly, "as do I. But we have obligations, do we not?"

Marius nodded. Waslo's face changed suddenly, the hardness fading away. He smiled at her, eyes glistening in a way I found especially unnerving.

"My charming little thing," he said. Then he put his lips to hers.

I'd thought such tenderness was not in Waslo's character. And to others, it wasn't. Soon after, his voice became gruffer when addressing Governess. "Must she dress like this?" he asked, noticing my stained smock and muddy bloomers. Governess acquiesced and forced me into a frilly frock that pinched in strange places. "Have you not groomed her hair?" Waslo would say, and soon after Governess would be drawing screams from my throat with each pull through my tangles.

I began to understand: when Waslo came calling, misfortune soon followed.

I would hide when the maid announced his arrival. In the end, Marius would find me, for which I would be grateful. As much as I disliked Waslo, missing Marius's visits would have been devastating.

Waslo and Marius might live on another island, but they visited Helix often. It seemed unfair, I thought, that they must be taken as a pair.

To cohabitate, I decided, meant spending all your time with someone awful.

"There you are!" Marius would squeal, kneeling low enough to see me underneath the desk in Father's study or buried under the fringed pillows at the base of Mother's air harp. "Found you, my little firefly!" She would open her arms and I would crawl into the warmth of her embrace.

She was well aware, I suppose, of my locations: the places I felt safest were the ones that had belonged to them.

Mother and Father. Governess used the words often, yet never explained their significance. Terms as familiar to me as my left and right foot, yet as foreign as the world beyond Helix. They were mysterious strangers, like characters in a make-believe. They had lived here on Helix Island, and now they didn't. They were connected to me, yet somehow not.

And yet, their rooms remained untouched shrines. As though they would return at any moment, Father to revisit his most recent deductions, Mother to compose a new aria.

Marius would never be angry when she discovered me, only wrinkle her nose at my misbehavior. Even her chiding was playful. "You mustn't run off like that, or perhaps one day we will not be able to find you."

"You will always find me!" I would squeal.

"My love, what will we do with you?"

In the end, Waslo would be the one to answer that question. And his solution would be far worse than new frocks and tangles.

I was going somewhere special. That is what Governess had told me that morning.

I was excited. Not excited enough to overlook being pinched in all the wrong places, though.

"But why must I?" I asked.

"Because all the other girls will have dresses as pretty as these."

"But why should I look like everyone else?"

Governess didn't answer, just kept buttoning. There were so

many buttons running up my back, each tiny and difficult to fasten. I'd come to believe she might never finish and I would stand in this same spot until I grew up, the unfastened buttons popping off on their own accord as my body grew bigger.

"There," she said, finally finishing the last. Together we looked in the mirror.

I hated what I saw.

A pale pink frock to my knees, layers of fabric lifting the skirt until it rose in a stiff circle around me. Ribbons winding around the entire horrible costume, their ends tied into elaborate bows, as though to keep me escaping my own body.

"Lovely," said Governess.

"Yuck."

Still, I couldn't conceal my smile. I was going on *a journey*. This is what Marius had patiently explained. I would meet other girls my age and learn all sorts of fascinating things and no, I could not bring Veda, but she would be right there waiting upon my evening return.

Governess kneeled in front of me, overseeing the final adjustments. Tightening every inch of me. I sensed her sudden worry and reached out to touch her cheek.

"Why are you sad, Governess?"

"I am not sad."

"Yes, you are."

Gently, she removed my hand from her face. "Livia, it is not proper to touch Governess in this manner."

"What manner?"

"As though . . . she is your friend."

I wrinkled my nose. I had always touched Governess. She *was* my friend. A friend who sometimes forced orders upon me that I found rather displeasing—demanding I finish a dish I disliked or go to my sleeper when I hadn't yet finished playing—but still a friend.

For a moment, I thought Governess might cry, something I had never seen her do. Instead, she squeezed my hand, fluffed my ruffles, and stood abruptly.

"Time to go, little one," she said.

Waslo looked me up and down, as he often did, though his reaction was somewhat surprising: he appeared pleased.

"Very good, Governess," he said. "I am glad we had our discussion."

This was long before my own *Discussions* started, yet I already disliked the word.

The three—Marius, Waslo, and Governess—stared down at me in heavy silence, their expressions making me squirm

"The shuttle is ready," said Marius, breaking the quiet. She leaned down, giving me a comforting smile. "Are you ready, my love?"

For the first time, I wasn't quite sure.

The shuttle pod ride was a journey, just as Marius had promised, though one I could have done without. I had never left the island, let alone seen the point where its farthest reaches met the sky.

"You must stay within the designated edges of Helix," Governess often warned. She had shown me the posts stationed near the welcome gate and prohibited me from ever crossing them. She explained I would most likely be injured if I tried to go beyond. "There are traps to protect us from intruders near the edge, Livia. Invisible stinger barriers to deter trespassers. Hidden holes covered in synth-grass, large enough to swallow a tiny girl whole. You would end up at the bottom, alone in the dark, and we might never find you."

"I'm not afraid," I would say defiantly, though I did as I was told back then. I had never liked the dark. When I couldn't see my own hand in front of me, I felt strange, as though I might not even exist.

Now, here I was, detached from the ground where I had spent my entire life. Seeing the sky above Helix was one thing. Flying through it, something else.

I had never been so frightened in my life.

Our air transporter hurtled through the sky, dodging other shuttles and speeding around the edges of islands, my stomach jumping with each turn. I pushed my face against the window, but the view went by too quickly: clouds, blue sky, islands, transporters. The sky was more active when you were in it, not standing on solid ground.

Will we smash into something and explode? I wondered. *Will pieces of us shower the skies?* I pushed my lips together to keep from squealing, wrapping my hand around Marius's wrist and holding tight.

"Do not worry, love," she told me. "I will not let any harm come to you."

My legs were wobbly as I exited the shuttle. Standing on island ground, I wanted to lean over and hug the surface beneath my feet, until I recalled Waslo's final words before boarding the shuttle: *Do not draw attention to yourself, Livia. You must appear to be normal as everyone else. Just do as you are told and remain alert.*

I tried to forget the fear I had felt moments earlier. Now I followed Waslo's advice, my eyes hungrily taking in this new island.

"We are within a group of islands," said Marius, gently leading me forward. "The Education and Socialization Cluster, as they are referred to. This is the tiniest one, suitable for the youngest of trainees. You will start here and eventually progress to each one until your Emergence Ball."

I could see the island's edge from our location, not more than a quick sprint distant, and wondered if there were hidden holes ready to swallow little girls here as well.

This might be an island, but in no way did it resemble my home.

The synth-grass was short and sparse, and the gardens featured traditional white lilies. On Helix, we had strange crossbreeds of roots and flowers. I could feel the garden crew's confusion with our decisions on every visit. Why did we program such strange new growths? Why did we allow the foliage to grow so thick?

I once asked Governess this very question, to which her response was simple: "That is what your mother wanted."

I loved our gardens, my curiosity charged with every garden crew visitation, knowing soon the shocking pink blooms might be replaced by tiny purple buds, or our shiny nuts transformed to exotic, inedible fruits. How could the rest of Indra deny themselves the discovery that overnight, yellow blooms might burst forth from unexpected crevices, or disappear just as quickly?

When Governess made a rare attempt to program something less exotic, the results were never pretty. Hence the bitter-tasting apples.

The Helix gardens were my ever-changing playground, and at that moment, I would have given anything to be back there instead of on this tiny, unremarkable island where the growing things mirrored my unhappiness. Marius led us down a path lined with shrubs aggressively trimmed into stubby cubes and pyramids; I looked at their sharp angles and felt sorry for all who laid eyes on them.

We came to halt in a clearing where a shiny steel building rose to the sky. The light reflected strongly off its facade, obscuring the glowing hololetter sign: Socialization Club.

I had never seen other little girls, as strange as that seems now, and it was like encountering another species. Everything about them made me uncomfortable, from their high, tinkling laughter to their small hands. Not a bow untied or pleat untucked or strand of hair out of place. We all wore the same dress, with the same ribbons woven through our hair. Yet somehow, I knew we were nothing alike.

Silent, tall governesses watched from the edges with stony faces and stiff blue uniforms. These ones wore bulky utility holsters strapped over their broad shoulders, the ones I knew to be packed with emergency components and child-rearing devices, including a stunner that administered a quick, painful shock.

Years earlier Governess had a holster of her own. I'd shocked myself playing with the stunner, but the tears were meaningless when compared to the sparks! The electric blue arc between the prongs! Governess woke to find me streaking the various multicolored antisepticizers across the wall and, in a final touch, burning a constellation of holes across the entire spread with the healing laser.

"Livia!" she bellowed, and I stepped back, grinning, to allow her a better perspective. I remember the surge of pride. *Look at this masterpiece!*

The holster disappeared soon after, and I hadn't seen it again until a few days ago. I'd known something was different when Governess came to collect me for lunch, her footsteps slower and heavier in the hallway. When she appeared, I was greeted by the holster and her unhappy expression, her shoulder stooping under the weight. "Waslo deemed it necessary," she said before I could speak. Then she gave me a knowing look. "And I am sure he will notice if items are missing or misused."

I hadn't wanted to take anything except her pain. I could feel it coming off her in waves. And somehow, I knew the holster was only part of it.

In that moment, I had the distinct feeling everything was about to change.

Now, standing on this tiny, unfamiliar island, I took no pleasure in being correct. Especially without Governess by my side.

"Marius will serve as escort," Waslo said shortly before departure. As usual, he seemed unaware of my presence, though I was right in front of him tapping on the marble floor. I was inventing a song in my head, my feet keeping the rhythm, though I was careful not to miss a word. "Curiosity will be high, of course, but Marius and I do have a certain standing within Indra. Let the reports begin to circulate of our approval and the child's genetic well-being and pleasing manner. Is that agreeable?" He didn't wait for an answer. "Good. But what is causing that racket?"

I stopped tapping. Not for Waslo, but for Governess: the look on her face worried me.

Lately, smiles were less frequent and silence was becoming ordinary. I tried to barrage her with unnecessary questions and pointed out fresh stains as though surprised by them, but nothing got a reaction. I even hid her micro specs, the ones she used for her holoreader and to inspect for errant particles when the maids finished cleaning. She didn't even chastise me, just sighed heavily and said, "The time has come to cease with childish pranks."

One girl in particular caught my eye. A group was gathered tightly around her with adoring faces. When she giggled, they giggled as well. When she spoke, they leaned in close to listen.

"Do not worry," said Marius softly. "Your beauty is far superior to every last one of them. For that alone, they will want to be your friend."

I didn't find this comforting. Even less comforting, the sudden, overwhelming wave of curiosity. The others had taken notice, and I could feel their eyes boring into me.

"Do not look away from me," said Marius, catching my gaze. Her expression was unreadable. And in this face I knew so well, I couldn't help but see her as a stranger.

"You are doing just fine," she continued. "Now I will stop talking, and I want you to say something. Then we will laugh. Not too loud, mind you, but just a little. I go quiet, you speak in a conversational manner, we laugh. Do you understand?"

I nodded. Suddenly, I did understand: Marius was playing a part. Waslo had said she would escort me, so she must be playing at "Escort." Marius even had a costume, trading her usual shimmering

robes for simple beige ones. When I first saw her, I'd worried she
might choke on the tall collar, or that her hair, piled dangerously high
upon her head, might go toppling.

"Now I am done talking," Marius said. "Your turn."

"I do not know what to say," I responded.

To that, she laughed, and I knew it was my time to do the same.
We both laughed at nothing and it occurred to me this journey would
be full of complications and nonsense.

"Very good, Livia," she said. "They have all stopped looking by
now, I am sure, and have been made well aware they cannot unnerve
us. You may relax. Try to abstain from overtly gazing in their direction, I should say. Just for the time being."

I wouldn't be able to help myself, I was sure, and didn't know
in what direction to face. I chose the only safe place that came to
mind.

"Socialization Club," I said, reading the sign above my head.

I'd been able to read since finding a holoreader in Father's study. It
wouldn't be until much later that I discovered the zinger there.

I'd never used a holoreader myself, but I'd observed Governess's
daily reading breaks. I often peeped over her shoulder in anticipation of the tiny men and women who popped off the screen. They
wore elaborate dress and danced across the air in front of Governess. They frolicked through fields and reclined in their chambers,
arms and legs entwined. Sometimes, oddly, they weren't wearing
clothes at all.

"Why are they always napping?" I asked.

Governess started from her chair. "This is *not* for little girls," she
responded, snapping off the holoreader, the light of these little people's lives expiring.

Now I had Father's holoreader, and Governess would never know!

I carefully inserted a cartridge and the screen lit up. This one had no people, only bursts of light racing across the air in front of me. Words. Beautiful, luminous words.

I sounded them out as they skimmed the air, at first with much difficulty, then with growing ease, still not understanding their meanings, when I was interrupted with a gasp. Governess stared at me from the entrance. Her mouth dropped open. "Do not move," she said. "I must send word to Marius and Waslo."

Now I will have a Discussion, I thought sourly, wishing I'd never found the thing in the first place.

Soon after, all three gathered to listen to me recite the words.

"Before Indra, the study of genetics was elementary at best. At their most basic level, genetics are understood to be the traits passed from parent to child. Those early researchers, with their prehistoric notions, could not comprehend our modern Indrithian science, our ability to control and perfect these basic human elements, to choose the most appealing and beneficial, therefore creating a human specimen with the most preferential makeup—"

"Impossible," said Waslo, grabbing the holoreader from my small hands and scanning the screen furiously. He looked at Marius. "Word for word," he said, full of disbelief. "She is not yet four. How could she possibly—"

"Do not forget her heritage," Marius said, smiling at me. "Livia is special. We already knew that."

She made *special* sound like a good thing.

"What is a 'human specimen with the most preferential of makeup'?" I asked.

"You are, my love," said Marius, smiling.

Now, outside the Socialization Club, there was no smile. Here, I decided, being *special* was not a good thing. Between the rules and

Marius's playacting and the frightening ride from Helix, I wished I hadn't come in the first place.

Perhaps she saw my apprehension. Instantly, Marius's old self returned. She leaned over, face very close to mine, eyes wide and voice very low.

"Livia, I need you to promise me something."

I nodded.

"You might be asked to do strange things here. Things you do not always enjoy. But you must not complain or refuse. You must promise to do all that is required, no matter the difficulty, and behave as though every task is simple and pleasing. Above all, my love, you must be a very sweet, good girl, even when you do not feel that way. Do you trust me?"

I nodded. Of course I trusted Marius.

"Then you must promise to try. Will you? For me?"

"Yes," I said fiercely.

I sensed her wanting to reach out and pull me into her embrace. *Please*, I thought, imagining the comfort of her warmth. Instead, she stood abruptly, the "Escort" character returning. "You will be fine," she said, giving me a tiny nod. "Now you must go inside."

Inside, I sat in a circle of girls wearing identical dresses, the only variation being the pastel shade. We sat silently, eyes downcast, and I wondered how I would keep my promise to Marius when I felt like asking, "Why is no one speaking?"

All I really wanted was to run home to Helix—not considering that running was not an option between islands—take off these pinching layers, climb on Veda, and gallop across Tranquillity Pastures fast as I could.

"Welcome, Little Girls of Upper Indra, to your first Socialization Club." As though materializing from empty air, a woman stood at the center of the circle. I had never seen anyone so tall, her body seeming to have been stretched upward. Her face was blank and unreadable, cheekbones high and sharp as blades. "I am Etiquette Tutor," she said. "And that is the only title by which I will be addressed."

The floor beneath her began rising. Once the circular platform was a few feet above us, it began a painfully slow rotation, allowing just enough time for this towering woman to stare at each girl until she was visibly discomforted. In that instant, Etiquette Tutor said the girl's name and moved on to the next.

"Emilia Johnsian," she said. Rotate. Stare. "Tirithia Lysander." Rotate. Stare.

On and on, for what felt like hours. I knew an hour, for this was the time I was forced to lie across my sleeper each day for what Governess referred to as "Rejuvenation." An hour was a very long time, and this felt like several of those.

"Margarite Fredrickus." Rotate. Stare. "Cybele Manius." Rotate. Stare.

Etiquette Tutor had skin smooth as ours, yet pulled tightly across her face, her eyes seeming to protrude, her stare all the more intimidating. Somehow, I knew she was very old, even more so than Governess. I tried not to stare at her, not knowing where else to focus. I fought the urge to fidget in my chair, to twist my frock ties around my fingers, to fill my cheeks with air and tap my fingers. There were so many things I could *not* be doing that, in that moment, they were what I desired to do more than anything else.

I looked at my feet and thought about *not* wiggling them.

I contemplated the possibility of merely wiggling my toes. This would be acceptable, I reasoned, for she could not see through shoes.

How does she know our names? She will not know my name, I thought, wiggling first the left toes and then the right. *For she has never met me. . . .*

"And you . . ."

The words were not loud, yet felt that way. I snapped upright as they reverberated through my body. I looked left and right for the source. Then I remembered.

Slowly, I lifted my chin upward.

Her gaze was penetrating, the prominent eyes giving me the distinct feeling I had no skin on my body. She did not flinch, nor did her focus shift. After a very long time—it felt like ten Rejuvenation naps, at least—she opened her pinched lips.

". . . are Livia Cosmo."

At my name, all the girls looked up from their own toes.

"What is your name?"

"Claudia Quintias," said the girl in pale violet.

"I cannot hear you."

"Claudia Quintias," she said, a tiny bit louder.

"Too loud. A Proper Little Girl of Indra must be heard, yet never offend the ear. Try again."

Claudia's knees shook. Etiquette Tutor moved in steady revolutions around the circle, as though we were locked in a cage and she our keeper.

She moved with grace, appearing to float across the floor. I had the unnerving feeling that, at any moment, she might creep up and shock us with a stunner. In reality, her words were more effective than that.

One by one, each girl mounted the platform for interrogation.

"Why are you standing like that, Nadine? Your knees turned together, back hunched over. Unattractive, to say the very least. A Proper Little Girl stands tall. Is that tall? Now you appear all the more repugnant. We have our work cut out for us, I daresay."

With some girls, this went on for a very long time. For others, the session ended as quickly as it had begun.

"What is your least favorite food, Daphne? Eggplant stew. I see. Your hair is a catastrophe. You may sit."

Immediately following, the dazed subject stumbled off the platform, stifling tears. No one wanted to repeat Cybele's unfortunate mistake.

"Crying is not only inappropriate but entirely unattractive. If you could see yourself, Cybele, you would be as offended as I am. Red-faced and sniveling. And you already will have to try much harder than the other girls, for you do not have the asset of being pleasing to the eye. Are you deaf as well as unappealing? Stop that abhorrent tearful display immediately."

I forced myself to sit still. *Be good*, I told myself, even though the pinched places on my skin were now raw, the tightly wound ribbons leaving my arms and legs numb and tingling. Even more, I needed to relieve myself. I knew I must stifle the urge, though, or be accused of vulgarity for asking to be excused.

You must be very sweet, good girl, I reminded myself, *even when you do not feel that way.*

"Ah. The Cosmo Airess herself."

"I do not know that word," I told her, standing as straight as I could.

"Admitting to ineptitude devalues your appeal. You must never admit to ignorance. The same is true of displaying excessive knowledge, which Proper Young Men find even less appealing. When you do not know a word, you mustn't let anyone know. So, once again. Are you, in fact, the Cosmo Airess?"

I nodded firmly.

"Do not bob your head like a ruffian." She demonstrated a slight, girlish nod. "It is not that difficult, Livia. This is not Genetic Engineering."

I nodded in my slightest, most girlish manner.

"You should not show agreement when there has not been a question. We are not off to a promising start, are we, Livia Cosmo?"

Slight, girlish nod.

"That was a rhetorical question. You are not meant to answer *those*. Do you understand?"

Now I was confused. Should I nod or not?

"Well?" she said.

"Is that a rhetorical question as well?"

"Are you an imbecile?"

This one, I could tell, was not meant to be answered. Besides, I did not know that word either.

"Perhaps you are. Odd, considering the genius of your father."

I was confused. How did she know Father? I opened my mouth to ask, then remembered the little girl in yellow who had displayed excessive curiosity. Within moments, Etiquette Tutor had reduced her to a sniveling mess.

I heard Waslo in my head telling me to be alert. I forced myself to look Etiquette Tutor directly in her bulbous eyes. Now she would know I was listening.

"Stop staring, Livia. Your rudeness is becoming unbearable. Once again: *Are you an imbecile?*"

"I . . . cannot answer."

"And why would that be?"

"I do not know what *imbecile* is or does, so I will be incorrect either way. If I ask for a definition, I will be admitting to ineptitude. If I give you an answer, I will be displaying an overly curious nature. Or perhaps," I say, proud of myself, "that was simply a rhetorical question."

I was delighted with my performance. *See, Marius? Now she knows I am a good girl, the kind who listens!*

Etiquette Tutor went silent. Since the beginning, I had found her as difficult to sense as Waslo. But in that moment, I felt a tiny fissure in her tightly sealed emotions.

Etiquette Tutor didn't understand me, and she found that profoundly disturbing.

Marius's voice echoed in my head: *You must act as though each task is simple and pleasing.*

I lifted my chin, looked Etiquette Tutor in the eyes, and smiled.

Just like that, the fissure cracked wide open. I had never felt someone so strongly.

Etiquette Tutor hated me. I think she had before she even met me.

"You, Livia Cosmo, are far less clever than you believe yourself to be," she said with an almost imperceptible quiver. "You will be a trial, but I will succeed. In due time, I will wipe that knowing expression off your pretty little face, drain the precocious, uncivilized brat right out of you. I will make you a Proper Little Girl. Not an easy task, by and by, but let me be clear: *I never fail.*"

There was a long pause in which my body, damp with perspiration under the many stiff layers, went icy.

"Now, you may sit."

Before the lesson ended, we were instructed to have a Pleasant Interaction. "This is a time to engage your fellow trainees in cordial conversation," Etiquette Tutor explained. "You must learn to entertain and enliven a room under any given scenario. Begin."

We stared at each other, looking shell-shocked and worn, our bodies seeming to droop despite our efforts to stand up straight.

"Now!" barked Etiquette Tutor. Everyone scattered, childlike voices rising before even finding a partner. I scanned the room, but no one would meet my eyes. Everyone had gathered in tiny groups already, voices overlapping and strained.

"Indeed, how lovely!"

"You do not say! How entirely delightful."

"Absolutely charming, I agree."

I had never met children, but couldn't imagine that they all spoke like Waslo. I stood there, both invisible and on display. Surrounded by more people than ever before, yet feeling utterly alone.

"Hello." I was startled to see a girl smiling at me. I knew her immediately: the sole trainee Etiquette Tutor hadn't chosen to demolish, dismissing her without insult after a few simple questions. The girl had glided back to her chair and sat gracefully, her lovely face calm.

She was also the girl I first saw outside, smiling faintly in the center of an adoring circle. Now the smile was aimed at me.

"You are Livia Cosmo," she said. "And I heard you have the most glorious estate in all of Indra! Yet no one has seen it in years, I have heard . . . how very delicious! Oh, you must tell me all about, well . . . *absolutely everything!*" Suddenly, her demeanor changed. She appeared devastated. "Oh, how could I? Livia, you must excuse my dreadful manners!"

She stretched out her hand and waited. After a moment, I understood what she wanted, for me to take her tiny grip in my own. We shook hands.

"I am Mica," she said. "And it is *terribly* lovely to make your acquaintance."

Once Mica had taken me under her wing, the others quickly followed. I was bestowed admittance into her exclusive circle, allowing me to gaze upon her adoringly, often during Pleasant Interaction, an exercise that grew far less pleasant with each passing day.

"Communication among your peers is of the utmost importance," Etiquette Tutor reminded us. "Begin."

Within moments, Mica's admirers gathered, standing elbow to elbow.

"Make room for Livia," she said, and that's all it took. On occasion, I was even invited to the most prime location, twining Mica's arm in mine.

"Livia is strikingly pretty, is she not?" she said to the others. "Yes," they would echo with carefully monitored enthusiasm. "Pretty," I soon learned, was of the utmost value, and Mica surrounded herself with what she found valuable.

The most winsome of us all, of course, was Mica herself. On this we all agreed.

"Yes, and hasn't she the loveliest bloom upon her cheeks?" Mica said, then placed her attentions elsewhere. Mica's questions were all rhetorical.

For the first few sessions, I didn't understand what was expected of me. I made the mistake of laughing too loudly at an amusing anecdote, to which Mica gazed off in embarrassment. On another occasion, I stated an opinion contrary to hers, the circle collapsing into deadly silence until she raised a new topic to discuss. I learned from the error of my ways, deciding it best to speak as infrequently as possible.

I mimicked the others, laughing with their laughter, raising my eyebrows in disbelief the moment one of theirs had lifted. I leaned in close to hear a secret, put my hand to my mouth in shock at their startling revelations.

Fitting in, I realized, was easy. Do as the others do. Act as though you share a brain.

In no time at all, I knew what was expected of me; ultimately, it boiled down to a single requirement.

Requirement: you must listen to Mica's opinion on various topics and express complete, unwavering agreement.

Topic One: Garment Selection and Physical Maintenance

Purple is far more fetching than blue. Curls are more fetching than braids, unless the braids are twisted in a certain manner, and few can achieve the intricacies of this correctly. Best to let your curls fall loosely and be easily admired. Unless you are Cybele, of course, who has been bequeathed locks of an unfortunate disposition. Poor dear.

A Proper Little Girl of Indra has seven dresses at the very least, one being a shade of purple, preferably lilac. If she has made the grave mistake of partaking in yellow, the garment should be disposed of immediately, yellow being fit for only the low-level Middler. "I do not mean you, of course, Claudia. Your dress is lovely. And perfectly suited to your rather unique complexion."

Topic Two: The Superiority of Your Family Estate

"Our sitting room was just installed with the latest in live animatics, seasonal projections! Yesterday we had the most glorious sunset, and tomorrow there will be rain! My father says it happened often before the Great Catastrophe."

Topic Three: The Male Species and What They Prefer

All things Mica, obviously.

Topic Four: The Other Young Girls of Indra

"That one"—and then Mica would point at her chosen—"gave me a rather unwelcoming look yesterday. I wouldn't do such a thing if my nose was an absolute monstrosity. Her family, I hear, is completely devoid of class and manners. A stain upon the Indrithian sky, according to Governess. Needless to say, I find her presence rather unsavory."

To each and every one, I forced an expression of fascination, as did the others, taking little notice of said Chosen Girl, despite her close proximity. More often than not, Chosen Girl appeared devastated. *I am nothing like them*, I wanted to explain, though we would both know that to be untrue.

I was just like them because of my silence.

More often than not, Chosen Girl would be fighting back tears. To which Mica would inevitably say, "She is just making herself look more ridiculous."

I despised Mica.

Even more, I despised the topics.

Above all, I despised myself for following the requirement.

I told myself I had no other options. Follow Mica or risk the danger of being one of her Chosen Girls, and that was a fate I feared not surviving.

I was barely surviving already.

And in truth, I had already been chosen. Etiquette Tutor had seen to that.

CHAPTER 4

The Academy

Lex

On my twelfth birthday, Recruiter entered the dorm after uniform inspection. I hadn't seen him since the year before—his appearance was the only way I could track the passage of years—and it wasn't an emotional reunion.

His outfit that day was the same blue as his work uniform, but with a higher collar, and his brown boots were shined to perfection. The badge on his armband now had a second star.

My contempt for his straight-faced militancy had grown easier to conceal. But today his arrogance lightened his step and a smile almost broke his lips. He looked at me and shook his head as if he couldn't believe I had made it this far.

"Approved," he said to himself.

I followed him without asking questions. Answers were hard to come by and I'd given up playing that game long ago. Since the moment I saw Samantha's empty cot.

I treated everyone around me exactly how I felt about them: like they didn't exist.

It wasn't hard to do. They knew how wild I could get with my fists. They kept their distance. Everyone here already had so little, they couldn't afford to lose their teeth.

I figured the change in Recruiter's disposition was because he was getting rid of me.

Today was my graduation from the Orphanage, if you could call it that. And I was going somewhere, though I wasn't sure where. Most went to the Hub, and the stories of the orphans that went there were passed along the cots before lights-out. A lifetime spent in ration assembly lines and sanitation facilities, only to return to a cramped Hubber barracks with the rest of the unseen and forgotten. Who were deemed uncohabitable and functionally useless. And those were the freaks who hadn't even hit Rock Bottom.

I couldn't keep track of those who bottomed out, there have been too many.

Still, I knew I was headed for something different. I wasn't sure what, but I felt pretty certain change was coming. And that part was kind of exciting.

As we neared the last security gate before the Orphanage's outer walls, Recruiter said, "You'll thank me one day, Lexie."

"Lex," I said. "How's my memory better than yours?"

"Your holofile reports your identity—"

"I don't care what my holofile says! And I'll never thank you. For *anything*."

He raised his eyebrows but didn't respond. For some reason, this weak, desperate man was no better than any of us. He needed *me*! His quality of life depended on just one of us paying off. Guess that's why he overlooked the fact that I was unpredictable and obviously hated his breathing guts. Secretly, I was as proud as he was. But I'd never let him see that.

An all-terrain transporter idled outside the gate. Recruiter flashed the driver his badge, then opened the back door for me. "Didn't you want to say good-bye to anyone?" he said mockingly. I boarded without looking back.

Then we were traveling, the transporter rumbling beyond the Orphanage walls, and I got a rush, a taste of freedom looking back on my former home.

The Orphanage was bright. Flooded by luminators so strong my skin glowed yellow. But beyond the lights there was almost nothing. Was the world really this dark?

My eyes hurt for a moment as they adjusted to the darkness. Only the beamers of our transporter lit our path. Ahead patrol tower spotlights became beacons that kept us on track, the towers themselves isolated and rising through the murky black. Men in bright orange uniforms appeared through the fog, blasters slung over their shoulders, keeping watch on us through their goggles until we were no longer visible to each other. Occasionally another transporter bounced along the rocky surface beside us, beamers cutting through black, and we would swerve to avoid it. I had a million questions. Not that I'd give Recruiter the satisfaction.

"Approved!" he kept saying, then mumbling about promotions and honors and chuckling to himself.

The darkness seemed to go forever in the tunnels. It seemed impossible that anyone could have constructed this network. Then there was light. Faint. Coming closer.

Then blazing.

A huge gate, sizzling with electricity. A sign: PCF ACADEMY.

Underneath the sign: Be Industrious. Be Vigilant. Behave.

Before I could even register the words, I was inside. Recruiter dropped me off at the gate, his smile even greater than before. Here I was, dropped at another set of huge doors, and this monstrosity would've dwarfed ten Orphanages.

We parted without further words. Just like with the transfer processing at the Orphanage, they gave me a uniform. Unlike before, this one fit perfectly.

They gave me new shoes. Real ones instead of pass-me-down slippers.

They gave me a cadet badge. They gave me a sleeper pod.

They gave me Cassina right next door.

Well, you can't get everything.

I'm not sure just why I'm here.

Cadets are hand chosen, the best of the best. Maybe I'm the best of the worst.

To be a cadet, you just need to be born that way. It doesn't matter where you come from. You can be the offspring of Islanders, your childhood spent floating in the air like some Airess, or you could be some Middlers' child. It's not likely, but even a spawn of the lowliest Hub worker might be selected.

"What you have in common," the senior lieutenant says at our initiation, "is that you are the most promising youth Indrithian Society has to offer."

Middlers, Hubbies, Islanders: they all look proud.

No one like me. I'm the only one of my kind.

Cassina is from the Upper Levels. She grew up on her own island. Even at twelve, I knew Cassina's goal: to get me kicked out of the Academy. I'd been assigned pod 13, right next to hers.

"Great!" she'd said, her voice echoing through the cadet quarters. "They put me next to the dirt squirt!"

"What'd you say?" I was standing over my sleeper, for the first time having one my size.

"You're gonna make my pod reek," she said, moving closer. Her thin, venomous lips were pulled into white lines, her nostrils flaring. "You stink like mud, girl. You subbies can't ever wash away *that* stank."

So I punched her. Right across that pointy little chin. Her jaw slammed shut on her tongue and blood fell over her lip. She stumbled back against her sleeper, embarrassment rushing to her cheeks.

Not so tough now, I thought, watching her stumble up to her sleeper, shock turning to hatred. She glared up at me.

"You'll pay . . . *orphan*."

I lunged for her, but someone pulled me back before I could do more damage.

Welcome to the Academy, I thought as the pod captain led me to her office for my first disciplinary meeting of many.

"Not a promising start, Cadet," she'd said, staring at me from behind the shiny metallic desk. She wasn't old, but life belowground had drained her youth, and the blond hair sticking out from beneath her cap was brittle and dry. *I will never be like her*, I thought.

The rage still bubbled within me, my knees shaking.

"I know you come from a unique situation, Cadet Lexie."

"Lex," I said.

She ignored me. "The first recruit via the Orphanage. Unprecedented situation, yes, but let me make this clear: here you are just a cadet. You are just like everyone else."

It was the nicest thing anyone had ever said to me.

However, we both knew it was a lie.

"We have rules," she said, expressionless. "We have procedure. A way of doing things. You are a cadet now, and you have to play by Academy rules. If you plan on staying, that is."

I tried to look like I wasn't still thinking about doing Cassina serious harm.

Mudgirl. Subbies. Dirt. That's what you called someone who wasn't even a person.

I tried to look remorseful.

Inside, I didn't feel sorry. Not one bit.

"Is that understood?" Captain said, slow and loud like I didn't speak her language. Like I wasn't smart enough to understand. *She thinks I'm a mudgirl, too. They all do.*

"Absolutely," I said, with more than a little disdain in my voice. She raised her eyebrows. I looked her dead-on. "Yes, Captain, I understand and appreciate the concise yet thorough clarification regarding this issue."

See? I use a lot of words and say absolutely nothing. Just like you.

She stared at me for a moment. "Maybe you need more time to contemplate the seriousness of this offense."

I got Pod Confinement for the rest of the evening.

I spent those long hours pacing the tiny circular unit. Part of me was thrilled. *My own room!* With a desk for my studies, a sleeper twice as big as my Orphanage one hovering in the corner. My own pod, all for my belongings. Not that I owned anything, but it was still pretty strato.

Then again, I'd already made an enemy. In less than a day. I'd hurt her, but that didn't change her mind any. That look in Cassina's eyes, the one that made my fist fly without thinking, promised she wouldn't quit. And if I punched her again, they'd bottom me out of the Academy before I wiped the blood off my knuckles.

Next stop: the Hub, where they'd bury me in the lowest of the low jobs.

I kicked the wall. *No way I'll spend the rest of my life scrubbing at Hubber waste. Not 'cause of some spoiled Upper Level synth priss. Not some brain-damaged air sucker.*

I'll prove her wrong, I thought, practically bouncing off the metal walls. *I'll prove them all wrong. I'll be stronger, smarter. I'll be the best cadet the Academy ever saw. No one will remember I came from the Orphanage.*

I knew that last part was a lie. Sounded good, though.

I don't need anyone. I never will.

But that part I still believed. Lived by. A promise I'd made myself long ago.

Of course, that was before I met Kane.

◊   ◊   ◊

I'd been so hardheaded in proving that I wasn't some dirt eater in my first week that I wasn't prepared for someone like Kane. Taking laps around the rec grounds, pushing myself even during break time, I saw him out of the corner of my eye, running up on me from behind.

I wheeled around on him, and in seeing my raised fists, he put his hands in front of his face. "Easy, Cadet!"

When I lowered them, he was grinning, his lip curled up in the way that I realize now is his thing. I felt my face relax.

Kane, already beautiful at twelve, even when the rest of us were growing into our awkward bodies. Only a week in and the girls followed him in a giggling pack, fighting to sit next to him at lunch, offering him bites of their rations.

Drooling over a guy? Absurd. But giving away food? Completely insane. That's not what we were here for. Cassina needed to save her rations for herself. She'd never seen an orphan wither away to nothing.

I hated her face already, but her pointed features became more intolerable the more lovesick she got. But Kane was never rude to her or anyone else, his patience seemingly unexhausted by her babble or adoring smiles.

The one thing about not needing anyone: you spend a lot of time watching the very people you don't need. And I could spot disinterest. Twitches. Eye rolls. Someone chewing the inside of their cheek.

I watched Cassina and Kane talk and his eyes would look right through her. In his head, he'd gone somewhere else. I knew that place well. I went there as often as I could.

Sure, his approaching me could've been a setup. But he wasn't much bigger than me. I could take him if I had to, and honestly, it might do a few things for my rep.

"C'mere," he said.

I followed him down the path as Cassina slaughtered me from afar with jealous whispers.

That made me smile. I didn't let him see, of course.

We came into a clearing and he led me toward the storage units that held the Academy's supplies. Everyone knew they were off-limits and alarmed.

"You can break the rules all you want, tough guy, but don't involve me."

"Tough guy?" He grinned at me. "All that's in there is used zip-ball equipment. You got to look behind it to get to the good stuff."

He disappeared into a narrow passage between the units. Of course, intrigued, I followed. I squeezed through the containers and found myself moving underground. The trail led downward into a pitch-black passageway.

"What smells?" I asked.

"Waste disposal facility," said Kane.

"You take all the girls here?" I muttered. But the truth? I was impressed that Kane had discovered his own personal sanctuary under all this surveillance. That he'd found someplace he could call his own.

Since the Academy was located so far below the crust—beneath even the Hub—the only lights were artificial, just like at the Orphanage. And they were everywhere, a sodium-yellow hue constantly broadcasting across our skin. Lights are a luxury in the lower regions. Light means you matter. They say Rock Bottom is pitch-black.

Kane stared at me. Even in the black, I could make out his face. This sensory thing that I hide from everyone. I can see pretty well in the dark, freakishly well. And my hearing's not bad either. Freakishly not bad. But these things are best kept to myself. There are parts of yourself that are better off hidden.

He switched on his beamer, his face hovering just inches from mine. He's just a regular person, Kane. He grinned at me in his spotlight.

"Laugh," he said, pulling something from his jacket.

"Why?"

"Trust me, just laugh. You can laugh, can't you?"

"I guess," I said. I didn't do it that often, that was for sure. "But there isn't anything . . . to laugh at."

He nodded. "Wanna see my impression of Cassina?"

"Not really."

He did it anyway. Sucked in his cheeks, pushed out his chin, gave me her sharp, love-struck stare. Like an infatuated Hubber with serious mental issues.

People said Cassina was beautiful. Her friends said it a lot. Apparently, the guys thought so, too. The whole thing was strange. Like a mass delusion. *Cassina is beautiful*, someone says. And everyone believes it.

I saw her ugliness from the very beginning. The cruelness in her cells. Could that be transmitted through her genetics? Perhaps I wanted to believe this, to confirm that my parents were stronger people, which bore out in my nature. It also probably meant they'd passed along their anger as well.

Kane's impression made me laugh. Not because it was that funny, but because it was the first time I'd felt it was even okay to do so since getting to the Academy. This weird kid—Kane—made me feel *okay*.

As I laughed he pointed a device in my direction that suddenly made a sharp sucking sound, all so quick I almost missed it.

"Got it," he said.

"Got what?"

"The pattern. Of your laugh." He pointed his beamer and sprayed the wall in front of us with the other device, and I watched the explosion of light and color hit the air. Purples and blues crashing into each other, dripping down in vibrant streaks before they hit the ground and flowed into the floor grates. The surprise took my breath away. That almost never happened either.

I don't do *surprise*.

"Sound painting," he said, smiling. "That's what your laugh looks like."

He looked a little surprised himself. "I've never seen those colors before. Not for a laugh."

"Stop looking at me," I said.

"You're looking at me," he said. I turned away, kicked at the ground. "Besides, you must be used to it. If you haven't noticed, everyone looks at you. We just can't help it."

"Of course I noticed."

"Maybe because you're pretty," he said.

Pretty? I'd been called lots of things, but never that. "Shut your mouth."

"Well, it could be that, but maybe it's something else."

I almost lost my words for a second. "What?"

"Your horns."

"Horns?"

"Orphans have horns, don't they? You all hide them under your hair."

He was smiling. Then I noticed I was, too.

"I wish," I said. "That would be cool."

"I know," he said. We were quiet for a second. Thinking about our horns, probably. Mine would be really sharp. Cassina wouldn't dare be on the other end of a head butt.

"I liked your . . . color thingy," I said finally. I motioned where the colors had been. "How'd you do all that?"

"Practice," he said. "My brush transfers the sound waves into pure aerosol pigment. You control what comes out by being very selective of what you take in. I've been doing them since I was a kid."

It occurred to me he was still a kid, and so was I.

"I'm not supposed to do it here. 'No paints or personal items.' I think they're all worried we'll get personalities. You'd get into more trouble with one of those."

"Then why did you show *me*?"

"I just thought you'd like it. I don't know. I thought you'd create something beautiful. I guess . . . I wanted to talk to you."

"Don't you know I'm dangerous? Haven't you heard? *Core-low mudgirl*, all that?"

"Yeah," he said. "I think that's pretty strato, to tell you the truth. That you aren't like everyone else."

We stared at each other. He looked normal, but this kid was weird. Even weirder than me maybe. I kind of liked him.

"I won't tell anyone," I said. "If you promise one thing."

"What?"

"Promise me you'll do it again." For a second, we were quiet. We just smiled at each other.

"Just wait," he said, "till I paint your scream."

I couldn't help sticking out. And it wasn't just because Cassina hated me. The second classes started, it was obvious I didn't know anything.

Our first week, the cadet instructor showed us holo-images in the Great Indra: Geography of Fulfillment. We walked around the 3-D projection of the City of Indra. Not the Lower Levels, but everything aboveground. The buildings rising into the sky. The clouds and floating islands above that. The others looked bored. They'd seen it before. But I moved in close, trying to make out the tiniest details. I'd never imagined anything like this. The most you could dream of in the Orphanage was the Hub.

The Islands looked like a make-believe, like the one we'd visited in the Orphanage Archive, "The Girl Tied with Rope." Our one access chip, given as charity from the Independent High Council. We all had Archive slots on our wrists, of course. Even if you didn't arrive to the Orphanage with one, they fixed that. If they were going to keep you, that is. You had to at least make it to Infant Surveillance.

Kane doesn't remember his Archive slot insertion. "No one I know does," he told me. "I think they put you to sleep first."

"Lucky you," I said. I knew he wanted to ask questions, but he didn't. I rarely talked about the Orphanage. And somehow, he knew not to ask.

Of course, I have a great memory. That isn't always a good thing.

They strapped down my little wrists, so I kicked. In the end, they had to bring in three caretakers to hold me down. I saw Infant Supervisor lift a sharp, silver instrument. It let off a few sparks, which scared me even more.

I think he wanted me to see that.

He lowered the instrument. Not seeing was even worse. Then there was a hiss.

I screamed so loud they had to cover my mouth.

It might not have been the worst pain in the world, but that's how I remember it.

The slots are nearly invisible. Just a faint mark across your wrist. We all used "The Girl Tied with Rope." You just tap your wrist and then press your thumb there. After that, the access chip slides right in.

Other than that one make-believe, we really had no use for the wrist slots. If we made it out of the Orphanage one day, we would visit other Archives. *If* being the key word.

But we all loved it. Loved it so much the Archive was pretty beaten up. The orphans visited so many times that we'd trampled a path though the untouched forest. The leaves wilted, the branches drooped. Even the princess—tied to a tree, waiting for the prince to rescue her from outlaws—looked annoyed. We'd ignored her for so long that over the years, her cries for help sounded bored.

Besides, I'd always been more interested in the shadowy man with the black cloak. Sometimes I'd turn, and there he was, slipping through the forest. I didn't care about the princess. I wanted to run after him. But before I had a chance, he'd disappear.

"Help!" the princess would shout. Then she'd sigh and roll her eyes. A shadow person.

I didn't know what that was until the Academy. "Shadow people are living human beings like us," Instructor told us. "But they have committed great crimes against Indra."

These dark figures, she explained, are forced to wander the Archives, unable to interact. Voiceless and directionless, destined to live the same scenario over and over. The worse the crime, the more awful their Archive prison.

I imagined my entire lifetime spent trapped in the same location. The middle of the desert or a freezing dungeon. The Orphanage. It was horrible. The only perk, I figured, would be no Cassina.

"The shadow people," the instructor said, "serve as living reminders to the rest of us. Indra's greatness is to be appreciated through our loyalty. We must follow rules and be proper citizens."

My head spun. "They can't be real!" I said before I could stop the words from coming.

Cassina giggled. Her friends followed suit. "How dumb is she?" she whispered.

"Of course they're real," said Instructor.

"Then where are their bodies?"

"Excuse me?"

"If they're in the Archives, where are their bodies? How do they eat? How many are there? Are they aware they're being punished." My mind spiraled away from me, my mouth moving faster than my brain. "I mean, how big is Indra? Does it have that many enemies?"

I looked around. No one was laughing anymore. Just staring at me like I was crazy.

"All you need to know is right in front of you." She pointed with a sharp fingernail at the 3-D image. "The City of Indra." She pointed higher. "The Islands."

She didn't know any of the answers herself. I could tell.

The others looked annoyed at my silly questions. They already knew about the City of Indra. They'd been there, and many had grown up on the Islands. But here they were, accepting all that was recited before them, not questioning how long it would take to travel by ground transporter around the outer borders, or what laid outside of them.

But if you were to, say, take advantage of the Governmental Educational Archives after class, which are completely unrestricted, and referenced the reports of the Independent High Council, you could learn what you weren't being taught. For example:

Indra's greatness makes travel beyond unnecessary. Even more, the repercussions would be enormous. Certain death would occur upon encountering the edges, if not before. Indra provides more than enough resources to serve as a self-sustaining biosphere. It is far larger than the major metropolitan hubs of former Earth and estimated to be the size of the East Coast of former America (see appendix 34A for historic maps). The great Indra was built from the barren, scorched Earth of the old world. A world so flawed in nature that it failed. Our ancestors learned from former Earth's shortcomings and built Indra to be much stronger and more resilient than the cities of the past. The City of Indra is a centerpiece to the sophisticated modern age. The City of Indra is The City.

I'd looked at the map. The East Coast of former America? That was enormous. And Instructor said none of it mattered. Except the City of Indra, that is. And the Lower Levels right below, where we stood now.

Terraforming the rotted former world into the great Indra had taken a thousand years. The founders of Indra had once sought safety below the Earth, then built upward in search of water. Just creating the foundations of the City of Indra took centuries.

At least, that's what Instructor told us. As to the mechanics of how they did that, she offered no explanation. I held my tongue in class and resolved to find answers to my own questions outside of it.

When they were young, my classmates learned Indra's history from *The Book of Indra*. There was no book of anything in the Orphanage. What knowledge of Indra would be useful to them in Rock Bottom? Would dreams of a better life only lead to more heartbreak and disappointment?

The Indrithians had risen above Rock Bottom. They'd built day and night—both marked by never-ending darkness—for hundreds of years, reaching upward, and pulled themselves from beneath the Earth and into daylight. Leaving the unworthy and unaccomplished behind to fester in the chaos of Rock Bottom below, forever jealous of the glimpse of star shine they'd seen miles above, before that world was sealed off once more.

I'd never been aboveground, but I would make it, just like the founders of Indra.

I knew nothing back then. During *The Book of Indra*: Worship and Recitation, everyone brought their own copies of *The Book*. "No personal items" had one exception, I guess. The girls passed theirs around, comparing.

"Yours is so stratosphere," said one of Cassina's followers to another. "I've never seen so many dried leaves. Are they real?"

Those were real leaves on her book, not synth-leaves. They were remnants of a time before the Great Catastrophe. Very little real nature existed, and only the most powerful Indrithians owned a piece. Having one leaf was a big deal. Covering *The Book of Indra* in them? I never imagined such riches.

"Butterfly wings," said another, holding hers out for all to see.

"Feathers," said another. That one looked soft. Everyone went "ooh" and "ahh," but I knew they were just waiting for the chance to show off their own.

Pollen. Petals. Beetles.

"It used to be alive!" squealed the owner. "I mean, it actually walked around!"

Someone cleared their throat. Faces turned. The room went quiet.

Cassina held up her copy nonchalantly. Hers was shiny, with complicated patterns swirling into each other. "Reptilian," she said smugly. "Snakeskin. Only one in all of Indra."

I'm not sure if anyone else knew what a *snake* was, but they all looked impressed. You could observe an Archive full of snakes and immediately see how well Cassina belonged to their world.

"What about Lex's copy?" said Cassina. Everyone turned to stare at me.

I shrugged.

"You don't even have *The Book of Indra*?" she said. "If you don't have one, how do you prove your existence? I mean, like, even Hubbies have them!" She shot a look at three kids in the back of the class who never strayed far from one another, as misplaced as me, but at least they had standard-issue copies. Even if I had one of those, I'd probably be dismissed because the pages weren't real paper like those of the Islanders, instead of rice paper or some other substitute.

"Just be glad you're in the Academy, Lex, or you wouldn't have clothes either."

Everyone laughed. Even the Hubbies! Who had never been aboveground or seen the City of Indra either!

That didn't keep them from laughing. Two of them, at least. Not the tiny one with shiny black hair. "How'd she even get in the Academy?" I'd heard people say. "She's so little she can hardly see a target."

Her name was Vipsinia. Vippy for short. She was always staring at me. Watching me blast targets, following the route I took to class. Popping up when I least expected her. "She just thinks you're cool," Kane said.

"Or she's gonna smother me in my sleep," I said.

Vippy just lifted her own plain copy defiantly, flipped the pages. Held it in front of her like it was made of gold and glared defiantly at Cassina over the top.

Gutsy for someone you could snap in half.

What really mattered was that Hubber Vippy had her own book, and I had zip.

"*The Book of Indra*," Kane explained later, "is made of real materials. No holo-anything. Real words on real paper."

"*The Book of Indra*," as the instructor put it, "contains the words by which we aspire to live."

In the Orphanage, our only aspiration was to make it to twelve.

Vippy flipped a page forcefully. Everyone else stared at me like I had ration gravy on my face.

"Hey, Lex!" said a voice. "You can share mine."

Kane. Rescuing me. No one would laugh at Kane. Cassina just stared at him, the mean melting off her pointy face. Then she looked at me. From dreamy-eyed to death stare.

I moved next to him. "Thanks," I mumbled.

"Whatever," he said. "It wasn't for you. I just don't wanna get crap about my book."

I knew he was lying. Kane didn't care what anyone thought.

"Scrubber wimp," I said. He grinned, knowing I didn't mean it.

For a second, I wanted to hold his hand. Reach under the desk and squeeze it.

That was the first time I ever wanted to touch someone.

We both looked at his book. There were no strange patterns. No feathers or leaves or skins.

Just colors, swirling into each other. Colors I'd never seen before or even imagined.

"I did it myself," he said. "It's the sound of my breathing."

CHAPTER 5

Countdown to Emergence Ball: 6 Years

Livia

When Etiquette Tutor demanded to know the foods we found most reprehensible, I told the truth. In retrospect, I should not have been so honest.

Etiquette Tutor watched as I lifted the spoon to my mouth, a blob of slimy kidney meat quivering before me.

"Leisure Skills," according to Etiquette Tutor, "are our birthright and duty as females. A Proper Little Girl of Indra must be adept in showing delight, even while enduring the most disagreeable of experiences."

The others whispered excitedly upon first seeing the dining table, cooing over the candelabra and polished silverware, giddily pointing out the delicate roses engraved on the fine china. We sat completely straight, as instructed, and daintily unfolded the linens edged in fine lace and placed them on our laps.

I knew this would not end well.

"The key to expressing delight is simple: you must always maintain a smile."

I heard the gasps before I even lifted the domed lid of my serving tray. Claudia took Etiquette Tutor's words to heart. Within moments, she retched violently through a smile.

My spoon was poised yet unmoving, the shiny lump gleaming in the candlelight. My hand appeared to be frozen.

Now, Livia, I told myself. *Just open your mouth. These dishes are not made from real animals.*

Real animals had been extinct for centuries, except for Veda. This meat was synthesized by bioengineers in sky labs. The vegetables were grown in the Aero-Crown, perched in the atmosphere even higher than the Islands.

In the City of Indra, the food was more functional: protein cubes, dehydrated vegetables, powdered vitamin supplements. Here, we were given re-creations of former Earth's delicacies. Eating such fine replications was considered an honor.

I didn't care to be honored. I just cared to be excused.

When Etiquette Tutor asked our least favorite food, the majority of us were quick to please, each naming a dish more horrendous than the last. Staring down at the kidney, I believed myself to have been most successful.

"Consume the kidney, Livia," said Etiquette Tutor, and I knew there would be no more stalling.

I closed my eyes and, for barely an instant, brought forth Marius's voice in my head. I often did this during etiquette lessons that caused me distress, meaning nearly every single one.

You must be a very sweet, good girl. Even when you do not feel that way.

I shoved the blob into my mouth.

"Not so fast. You must appear to savor your meal. And your smile must be believed."

I took another bite, this time slower. The glutinous kidney was cold on my tongue, and its bitter juice pooled at the back of my throat.

"Smile," barked Etiquette Tutor.

Do not vomit. I forced a swallow, my lips pulled upward.

Across from me, Mica took dainty bites of her banana soufflé. She simply hated dessert. It was so fattening and sugary.

Etiquette Tutor watched me swallow, shook her head, and nodded to my plate. "Again, Livia. Your countenance should say, 'This kidney is divine. More kidney. *More kidney.*'"

Bite after bite, smiling till the corners of my lips ached. And yet, Etiquette Tutor deemed my performance unsatisfactory, even more so than that of Bettina, who, after vomiting pig trotters across the floor, was simply told to wipe up and begin with a fresh pair of feet.

"Perhaps, Livia, you have never experienced delight. Or even an emotion that would lead you to keep your mouth closed when you chew, for I do not care to see what you are digesting."

I finished the kidney, worried that I would now be forced to lick the plate clean as well. I gulped down a glass of water and took a deep breath and gave my first real smile.

It was worth every horrendous moment—Mica's requirement, kidney, Etiquette Tutor—for Marius's support.

"Today we learned Reliance on Others to Affirm Our Femininity," I told her. "And Etiquette Tutor had us affect the state of one who has become incapacitated due to physical injury and must remain fetching while awaiting a Proper Young Gentleman to rescue her."

In actuality, I was fully aware I could rescue myself, though had long ago given up questioning the need for our lessons. Need, I had come to realize, was beside the point.

"Ah, yes. Indeed, I remember the exercise well," Marius said.

"And I kept my wits about me under duress, just as instructed."

Of course, the reality had been quite different. Etiquette Tutor had assigned Claudia an arm injury, strapping it to her side and telling her to pretend it had been broken. Emilia was asked to elevate her leg due to a splinter. Both waited patiently for help, not seeming put out in the slightest.

I had been restrained, blindfolded, and told to silently wait for relief. "You have suffered a great shock and fainted," Etiquette Tutor said.

My relief was a long time coming.

"And it was terribly easy. And Etiquette Tutor was very pleased with me, I could tell. Told the others I had shown 'serenity under pressure.'"

If serenity entails withstanding uncontrollable shaking in complete darkness.

Marius gave me a strange look. *I mustn't go so far,* I told myself.

"Though it was a tad bit scary," I said.

"I knew you would shine, my love." Marius reached out and took my hand. Just as Governess had ceased smiling, Marius no longer embraced me. I knew not to question, just hold tight to the most minuscule slivers of affection: an appreciative smile, a hand in mine. These must keep me going.

"Grace is about maintaining your dignity," said Etiquette Tutor. "Stand with purpose and you will not fall."

We all stared at the small circular platform sixty feet above us.

"The key to Maintaining Grace under Difficult Circumstances is to not appear under duress. Act the part, and you will succeed. Your elegance will be your safety."

Luckily, there was also a massive inflatable cushion below to serve the same purpose.

My training with Master had improved my flexibility and endurance. While the other girls spent their childhoods avoiding stained frocks, I'd grown up racing through gardens and riding Veda and scaling synth-trees that towered higher than that platform.

This was my chance to show Etiquette Tutor she had underestimated my abilities and impress her. She wouldn't say so, of course, and still wouldn't like me, but she would respect me.

I was still a child, I suppose. I believed in make-believe, even my own.

Cybele was the first to step aboard the lift and be raised to the platform. I could feel her fear surge, the expectation for failure tangible. Plummeting to the ground, in front of her peers? Even if the fall was cushioned, the humiliation would not be.

"Begin!" said Etiquette Tutor, and Cybele lifted her chin and forced a pleasant smile. With that, Etiquette Tutor raised the small black remote in her hand and pressed a button with her long, thin finger.

Immediately, the platform began to rotate, spinning slowly at first and gaining speed with each revolution. Cybele attempted to find her footing, only to stumble.

Below, Etiquette Tutor clicked away, her face utterly devoid of emotion.

Cybele never quite found her balance, though she lasted immeasurably longer than we thought in the moment. She fell, but she wasn't alone in her failure.

For some, this trial lasted quite a while as Etiquette Tutor taunted them with her controller. She spun them one way and then the other, going from slow to fast to frenzied in an instant. For others, she began full force, watching them stumble and fall within a few seconds of stepping onto the platform. Bodies tumbled through the air, bloomers on display and limbs splayed at angles not befitting Proper Young Girls. We watched as each girl sat up awkwardly, her equilibrium destabilized, rising red-faced and dress askew. Often the girl would stumble a few steps before regaining her balance.

More than one hurried away, knowing it improper to become

sick in front of the others. This lack of control, as Etiquette Tutor often reminded us, was highly disagreeable and outright disgusting in nature.

Immediately, the trials would continue.

Click. Click. Click.

When it came time for Mica, there was a palpable sigh of relief. She would set a glowing example for us all.

Mica smiled pleasantly to herself on the way up. Once she reached the top, she gave a tiny sigh, as though the task were simply another banana soufflé.

Her body held tall, she took her place on the platform. A dainty smile played on her bottom lip as she began to spin very, very slowly.

She fell almost immediately.

The girls sucked in their breath, a few even squealing. The fall seemed to take an eternity. When she landed, dress over her head and undergarments on display, the girls fought the urge to look away. Of course, that would have been against the rules. According to Etiquette Tutor, we must learn from the mistakes of others by fully observing their failures. I drank hers in.

Even Etiquette Tutor seemed taken aback, signaled by a momentary flicker of her left eyebrow. Mica pulled herself together, unharmed but shaken. She glided back to her seat in graceful strides, just as we had all been taught, instantly regaining her self-satisfied smile and regal manner.

I could sense her utter humiliation. Even more, her powerful fury.

Etiquette Tutor opened her mouth to speak, and we sucked in our breath in preparation. Even Mica was not above critique, we were sure of that, though the theory had yet to be proven.

Perhaps this was her destined moment.

"Next up will be Livia Cosmo."

◊ ◊ ◊

Focus, Livia.

The spin began slow and steady, the pace increasing in gradual increments that allowed me to adjust.

Nimble, Livia.

Steady, Livia.

Beneath me, I heard Etiquette Tutor click the device, careful not to tense in anticipation of a change in speed. It could go slower, but it never did.

I spun a little faster. Then even faster than that, as if I were at the center of a whirlwind.

Click.

The platform hurled me in frenzied circles, and all the while I could hear Etiquette Tutor's click. Click-click-click.

Don't look down. Don't think of their faces sixty feet below you. You won't find compassion or support there. Imagine your legs are heavy as stones beneath you.

Nimble, Livia.

Steady, Livia.

One direction, then another. Whirling in rapid circles, then suddenly decreasing in speed. Going slower and even slower . . . then fast again, the world disappearing into blurry color bands everywhere I looked.

I slipped.

Faster than thought I dug in and caught myself on the edge. My whole body rushed with adrenaline. Instead of Marius, I could hear Etiquette Tutor in my head.

Imbecile. Livia, you are utterly hopeless. Ridiculous.

Then it occurred to me, balancing on the air above her: Who was Etiquette Tutor, really? A very tall woman with sharp cheekbones and an unpleasant disposition, who had never been celebrated at an Emergence Ball and never cohabitated. She led not by example.

Focus, Livia. I sought to find empty space in my mind, just as Master informed me true warriors do. Everything kept revolving around me. Yet at the center, I was unmovable.

Rotating in never-ending circles, where nothing could touch me.

No one said a word as I descended on the lift and disembarked. Their faces betrayed their awe and confusion.

How long had I been up there? It must have been quite a while for Etiquette Tutor to finally cease turning me. Anticipating a throw that would never come. Everyone turned to her, awaiting her response. I had done well, we all knew that. For once, she had no other choice but to compliment me.

"Let us move on to Pleasant Interaction," she said.

One person was looking at me, though. I caught her eye before her gaze flickered away. I had never seen an expression like that, not even on Etiquette Tutor's face. In that split second, I sensed everything.

Mica.

And the feelings were far from proper.

In that moment, she chose to despise me.

I had a sudden revelation: I could try to be like the others, but I would never succeed.

Even more surprising? I had no desire to try. Not anymore.

In that way, my fate was sealed.

CHAPTER 6

Countdown to Final Simulation Exam: 4 Years

Lex

Be Industrious. Be Vigilant. Behave.

It was upon these three principles that all cadets were molded.

Be Industrious: We woke promptly and groomed before morning rations. We attended two block classes, were given an hour's rec time—time enough to eat afternoon rations and do some light training—before two more block classes. Followed by evening rations and rec time, usually spent reading and on homework for the next day's lessons. Then lights-out.

Every day of the week, every minute of it, our lives were accounted for. The PCF Academy's regimen had successfully shaped its graduates into becoming Indra's foundation.

Be Vigilant: First, you hold yourself accountable. Always show up on time. Always get your work done. Then, you hold your fellow cadets accountable. Their failure is your failure. Otherwise, all of you are doing laps around the track and no one's happy with the cadet who's to blame.

Behave: This one, I had trouble with. No further explanation needed.

The most promising youth. That's what Senior Lieutenant called us. And he meant me, too. Even if they'd never had an orphan in their ranks.

After the pod confinement from my altercation with Cassina, I threw myself into Academy life. I was going to stick to my promise. *Work harder. Be smarter. Be stronger.*

Cassina stuck to her promise, too. She planned on making me pay. At least, she'd spend every waking hour trying.

Cassina was sure I'd been an Academy mistake. She told everyone within earshot. Those first weeks, it took everything I had not to make her bleed again.

The worst part? Secretly, I wondered if she might be right. It had always felt like an accident, being *special*. Maybe this charade was at its end. I could be found out at any moment. Bottom out, as if I'd escaped my true fate and was living on borrowed time.

Not if I could help it, though.

No way I was gonna mess this up. Not a chance.

I learned to ignore her. I learned to ignore the names.

Mudgirl. Orphan waste. Dirtbaby.

At all times I could feel their eyes burning into me, Cassina and her pack.

"I heard she was born Low Level," one said. "Like, core-low."

I knew what "core-low" meant. Down here, we were nearer to the crust of the Earth. Being "crust" was a good thing. Core? Not so much. That meant Rock Bottom, way down below us, near the center of the Earth. That's where Indra started a thousand years ago. Before the population grew and the citizens reached for the sky.

A thousand years ago, only the worst of the worst chose to remain below. I couldn't imagine why they would do such a thing. And generations later, the worst of the worst were still there, causing damage and creating chaos for those of us above. That was why the PCF existed. To preserve the peace above and to quell the troubles below.

Where everyone thought I came from.

"In a brothel," said one. "Her mom was, like, a prostitute. A Mud-town brothel, dirt walls, dirt on her back and knees. Can you imagine?"

"Of course I can," said Cassina. "So low she'd probably even engaged a mutation."

As if she'd ever seen a dirt wall. She sounded sure of herself. When she spoke, everyone shut up. Didn't want to miss a word. Less than a week, and she was already their queen. "I'm not surprised," she continued. "She reeks of Low Level. Not something you can hide. That's what happens when they recruit from outside Indra. Looks bad for the Academy. For all of us. She's an experiment . . . and it's not gonna work. Just wait and see."

I could hear every whisper. Of course, they didn't know that.

Not all of us would become PCF. Not all of us wanted to. Some would be happy to join a policy committee within the lower ranks of the High Council. Not me. Not since Commander Hauser visited us in our first year.

I had never seen a sharper haircut, or cleaner uniform, or so many medals within the Academy's halls. He was tall and handsome, even if he didn't smile. He instantly made me feel safe, if that wasn't already high on his list of priorities.

"Yesterday morning," he said, standing at the front of our first block classroom, "at oh seven hundred hours, the Hub came under attack. A team of two, disguised as maintenance workers, planted an explosive charge in a transport tube. If you haven't already noticed, Cadet Forza is absent today. His older brother was killed while traveling to work. One hundred and twenty-one others died alongside him. It is the largest rebel attack in Indra's history. It is all of our jobs to make sure that it is the last.

"You wouldn't be here if Indra didn't see something more in you," Hauser continued. "Your acceptance here is a privilege, and with that privilege comes responsibility. To yourself, your fellow cadets, your instructors, your city. *Our* city. The Founders settled Indra to learn from the mistakes of former Earth, to continue to reach and strive to greater heights. And yet, there is a pocket within us that would rather see us die. For that reality to shatter. As I stand here before you, I will not let that happen. And you will not let that happen. We will retain solidarity in the face of those that seek to endanger our lives and destroy what we have built."

It felt at that moment as if he were speaking directly to me, his eyes hard beacons into the heart of Indra. I wanted nothing more than to serve at his behest, and to show all who'd doubted me that I was still there to protect them.

"Otherwise, we do not deserve what the Founders fought for."

No longer could we inoculate ourselves from the reality of what we were training for.

Rebel.

It was the first time I truly understood the word, or learned of people who held Indra in such contempt. I became restless. Placements were so far away and we could only play at soldier here. It was all anyone could talk of, and for an orphan like me, I was curious about how much the other cadets knew about the world. It seemed like everybody knew somebody who had been affected. I'd thought Indra was much larger than that.

Perhaps in light of Commander Hauser's visit and the Hub attack, a good game of zip ball was either the worst or best thing we could do.

I felt the tension as I strapped on the gloves. I had no love for the game, but at the Orphanage I'd grown good at it. There, the field was pockmarked with gaping holes you could break your ankle on, and those electrodes on your fingertips would drop signal unexpectedly. You lose control of a fifteen-pound metal zip ball in midair, you could get real hurt. But if you learn under those circumstances, you can play out of your mind on a real field, like the one at the Academy.

We lined up on the sidelines as Cassina and Vipsinia chose teams. Cassina chose Kane first and he looked back at me as he jogged over to join her, shrugging his shoulders in amusement. It wasn't a surprising choice. Whenever she was captain, the other team would just pick me last, knowing she would never take me for her team. This didn't really hurt my feelings. Except Vippy, out of some weird pride, couldn't help picking me first. I wasn't happy—she could've spent that pick more wisely—and I'd always clearly shown my emotions on my face.

For today's five-a-side game, we had Vippy, her two fellow Hubbers, and Caesar, who was from somewhere in the Lower Levels. Not exactly an ace squad.

I like to play a fast game. Keep the ball moving between my teammates, keep it out of your opponents' hands, and tire them out. My team wasn't quite built for that. Vippy's loyalty to her fellow Hubbers sabotaged a truly competitive match, but as long as I was out there, we had a shot. We put on our helmets and jogged onto the field, the electro fields humming from the skin of our gloves. You never actually touch the ball, but you can feel it, if that makes sense. Not it's full weight, but it's . . . potential.

The scoring buzzer sounded quickly. Cassina may be confident, she may have been the captain, but she always plays the player, never the ball. I got the ball to Caesar, who cut it right back to me. High sidewalls allow great bank shots if you play the angles right. There can be as much as five feet between a zip ball and the person controlling it. You can get faked out that way. You can also fake yourself out if you stretch your electro field too thin and get too cocky. Kane didn't even have a shot at redirecting it; it was already passing through the goal as he was diving for it.

That could've been our only goal, but it still would've been worth it to see Cassina's despair. She immediately shouted at her team while I forgot just how much I didn't believe in my own and gave them all pounds. Caught up in our own celebration, I couldn't have anticipated just how angry Cassina was.

The zip ball slammed directly into the back of my head, cracking the helmet where it hit. I fell face-first into the ground and my head exploded with pain. So much pain I couldn't even see.

Kane was kneeling by my side, but I could hear the rest of Cassina's team laughing. All I could do was hear. "What the hell, Cassina?!"

"It was a live ball," she said. "Not my fault."

You get scored on, you have to run it out from your end. It makes it that much easier for the scorers to go on a quick run if they mount a press and steal the ball so close to the goal. My team should've immediately gone up to press. Cassina wasn't wrong about it being a live ball, but you don't ever headhunt. On that, she knew better.

"Stay right there," Kane said to me. I rolled onto my side and could make out only the blurred shapes of my teammates. "Your visor's all cracked. Wait right here."

He should've known me better. I sat up.

"Lex, game's over. Let's go get you checked out."

"No . . . damn way," I said, my head feeling as if it had broken right open. Everything I did made it feel like the crack was getting wider. Kane helped me to my feet. I couldn't see a damn thing.

But I could hear the zip ball clearly, several feet away. It hummed at a low cycling rate.

Kane waved his hand in front of my face. His glove's electro field hummed at a much higher one. If I could concentrate away from the pain, which truthfully is all I could feel, maybe I could hear the individual electro fields of every player. Possibly . . .

I slowly walked over to the zip ball and rolled it toward . . . someone, with the tip of my foot.

"One-nil, us."

Someone's electro field engaged and I could hear the ball several feet higher than my head. I tried to make a play for it, but it was already thrown downfield. I ran blindly, focusing so hard on the sound of the ball that I crashed right into . . . someone. We both fell to the ground.

"You okay, Lex?"

"I'm fine, Vip."

The goal buzzer sounded. Cassina and her laughter just had to be even louder.

One of the Hubbers retrieved the ball and brought it back out. She avoided me and passed it off. They didn't even get it to midfield when the ball sailed for too long and then someone grunted as they ate it on the field.

"I got it!" Kane yelled. His legs pumped down the field, his footfall sounding far closer than anyone else's, the ball secured in his electro field, which buzzed brightly as it hyperextended—the energy positively crackling—and pulled the ball back and forth. Another couple seconds and he had a clear shot. Just my impaired self and the goal.

He hesitated. No way was this fool going to go easy on me. He wouldn't dare do me that way. No way. *What a—*

He sidearmed it and launched it on my strong side, low and fast. The ball's electric whine whistled as it shot toward me. My gloves' field couldn't slow it from this range, but damn if it couldn't redirect its trajectory.

I reached out and could feel the tension between field and ball, catching ever so slightly . . . right before it blasted past the electro and hit just wide of the goal. I brought it back and signaled for a time-out.

"Guys, huddle up."

They huddled closely around me. The two Hubbers were huffing hard from their exertion. My vision had improved to a complete blur deadened by black spots that shifted every time I blinked.

"This is going to be hard, but I think we can win this. We just need one goal. If you can get me one goal, I will make sure they don't score any more."

"You're going to be goalie?" Caesar asked.

"You're the best player we got," Vippy said.

"Yeah. If she *scores*." Caesar's heart was beating hard. What he didn't know was that with my hearing, at least from an offensive perspective, I couldn't detect the goals. They weren't electric, so they made absolutely no sound. There was no way I was going to thread a zip ball through one of those. But defending one?

That played into my sets of gifts very well.

"So tell me, who's gonna get the goal?"

There was no rush of hands being raised. But there was one.

Vippy.

I looked in the direction of her raised hand.

"You better."

Well, she didn't score. She didn't even come close. But neither did Cassina's team, so I counted a tie game as a personal victory. Even though my head ached like a groundquake, my sight was improving. I mean, I could at least tell that Kane's smile was incredulous. The amount of pain I was in, it didn't even give him problems about thinking twice about scoring on me. He wasn't soft, he was just . . . Kane.

Later that week, we settled in for afternoon rations when I heard the chatter.

The chatter quickly grew to a roar, and I thought that if there was any real trouble happening, the instructors would step in. Even Kane shrugged it off when it first began. But when I saw the instructors step out of the lunchroom and actively ignore what was clearly an out-of-control situation, I couldn't ignore it any further. Perhaps they thought a fight would expend our energy. Perhaps one death, or two, was a necessary sacrifice.

Cassina and several of her paramours were gathered around a table. Vipsinia was on the ground next to it, one cheek puffy from being hit, her Hubber friends having already retreated way across the room. So much for loyalty

"Are you a rebel?!" Cassina shouted at her.

Vippy was nearly in tears.

"Well?! Are *you*?"

Vippy was shaking her head furiously, but couldn't get them to leave her alone.

I pushed my way through the growing crowd.

"Back off," I told Cassina.

"One of the rebels came from her zone!"

"So?"

"Of course a dirtgirl like you—"

"—would be too high-minded not to jump to conclusions? If that whole zone was rebels, don't you think the PCF would've imprisoned them by now? Who'd allow Vippy to even be here if that were true?"

Cassina screwed up her face, nearly out of her mind. "Maybe *you're one*, too."

I pushed her hard against the wall, taking her off her feet. One of her male companions put his hand on me, not seeing Kane right behind him. Kane tripped him, and sent him sprawling onto the ground. The other companion helped Cassina up, which she didn't appreciate, red-faced.

"A rebel!" she yelled. "At least we all know it now!"

"If you ever call me that again, you will see just how rebellious I can get."

As much as I didn't let her see it, her words stung and there was nothing I could do to reverse their effect on the other cadets. The break time buzzer sounded and that was all it took for the mob to disperse.

Vippy still hadn't moved, so I told her, "Get up."

She wiped the tears from her face, and Kane took her hand and pulled her up. She sniffled. "Thank you."

I had been angry for most of my life. It was the sort of thing Samantha had curbed just with her presence, and Kane was growing to fill that role as well. But here—in the wake of the past week, of the past year, and all those that came before—I felt those instincts become completely unhinged. I was beyond thought, beyond compassion. I looked at Vipsinia and all I could see were the same doubts Cassina had.

A rebel. I feared that I had stuck my neck out for one.

I used my size to show her how serious I was, and she held her ground as I pinned her back. "On your life, you better not be one," I said.

CHAPTER 7

Countdown to Emergence Ball: 1 Week

Livia

The sun warms my back as Veda and I trot the winding dirt pathways through the village, passing weeping cherry trees and thatched huts. Outside one thatched hut, an aged woman hunches over a loom weaving iridescent patterns. Farther ahead, others gather at the river to rinse their garments, wringing water from them and gossiping loudly in their ancient tongue.

As of yet, we've gone unnoticed.

I halt Veda just beyond a prayer garden. "Rest," I tell her. She shakes her ivory mane. Veda loves it here.

My mother adored Veda, often wishing she could take her into the Archives. In the end, my father implanted a personalized access chip in Veda's hoof that would mirror my mother's Archive experience. She simply led her to the reader pad built especially for Veda and placed her front right leg on the sensor, and they would enter the Archives together.

For some reason, Veda's chip also works for me. Just as she entered my mother's Archives, she can enter mine. This is not logical, a fact of which I'm well aware. Yet I have kept it a secret as long as I have known.

If I want Veda to join me in the Archives, I simply send the thought to her and soon she is there beside me. I could be in the main quarters and she in the stable, and we will be together. I have always felt the emotions of others, but Veda is the first being who could sense me as well. She's the only animal in existence, and I often feel just as alone.

Now she looks at me, concerned. *Where are you going?*

"Don't worry," I tell her. "Rest." She stomps the ground a few times, showing me her dissatisfaction, yet she complies.

I leap the wooden gates and cut through a thicket of brush. Bushes are trimmed into strange, slanting angles. Squat trees, their trunks twisting and coiling. A trickling brook weaves through the lush foliage, the water swarming with glimmering neon fish.

If only this were real. Still, the Archive training simulation is perfect, down to what I think is the sweet smell of cherry blossoms on the gentle breeze.

This simulation is part of my swordsmanship training program, yet strictly prohibited by Master. "You are not ready for opponents who fight with both sword and mind," he's told me. "Perhaps one day, but not yet. You think too much, Livia, to engage in real battle."

For all his warnings, Master never fails to leave the access chips unguarded. A test of my will, perhaps. A test I have chosen to fail.

This may well be my last chance. At least, this is what I told myself as I slipped the chip from the black box this very morning. Next week I will have my Emergence Ball, and soon after I will cohabitate. Proper Cohabitated Women of Indrithian Society don't practice swordsmanship, even though my mother did.

Now I'm somewhere I have never been, with no concept of what awaits me. For just a moment, I recline on a flat black rock. The surface is pleasantly cool, though I'm far from relaxed. This isn't a retreat, I remind myself.

The wait is short.

I'm on my feet, hands grasping the hilt of my zinger, when I hear the first footstep.

I have fought all breeds of enemy in the Archives . . . but this is something altogether different.

For a brief moment, I wonder if perhaps Master was correct. The opponent is unexpected, to say the very least.

He stands there dressed in a kimono, smiling at me calmly, as though ready to initiate a warm conversation, perhaps even invite me to tea.

I will myself to focus. I won't let his appearance deceive me. A samurai is never unarmed, even when taken off guard. As though he can read my thoughts, he draws a sword from the obi tied around his waist, the pleasant expression dropping as the sword rises. We both stare at its edge gleaming in the sunlight. He glares at me, his eyes as sharp as the blade itself.

I pose, zinger drawn and humming, my body prickling with energy. The samurai's face is rigid with concentration, barely a muscle flickering. His mind is clear, I know this from Master. He's been telling me since we first began training when I was a little girl: *The true warrior is empty of emotion.*

I close my eyes and force my mind to go blank.

No Emergence Ball. No sashes. No Mica. No Etiquette Tutor or Life Guide or Helix Island. Only now. Only the battle.

An almost indiscernible rush of wind: I know he has launched into midair. I'm poised to attack before even opening my eyes.

I leap, my rigid body cutting through space. In that brief moment of flight, I feel every hair on my arm rising. All it takes is the space between two heartbeats.

Our blades clash.

We spin away from each other, our weapons locked the whole while. Our dance is violent. His face is inches from mine, lips drawn over his teeth, a growl rising from his throat.

The zinger releases a low note as I force him away. The impact throws me off balance. I land on my feet and stumble, disoriented, trying to catch my breath and regain focus. My eyes scan the garden frantically. Where could he have gone?

A low groan. I turn just as he charges, eyes mellow, his form perfect. An unexpected beam of sunlight glints off his katana's edge, blinding me.

Do not think.

Forward thrust. I slice empty air. A faint whizzing to my left and I duck the instant his blade slashes down.

He trims a lock of hair from over my ear. It floats to the ground.

He was aiming for my head.

His emotional armor cracks. Now I can feel his fury rising. His programming is so real that he's incapable of controlling himself. I have gone from a mild annoyance to a skilled opponent. A mere child—*a girl, even worse*—has dared force him to work for his victory.

Master didn't teach me to do this. To *feel* people. I have read emotions since I was a child. At first, I could only read Veda. I would go to her stable when I was confused or sad, and feel her fret over me. She would try to cheer me up with a little galloping dance. When I finally smiled, I could feel her satisfaction.

I assumed it was only Veda I could feel. Perhaps because my father created her, I reasoned. Because she is the only one of her kind. Then one day, I hid from Life Guide in the synth-orchard, and I could sense his frustration growing from the other side of the island. I knew when Master was planning an intense training, or Governess worried over my eating habits.

I've always felt people, but never in an Archive.

He isn't real, I remind myself.

Archive simulations are meant to train and entertain Indrithian citizens. Archive memories are different. They are a record of your past, allowing you to enter your own experiences. Archive memories replicate real events as you lived them.

I had attempted to access my own memories countless times. I'd hoped to see my mother and father, though I don't remember either. *Perhaps they held me as a child*, I reasoned, *and the memory remains buried right beneath the surface of my consciousness*. With every try, I would end up in a thick fog, a faint buzzing noise surrounding me.

I have cycled through every day of my existence, painstakingly tapping each date into the personal memory chip we're each issued as children. In the end, I found a few uninteresting moments, but none of importance. In one, Governess towered over my six-year-old self, encouraging me to eat my pudding. Even simulated, I found her very demanding. In another, I was picking synth-flowers in the orchard and winding them into a crown.

This cannot make up the entirety of my life experiences, I thought.

One day I asked Marius about my memory blanks, and she merely gave a faint smile. "I do not know, my love. Some have many archived memories. Others have few."

"But who decides?"

"The High Council," she responded. By the tone of her voice, I knew not to inquire further.

In all truth, little is known of the Archives and their origin. Yet there are a few facts of which everyone is made aware: despite feeling fear or pain, you cannot be permanently injured. You may be stabbed by a simulated enemy, yet you will wake unscathed. As for the human simulations, they do not have emotion. As real as they may feel, they feel nothing in the slightest.

Yet here in the garden, I can feel this samurai. For a mere second, he seems to wallow in a hatred that almost feels authentic. Is this possible?

Who is this girl? he wonders. *Why does she fight so well?*

In that moment, he hesitates. In that moment, I swing.

He gasps. We both gaze downward. A drop of blood blossoms across his white kimono.

It's a flesh wound, yet I have caught him off guard. He stumbles backward and regains his footing, but not his composure. He grimaces at me, his face pained. His surprise turns to anger. Then he does something unexpected.

He smirks.

I follow his gaze over my shoulder. Four more samurai stand poised, swords drawn, eyes targeted on me. One opens his mouth wide and gives a bloodcurdling screech.

"Liv—"

"—ia!"

I blink. The samurai are gone, as is the garden. The brook, the winding trees, and the neon fish all have disappeared. I'm stretched across my hovering four-poster sleeper, covered in a sheen of sweat, every muscle aching. Instinctively, I reach for my sheathed zinger hanging on the post next to me.

"Do not," says a voice, low and lethal. I drop my hand and look upward.

Governess is holding my access chip between two fingers. She has removed it from my wrist, instantly ending the program. Even if I could immediately return to it, my progress wouldn't have been saved and I'd have to start the encounter all over. Her expression is disagreeable, to say the very least.

"I hope you found that activity a suitable distraction. Perhaps there are more appropriate uses of your time?"

"I was fighting a class-five samurai, Governess. Higher than Master even allows!"

I know the last part was a mistake the moment it comes out of my mouth.

"Indeed. Oh, Livia . . ."

Governess believes swordsmanship to be an intolerable waste of time. As for the Archives, they should be used solely for enrichment, as a means of accessing ancient ruins and places of worship that vanished centuries ago.

The Sistine Chapel. Taj Mahal. The Gardens of Babylon.

Places of refinement, she calls them. Places of unimaginable boredom, I say.

I can't tell Governess this, or anything else that matters. Especially not now, a week before what she calls "the most important day of my life."

"Can you begin to fathom the extraordinary number of preparations necessary that—"

"Yes," I say.

"—an event of this magnitude—"

"Yes," I say again.

"—entails?" she finishes on a high note. *Cue the guilt*, I think. "I daresay, you do not consider my feelings. Not for one moment. The utter exhaustion innate in overseeing the multitude of obligations necessary for a ball thrown in *your honor* . . ."

"Of course I do, Governess dear," I say halfheartedly.

Cue the indignant lecture.

"There is preparation," she says. "You have obligations, Livia. You are well aware you should be en route to Etiquette Training, and I turn my back for one—"

"What did she do now?"

Marius stands in the doorway, a placid smile on her face.

"Marius! How lovely!" I say, sitting up quickly. *Saved*.

Marius glides over, putting a tiny, delicate hand to Governess's large, bony shoulder. Instantly, the tension drains from her face. Marius has this effect on people. Her voice is rich and smooth, and her face shines like sunlight has been implanted under her skin. But for her it's natural, not an enhancement. Her robes are always perfectly draped around her tiny frame, and her laughter contains just the right amount of music.

Governess welcomes Marius as warmly as I do, but for different reasons. Marius is an outlet to share her vexations, of which I am usually the cause. "A week until her debut," Governess tells Marius, "and where do you suppose I find her? In the Archives, of all places!"

"Indeed," says Marius calmly.

"And she has Etiquette Training! Not to mention the various—"

"Poor Governess! You are a wonder. All those preparations! I cannot fathom the enormity of the pressure, my dear." Governess nods vigorously and gives a dramatic sigh. "And somehow, you persevere. And look lovely doing so."

Governess glows, and I marvel at Marius. She is most likely the only woman in all of Indra capable of silencing Governess.

"Tell you what. I shall have my driver transport her in our sky speeder. She might well arrive just in time. He is wonderful, my driver. Chauffeured for the High Council chancellor, as you know." Governess nods, as though the plan has already been agreed upon. "And that will afford you a well-deserved break. Must not wear yourself down, my dear. We need your strength. I will take the young lady off your hands. A small outing, I think, will serve both of you well."

My heart soars.

"Lovely of you, Marius, but entirely unnecessary," says Governess.

"Yes, of course it is necessary. Even *you* need to recharge." At this, Governess smiles, which is a rare gesture indeed. Marius turns to me. "How does that sound, my love? Shall we? I found an enchanting little hideout in the Archives where we can stop afterward."

"Yes!" I say quickly. "I mean, that sounds absolutely delightful, Marius."

Governess sighs again. I know that sigh. It is the sound Waslo has made too many times.

I hate Etiquette on a good day, and today is not one of those.

Today is cinching.

Though it is one of my last days, it will be a long and painful one.

Marius's driver is as skilled as she proclaims. He races across the sky, dodging shuttles and rigs, swooping through clouds. Due to our status, we are allowed to cut through other islands' restricted airspace. Rigs and other craft must secure permits; that is why Helix is often left unlooked upon, except from afar. The ride is so exciting, I nearly forget where I'm headed. If it were only so easy.

Anything is preferential to cinching. Even dining instruction, which consists of everything *but* food consumption. According to Etiquette Tutor, "Silverware must be properly positioned. Salad fork to the left of plate, then meat fork accompanied by fish fork. Salad knife to the right of plate, then meat knife, then soup spoon. Of this be wary: soup spoon, not fruit spoon. The incorrect utensil speaks volumes."

Conversational Intercourse is even worse. Endless simulations from centuries predating the Great Catastrophe. A time, I come to understand, when the human species took great pleasure in posing charmingly in ball gowns and discussing *absolutely nothing*. It seems we have adopted the very worst of their habits.

"Lovely to make your acquaintance, Lady Ingrasol," I say to my partner. "Indeed, the weather is divine. I do so enjoy these summer evenings. And do tell, what of the progress on your lavish garden?"

There is only so much inconsequential chatter I can withstand before I find myself telling Lady Ingrasol that if she doesn't refrain from another speech pertaining to this season's glove length, I would, quite regrettably, be forced to enhance her eye with my salad fork.

I failed that unit. Incorrect utensil usage, I suppose.

◊   ◊   ◊

"Breathe," Etiquette Tutor says, "drawing from your diaphragm, slowly and deliberately. Remember to be calm. Remember, you are ladies."

I glance at the other "ladies." We are all strapped into our cinchers, a network of cords restraining our bodies. Each of us is plagued by deficient skeletal structures. For some girls, the straps are tighter over their belly or chest, while others have the pressure focused on their pelvis and hips.

The overall purpose: ensuring our waists are shrunk to the absolute minimum.

Etiquette Tutor has an impossible figure. It is stated to be our ideal, yet she has no cohabitant. The closest she has is her enhancement specialist.

The other girls don't appear the least bit uncomfortable, smiling at each other and engaging in polite conversation. They practice for their own Emergence Ball Grand Dinner, daintily holding tiny cakes between thumb and forefinger, nibbling and perfecting the art of being utterly enchanting. Each is thinking of how their own ball will unfold, dreams of perfection almost overcrowding her learned manners.

The pain, it seems, doesn't affect them. Or perhaps they hide it better than I do. Despite the niceties, one must keep in mind that this is a competition.

Somehow, Marius has arranged my ball to be the first of the season. It is apparently quite the honor to have at my whim a full complement of suitors. To me that only means more of them to dispatch.

"Another pull," says Etiquette Tutor. "Big smiles, girls." She circles the room, adjusting each cincher with a gradual increase of pressure. We will bend, but not break, before her. I wince before she even touches my crank. When she does, it's swift and forceful.

The pain shoots up my spine. I clench my teeth, my eyes watering. *Control yourself*, I think, as if it's a viable option.

A moan escapes my mouth. It draws every eye in the room. The girls act completely surprised, though I know they are not. My failure is expected. As are their whispers and giggles.

Next to me, Mica makes no effort to hide her utter disgust. Of all the girls, she's the one I despise the most.

"Livia!" Etiquette Tutor calls in her moderately toned way. "Show some control. Do you plan on making such unattractive vocalizations at your ball? With thousands of eyes upon you?"

We are taught that politeness is of the utmost importance. Yet I find the concept difficult to master, especially when verging on the loss of consciousness due to a lack of oxygen. Or maybe it was the endless monotony of years of lessons I deemed a waste of time; I could no longer bite my tongue.

"I do not plan . . . on wearing . . . a cincher . . . . at my ball!" I gasp, my ribs grinding together.

"Is that so, Livia?"

"I will wear my corset if I must."

"A Proper Young Woman needn't use the corset. You cannot be dependent on the corset!"

With that, Etiquette Tutor gives me another crank. To which I give her an even louder groan.

"Your fellow trainees are undergoing precisely the same exercise, yet they do not appear distorted in the slightest. What value in a tiny waist do they see that you do not? I must assume you believe your fellow trainees to be fools, am I not correct?"

I glance around the room, but the girls avoid my gaze. Glaring, as they are well aware, would be highly distasteful.

Mica makes little effort to hide hers; she was always the pioneer when it came to hating me.

The others believe in the value of cinching because each has practiced it religiously since receiving her first training cincher at age six. Governess saw to it I wouldn't be deprived the same honor, though I promptly hid mine in the storage quarters. I put her replacement to good use as well: target practice. After four more attempts, Governess conceded. "Fortunately, your waist is already smaller than average," she said, exasperated.

"Due to swordsmanship," I told her. "Lucky for you, I didn't choose needlepoint."

"Are you not seeking a wide choice of cohabitant?" says Etiquette Tutor. "Or do you find it dismissible that the Proper Young Men deem you attractive?"

The pain only grows in intensity. They're all watching me now and enjoying the spectacle. An enticing distraction, their favorite folly: watching the Cosmo Airess be put in her rightful place.

The least I can do is give them a spectacle par excellence. I catch Etiquette Tutor's gaze and stare at her, unflinching, as I force my words to sound calm and measured.

"My cohabitant of choice . . . will care about things that truly matter."

Silence. One of the girls flattens her tiny cake between two fingers, her jaw dropping at my utter audacity. Another gasps, and I wonder where she found the breath.

I force my face high, giving them a sufficient view. *I am Livia Cosmo. And yes, I am as incorrect and inappropriate and, I daresay, improper as you imagined. And your opinions do not matter to me. Not in the least.*

I force a smile. My last day brings with it the promise that the pain will stop. It just feels like it won't happen anytime soon.

Her eyes flashing, Etiquette Tutor strides to my contraption and makes a swift adjustment. I choke on my own disobedience.

"Manners," she hisses.

Mica catches my eye and mouths a single word, her lips puckering as though the word is sour.

Orphan.

Once, a very long time ago, Mica didn't consider *orphan* to be a dirty word.

I was very little then. For all I knew, the entire universe was Helix Island, the population consisting of Veda, Governess, and myself. There were many others, of course—Marius and Waslo, Life Guide and maids and gardeners. Still, it never occurred to me that they came from somewhere beyond. I believed Helix to be the center of existence, and myself the center of Helix.

That was before I knew better.

A time when I ran the grounds in bloomers without worrying at soiling the whiteness. I climbed synth-trees and scraped my knees. This was a time when Governess knew how to comfort. When hungry, I ate. Tired, I curled up in my tiny sleeper and fell into a dreamless state. Before I knew what it meant to be a Proper Young Woman.

I did as I pleased and there were no questions. They pitied me, perhaps, and believed the coddling necessary. Poor little orphan Livia, motherless and fatherless and all alone in the world. Yet I never felt alone, with Veda and Governess and endless gardens and an entire island of secrets.

Perhaps I'm making a romance of memory and warming my recollection. For soon I would come to understand the world beyond Helix—the one I never knew existed—would be far crueler than I could have imagined.

The first time I stood at the edge of Helix Island was after Sash Training. I was still in Mica's favor then.

"Sash binding is meant to challenge, thus replicating the transition from innocence to womanly obligation," Etiquette Tutor told us, watching us fumble. "Your sash is a true sign you are a Proper Indrithian Woman."

Long after the others had finished their tidy bows, I was still at work. I couldn't get it right, smiling through my frustration, fingers growing dumb and slow, unable to solve this puzzle on my back.

There was too much to remember.

Sash horizontal to belly. Wrap counterclockwise in steady revolutions. Shift fabric to left, position at rear of body. Grasp edges between thumb and forefinger, measure for evenness. Left draped over right, right pulled under left; loop, pinch, and hold tightly. Wrap clockwise this time, revolutions still steady.

Hold ends firmly and do not forget to smile.

Pull.

And yet, I couldn't make it work. Not that Etiquette Tutor made the task any easier, spitting insults, the other girls forming a perfectly sashed, glaring circle around me.

"You look like an uncultivated fool, Livia. Again. Once again."

The process went on for what seemed like hours.

I didn't succeed in tying my sash that day.

"Do not worry," Mica told me later. She took me aside during Pleasant Interactions. That day, Etiquette Tutor had excused herself at the end of our session. She did this often, knowing we would continue our silly, vapid conversations with or without her presence. That is how well she'd trained us.

"Follow me," Mica whispered, and we ran off, the other girls pretending not to notice us in the clearing behind the bushes.

"Tying the sash means nothing," she told me. "We have maids to do that, after all. This will be your real test. Are we friends, Livia?"

"Yes."

"Do you trust me?"

"Yes," I lied again.

"Close your eyes," she said. I did as I was told. I felt her reach for my hand and hold it in her own soft one. "Do not scream," she said. There was a sharp pain, and I held back my shriek.

"Open your eyes now," she said. I looked down to see blood on my thumb. She had cut me with something. "Look," she said. "I am bleeding, too." She held up her own thumb. While crimson fell down the length of my thumb, hers contained merely a droplet.

"Now I will put my thumbprint inside your sash, and you will do the same for me. In that way, we will be eternally bound. You will be my friend forever, do you understand?"

I nodded and did as I was told, believing her lie. When we were finished, she nodded in satisfaction.

When we returned to the end of Pleasant Interaction, Mica's smile was smugger than ever.

I didn't fully understand then, but I do now. She was proving her power. Mica was powerful enough to cut me. Powerful enough that I was afraid what would happen if I didn't let her.

I kept my thumb wrapped in the corner of my sash. It took a long time to stop bleeding, yet Mica's wound was so superficial it hadn't continued past that first drop. Somehow I was able to hold back my tears until I returned to Helix Island. Even in the transporter ride home, I kept my face impassable.

The instant I set foot on my home island, I took off. Ran fast enough that no one had a chance to see me. Tears streaking off the side of my face, no idea where I was headed, only sure I must keep running.

I decided there had to be a way to escape Mica and Etiquette Tutor. Their conniving eyes and judgmental voices I knew would never stop.

Then I passed the designated borders and came to a sudden stop. I finally understood: I had known the whole time.

I stood at the end of Helix Island and stared out into the clouds.

There had been no stinger barriers, as I'd been warned. No grass-covered holes waiting to eat me. No need to fall into a dark hole. I had always been in one.

There was only the edge, where island met sky.

An entire universe that I would never know.

CHAPTER 8

Countdown to Final Simulation Exam: 3 Weeks

Lex

"Three more weeks," says Kane, "and I won't have to hide my art anymore."

We stare at the ceiling. It's crazy, hearing him say that. Especially the "three weeks" part.

Three weeks from now, Kane and I will receive our placements. He'll probably go to Upper Indra. Back to the air. I have no idea where I'll go. But it won't be aboveground, I'm pretty sure of that. I won't see Kane every day anymore. No more hiding away in his creation studio. No more painting with snorts and shouts and buzzes.

Just three weeks. If everything goes right.

I stare at the ceiling of the abandoned weapons armory, mellowed out from boosters. Kane calls it the COC: the Center of Creation. This is where he makes his sound paintings. Sometimes he even makes sculptures from wreckage I help him collect.

That first year we got to know the Academy inside out. The spaces no one used. The forgotten hallways and hidden corners, those places were ours. They belonged to Kane and me.

When we found this one, we didn't need the others.

This place is stacked with all the stuff Kane has swiped over the years. Even with the strict intake and supply monitoring, instructors still misplace inventory. Only since Kane entered the Academy, though.

Kane can swipe as fast as he can rewire. Gone before you remembered it was there. No one suspects a thing. He just shoots them that innocent smile. It works on everyone. Other cadets, instructors, even the Middler ration distributor blushes, piling his tray with extra helpings.

That kid gets away with everything.

Cassina long stopped acknowledging him. "If he chooses to spend his time with a core-low smudger, then he is not worth mine. Spend time with a dirtgirl, you are bound to get filthy."

Still, I catch her watching him. Her eyes follow him when he leaves a room. She loves him, I can tell. And it kills her that it only goes one way.

Instead, she attaches herself to a new guy every rotation. She giggles and blushes, clings to his arm on the way to classes. Stares at him in a way that makes me want to puke. "He will make a wonderful cohabitant!" she tells the others, then dumps him. The breakup is always dramatic, usually in a crowd. "You will never understand me!" she cries, then races from the Rations Hall, tears streaming. Her followers rush to support her.

It seems to me Cassina's relationships have little to do with understanding.

The only one who doesn't care about Kane? Little Vippy. She only has eyes for me. This has been going on since the Book of Indra show-off session.

Of course, it's me they suspect. Of everything.

My admittance to the Academy still can't be explained. Even after all these years, I hear their complaints about this outcast orphan with top performance marks, beating records on her air speeder. There has to be a reason, though no one can figure out what it might be. How does someone like Lex end up here? And what does Kane see in her?

"Maybe he has, like, this weird thing for orphans," they say with smirks. "Likes to Rock Bottom it, you know? I've heard of guys like that. He'll never cohabitate with her, though. Those kinds of things you keep secret. What, he's going to move her to his estate? No way. He's engaging with her, no doubt."

They're wrong, of course. We've never engaged. Not in the way they're thinking.

Not that I haven't thought about it. Everyone thinks it's happening anyway. It would be easy, I figure. We spend all our time together. One day, while he's talking, I could just lean over and . . .

But that's when my mind goes blank. Or I force it to.

This is Kane, I remind myself. My only friend. I'd do nothing to mess with that.

Besides, I tell myself, *I don't want to.*

Do I?

I look over at Kane, still contemplating a creation studio he doesn't have to hide in an abandoned weapons armory.

I don't care about cohabitation like the other girls. It's not required of cadets. Some do it anyway, but they mainly end up with Academy grads. Like meets like. Nothing changes.

One girl from the Islands locked herself in her pod for two days, crying hysterically.

"Debut ball season," I heard her podmate mutter. "She'd be having hers if the PCF hadn't recruited her."

When Kane explained a debut ball, I just started laughing. I'd never heard of anything so crazy. Didn't that girl know how lucky she was? She was a cadet. She was chosen. He told me this girl's parents had lost their social standing, had lost their means to throw her a proper ball. She was chosen, sure, but it wasn't her choice. Still, she really wanted to prance around in a dress instead of blasting rebels?

"And what about you?" I asked Kane. "Would you have gone to those balls if you were still on your island?"

"Yes," he said. "Not even negotiable."

Being without him? That scared me. That was nonnegotiable, too.

In three weeks, I'll be right back where I started. Alone like in the Orphanage.

Kane sighs. I still refuse to mention his weird behavior. He's distracted a lot, disappearing for long stretches, showing up suddenly without an explanation. He doesn't smile as much.

I keep thinking he'll tell me on his own. Or maybe he's worried about the Final Simulation, just like me. Even though he pretends it doesn't matter. Besides, questions won't make anything better.

Boosters do, though. Boosters make everything better.

Like I never realized how fascinating the ceiling is.

"I can't believe you just walked in the medical unit and took them," I say. My voice sounds faraway, like it belongs to another Lex entirely.

"No one ever notices."

Of course, we'd scored boosters before. The first time we ever boosted, a cadet had smuggled them back from the City of Indra after midterm break. These ones—Kane found Sergeant's private stash in a storage unit. "How could you take that kind of risk?" I asked him, furious. "Why don't you just ask them to expel you!? You're crazy!"

"You might be right," he said. "You want some?"

"Of course," I said, palm already extended.

Sometimes we just need a release.

Boosters have all kinds of medical and tactical uses, but the bright pink ones made us laugh for hours about the stupidest thing. The yellows make me so relaxed I can melt into the steel floor like it's a feather sleeper.

But the ones he handed me now were different. Medical boosters, I realized, were far more powerful.

Kane's secret studio is a hollow room beneath the main building. I can hear cadets running the halls above us, their thuds like the steps of giants. Smell the sharp, bitter odor of formulas mixed in the student lab two quadrants over.

Heat emanates from Kane's skin, warming me from across the room.

"Wow," I say. "What kind are these?"

"Sensory, I think," he says. "What you think they use them for?"

"Maybe on missions," I guess. "To hear enemies miles away? To smell out explosives?"

"Intense," says Kane "Especially for you, I bet. I mean, you can already do that stuff. Like, how I feel right now . . . must be, like, how you feel *all the time*."

"Yeah," I agree. "Probably."

"Is it too much?"

"Nah," I say. "You'd be surprised what you can get used to."

"Sometimes I wish I could do that stuff. Hear people whispering, see stuff through the dark."

"No, you don't," I say. "You'd be as big a freak as me. And you're already close."

"True," he says with a chuckle. A few seconds pass. "Hey!" he says, sitting up suddenly. "You'd tell me if I smelled bad, right? 'Cause you'd be the first to know, right?"

That makes me laugh, and then he laughs, too. I can't stop. He's the only one who does that to me. Then he snorts, or maybe I do. Either way, it starts a whole new round of laughing.

We finally settle down, and then for a while, we're quiet.

I can hear his heart beating in his chest, and my own syncs with the beat. Kane is staring at his newest sculpture hanging from the ceiling above him. The sculptures are so different from his sound paintings. Still beautiful, but in a way that makes me uncomfortable.

Horrifyingly beautiful.

"Come look at this," he says, motioning to his newest one. I already have, you can't exactly miss it. Still, I go over anyway and sprawl out next to him.

Together, we look up.

Bolts, wires, and empty rounds left over from Target Instruction, all fused together into the shape of a body. A face with spikes coming out of the eye sockets.

The sculpture glares down at us.

"Who's that supposed to be?" I ask him.

"You, me. Everyone, I guess."

I give him a serious look. "Is it tough on you? I mean, being so genetically dysfunctional?"

"Liberating," he says, grinning. "And it keeps me occupied. But maybe I should ask you the same question."

I sigh. "Maybe you should."

"I was just kidding," he says. We're silent for a moment.

"It really is everyone. The instructors. The cadets. The whole core-low Academy."

"Yeah, but not for much longer. Pretty soon we'll be running the Final Simulation. And then we'll be out there, doing something. For real. Taking out real enemies." I feel the intensity rising inside me. "Finding real Rock Bottom scavs and . . ."

"And what?" he says.

"Punishing them. Decimating them."

There's a long pause.

"Sure. Pretty soon the unreal will be real. And the real, well, I guess that never existed in the first place. Not here. But I want to ask you a question. Why? What's the point? Why take out anyone? I mean, it won't make a difference."

"Wow, Kane. You sure are smart. Specially on boosters." I sit up. "All those raiding parties rising up from the core? If the core-low rebels had their way, everyone above would be forced to join them.

They want to bring civilization back to the way it was before, before Indra gave us something to look up to, and they won't think twice about blasting first."

I pull out my blaster and place the tip on his forehead. "Just like that. It's a real situation out there. Our people are getting killed."

"Just who are *your* people?" he says.

It's mean but I'm angrier because it's true. My people don't exist. But if I can't believe in progress, if I'm always going to just be an orphan, what's this life for? I want something better.

I look away from him and he knows he's gone too far. I can hear his heart pick up in his chest and he's pushing off more body heat than before, so much it makes me feel uncomfortable.

"If that wasn't a simulation blaster, maybe I'd take you a little more seriously," he says.

"I always take you seriously."

He laughs and it breaks the tension. I can't stay angry. I break, too. My body is suddenly pulsing with energy. *The boosters*, I think. The idea of real missions. Making those Rock Bottom scrubbers bow before the force of our superior firepower.

"You really hate them, don't you?" says Kane. Like he can hear my thoughts. Sometimes I wonder if he actually can. "I mean, I've never met anyone from Rock Bottom. It's hard to hate someone you've never met."

"Not that hard," I say. A memory plays in my head: an empty cot being sprayed with antisepticizer. All that's left is a number: 374.

They sent 374 back where they found her, back to Rock Bottom. I'll bet those core-low dirtmongers decimated her within seconds of her arrival.

I hate the Rock Bottom. I hate every monster in that place. I want to destroy them with every fiber of my being.

I've never told Kane about Samantha or the Orphanage and the kids left outside the gates for the mutants. He doesn't talk about his home island, or clear up the gossip that his father's a recluse and his mother long dead.

There are some things you don't need to talk about. Somehow we both kind of know the truths already.

I know his face so well. In the first year, when I felt like a shadow person roaming the Academy halls, I'd see it and his crazy grin would pull me into existence.

That same face stares at me now, unsmiling and just a little less boyish. That face I know as well as my own, inches away, our eyes level.

"I'll never see you again," he says softly. "I'll be doing security in the Hub. Maybe in the City of Indra. And you . . . they'll put you somewhere important, I know it. Doing something hidden. Secret. And I don't know when and if we'll ever see each other again."

"No," I say. "Not like that, just like we promised. We'll see each other, Kane."

We've gone over this.

"I know," he says. "I would never forget that. I just meant—"

"Two weeks after the Final Simulation," I say, cutting him off. *I'll tell you again. I'll tell you until you can't think of anything else.* "We meet in the Archives in the memory of your eighth birthday. On your estate, behind your grand obelisk. You'll remember, right?"

"Of course. Eight years old. My birthday. Estate. But what if *you* forget?"

"How could I?"

"No," he says, his face serious. "Me."

His expression makes me feel strange. "Yeah," I say. "I wish."

He doesn't laugh and neither do I. Our eyes lock.

Then I want to do something crazy. Something I could've never imagined wanting.

I want Kane to kiss me. Or for me to lean over and kiss him. Either or both or whichever comes first.

Lex, don't be crazy.

I turn away quickly, my pulse racing like a speeder. I pull myself to sitting, my face flushed and tingling. Boosters. It's got to be the boosters. "We'll be late for rations," I say.

Kane has turned back to face the ceiling. He stares into the sculpture's spiked eyes.

"If you say so," he says.

I don't look at him. I'm afraid I'll see it again. That flash across his face.

"Get up, Cadet!" I say, trying to sound normal. I give him a kick in the ribs. Not hard enough to really hurt.

"Okay, killer. I hear you."

I immediately erase everything that just happened. I have to focus on what matters: the Final Simulation.

Still, I'm sure I saw it. That split second, his expression was unmistakable.

He wanted the same thing. He wanted to kiss me.

I give the ceiling a push and the fluorescent light irritates my boosted senses. I hoist myself up first. I look back at Kane, still in the Center of Creation below. I reach out my hand, and he takes it.

"Remember: eighth birthday. Behind the grand obelisk."

"You know I'll be there," he says, and I pull him into the real world.

CHAPTER 9

Countdown to Emergence Ball: 1 Week

Livia

I can barely walk. I limp a few steps, Marius watching pityingly.

"Ah, the cincher, I daresay," she says. "Not the most appealing of lessons."

My heavy sigh serves as answer enough. I long ago ceased my fibs of successful lesson completions and Etiquette Tutor's accolades. The day I stood on a platform sixty feet in the sky, to be precise.

"I don't understand the necessity," I say.

"And you are not meant to, my love. Have all these years taught you nothing?"

What it feels like to be despised, I think. *What it feels like to have an enemy.*

"Perhaps," I say.

"Well, it will be of no concern where we are headed. Let us enjoy some time together."

Marius and I are in the living quarters on Helix, surrounded by white walls. I wear my white evening gown, reclining vertically across the white reposer. The only pigment is the synth-dirt-stained soles of my feet. There was no time to groom before Etiquette, not that I would have. Etiquette Tutor cannot see through shoes, after all.

Marius pretends not to notice, though. Having also been trained by Etiquette Tutor, she is well versed in Portrayal of Obliviousness upon Encountering Unpleasantness.

I wonder if Etiquette Tutor will ever retire. I doubt it. She clearly relishes the power too much.

"Shall we?" she asks. I nod, tap my wrist, and press my thumb to my pulse. Then Marius reaches over, inserting the access chip into my wrist with a satisfying click.

"Take me anywhere that is very far from here," I tell her. I lean back and gaze upward.

Within moments, the white ceiling has gone black.

The darkness is broken by a pinprick of light spreading outward, seeping brightness across my vision.

When I gather my bearings, I can see we're in an enormous domed room embellished with gold. There are fragments of melody, and I discover the source below, men with strange instruments plucking out uneven notes. "They are tuning them," Marius says. I turn, and she's watching me, smiling at my wonderment. "We are at the theater."

"But why?"

"For pure enjoyment. The viewers wish to be, I suppose, taken to a place they have never seen."

This part I understand.

"Rather popular charade, this one," she adds, gazing downward. Below us, the patrons are seated and waiting. The men wear strange uniforms and long coats; the women are an eternity of sparkling beads and plumed feathers. They whisper behind their hands, faces disappearing behind sleeves bloated to gigantic puffed orbs.

"This is Russia," Marius says. "A place that is very cold and dark. So chilling, in fact, the citizens must ingest medicine to avoid freezing—vodka."

We are seated high above the others in an area reserved for those worthy of notice. Box seats, Marius calls them. Part of me yearns to be below with the others, close enough to smell their perfume, hear the silk of their dresses rustle.

Perhaps I am destined to always be in the air, even within an Archive; fated to eternal isolation on varying makes of island.

The theater lights fade around us. "Is it over?" I ask helplessly.

"It has just begun," says Marius, the music rising.

Despite my dislike of Waslo, for two things I am grateful: his extended Archive access and Marius herself. Marius need not be relegated to dusty archival ruins with tedious images scrawled on the ceiling. Because of Waslo's stature, she's allowed into historic re-creations unavailable to the average Indrithian citizen. Locations created for only the most high-level scholars and meant to entertain Indrithians of the Utmost Importance. And on occasion, she will take me with her.

Marius has shown me Archives I never imagined possible. Places deemed too provocative for the average citizen. A hub of flashing lights, the technology rudimentary. Yet the citizens find the site so overwhelming they are forced to halt midstep and stare upward. She pointed out the ancient form of holo-imaging spanning across the buildings of Times Square. A frenzy of distractions: food products and electric smiling faces and garish fashions. An early hololettering runs across the whole disconcerting collage. "This is where they exhibit and honor those societal artifacts they deem most meaningful."

I have seen a jungle, where the growing things are more powerful than the people. I have slid across ice caps, seen a mountain explode and bleed fire. We have watched figures travel the desert upon strange, long-necked creatures.

I have seen things that startled me, images so odd I could hardly believe they existed. "Why can others not see them?" I asked.

"They are saved for those believed worthy," Marius said, smiling as though I was one of them.

She's mistaken, I thought, listing various failures in my head: the girls who abhorred me, failed etiquette lessons, stains and dirty soles and Mica.

I would never argue, of course. I needed these excursions, even if they were just simulations.

I had come to like these fabricated worlds better than my real one.

Yet never as much as this one. I want the ballet to last forever.

Onstage, the women prance like Veda. They stand on the very ends of their toes, their chins lifted high, and spin in dizzying circles. They are strong, their muscles lean and hard, yet they move weightlessly, unrestrained as the clouds around Helix.

"They are beautiful, are they not?" says Marius.

I nod, watching through the crude magnifying device. I can only imagine what their skill with a zinger could be. The music intensifies, the dancers moving faster, seeming to barely skim the ground. Marius, her voice low and gentle, tells me the story as I watch. "And now it is the princess's birthday. She is blissful, you see?"

The princess dances across the stage on her pointed toes, elated. A crowd gathers to observe, the king and queen and their many Middlers, all infected by her happiness and smiling.

"She's about your age. Young and beautiful and holding the world in her palm. And this is her special day, just as your Emergence Ball will be."

Those two words suck the happy right out of me.

Marius must see the change, so she rests her soft, small hand over mine. "You have no idea, my love, of your own power."

I have no power.

"Just look at her, Livia. Beloved and worshipped by all."

I watch as the princess dances on air, a skill not taught in the Islands. There are so many things I do not know and will never learn.

"The princess is sweet and gracious, just as you will be at your ball. And observe those watching. They are transfixed by her. See the faces of the men? They cannot look away. The Proper Young Men will do the same for you, my dear."

"And she's not even wearing a cincher," I state.

"Touché. But do not underestimate the power of having the right man beside you. Pick the right cohabitant, and you can have everything. Not just an island, my love, but power far beyond any you could ever imagine."

Marius has never spoken in this manner, the urgency in her voice making me uneasy.

I do not wish for a man beside me, I want to tell her, *be him the right or wrong one. And what use is power when it comes with designated borders?*

Onstage, the princess spins in circles.

"It's not what you sacrifice," Marius says, "but what you gain. And you, my love, can gain *everything*."

Marius leans back, gazing toward the stage. The princess leaps, her body lithe and strong. For a moment, she appears to hover, body suspended in space.

I know she must come down. That kind of happiness cannot last.

A bit later, I find my assertion to be correct. A disfigured sorceress arrives to cast evil spells. The princess ends her birth celebration lifeless, sprawled prettily across the castle floor.

"She will remain in this state for a hundred years, until a cohabitant arrives to wake her with a kiss," Marius whispers. "Rescuing her from the cage of eternal darkness."

Reliance on Others to Affirm Our Femininity, I think. *Etiquette Tutor would approve.*

The pantomime ends. The lights lift and the bodies rise from their seats. The men replace their hats, the women adjust their trains. They chat while exiting, the crowd growing thinner by the moment.

The ending has come far too soon.

"I wish to stay here forever," I tell Marius.

"You silly thing. Eventually, you would be flung. And besides, who wishes to live in an Archive?"

"Perhaps they haven't seen this one," I say. I turn to her, suddenly frantic. "One more place, Marius. Please. Take me anywhere, I don't care where. I can't return to Helix, not just yet."

Marius raises her eyebrow. She sighs, smiles, and reaches for my access chip.

Ocean is far grander than Life Guide had described. I don't fear the edge of the cliff, or the waves that break upon its rocky base hundreds of feet below. All I can do is stare and get lost and wonder where it begins and where it ends. "How does a mass of such vastness simply vanish?" I ask.

"The Great Catastrophe," Marius says as I remove my slippers. She sees me do this, and with a girlish smile that signals a secret that must be kept between us, she does the same.

The earth is soft and wet under my bare feet, the sun a ball of fire setting in the distance, casting its orange-gold across the water's glistening surface. They are perfect cohabitants, the sun and the sea.

"Ocean hasn't existed for centuries," Marius says. "Before the Great Catastrophe, nature could not be controlled. Nature could hurt you, for it was violent and untamed, just as we once were as well."

Now the sun is harvested, rain collected, and wind harnessed for proper use. It all occurs far above the highest island in the Aero-Crown. If Indra were a living being, the Aero-Crown would be the heart. The blood it pumps gives power and light. But it is a machine. Its power can't match that of the sun or the ocean. The grand fountain atop the Independent High Council, a wonder only Indrithians of the Utmost Importance are privileged enough to see, would be but a drop in this ocean.

I try to mentally record this moment high up on the cliff, knowing that, most likely, this will be the last of my Archive adventures with Marius.

Proper Cohabitated Women have obligations. They don't play with zingers, and they don't muck about in Archives. These activities are not considered Proper and they certainty don't serve the Greater Indrithian Good.

As soon as I understood Mother was an idea greater than an air harp, I had come to wish Marius was mine. Then we could visit Archives, even after I had cohabitated, and few would dare question. But Marius isn't my mother, couldn't be even if she wanted. According to *The Book of Indra*, "A solitary offspring is permitted per Cohabitated Unit, and that child must originate from said Cohabited Unit's genetic resources."

Etiquette Tutor forced us to memorize this section.

And then there is the unspoken secret: Marius already has a child. I have overheard the gossip since I was young, though Waslo and Marius have never confirmed it. Perhaps a genetic mutation, I conclude—a child even smaller than Marius—they have chosen to conceal for fear of public ridicule.

In a strange way, I'm jealous of her. Or him. Perhaps we could have been good friends.

"It's not so bad," says Marius suddenly. "Cohabitation." Her voice ricochets across the water, then surprisingly returns to her. "Perhaps you will fancy one of the Young Men."

"Perhaps I will find my own Waslo," I say, imagining no fate worse.

She laughs, a tinkling sound. "You will do better," she says. I turn to her, eyes wide. "Do not appear so greatly shocked, Livia. You are a smart young woman. You must know that Waslo has given me a great deal, elevated me to an enviable status. Of course, due in large part to my own guidance of him, but that is beside the point."

"Do you love him?" I say, the words slipping out before I realize what's been said.

"In a manner of speaking, I suppose. I respect him. I applaud his success. I bask in the light of his accolades. That is love enough for me." She sighs. "I love him for choosing me. I was lucky to find anyone at all."

I nod, understanding. She looks off into the ocean.

"Waslo saw something no one else was capable of seeing. 'You are little on the outside,' he told me. 'But inside you tower over the others.' He let me be strong. In fact, he welcomed the strength."

Marius turns to me. I've never seen her expression so fierce.

"He worshipped your father, of course. Would have followed Armand to the ends of Indra and beyond. Your father was a brilliant man, and Waslo was devastated when . . ." She shakes her head. "When it was over."

Please keep going, I think. *Tell me. What happened to my mother and father?*

I don't say that of course, for I already know her response. The same I have been given for as long as I remember.

"You will be a Citizen of Importance, my dear. Just like Waslo. Just like your father before you. After you cohabitate, you will carry out his legacy."

"Genetics? Unlikely, since Life Guide refuses to impart this knowledge. Perhaps if I had access to my father's research . . ."

"Is that what you want? Truly?"

I nod. I feel I want his research more than anything. It's my birthright.

"I'm sorry, my dear, but I was told that disappeared when your father . . ." Suddenly, she grows pained.

"Perhaps the High Council recovered it. Waslo could speak with them."

"Perhaps. We have petitioned for anything they may have found, but all we hear back are empty promises. Remember, you'll be a woman soon, and now is the time to wipe the slate clean." Her mood shifts more drastically than I expect, and it's clear what the loss of my father's friendship meant to her. "I'm being silly," she says, brushing hair from my face. "I'm spoiling our time together."

"No," I say, trying to hide how crushed I feel inside.

"There was a great deal of power in knowledge, your father's knowledge especially. He was . . . visionary." Marius reaches out, takes my hand in her own. "But you . . . you are his finest creation."

Now we are facing each other. Even the ocean is overwhelmed by the privacy of our council. "Promise me one thing," she says, staring into my eyes, distracted by what she sees there for a second. How my eyes do not match.

We have done this before, I think, remembering suddenly. *The first day of Socialization Club, when I worried your collar might choke you.* Only then I was looking up at Marius, and now I must look downward.

I nod, just as I had then.

"You must be the ideal Proper Young Woman at your ball. For Waslo. For me. Because we owe it . . . to the memory of your father. And to the citizens of Indra."

At that moment, I understand: she may love me, but that is beside the point. Above all else, I am her duty. The obligation she has spent my lifetime fulfilling.

It is almost freeing, the sudden knowledge: I'm completely alone in the world, even more so than I imagined.

"I promise," I tell her, and she smiles as the sun is replaced by the moon.

I stare into the horizon, the reflections of long-extinct stars shining off the long-evaporated ocean water.

That is when I sense the desperation. *Someone is watching*, I think, turning quickly. Just fast enough to glimpse a black-cloaked figure, hood pulled low, eyes peering out from beneath, glimmering and alive.

Shadow people have dead eyes, I think. Or so we have been taught.

Marius follows my gaze. "Splendid, Livia!" she says quickly. "I knew you would understand."

She pulls out my access chip and everything disappears.

CHAPTER 10

Final Simulation Exam

Excerpted from The Population Control Forces
Academy Cadet Holo-Handbook, *Chapter 45, Section 8*

FINAL SIMULATION

Immediately following completion of Final Simulation, Cadet
will appear before Population Control Forces Panel for performance assessment. At that time, Cadet will receive orders of
their placement within the PCF.

Immediately following placement orders, Cadet is granted
twenty-four hours in which to collect belongings, clear out pod,
and report for active duty.

As ordered by the Independent High Council, Cadets' placements are permanent. Cadets have been carefully chosen, and
PCF placement is nonnegotiable.

As a PCF Cadet, you have been carefully chosen and rigorously
trained for one purpose: protecting our Great Indrithian Society.

This is the greatest honor of all.

Lex

I'm ready to kick dustball ass. Now I just need the signal.

My black mission suit gleams, the silitex molding to my curves like a second skin. I've secured my body plates, pulled the straps extra snug. My new blaster, the Dust2Dust Model 750 they hand out before exams, is packed with four hundred charges.

I straddle my air speeder, the engine humming beneath me. Kane straddles his ride beside me, grinning in that way he has, upper lip curling like nothing matters. Like this exam won't determine our entire forsaken futures.

I narrow my eyes at him. He's still grinning. He'll do what he wants, always has. It makes me crazy. It's also the reason he's my best friend.

"Focus on yourself, mudgirl." I don't have to turn. I can picture Cassina's cold blue eyes staring through the security goggles. Her hair, so blond it's almost white, is sheared at her chin like a helmet, with ends sharp enough to cut you.

My hair is long, dark, and wild. The cadet groomer gave up on me years ago. Set his clippers down and said, "Not much I can do here."

If only Cassina had done the same thing.

"Too much mud in your ears?" she says, her voice ringing clearly through my earfeed. Even above two dozen engines I can hear her say, "You make me sick."

She's trying to psych me out, of course. I know how that airborne princess works.

"You bottom out here, they'll dump you back to the very bottom. Let the mudpeople eat you alive. But does anyone want you?" Her voice plays at being hard. "You just appeared one day. All alone in the world, no one giving a damn whether you lived or died." She laughs. "Not much has changed, I suppose."

I will smash your face in, I think for the first time today. It's not a new thing. She's rabid because she doesn't have my focus. She's a victim to her nerves. She throttles her air speeder at the head of the pack.

We're all waiting for the green light.

For our final exam, Cassina's leading this mission. Indra help us all!

Indra has put miles between civilization as we know it and Rock Bottom. This is to ensure that only those who want to get there have the determination to traverse the tunnelways and suffer through the heat that builds the deeper you go. The silitex regulates our body temperatures, but it never feels completely comfortable.

Cassina leads the pack, and the rest of us stay in formation as we bend around the turns and merge into the narrowing passage. One mile out and we go into silent running, cutting down our engine power to mask our approach. We cut our illuminators by 90 percent, but my eyes have no trouble with the darkness. The rest do their best to avoid sheer drops that go express to the core. The placement panel will examine our recorded biorhythms on our return. My adrenaline is off the charts.

Like I said, you have to want to be down here. I do and I have much to prove.

Cassina signals for a full stop. We hold in silence, awaiting her next order. What's come so far was the easy part. Now we have to track down the scavenger leader and detain the locals.

Kane's head is bopping up and down, as if he's saying, *Come on already.* Even now he keeps it light.

"Lex? You'll take point from here on in," Cassina says.

I look at her. She mistakes it for confusion.

"That means you'll be scouting the perimeter."

I heard her the first time. There is silence on the earfeed.

A one-way. No return. A ride to failure. That's what all the cadets are thinking.

Clearing a room is dangerous enough. Clearing an entire mud cell is even worse.

Being the first one in? Suicide.

There are other options. Logical options. Send in a recon team for initial surveillance, disorient the enemy with a warning flash-buster. But sending in a single cadet? We all know that is core-low crazy.

It's a setup. Of course I know that. Everyone does. Send me in, get me killed off.

I know the others are waiting on the earfeed to hear my okay. My mind is racing. The fear is very real.

I go in first, I think. *Get demolished immediately. Cassina orders team to rush location, surprising already disoriented enemy and taking the mud cell out.*

Cassina leads us to victory.

I fail.

Theoretically, she could make this work. But it goes against every-thing we've been taught to value. The plan shows blatant disregard for her fellow cadets. For the people who have been trained to have her back.

That's about as core-low as you get.

Cassina hates me even more than I thought. She hates me enough to jeopardize her mission captain status.

Of course. It isn't that big a risk. Not for her.

She'll risk low results and still get a great placement. Either way, she'll be fine. And chances are she's probably thinking everyone will remember the victory. Not the sacrifice that made it possible.

Then I notice something. I'm smiling.

"Okay," I say, breaking the awkward silence. I hear someone gasp. "Order received, Mission Captain."

I'll take out every single one of them. Every single dirt scavenger. By myself. Just me blasting my way through those dirtmongers.

I'm ready. I've always been ready.

And being alone? That's nothing new.

"Okay, Cadet," says Cassina, uneasy.

Maybe she thought I didn't have the guts. Maybe she's realizing the truth. Maybe Cassina's thinking: *Wow, I really am evil.*

Most likely not.

"Cadet," she says, her voice strong again. "Take defensive position and await the go—"

A voice buzzes in. "No," it says. "No, Cassina."

Kane.

"Excuse me, Mission Captain," he says. "What I mean . . . I'd like to volunteer to accompany Cadet Lex. Make it a two-man clearing mission."

"Wait," I say. "I can do it by my—"

"Mission Captain?" says Kane, his voice rising over mine. "Do I have the go-ahead?"

He called her out. Stepped up for a fellow cadet. In that moment, I know she hates Kane as much as she hates me.

"Fine," she hisses. "Just get the job done."

Rock and concrete. The smell of human waste. Leftover bits of humanity: a deflated zip ball, mounds of stinking, soiled clothing. Thick black mud bubbles up to our ankles. Some sort of rubbish dump. Or maybe this is just another day in Rock Bottom.

Kane and I crouch behind a mound of scrap and wait for the signal. We left our air speeders outside the tunnel entrance and trekked down here on foot. My hand mutes the earfeed. "What were you thinking?" I spit.

"Calm down," he says, covering his own.

"Now we'll both get bad placements if you survive this."

"I don't care," he says. "Do you understand?"

I've never heard Kane like this. His intensity shuts me up quick. "I don't care about my placement, Lex. Don't you get that? I never have. I could have gotten myself kicked out of the Academy long ago."

"Why didn't you?"

He doesn't say anything back. He doesn't have to. I can see the answer in his eyes.

I don't need you, I want to say. *I don't need anybody.*

The earfeed buzzes a mission update alert.

"You will infiltrate the headquarters and take recon. Other cadets, take positions bordering the area. Cadet Lex and Cadet Kane, we will await your signal. Understood?"

"Absolutely," I say.

Silence.

"Kane?" says Cassina.

"Copy," he repeats, though his silence already said everything.

"Good. Then stabilize and await four count," says Cassina, having regained a measure of self-delusional swagger. Kane and I stare at each other, both holding our breath.

"Four . . . three . . ."

Instantly, we rush for the target, our bodies hunched low in the dark. We stop, push up against a slab of rock. I check coordinates on my wrist monitor. "Less than ten feet around this corner," I say. "You ready?"

"For anything," he says.

Then he grins. The lip curls. It's exactly what I need. The power surges up through me.

We sprint from cover and don't stop until we reach a tall building jutting out from the side of the tunnel. It's then I realize the tunnel is a wide boulevard. There are thousands of tracks trampled into the earth, all migrating here. Most of them are fresh.

The building was white once, in the long, long ago, and the front steeples up. At the top hangs a large, rusty bell. If you rang it, it would probably fall and smash through to ground level—that's what condition this place is in.

The dirt scavengers hide in this house of worship. Wooden shingles hang like broken teeth. Dust storms have torn gaping holes in the roof. What remains was blackened by fire.

Just like a Rock Bottomer, I think. *Taking something nice and sucking the beauty right out of it.*

Kane and I could sit here and let time solve our problem for us. One blast to the bell and it would fall, maybe destabilize the whole structure. Seal the scavs and their blasted leader inside.

That's when we hear the grating notes. Clanking and banging so loud I think my ears might split open.

I freeze for a second.

"Are you okay?" says Kane

"Of course," I say as my blaster hums to full power. Kane has his at the ready, too, as we skirt the perimeter until we find a broken window along the side.

I clear away the glass shards with the butt end of my blaster—the racket coming from inside so loud you couldn't hear a transporter landing—then sling my weapon back over my shoulder.

I reach up, bracing myself on the edges of the opening.

"Wait," says Kane. I feel his hand on my back. "I'll go first."

I turn around. "No way," I say. "I have to go first, you know that. That's the assignment. I'm First Cadet."

He nods but doesn't take away his hand. I look straight in his eyes. "I'm glad, though. That you came with me."

Kane nods and boosts me up.

I drop down into the pitch-black. He lands beside me and we stay crouched on the sticky floor.

"I can't see anything," yells Kane. The music—if you could call it that—is louder. I feel my teeth vibrating. "Should I turn on our beamers?"

"No," I say. "It'll give us away. Just follow me. And stay close." He rolls his eyes like he always does when he thinks I'm being bossy. "And don't make that face either." He almost grins.

We scuttle along the ground, pushing through garbage and debris. My hands are coated in a thick, sticky fluid. I cut my leg on something sharp. Straight through my uniform. I see the blood rising through my silitex. I know the wound is deep. *This must hurt*, I think.

All I feel is electricity running through my body.

Kane tries to give Cassina information through his earfeed. It's useless. We can't even hear ourselves think, that's how loud it is.

The clanging and grinding is overwhelming, inescapable. My temples throb.

Kane grabs my foot. He means *stop*. I know him that well. I turn to look at him. Something is about to happen. I know that's what he's thinking.

Be careful.

Light bursts from the monstrous gaping hole in front of us, a fiery mouth blazing inches from our faces.

Kane and I look at each other. His eyes are wild, his face lit up bright.

I trust you more than anyone in the world, I think. *And I hate that. That I need to depend on anyone.*

We rise to our feet at the same time, blasters aimed.

Now or never.

Together, we rush into the light.

It's too much to take in all at once. I feel something snap in my brain. I circle the room with my eyes, trying to get my bearings, trying to keep my cool when everything I see is horrible and new. They never taught us about this.

I wonder if I'm going crazy.

The screeching music is coming from the top of the huge cavern. An enormous pipe organ hangs from the ceiling, a man pummeling the keys like he's committing murder.

They're all dancing. Horrible, disfigured bodies writhing together. If you totaled up all their missing limbs, you could probably build a dozen more of these scavs. An old man is speaking to a half-naked woman. He opens his mouth wide, showing rotted teeth and half a blackened tongue. The woman is huge, her fat gathered in strange, uneven lumps on her body. She laughs at us through bright pink lips. Her laugh sounds more like a backfiring speeder.

Someone passes a bottle to a man with a scarred face. He gulps it down, then smashes it on his companion's head. Bright red blood squirts from the wound. No one takes notice except us. The scarred face erupts into cackles and moves on.

Over his head sails a firebomb.

A bare-chested man with an exoskeleton mutation hunkers nearby, parts of his heavy bone structure outside instead of in. The firebomb breaks on his back. Instantly, he's on fire. He makes a hollow, shrieking sound and the flesh melts beneath his bones.

Above, the man continues to play music. Below, everyone keeps dancing.

Next to me, Kane tries to keep his breathing steady. I can't unsee this either—the true face of the scavs, the savagery of Rock Bottom—but I can make it no longer exist. Which one is the leader, I couldn't begin to guess. If we are to survive, we'll probably have to take them all down.

Then a loud moan echoes through the room. Loud enough to hear over the music. It doesn't seem human. Everything stops. Heads turn in our direction. We've been spotted.

Everyone is looking at us. The ones with no eyes stare through empty sockets.

Then they're coming. For us. All of them. All at once.

"Now," I say to Kane, our blasters already aimed. Our blasters are the loudest music of all.

If that organist doesn't stop playing, I'll go mad. Kane's shooting at their feet, keeping them away, while I aim at the organ on the balcony. It's so patched together, the support struts are calling my name. I'll feel stupid if I don't do this, and probably die, too. You have to take advantage of every opportunity your environment affords.

I blast the first strut and the rusty metal snaps. The organist plays a harsh cord as the balcony shifts, and that might be enough to bring it down, but I'm not interested in half measures. I blast the other strut and it doesn't take but one second for the organ's massive weight to bring it all down. Kane sees what I'm doing and he's backpedaling with me.

The organ tears a hole through the floor, and the sound of its destruction—of colliding metal and rending and groaning—is the best thing I've heard so far. Except now the scavs not caught under the organ are running crazed out of their minds straight for us.

I take out the closest one and the blast sends him flying through the cloud of devastation.

For a second, I feel sick. Until I remember they aren't human. They're Rock Bottom. And it's them or it's me.

I hear a blast and an enormous man stops suddenly, so close his hot breath fogs my face shield. He's covered in hair, even his face. The hair on his chest is smoking and smells like burned rations. His eyes roll backward, and the rest of his body follows.

I turn. Kane's face is a mask of fury, his blaster fuming. He gives me a look. "Careful, Lex!" he says, just as two blistered arms wrap around his waist.

They belong to a shriveled old lady. She's strong—only survivors live long down here—pulling him to the ground. Instantly, two men are on him, kicking and bellowing. Spittle launches from their mouths. Kane groans. A bodysuit and face shield can only protect him so much. I aim my blaster, but something's got me by the arm.

I spin, coming face-to-face with my attacker, only his is half a face. He screams and Kane screams, and my miscalculation—my appetite for destruction—has put my best friend at death's door.

I slam my head against his half face, and pus and blood smear against my face shield. His scream's cut short by my blaster. The guys pummeling Kane are next to fall. Kane rolls over, pretty ragged, but manages to get on his feet with my help. I won't let go.

"Welcome to the Lower Levels," he mutters.

The chaos I've created has done something right. The scavs have turned on each other. They haven't forgotten us either, but they're willing to kill anything within reach to . . . to . . . I don't understand them. Any of this.

Back-to-back, the weight of each other propping us up, Kane and I blast full force at everything in sight. We give it everything we got. As soon as one falls, another is coming.

"What do we do?" I say.

"Mission Captain! We need backup!" shouts Kane into the earfeed. "We need backup!"

No answer. They won't come without the signal. Maybe the earfeed has been compromised. Or maybe they're ignoring us. After the head butt to pus face, all I get is static in my ear.

The room is roaring. My head throbs like it might explode.

Then I get it.

"The sound paint!" I scream.

"The what?"

I turn to him, still blasting. The blaster's energy bar is flashing red. I'm going to run out of a charge real soon. I flip open my face shield. *"Sound paint!"* I shout. *"Sound! Paint!"*

His face lights up through the drying blood. He always carries some, even here. Even though we're prohibited from carrying personal items. How he snuck it in past the instructors and the sensors, now that's a secret he'd delight in not telling me.

My blaster stops firing, and even spent, I can use it as a club. I crack a scav in the head, but another rips the dead blaster out of my hands. Kane hands his off in my gut, and I shield him and keep firing. Hope still lives in this hopeless place. The blaster is the only instrument I've ever played, but I'm sure it's the most beautiful in all of Indra.

I look over at Kane. He's the same twelve-year-old I met, with the same face, aged some but more confident. I think he's even having fun. He's always known how to do that.

His arm is lifted high and he takes a deep breath before he starts spraying.

Instantly, there's color.

Not the colors of my laugh, no purples or blues. Not the swirling reds and amber on his *Book of Indra*, but colors I've never seen. Colors I hope never to see again.

The color of rot and decay. Infected yellows and festering greens.

The first sound cloud rises. I hold my breath because the mixture of the sight and the smell is enough to make my eyes bleed.

Fists freeze in midair, and finally, there's dumbfounded silence.

I love this silence so much. . . .

At least until mayhem returns. It turns out even scavs get scared. Or maybe they're screaming in excitement. Or just for the sake of screaming.

Kane keeps spraying. The painting becomes more putrid and cancerous, a sickening feedback loop between artist and subject.

No one knows what's happening. There's no art down here. Nothing worth living for, so they devote themselves to destruction.

We can't see in front of our faces, and the scavs are swiping their deformed hands and half limbs at the colors, bellowing in confusion and amazement.

As the volume increases, new clouds erupt and spread. Kane is a craftsman. The room is thick with color.

"C'mon," says Kane, grabbing my hand. I blast a hole in the

church wall and we charge through. We keep running, me leading the way because Kane's eyes haven't adjusted to the darkness yet. We stop and Kane tries his earfeed.

"Mission Captain?" says Kane "Hello? Anyone copy?" He looks at me. "Forget this. We gotta go. Before the colors die out. I only have one canister. There's hardly any left."

"Wait," I say. "We didn't take out the leader."

"We can't go in there again. Not without backup."

"No!" I say. "We have to!" He grabs my arm.

"Stop, Lex. Don't be an idiot."

I shake him off. "We have to finish the mission!"

"We did our part!" he screams in my face.

We glare at each other. He won't back down and I won't either.

Lucky for us, we're in no position to make a choice.

Standing behind us is the greasiest, nastiest scav birthed in the Bottom. His guts rumble and he belches. His face is almost all skull, his flesh having dissolved long before we brought thunder to his home. He's got an illuminator attached to his left eye, which blinds us. Most of all, he smells like waste. Probably his own.

Their leader, obviously.

"Gross."

"Oh great," says Kane. "We couldn't just leave, huh? Why are you so core-low stubborn?"

I open my mouth to argue. "Shut up," says the dirtmonger, oozing foam from his rotting mouth, covered in dead man's sores.

He reaches behind and pulls something from his back. A weapon, crudely constructed of cast-off materials. A makeshift blaster that sparks with fused power cells.

I'm reaching for my borrowed blaster, but Kane is quicker. His arm is already lifted high.

"Scream," he says, just as the dirtmonger is pulling the trigger.

I scream harder than I've ever done anything in my life.

My sound cloud is instant and overwhelming.

The dirtmonger stumbles backward, and I blast him, right between his rotten eyes. He drops dead. At least he looks that way.

We escape through flecks of my golden scream just as Cassina and the rest of the cadets finally storm in.

My body jerks in the blinding light. Above me, the sooty sky fades to a white dome. My weapon fades with it, and so does my leg wound. The only thing real is me.

I blink a few times and look down. My body is untouched. Even my fingernails are clean.

It wasn't real. But it felt that way. I unstrap myself from my simulation capsule, and all my fellow cadets look as dazed as I do, even though they didn't see any real action. One by one, they stare at me. Their eyes are wide with surprise. No one says a word.

"Hey, Lex," says a voice. Everyone turns toward Vipsinia, so little she almost disappears in her capsule. "You are so stratosphere," she says.

Then Exdrilla, one of Cassina's most loyal followers, looks at us. Something in her eyes, maybe a sense of recognition that Kane and I did the unexpected. We succeeded. And yet, she's scared to recognize that. They all are.

The dried blood from Kane's face is gone. Just plain old Kane, his combat uniform as spotless as mine. The nightmare world and the nightmare people of the Rock Bottom are only memories now, locked away in their electric Archive chips, at least until the next class takes their Final Simulation.

I smile at Kane. I feel my face glowing. *Pretty good for an orphan, huh?*

He smiles right back. Only he isn't glowing. There's something underneath his smile. Something I've never seen before. It scares me.

Cassina remains in her simulation capsule, the look in her eyes distant and cold. We made her look good and still her pointy face is pulled tight.

"Cadets." The senior lieutenant booms through the speakerfeed. "Congratulations. You have completed your Final Simulation. Report to Academy headquarters immediately to receive your placement."

No one makes a noise.

It no longer matters how we feel inside. We are cadets. We serve a higher purpose.

Kane and I are last to exit the Simulation Room. I wish I could say something to him. Just a few words. But we can't speak. Placements await. It's a serious occasion, walking toward your future. The cadets stand tall. We walk in drill lines toward headquarters. I wonder if they're all as nervous as I am.

Paint me, I want to say to Kane. Just one more time. *Paint me saying good-bye.*

"Cadet Kane," says an authoritative voice. Kane and I stop. I turn, Kane doesn't. He just stares ahead into nothing.

Three Population Control Forces officers stand shoulder to shoulder. They aren't part of the Academy. They wear the dark blue PCF uniforms, but there are no insignia patches. Weird. All members of the PCF wear patches to show rank, even the lowliest, floor-scrubbing slabbers.

"Cadet, it's time to go," says one of them.

"What is this?" I say to Kane

Kane's shoulders slump, like somebody just lifted a weight off them.

"Can I say good-bye?" he says.

"Good-bye?" I say.

The rest of the cadets are long gone. It's just Kane and me. And these officers, telling him it's time to go. Go where?

Fear rises up inside of me. Fear of what's about to happen.

It catches me off guard. I don't do *fear*.

"Make it quick," says the lead officer. He and the other two don't move. Don't even look away.

"What's going on?" I say to Kane, out here in front of these strangers. "Did you know this was going to happen?"

"Lex," he says, accepting my anger. "I couldn't tell you. I took an oath. I couldn't tell anyone. I got my placement already." *What?* "I can't tell you more. I've already been doing it for a while—"

"That's where you've been?"

"Yes," he says. "I wanted to tell you more than anything, but—"

"Wrap it up, Cadet," says the lead officer.

"But we'll meet, right?" he says. "Meet as planned. Two weeks. Same as before."

Kane's stares at me, so much left unfinished between us. But we'll meet. We will. I look into his eyes and wonder how much else he's hidden. What else he could say that would leave me as speechless as I am right now. What else he could do . . .

He reaches for me and pulls me in tightly and kisses me.

My whole body blushes, and I kiss him back.

I kiss him back.

He steps away and salutes the officers.

"Kane," I say. "Why did you—?"

Over his shoulder he looks at me. "Because I wanted my first kiss to be with someone I actually care about."

"That's enough," the lead officer says.

Kane faces the men, his expression suddenly hard. "Agent Kane reporting for duty, sir," he says, never sounding more official.

He sounds like a man, I think.

Then he marches forward, and just like that, he's gone.

◊   ◊   ◊

"An inability to follow orders. A blatant disregard for standard protocol. Habitual and premeditated departures during simulation training . . ."

I have to stand before the Official Placement Panel and listen to Senior Lieutenant list my offenses while everyone glares at me. These are bad things he's saying. I know that. I'm neither proud nor ashamed of my disobedience. I've just proven that I can't be changed. This is me, and I will always be this way.

As soon as he's stopped talking, I'll get my placement, and I'll accept it. It's not gonna be pretty. A lifetime filling out PCF forms for people who matter. Cleaning up after people who matter. Serving others who mean something more than I ever will.

And all I can think about is Kane.

He's gone, and he knew it would end this way.

"All that said, graduate, you've shown remarkable skill today. Unexpected circumstances. Unique aptitude. Unprecedented ability . . ."

Kane already knew his placement.

"This knowledge has led the committee to contemplate the possibility . . ."

And he didn't tell me. Senior Lieutenant replaces my armband with a new red one.

"With training, you could be of great use to Special Operations . . ."

Kane.

". . . of the Rock Bottom Patrol."

I'm finally headed to where I was always meant to be.

CHAPTER II

Special Operations: Apprenticeship

Excerpted from The Book of Indra, *Chapter VIII:*
"Indra: Protecting Our Great Society"

THE POPULATION CONTROL FORCES ARMY:
PROTECTORS AND SERVANTS OF INDRA

The elite soldiers that make up the Population Control Forces are painstakingly chosen through a process veiled in secrecy. These select individuals are trained at the Population Control Forces Academy. Once graduated, they will go on to some of the most important positions Indra has to offer—some will serve as the leaders of the City of Indra, overseeing the safety of all Indrithians. Others will serve in intelligence and security roles, overseeing the Horizon Checkpoint. The most elusive and lethal members of this highly exclusive force will work in Special Operations in the lowest levels, also known as Rock Bottom.

Lex

Two weeks and I haven't been permitted to leave the Academy. "This training is so specialized," Senior Lieutenant tells me, "that you'll do it here. When you are deemed adequately prepared, you'll be relocated to your new base of operations."

They don't even tell me where that will be.

I'm still on Academy grounds, only far away from the students. Even farther than where the instructors live. A place not even Kane and I knew existed.

There hasn't been an Academy graduate placed in the Rock Bottom Patrol in almost ten years. It takes a couple days before all new training equipment arrives. My placement reflects well upon the instructors. I'm even permitted to dine with them, if I choose. I don't. Still, I should feel honored.

Rock Bottom Patrol is the elite. If I pass the apprenticeship, I'll be a Special Operative.

SpecOp Lex. It sounds pretty good, but for some reason, I'm not that excited. Moving on is harder than I supposed.

I have a home pod. Just like my sleeper pod, only bigger. For the first time, food is brought to me. And I have choices. "I'll have the turkey ration," I tell the woman who takes my order. Sometimes I choose the beef. There are choices, but not that many.

She just shoves the tray of turkey into my hand. Then she wheels her meal cart away. It's pretty much my only normal interaction of the day.

I don't see many people besides Special Operative Langhorn. He appeared at my door one day, earlier than my alarm. "I'm here to train you," he said. I knew not to ask questions.

I spend my days in a small facility just down the hall from my pod room. There's a sim capsule in one quadrant, and strengthening and cardio trainers spread among the other three.

I have no friends. SpecOp Langhorn trains me. I'm not in as good shape as I thought I was. My only rest is when I return to my sleeper to review rules and regulations on my holoreader.

For a week, he explains how to use the new equipment and technology. I complete weapons training and grow to like using pacifiers and decoys, even though blasters are more efficient. When I can finally plug myself in and operate the transmission valves, he leaves. No good-bye, nothing. He's programmed me to follow my daily schedule.

After my morning workout, I spend my days observing SpecOps training on the earfeed. No visual projections, not yet. I just sit there with my earfeed turned up. I record the team's actions and file my report at the end of every day. I should listen and learn. That's what Langhorn instructed.

I'm alone at night, too. This is not forever, I know that. But sometimes it feels that way.

I've been listening to the guys as they prepare for their next mission. They do not give me their names, simply tell me to refer to them as "Op O" and "Op C." To them, I'm "Apprentice L." They run diagnostics on equipment and discuss tactical strategies endlessly. They know I'm here, but they mostly ignore me. I don't ask questions, just like Langhorn told me. "Don't ask, don't speak." That's the apprentice motto.

From what I can put together, they're targeting a rebel troublemaker. Not to take him out, not yet. This first mission is just recon. The rebels control a small base that distributes supplies throughout their entire network. It's been designated a Class 2 scenario.

I think about the final exam. The scenario we faced was built off a real SpecOp mission. That one was rated Class 4. Lunatic fringe elements. Cannibalistic proclivities. Even the Islanders don't get real meat—no one does—but these savages do us one better and take it from each other. If someone's missing a limb, it's probably because someone else got hungry.

I don't sleep the night before. I pace my room. I want to be down there with them. I want to hurt someone.

I want to destroy those dirtmongers. This time for real.

By the time O and C finally hit the ground, I've been granted access to the visual feed. The feed is so dark I can hardly see anything.

"Apprentice L, do you copy?" says O.

"Yes."

"We're currently en route," he says. His voice is low, even when I increase the audio. Both O's and C's feeds are running simultaneously on my monitors, but I can barely discern their outlines, despite my sensory gifts.

They're sitting in a powered-down dirt ranger scouter. The parameters of their mission are basic: Survey the target location. Paint suspected rebel bases of operation with guidance lasers. Return to headquarters.

So far, all there's been is silence and darkness.

I strain to see something on the monitor. I think I can see C's hand moving across the controls of their stolen vehicle. I can't be sure. I wasn't expecting fun, but it's almost painful to be this powerless. I chart their location on a known map of the area. Cave-ins and the shifting of the Earth's plates change the terrain of the Lower Levels frequently, so for all we know, this map is useless by now. Now would be a terrible time to find that to be true.

"Nearing quadrant minus eighty-three," says O.

There's a long enough silence for me to doubt myself. To know if what I'm doing is right.

"Approaching suspected rebel HQ."

There's a faint light ahead of them. They've switched on the scouter's antique beamers, but its range is so limited. Then I see it: the target.

A mountain of stones rises from the void. The map indicates the tunnel should not have ended so abruptly.

Transporters rumble through the uncharted blackness ahead. They cross the scouter's path, but no one identifies the stolen vehicle for what it is.

The mountain grows closer in the dark, then I see it. Coming from the left side on the projector feed. A shadow, barely detectable.

They must see that, I think. I can't be the only one seeing that. O and C don't speak.

The shadow approaches. I'm so close to the monitor projection I almost bump my nose on it. I feel my eyeballs expanding.

An enemy craft. That's what it is. Crude blasters attached to the sides, pointed and ready.

"Armored craft, vectoring at minus sixty-three," I bark before I can stop myself. "Aiming to fire!"

Within a millisecond, the scouter redirects and the videofeed goes ballistic with live fire. I bolt up and throw the headset off, my ears splitting with the first barrage of the firefight. My senses can get overloaded easily. It's part of the reason I keep these abilities to myself. By the time I stop reeling, the feed's gone out.

I wait by the monitor as patiently as I can to hear from O and C. Instead, Langhorn buzzes in on my earfeed and says, "I told you not to speak." I've waited three hours for this reprimand, and I'm still grateful.

"Affirmative," I say. "I saw the craft and—"

"Quiet, Apprentice," he barks. I shut up. "You alerted the Ops just in time," he says, calmer. "They retreated unharmed."

My pride surges, but I'm not expecting a compliment. I just do the work that needs to be done.

"Your training isn't complete, but higher-ups believe you're ready to be called up. In two days, you'll be taken to your forward operating base."

My stomach jumps. I wait for his kudos.

The line goes dead. Even with his lack of warmth, I'm still elated.

Two days to report. Enough time to meet Kane, just like we planned.

I'll get to tell him about the end of my apprenticeship. I'll get to see him before I begin my new life.

I'm waiting for Kane in his childhood memory. Everything is too bright, the edges all blurred. Still, it beats anything I've got.

I was taught that your experiences are filed away by the High Council, and a handful are made available to you. How they get them, I'm still not sure. These are the incidents they deem important, pivotal points in your growth and development. Good times, bad times, I hope they've captured it all. You're issued a memory chip as soon as you're old enough for the experiences not to induce trauma and you're expected to learn from these highlights of your life.

Recruiter gave me my first one on the way to the Academy. I put it in, expecting some massive understanding to how life screwed me over, and then I just got the same thing I always got: nothing. Complete and utter darkness. It was like the Orphanage had never happened. I kind of wished that were true.

Memory Archives are personal. It's strictly forbidden to go into someone else's. "You wouldn't understand their memory anyway," Instructor explained during our unit on Archives: The Universe in an Access Chip. "The memory is personalized, their emotions captured instantaneously to be infused into the database. The colors and sounds will reflect their inner state. Archives aren't duplicated experiences, they're subjective. Without the proper framework, going in as a stranger could induce brain trauma, and remains strictly prohibited by the High Council."

Not that Kane ever cared about rules. Not that I don't already feel brain damaged.

Now, waiting for Kane in his eighth birthday, I understand. The colors are so vivid they hurt my eyes.

Maybe all memory Archives are like this. Maybe everything is brighter in our memory. Or maybe it's so bright because Kane never came here before. Something not worth revisiting or something he wanted to stay away from. You degrade an Archive every time you visit, just like the make-believe at the Orphanage. That's the only memory I could keep returning to.

I hear Kane's voice in my head. *I'll meet you on my eighth birthday. On my family island. Behind the obelisk.*

I'm on his island and I found the obelisk. *Now where's Kane?*

I'm in a small clearing bordered by a copse of trees. Everything seems enormous. I've always wanted to see a real synth-tree, but I'm sure they're nothing like these ones. They tower over me. You can drown in their shade.

I must be seeing everything from Kane's eight-year-old eyes. The world seems too big around me, and too small at the same time.

I've been circling the same grounds since I got here, unable to get a glimpse past its border.

I can only imagine how far his childhood estate stretches. I reach out, the rubbery surface buzzing under my touch, but then it pushes my hand back. If I try again, I might be flung from the memory. Then I'd never see Kane.

Breaking into the Archive access room was risky enough. I waited until late at night and snuck through the Cadet Quarters. I briefly stopped to look at the entrance to rooming pod 13, my former home. It hadn't changed. Neither had the camera positions or the instructor floor sweeps. Their patterns Kane and I had long ago memorized.

The quarters were quiet, the cadets dead asleep. I didn't belong there. Not anymore.

I felt stupid for even thinking it possible. I moved on, crept my way to the Archive access room.

Breaking the code on the room itself was easy; Kane taught me a dozen ways to bypass. The chip locker was a little tougher, but SpecOps training has its advantages.

"I build stuff," Kane once said while rewiring a beamer to glow green, "and you take them apart."

That made me smile. In the times I'm not actively apprenticing, I learn stuff from the patrol Archives. Stuff that would be considered illegal in the hands of others. I cracked the code. The chip locker slid open. I scanned the names, finding Kane's memory box. They keep them here until we graduate and have served out our probationary period in our official placement. "But don't worry," Kane told me. "You can just keep it for me. Give it back when you see me."

I punched in the code he gave me. The box buzzed and popped open. I locked the door behind me and sat on the cold steel floor. Heart thumping wildly, I'd tapped my wrist, put my thumb tip to my pulse, inserted the chip, and closed my eyes.

Instantly, I was here. On the memory of soft synth-grass. I was in Upper Indra for the first time. Even in someone else's memory, it felt real. Not to mention strange.

Time works funny here. However long I'm here, only a fraction of that time will have passed in the real world. Still, I've got to worry about someone discovering me.

Pretty soon, the cadets will get up. They'll do appearance maintenance, eat their rations, and head off to class. I'll be found out eventually, I know.

I kill time walking the memory perimeter. Its border looks like dense fog. *C'mon, Kane. Where are you?*

I find a makeshift campsite: bedding, a supply of wafers. Kane spent a lot of time here, I can tell. Probably even slept here sometimes.

It's his birthday. Why would he remember being at this place? Where is everyone?

Birthdays are important, I've learned. At least, they are to people outside the Orphanage. Funny, since I don't even know the date of mine. All I got every year was a visit from the recruiter.

From what I've seen at the Academy, everyone wants to be around you on your birthday. Yet Kane spent his eighth one here. By himself.

Kane was alone a lot, I guess. Just like me.

This was the place he made sculptures and sound paintings before he had a Center of Creation. These sculptures are made of cast-off scraps, just like at the Academy. Only the materials are different: Tree limbs, fancy ration plates broken in half. Pieces of shiny metal. High-quality stuff. Stuff people would miss if they cared. But obviously, they don't.

I think of Kane's sculpture in the Center of Creation studio. The metal face he made with the eyes protruding on spikes. These pieces are frightening too, but different. More childlike and obvious: monsters from bad dreams that hide under your sleeping pod.

Kane was weird. Even as a kid. That makes me smile.

"Looking for me?" says a voice. I spin around quickly, already on edge, knowing immediately that something's gone wrong.

A shadow steps out from behind the obelisk, and then Cassina's standing in front of me. "Not who you were expecting?" She pouts like she's sad for me.

I don't answer.

She's wearing her new PCF Security uniform. How predictable. *She's* protecting Indra. Assigned to the public projects, news of them running along holoscreens to make the Indrithians feel secure, like installing defense gates in the Hub. I can see her pained smile on an awareness campaign projected on the side of Indra's glass towers: "Indra Gives You What You Need."

She's holding her pointy chin high, which makes it plenty exposed. The pride of holding an official public position. Her main obligation? Look important, probably. They don't even carry blasters on them in most sectors.

She's probably living on Apprentice Island with all the other cadets. Her same group, following her around. Just killing time till they cohabitate and relocate to an island. Things change, but not really.

I wonder if Kane is on Apprentice Island with her.

I wait for her to speak. I think of the small blaster on my hip. It won't kill her here, but it will boot her quick and give her a massive headache.

"Wow," she says, looking at a spiky sculpture made of ration forks. "Kane did this? He was always . . . different."

"Why are you here?" I say.

"Isn't that the question I should be asking *you*? In case you haven't picked up on it, my family is very, very, very important. Therefore, I matter." She smiles. Her chin has gotten even pointer. "More than an orphan ever could."

I've had enough. I start for her and she backs up, eyes wide. "Stop," she says, her voice catching. "Kane! Kane!"

I'm so close, she's shrinking back.

"Where's Kane?" I ask. Get any closer to her and we'd be cohabitants.

"Take out his access chip and I'll show you."

"Why not show me here?"

"You can't access an Archive within another Archive, so . . ."

"You first."

She nods.

"There're no instructors here to save you if you're lying," I say.

She nods again.

It's not a trap, I tell myself.

I narrow my eyes. I have no choice. I reach for my chip, but only after she reaches for her own.

◊　◊　◊

I'm back in the Archive access room, getting up from my resting position. Cassina stands too, right across the room from me, both of us
holding the Archive access chips.

"How'd you find me?" I ask.

She grins. "Indra has its way of finding you all. Even if you didn't
stray that far. Don't you get that by now? My security placement grants
me total access. Whereas yours grants you a one-way trip core-low."

She thinks her life is all sweet. Out here in the real world, somehow she has more control.

"How'd you get a copy of it?" I ask her. She just stares at me.
"Where is he? Tell me!"

She reaches into her pocket and holds out another access chip.
"Put this in and you'll see for yourself. It's another of Kane's memories."

"You first."

"I only have one. It's hard enough sharing this with you, I don't
want to *share* it with you."

"And he gave it to you?"

She nods. I have no idea if she's telling the truth. She's only ever
wanted me to fail. Why stop now?

We stare at each other and her face softens. She's never been a
good actress.

"Because," she says quietly, "he's hurt."

I've never seen so much hate in her eyes, but this time they're
telling the truth. My mind clouds whenever I try to figure her out.
But she seems to be worried about Kane, and that makes me worried.

"After all your training, haven't you learned that rebels never
win?" she says, holding out the chip.

In my after-hours I've learned how you can weaponize everything, even an access chip. Once an Archive starts, you're supposed
to be able to jump out at any time. But there are ways around it.

False memories could wreck your mind for a lifetime. You could get trapped and never know you were out of touch with the real. You'd be lost in there just like a shadow person for all eternity.

I hold out my upturned palm. She drops the chip in my hand, pinching her lips at the thought of touching me.

Using the chip could be dangerous for all those reasons. But most of all, I fear that learning the truth may be the most dangerous thing of all. But it's Kane, so I have no choice.

CHAPTER 12

Emergence Ball

Excerpted from The Book of Indra, *Chapter V:*
"Indra: Society and Customs"

The Indrithian upper elite abide by a given set of unspoken laws.
The young people are allowed monitored interaction in the form
of Socialization Clubs and balls. At seventeen, the young women
will be introduced to society through their Emergence Ball, and
soon after they must choose a mate, cohabitate, and embark on
the journey of being Proper Indrithian Citizens.

Livia

I'm spinning and the world is watching.

Elevated high above the Helix Grand Ballroom, with each rotation I alter my pose. I move as slowly as the platform itself, my face
emotionless, yet projecting the countenance of an esteemed Proper
Young Woman.

In the words of Etiquette Tutor, "As though you have barely a thought in your head."

My body may be languid, but my mind is speeding.

I look beautiful, of this I'm sure, Marius and Governess having lavished me with endless praise; even more, I have seen my own startling reflection.

I don't know this girl, I thought, considering the stranger before me. A Proper Young Woman, to be sure. The dress every shade of blue, trailing in long and filmy waves, shimmering like the simulated ocean. Skin flawlessly creamy, lips rose pink. Every inch of her fretted over and perfected, every flaw deliberated over and eliminated, each hair glossed and painstakingly coiled.

Proper Young Women are built.

It takes more than a day, it takes a lifetime.

In terms of competition, there is none. I am immaculate, all except for my thoughts.

Below, the guests observe me with alarming intensity. Not all of Upper Indra, of course, but their eyes make me feel that way. "A record turnout in Emergence Ball history," Marius informed me, moments before my grand reveal. "Remember, my love, tonight is the night for you to have everything you've ever wanted. Do your best, for me, for your parents. Just look at you. You'll take their breath away."

When the music began, the room hushed. The curtains parted from around me, the invitees giving their requisite intake of breath, and I began my slow ascent upward.

Faces rapt, they watched me rise.

Now, they watch me spin.

"Do not show pain," said Etiquette Tutor. "Nor discomfort. Nothing is less appealing to a Proper Young Man than a woman lacking in endurance. Clear your head of needless concerns and focus on the task at hand."

The truth is far less simple. I'd heard the frightful tales during Pleasant Interaction, whispered recounts brimming with nervousness. With our debuts growing closer, little else seemed worthy of discussion. Clearing our heads was easier said than done.

"Yes, an utter debacle," Mica told the others, too willing to recount the details of disastrous debuts and reputations never to recover, never failing to throw a glance in my direction. "She proved herself an utter fool."

I'd been Chosen Girl for so long I couldn't imagine being unchosen. Since the moment I succeeded in staying on that platform sixty feet in the air, Mica had stopped speaking to me, not even for a Pleasant Interaction.

Mica hadn't spoken to me, but she spoke about me plenty.

That day and every day following, I was relegated to pleasantly interacting with Cybele. Despite have grown into a lovely Young Woman, she'd never shaken Etiquette Tutor's curse, destined to be "of unappealing physical appearance." Yet even she seemed disturbed at having to speak with me. Of course, I made little effort to change her mind.

"The weather is lovely, do you not agree?"

"If you say so," I responded.

"Very mild, I have noticed, with the slightest of breeze."

"As mild as yesterday and the day before," I said. "As mild as it will remain, every day until eternity, as so dictated by the Aero-Crown."

She sighed, never losing the strained smile. We went on like this for some time, I all the while catching the whispers of Mica's still-exclusive circle. They told the same few stories, growing more horrific with each retelling, but always came back to their favorite. "The Girl Who Fell," according to Mica, happened two debut cycles ago.

"Six foot two and from excellent genetic stock, graced with a delightful bone structure and pleasant manner. She collapsed on the platform," she told them, "and was lowered immediately. Slapped her until she regained consciousness, lifted right back up. She finished the rotation, but never once ceased her incessant sobbing. Turning and turning, all eyes on her, tears streaking down her face. Could not even wipe her running nose for fear of breaking the poses.

"In the end," Mica said, voice bursting with foreboding, "the only cohabitant available was under six feet! Even worse, he secretly preferred the company of other Young Men to her own! Now she is left alone on her estate, as he spends his days on a faraway one frolicking away the time with another Young Man of similar interests."

In the old world, before the Great Catastrophe, this kind of life choice was considered acceptable. You were free to love who you pleased and spend your life with the mate of your choosing. And yet, somehow we have regressed in Indra because of the IHC's pursuit of perfecting our population through controlled procreation. For all the warnings of the world before the Great Catastrophe, I often question whether they were more evolved than us in some capacities.

I'm sure they didn't spin on platforms for audiences brought in to judge them. At least, unless that was of their own choosing.

Of course, saying such things would be considered Anti-Indrithian Hate Speech and is highly illegal. But how can the High Council control my thoughts, when even *I* can't?

"Her own fault," the others would say to Mica's every retelling of the story, voices rising in a chorus of pity. "Perhaps she never took etiquette lessons seriously."

It seemed odd, Mica choosing this story. After all, she had fallen off the platform that day herself and many times after until she had perfected it. And yet, these rules of logic didn't apply to her as they did to others. Just as Mica's failure was never mentioned, my ousting from her circle went unquestioned.

At some point, I repeated the tale of "The Girl Who Fell" to Marius, and then waited for the confirmation it was only gossip. Instead, she shook her head tragically. "I saw the whole unfortunate event, the poor thing. I only wished I could pass her a handkerchief."

She needn't elaborate further. Besides, Mica had already been successful: I was suitably terrified. This platform spin would be far worse than the one Etiquette Tutor had given us, of that I was certain.

After only a few spins, becoming the new Girl Who Fell seems a distinct possibility. It is one thing to keep yourself balanced on a spinning platform in class, but doing so while holding elegant poses and pretending a hundred sets of eyes aren't blazing into you? That is entirely different.

"You'll take their breath away," Marius told me. Yet the cincher that Governess insisted on is pulled so tight, I am gasping for my own.

I rotate, comforted by the knowledge my Debut Spin will take less than an hour, yet knowing that at any moment the cincher might cease my breathing altogether. The dress, weighted down with countless layers and intricate beading, is threatening to pull me to my knees. I feel as though I've embarked on a battle with my own attire, and the gown might well prove the victor.

And then there are the stares. The eyes burning into me, the mock whispers behind fans echoing upward, little being done to hide them. Are these not the most proper of Proper Indrithians?

The worst offender? Mica, of course. Surrounded by her gaggle of adoring admirers.

Not inviting her would've been disastrous for my reputation, Governess had warned me, not giving me a choice in the matter. But having her watch me is equally horrific.

Strangely enough, she doesn't say a word. She simply stares, I feel her urging me to fail.

This is an Emergence Ball, after all, and serves a single purpose: for the gathered crowd to come to judgment as to the quality of the goods set out before them. The goods, in this case, being Livia Cosmo.

Even from this high up, their voices carry. It's something Etiquette Tutor never prepared us for. The acoustics of the Grand Ballroom assault my heightened senses with incessant whispers.

"Well, there is the name, of course. The Cosmo legacy. That alone ups her value. . . ."

". . . and the estate is magnificent, you must agree on that. Could do with a more attentive garden crew, but still, the possibilities. If the cohabitant relocates here, perhaps he will see to these details. . . ."

"I have heard it said she is rather defiant. Pity, seeing as she is pleasing to the eye. Perhaps if she never spoke! Terribly wicked of me to say, I know, but there are procedures . . ."

I listen to their babble, their predictions for my future, all the time focused on steadying my breathing. I'm aware of my every last twitch. I can't lose control of myself.

I know what's expected: spin as to appear motionless, stare as into nothingness.

Keep movements slow and measured and nearly imperceptible. *Let this end*, I think, inching from one position to another.

Below, the Young Men are meant to be memorizing my poses. This is only tradition; every Proper Young Man was taught the Courting Dance in childhood.

Later, if later ever arrives, I will repeat this dance with each of them. There are so many, it will take hours and hours.

At least they cannot touch me.

"They will try to get close," Etiquette Tutor warned us. "As close as they can. And here is the secret: if you find one of them to be utterly unappealing, force him to touch you. This must appear accidental, of course, or you might incite scandal. But if carried out correctly, the Young Man will face immediate expulsion. In the case of Young Men to which you are drawn, those you would not mind touching you, never be overtly forward. Be available, yet withdrawn. Alluring, yet modest. Show too much interest and you will send the wrong message."

What's the wrong message? I had wanted to ask. *That you actually like them? Is that not the point of the whole miserable evening?*

It seems unfair that Proper Young Men don't have debut balls. Instead, they come to ours and watch us spin with smirks on their faces. We have the power, I've been told, for we may choose the Proper Young Man we like best. At the same time, they're allowed to reject us.

It makes little sense to me, the whole occasion. Choose a man you hardly know and await his acceptance or rejection? Yet on what basis is he accepting you? How well you turn in circles?

Another spin, another pose.

A few minutes pass. A few more.

The perspiration drips down my flesh, torturing me, the gown growing heavier with each passing moment. The cincher squeezes, my pain steadily intensifying.

My whole body aches; my insides are screaming. *Focus, Livia.*

Circle and pose. Circle and pose.

My future spins below me.

I try not to look down.

With the time it takes for the platform to lower, my admirers still silently pray for me to fall. But it is once the platform has secured me to the ground that the real torture begins.

There are so many Young Men they begin to blend together. I want to see all of them fail.

Some I have seen before, on the rare occasions of a required

Socialization Club mixer. Then there are the strangers. Young Men from the farthest islands, alternate education clusters. Many have come from across all of Indra simply to witness me.

Not *me*, of course. The idea of me.

The famous geneticist's daughter with a vast estate and legendary name.

The Cosmo Airess.

I am Livia, I want to tell them. *And I am strange and confused and prefer my horse to any person.*

Of course, I cannot say this, or little else of importance. I am well versed in the List of Acceptable Topics for Emergence Ball Conversation.

Hours off the revolving platform and I'm still spinning. It's unclear where I begin and the music ends.

I keep waiting to feel something. "A flame of passion," Etiquette Tutor calls it.

At this point, I would settle for even a weak spark.

As soon as one Young Man exits, another replaces him, immediately taking the Courting Dance initial position. At least I need not offer much in the way of conversation; they are happy to speak for the both of us. They only have a short time with me, and they're not about to waste it.

They tell me I'm beautiful. They love Helix Island. This is the best Emergence Ball they have ever seen. They love the color scheme, for white is their favorite color.

They try to impress me with their range of talents. Speak of their leisure pastimes. The numerous targets they hit in archery, the extraordinary lengths they throw the discus. They tell me how important their family is, how big their estate, how vast their wealth, how very much they matter.

Please say something interesting, I think.

An hour passes. And another. I'm exhausted, every muscle aching, the cincher still biting into my flesh. It has eaten more than I have.

The same answers, the same questions. The same musical refrain and poses.

"The party? Absolutely divine. Discus throw? How fascinating. You don't say! Is that so? Isn't that lovely. Wonderful. Intoxicating. Exhilarating. Yes, I'm having a lovely time. Yes, you are fascinating."

Yes, I want to die of boredom.

"I respect your legacy," this Proper Young Man says. "Your father was a genius. And might I add, blue is a color in which you are especially fetching."

You know my father as little as I do.

They fight to catch my glance between poses. Gaze intensely, trying to convey silent messages: *I am deeply sensitive, Livia. I understand you, Livia. I am the one for you, do you not see?*

All I see is the Ending. Of anything that ever mattered to me.

"My favorite flower sonnet is 'The Petunia,'" he says.

I smile so hard my jaw hurts.

Then something stops me. Someone.

"You despise every moment of this," he says. "Me included."

Hands in the air, palm facing palm.

"I do not . . . know you," I say, caught off guard.

"That makes little difference."

"I do not understand your meaning," I say.

"I mean *you hate this*. The ball, the attention. The whole *core-low* thing. I can tell. I can tell a lot of things about you."

Pivot and turn. Now he has my attention.

"For example?"

"Well, to start with, none of this means a thing to you," he says quickly. "You'd rather be anywhere else but here. And you think no one has anything interesting to say. A bit egotistical of you—"

"What did you—"

"But also correct. And you cannot stop thinking, I have to pick from these mindless Islanders and listen to them prattle about midday tea receptions and the importance of the status quo for the rest of my life."

Perhaps I'm hallucinating. For the first time, I really look at his eyes and they're unlike the other Young Men's. As though they have seen the unexpected.

He stares right back. For significantly longer than is proper. "You have such interesting eyes," he says.

Left arm up, chin to shoulder.

"If what you were saying was true," I say, "and I am not saying it is, but if it was . . . on what do you base your shockingly forward assumptions?"

Pivot and turn. Now we are closer. *Did he make that happen?* I wonder. *Did I?*

"On myself. I'm exactly the same, Livia. I'm just like you."

Hands in the air. We're almost done. Back where we started.

Palm to palm facing each other. The slightest movement. That's all it would take. Barely an inch and we would be touching.

It is as though he has a power source hidden inside of him, his skin almost seeming to crackle. And yet, I cannot sense him at all. As though he has built a wall around his true feelings.

"We aren't like the others," he says fiercely. "Nor would we choose to be."

The final pose, the final note. His turn is over. He steps back and smiles politely. A rush of cold air takes up the space where his heat was.

A deep curtsy, a manly bow.

Then he is gone, quicker than I would have liked. I strain to glimpse him through the crowd of bodies, then notice the faces.

Hundreds of them, staring at me with curiosity, oozing with judgment.

He didn't even say his name.

"May I?"

I swing around. My next partner, grinning at me. Six foot two, superior bone structure, all the signs of exemplary genetics.

Empty eyes on a face I have seen many times before.

"Is this not enchanting?" he says as we take our first pose.

The Helix Grand Ballroom is said to be the grandest in all of Indra, though I've never seen any others, except for what serves as one at the Socialization Club. I've never been invited, though Marius assures me that with the right cohabitant, the social snubs will cease, though I wonder for how long. I've never really cared about the Helix Grand Ballroom until now. I'm at my own dining platform, elevated above the others. The Finest of Indrithian Society are seated below me, their tables extending to the perimeter of the room.

I can't see him anywhere.

I scan the crowd, Young Men looking up expectantly as my eyes pass over them.

Dejected, I push the leg of lamb around my plate. More historical re-creations, only slightly less repulsive than the kidney, though it smells much the same.

I've lost my appetite completely.

I lift my fork—meat fork, not salad fork—and pretend to take a bite.

Where has he gone? Perhaps I only imagined him, the cincher completely cutting off oxygen to my brain. I put down my fork and pick up my fan to look sufficiently busy.

The guests engage in Polite Conversation Befitting a Formal Engagement. With so many guests, the volume is a polite roar. I notice a few Young Men have risen to their feet, milling about and chatting amicably, their eyes continuously flickering in my direction.

The fan, I think. Now I have unintentionally opened the door, given them a signal that I'm open to their attentions.

I fan slowly with the left hand: please do not approach, for I am otherwise engaged. Just a quick shift to the right hand and a more rapid movement—*now I'm ready for you*—and they will come racing, ready to smother me with their affection.

Will this ever end? I sense a wave of annoyance, and am not surprised at the source. Governess, sitting near the front of the table. A quick jaunt to Rejuvenation Island and now her skin is stretched so tightly that her eyes angle upward, which doesn't prevent her from glaring at me through her slits. I feel her desperation for me take some sort of action.

Next to her, Waslo holds court, entertaining half the table with his wit. With me, he's sullen, always scrutinizing for imperfections. Among other Indrithians of Importance, he expresses charm and mirth.

I don't like him either way.

Next to him, Marius is watching me. Despite her tiny frame, her grace seems to dwarf the others around her. Next to Marius, they appear to be practiced, laughing with strained faces, leaning forward, overly eager.

She catches my eye and smiles encouragingly. *She's worried. I made her a promise, yet I'm putting forth little effort.*

There's someone I wish to know more of, I imagine telling her, *but he disappeared as mysteriously as he arrived. He made the others seem even less interesting, if that's even possible.*

Without noticing, I've begun to fan faster. I slow myself down, but it's too late, for I have already attracted curiosity. The Young Men ease closer, seemingly poised to sprint toward me at any moment; the enormous ballroom feels smaller, the walls angling in on me. I look upward, swearing the massive chandelier is lower than before, wondering if, within moments, the ceiling will drop and crush me.

I'm suddenly dizzy. Long off the platform, yet everything is once again spinning. I fear I might faint. If I faint, at least I've been taught how to react.

Soon I will be a cautionary tale told during Pleasant Interaction.

That is when I see Mica. Not socializing or engaging in interaction, pleasant or otherwise. Simply staring at me from the far left side of the table. Surely *that's* a sign of rudeness.

I know exactly what she's thinking: I will never be one of them. I will never be an Indrithian of Importance, no matter how hard I try.

I know she's right. And even worse, I don't care to try.

I don't remember standing, yet I'm on my feet. They're sore and pinched, but they'll do.

The room has gone silent. Everyone is looking at me. Again.

Keep your wits about you, Livia.

I give a girlish sigh. Smile charmingly, lower my eyes bashfully. Tap my left cheek with my fan: *Might you be so kind as to pardon me?*

I don't give them time to answer.

I know Helix Island, even in the dark.

I exit the main quarters with graceful strides, chin lifted high, as though seeking a quick breath of fresh air.

"Overcome with emotion," I imagine Governess telling the table, her pained smile pulling her face to its breaking point. "She needs merely a moment to gather her thoughts. Grace and quiet composure, that is our Livia."

In the dark, I bound forward, stumble awkwardly over my train, and go tumbling. A grunt slipping from between my clenched teeth, I hoist myself back to standing, lift the sides of my gown, and knot them in front of me.

I kick off my dainty shoes. I watch them fly, making blue arcs through the darkness. I rub my feet in the dirt until I know they're absolutely filthy.

Only then do I run.

The air is chilly on my bare legs, the grass soft beneath me. I shake out my carefully constructed hair, pins flying, and rake my fingers through the strands, eager to annihilate each perfectly arranged coil.

I realize I'm still wearing my sash. I reach around and pull as hard as I can.

"I hate this sash," I tell the empty air, pulling as I run. The fabric unwinds from around me, the tail unfurling, growing longer and longer until it disappears into the darkness.

I hear laughter and realize it's me.

Intoxicated with my own freedom, I reach for my cincher. Hours to strap me in, and a few mere tugs to escape. Within moments, my rib cage expands, my chest rising. I breathe in the fresh air, taking in as much as I can possibly hold, the oxygen overwhelming me with giddiness.

Islanders are built for high altitudes, having adapted throughout the generations. Those who come from the Lower Levels face long adjustment periods, their lungs becoming starved for oxygen, Life Guide once explained.

What you mean to say, I hadn't dared respond, *is they should not have come in the first place.*

Everything is made a prison here. Even our own bodies. The price of beauty is hidden behind torture machines. I see my destination in the distance and move faster. A silver dome growing larger with each stride.

My father built Veda's stable and around it, a track. Veda can run, but only in circles. In that way, we have a lot in common.

Of course, I programmed Archives for her to access when I could not be with her. She could escape at any moment: to a field to romp through, hills to climb, rivers in which she could wade. Yet she knew these weren't real, just as I knew the ocean was lost to us forever.

"Veda!" I call, rushing into the stable. Her white face rises instantly, eyes warm in greeting. She whinnies and stamps her feet, turns a few quick circles. This happy dance has always been my greeting.

I run to her and rest my cheek against her silky mane. How many times have I done this? Run to Veda when there was nowhere else to go? As a child, she would rest her muzzle on top of my head, though now she must use my shoulder.

Things change, but very little. On this occasion, I'm grateful.

Now you may cry, I tell myself. The tears don't require more urging; they fall and disappear into Veda's silky mane.

"Livia."

His voice sends a shiver down my spine.

Veda lifts her head and peers over my shoulder. I'm safe, I know, or else she would have warned me. Instead of rearing up, she simply stares, her brown eyes warm and curious.

"How did you know where to find me?" I ask, unwilling to turn yet. *I will not be seen in this weakness.* I pull myself tall, use the backs of my hands to dry the wetness from my cheeks.

"This is where I would go," he says.

Even without turning, I can sense his feelings are strong. He's here to do something important, though I can't imagine anything of importance here, in Veda's stable.

Other than Veda, that is.

Only once I have returned to myself, made myself mimic a Proper Young Woman once more, am I ready to face him.

He's hiding something. The other boys are so open with their desires, but this one stares at me strangely and has secrets he would never share.

"I thought you might not exist," I say nonchalantly. "That perhaps I conjured you from my imagination simply to pass the time."

He doesn't answer or look away.

"Staring, as I am sure you are well aware, is a blatant disregard of proper etiquette," I say.

"Have you seen yourself lately?"

I glance down and realize he may have a point. A debutee with bare legs and dirty feet, gown knotted at her waist, hair permitted to go wild, isn't much of a debutee at all.

"I don't have to answer for my appearance," I tell him.

"I don't want you to," he says softly. "I like you much better like this."

For a second, I lose my train of thought. Who's he to make me uncomfortable?

"You don't belong here," I tell him, hearing the haughtiness in my own voice.

"True. I don't."

"You are the intruder, not I."

"Agreed," he says.

I wait for an explanation. He doesn't offer one.

"Well?" I say finally. "Have you nothing more to say to me?"

Apparently not. I pick up Veda's brush, turning my back to him, and neaten her mane. Veda looks at me oddly; I'm well aware she prefers to be untamed.

There's no sound from behind me. I only hope he's done the appropriate thing and left. So why do I feel a sudden heaviness upon me?

Veda looks past me and I know he's still there, but I finish her grooming before I turn.

He's so close I could touch his face. *Not that I want to.* He smiles as though hearing my thoughts.

None of this makes any sense—being in the stable during my own ball, my missing sash probably flying through the clouds by now. The fact that Veda, who is usually abhorrent of strangers, is playfully nudging the side of my face and giving a serene whinny.

Most implausible of all? This strange boy in front of me with a calm, self-satisfied smile. The fact that I can't sense his feelings, only guess, while my own frustration rises. Nothing is logical here, the whole situation utterly maddening.

He moved nearer when I wasn't looking.

"Don't come any closer," I tell him.

"Why?" he says, already inching forward.

"I don't want you to," I tell him, hearing the lie in my own voice. "And for a Proper Young Man, that should be reason enough."

"I am not a Proper Young Man," he says. "I'm Kane, and I certainly wouldn't mind another Courting Dance with you as my partner."

In that instant, I feel him. It's as though the wall he's maintained suddenly explodes, and his emotions rush toward me with a surprising intensity.

He wants to kiss me. The revelation is disconcerting, to say the very least.

"That's prohibited," I say.

"What is?" I can sense the heat coming off him.

"What you want."

"You *are* strange, Livia Cosmo," he whispers.

"That is a fact of which I am well aware and is rude of you to say." It would be so easy to reach for him.

"Funny," he says, "but you remind me a lot of someone."

"Then why are you here, with me? You've already pursued me across this entire island. Do what you came here to do, then leave."

He wants to kiss me, I think. *And I want to let him.*

Then the word is there again, flashing in my head: prohibited.

I am sick of *prohibited*. Prohibited from leaving the island, prohibited from asking questions. Prohibited from fighting or laughing too loud or even breathing in a natural manner.

Perhaps it's the whole pointless evening or the knowledge that, with each passing minute, my chances for a cohabitant grow slimmer.

Perhaps it's because I don't care.

"I can't do this," he says, almost to himself. His confidence turns to worry. He's backing away from me, more air between us with each passing second.

For once, I tell myself, *I will do exactly what I want.*

My mind goes blank, just as I have been taught, my final thought being that this isn't the use of training Master had intended.

I rush forward and his lips are on mine, his kiss somehow soft and hard in the very same moment. I'm buzzing all over. I don't want to come up for breath.

Then I'm melting. This surprises me, having never imagined any part of myself to be frozen. The more he pulls away, the more I draw him close.

Our mouths part wider and our kisses multiply. Then there's something small and round rolling around in my mouth. Something that he pushed in with his tongue.

It rolls into my mouth and he's now pulled away, his eyes widening—with horror? Mine must be doing the same. Whatever it is, it's caught at the back of my throat and I feel as if I might choke.

"Spit it out!" he says.

I'm confused, but I do it and a tiny white pearl lands at my feet. It's a pill, I think. My mouth is impossibly bitter, so I spit again, and with it comes rushing too much anger.

"What was that?!"

Veda rears up with a protective neigh, and the Young Man stumbles backward.

"Kane. What did you just do?"

"I changed my mind," he says. "I didn't want to go through with it . . . but then you kissed me. . . ."

I reach for my zinger, but of course it's not there. Hardly debut appropriate. "Start making sense," I say.

"I'm sorry," he says, the words growing thick in his mouth. As much as I wish it, it wasn't me who did this to him. His body grows unsteady and his emotions are blunted. He's not sure what he thinks, and neither am I.

His eyes have trouble remaining focused and the color drains from his face. "I'm so sorry . . . to spoil your special day." His palms clutch his temples, and he shakes his head to clear away the confusion, but it's not working.

I grab him, I'm so angry. "Did you just try to kill me?"

Half a pill dissolves at my feet, the rest of its poison flowing through my would-be assassin's veins. Did he hold it in his mouth too long? He collapses in my arms, falling forward, and I brace myself to catch his dead weight.

Blood drips from his nose onto my dress. I was never going to wear this again anyway. This day is probably best to be forgotten.

He looks up at me, almost gone, his eyes giving a final flicker of recognition. He smiles, his bloody lip curling upward. "Livia," he says softly.

His eyes go blank. His body shudders. I mean, someone should try to save him, I just don't think that's me.

Then someone else is shouting my name and it's Waslo standing outside the stable. He stares at us, trying to make sense of the chaos before him.

That's when I see the security team hired especially for my debut. They rush toward me in their PCF uniforms, blasters in hand, and I look around, expecting to see more assassins lurking in the eaves. Just who are they protecting me from?

"Step away from him," one bellows, Veda rearing up and bellowing right along with him.

"Facedown!" the PCF scream at him. "Hands on your back! Don't move!"

When he doesn't respond, they pull him from my arms, hurling his limp body to the ground.

They surround him, and Waslo takes my hand and pulls me away. They're beating this boy, and once more I can't get a read on him. I scream again and again for them to stop.

He's completely and utterly emotionless. He's unconscious as they continue to hit him.

At least he's no longer feeling any more pain I hope.

CHAPTER 13

Two Weeks Following Apprenticeship

Lex

A girl. She's air, I can tell, but some sort of weird fringe group, with the way her hair's tangled and her dress recalls some Rock Bottom scav. She doesn't even have shoes.

This doesn't seem important when you consider the white creature behind her—a horse, but not an Archive kind, even though it kind of is that, too. Except this one's real as this memory, massive and the purest white I could ever image. Not synth-white. Pure white.

You can get anything in the Upper Levels, I guess. This way of life I'm still trying to process.

Every time Kane or the airgirl speak, all I get is *buzzzzzzzz*, the audiofeed's all jacked, but I suspect Cassina wants it this way.

Something bad is going to happen. I know it. But I can't tear my eyes away.

The girl pretends to ignore Kane. She brushes the horse and I see her playing games, just like Cassina does. It's so transparently obvious.

Kane puts his hand to his lips. A yawn? I can't be sure.

The girl turns back to him. She's got an expression like she's doing him a favor. Lowering herself to offer a few words. Just like an airgirl.

But then she attacks him, right as he's backing away. He's not himself. I have to help him. My reflexes kick in and I bash against the enforcement wall and am reminded I'm just an observer.

By then I see they're kissing. Kane and the girl are kissing, and I feel foolish for rushing in. My training got the better of me. My emotions did, too.

I don't know why, but I'm even angrier than if she'd have punched him.

Kane's words pop into my head. *My first kiss with someone I care about.*

I look at the girl. She must be the second. He knew this assignment was coming. He's known about this for a long time. Was she on his mind when he was with me? Am I on his mind when he's with her?

He breaks the kiss. Yells at her. Probably for throwing herself on him.

That's when she spits on him.

Forget not caring for airgirl. *Hate* is a better word.

She's yelling now. Ferocious. Not so great with rejection, I guess.

Now she's pulling back her arm. . . .

Everything goes dim. I figure some glitch is going to boot me out, but then there's a flash and the girl's holding Kane in her outstretched arms. Like he isn't worthy of her touch. Looks down at him with disgust.

His eyes are closed, his body lifeless. And that's when PCF officers surround Kane and start kicking his already broken body. They don't touch her. I can't either. Not right now, but she's out there somewhere. Are they just going to pummel him until he's dead?

Someone is holding the girl back. Her father? He's not PCF, that's for sure. He's fancy, more put together than her. She tries to run toward Kane, but the guy has her good. She struggles against him, wanting back in on the action. But it's over already. The PCF step back, winded from swinging clubs against a defenseless kid.

Great work, guys.

My list of people to hate is growing.

They move aside, and if you didn't know it was a human lying there at their feet, you wouldn't be able to tell. Until he twitches, and you know there's still life, know that he's got more fight in him than everyone on that pathetic island.

I might puke. It feels like I have to, but my body just won't let me. The memory of the ball and Kane's beating lingers in a bad way and I might just heave all kinds of reality over this Archive access room. She set me up. I stepped right into her trap . . .

Though I asked for this, I really did.

Cassina's still standing there. She just had to stick around to see me this way. She takes the chip from my wrist and I'm too sick to resist. "I can't let anyone know where you got *this* from," she says.

I squeeze my eyes shut, but all it does is jog my memory, which is the last thing I need. Plugged into a restricted archive, all I could do was stand apart from it and bear witness to Kane's new life without me. I couldn't yell at him or warn him or even beg him to stop. All I could do was watch and see him with someone else, then be beaten so savagely that I can't believe he's still alive.

The nausea begins to pass as the memory fades. Cassina looks calm, but she's keeping her distance. That was a dirty trick. I'd be all over her if I didn't need her in a condition where she could still talk.

"He's alive," I say, not allowing myself to consider any other option.

"He could be. That's all *I* know."

"Where'd they take him?"

"With the rest of the traitors and dissidents. You're SpecOps. You have access to all sorts of secret knowledge."

Her eyes dart to the fist I'm making.

I lack discipline. I lack self-control. I lack satisfaction and answers.

I'm closer to her now, trying to keep my voice from exploding. "Is it real?"

She circles away and puts distance between us. "As you and me. Perhaps, in the past, I've understated how important I am. The man in the videofeed, the one wearing the mark of the Independent High Council, is my father. He has an island, bigger than that. That's where *I* was born."

"Well, if you're so important, why was your father with her? And why're you down here?"

She's silent for a moment. I've hurt her. Even she doesn't know the answer.

"Kane trespassed, impersonated a Proper Young Man, and then attempted to assassinate that debutee. But he failed, as was plainly apparent. More of an artist than a killer, our Kane."

Our Kane.

"Kane's not a killer."

"Not for a lack of trying," she says.

"And PCF, were *they* trying to kill him? Is it normal for them to attend fancy balls?"

"Of course. Do you know what would've happened if they weren't there?"

"Can't say I'm civilized enough to know the answer."

She swings around. "What exactly are you implying?"

"Those men sure looked like they were listening to that man you say is your father." I keep my voice measured, my face calm. But with each word, I'm moving steadily closer to her. "I mean, he was right there with them. He was watching."

"He was the host."

"As host, did he invite Kane?"

"My father had nothing to do with this! Even he wouldn't get in the way of PCF. He saved Livia Cosmo's life!"

Livia Cosmo. At least I have a name.

"How would you even know?" I say. She's starting to get worried, I can see it on her face.

"No way Kane was acting alone. He told me he had a secret assignment. Who gave the orders? I mean, why kill *her*? She's crazy, perhaps, but not exactly old enough to be an enemy of the Indrithian state."

She shakes her head. She hasn't bothered to ask herself these questions. She's baiting me. "As to that, I have no idea."

"Think," I say. "You didn't graduate just so you could stop using your head. We weren't brainwashed."

She turns her back on me, but only I say when we're finished.

I snatch her up and push her against the wall face-first to stun her. With a little pressure to the back of one knee, she falls forward. I drive my knee in her back and twist one of her arms behind her so it's coiled with enough tension that if she tries to escape, it'll snap.

"Now either I can recollect Kane's pain from that memory and share it with you, or you can tell me what you know about that girl *right now*."

She grunts and I apply more pressure to her arm.

"She's air, like you," I say.

"And do you know every orphan?!" she says through gritted teeth. "Of course not."

I twist.

"She's an orphan!" she nearly screams. "Just like you."

I whip her around on her back. Pin her with my arm across her throat, my weight and legs restraining the rest of her body. She makes *orphan* into such a hateful word. She doesn't flinch. I look for the signs: fluctuation of pupils, expansion of the nostrils, perspiration, faint twitching of the eyelids.

Nothing. She's not lying, I don't think.

Not a drop of sweat or an off beat in her heart.

Even if she's telling the truth, I'll still make her pay. But right now, she doesn't matter. Only Kane does.

"You just find this memory and you don't question why? Why it was there for you? And your first instinct was to give it to *me*? Of all people?"

When she finally speaks, her voice is a shadow of itself, her song gone. "I know how you feel about me, and I hate you even more. But you're the only one who can help him. I'd do it, but that's not possible in my position. Everyone knows me. But no one thinks twice about a . . ."

She doesn't dare call me that again. People think twice after they get roughed up.

"You're still in love with him," I say.

This time, her pupils flare. There's a hitch in her breath.

She needs me, I know that now. She needs me and she hates that. I need her too, and I hate it even more than she does.

I take a deep breath. "What do you know?"

"Will you let go of me already?"

I get up off her and she rolls away, massaging her throat. She pulls herself to standing and straightens her uniform. "I couldn't find out much, even in Security. He was sent to assassinate her, but I'm not sure why."

Assassinate and *Kane*. Those words don't go together.

"He's the perfect choice, really," she says, regaining her crustiness. "They had him on the construction rigs with proper air rights authority doing surveillance. He was monitoring this island for weeks. I have enough clearance to get his memory, obviously, or I wouldn't be here. Saw you two planning this meeting. Saw a great deal of you both, in fact." She looks disgusted. "Cute moment with the boosters," she adds.

She just can't help herself, even now.

"In terms of strategy, I understand why they chose Kane. Especially considering his talents. Who else could fit in on a rig? One step from mudpeople, those rig workers. Could tell a nonbuilder on sight. And Kane has the uncanny ability to keep from ruffling feathers. Even those of a rigger."

The riggers truly are the last of the air outlaws. How the IHC has allowed them to coexist with their society is an unimaginable feat. From what I've heard, they're practically scavs. Except they maintain the functionality of all the Islands and do all the jobs that the rest of proper society finds beneath them. Kane can be slick, but entrenched with a bunch of pseudo-scavs? It's almost too much. Yet to Cassina, it just is. You're either air, or you're not.

For the first time, I see her as the IHC higher-ups must. Sure of herself. Someone able to assert authority. The kind of person you trust to make things happen.

I don't trust her one bit, of course. But right now, she's all I have. The only way to get to Kane.

"They probably put Kane on a rig near her island. I don't know for sure. They were careful to block those areas of his memory. Seems logical, though. That way he could observe her, get to know her habits. Then attend her ball."

"Emergence Ball," I say. "Kane told me about them."

"All the island girls have one." She sighs. "Except me, of course. I was already at the Academy. But Kane knows how they go. He's from the air as well. You see? He was the perfect choice."

"Where is she—*Livia*—now?"

"They have her quarantined on Helix. No one knew about Kane's assignment, after all. A great many of Indra's Most Importance were there that evening and I'm sure the gossip is flying. Everyone discussing her attack by an uninvited guest, contemplating the threat to all the Islands. They have to put up a show of protecting her safety."

Her safety. It's so messed up I almost laugh.

"They'll keep her there for a while, I suppose. Make a big deal of investigating the incident."

"What else do you know about her?"

"Livia? I told you already. There's not much to know. Upper born and raised. She sticks to herself. Reclusive. She was never like the rest of us. I mean, what do you expect? After all, she's just—"

"What?"

"I don't know much else," she says.

"Just shut up then," I say. "And let me think."

Cassina goes silent. I pace the Archive room. There isn't time to weigh the options. Not that there are any.

I'll go after that girl. She'll lead me to Kane. There's no other way.

When I don't report for Rock Bottom Patrol, they'll come after me. They'll put me in confinement, maybe worse. But that's a risk I'm willing to take. A placement doesn't matter much, not compared to this.

Kane needs me, I tell myself.

And this is what I need: to find Livia Cosmo. Make that conniving airgirl suffer.

"How will I get to her?" I ask Cassina.

"I have a plan," she says. "Why else would I be here?"

CHAPTER 14

Rock Bottom Patrol Day 1: AWOL

Lex

I found the uniform right where Cassina told me, folded neatly on the floor of Kane's studio. *How did she know about the Center of Creation?*

Of course. She saw it in Kane's memory. The idea of her watching and seeing us made me feel naked.

Did she see the kiss, too?

I pushed the thought aside and slipped on my new identity.

Moments later, I was in the PCF carrier she'd arranged to pick me up at the edge of the Academy gates. It hadn't been easy getting there unseen, but Kane and I had found all the dark places long ago, the forgotten hallways and hidden corners. I only had to remember them.

I slipped into the abandoned carrier. Held my breath, put my thumb to the printscan. The Academy gates swung open and we rumbled forward.

The synth-print worked, just like she'd said. She said she had it made in the High Council labs, by a friend there who could be trusted. A duplicate of her very own thumbprint. "With my high-level position, you should have no problem with access. The print is infused with a liquid reserve of my DNA, but at some point, it will run out. So move quickly."

Cassina might be a cold, heartless airgirl, but she was good with details. I'd give her that.

The more ground I put between me and the Academy, the more I realize I've been here before. Or maybe just a place like it. I remember seeing the patrol towers after leaving the Orphanage. The armed soldiers safeguarding the darkness, me trapped inside the transporter with Recruiter, on my way to my new life.

I'd been burning with questions then. Now I'm possessed with a different type of fire.

Everything is the same here, only smaller. Everything is the same. Except for me.

I park the carrier and board the train at the nearest commuter station, amidst the Hubbers headed home after a night's work. A few PCF are scattered throughout my compartment. I keep waiting to be noticed. For a voice to tell me I don't belong.

The voice doesn't come. All it takes is a uniform and I can be like everyone else. If that's the secret to life, I should just give up now.

The doors slide shut and the hiss of pressure sealing them gets my attention. The transporter gains full velocity quickly, but my heart gets there quicker.

We shoot into oblivion. There's nothing out there for miles and miles. Then, there is the Hub.

I'd always imagined the Hub as enormous. I was wrong. *Enormous* isn't a big enough word.

I look up. Somewhere above me, this endless cavern actually ends, where the Lower Levels become the Upper. *I'll believe it when I see it*, I think. Then I remember how soon that will be.

There are so many layers of strata, so much rock and iron. Someone thought this up. Someone planned this. My own life is so small compared to this.

There are a lot of loose ends that don't add up. Cassina's father, the sudden arrival of PCF to beat down Kane. Orders from someone who knew where to assassinate Livia Cosmo, and just why did Kane agree to it? But I push those out of my head.

Right now, I have one clear mission. Make that two: find Kane and demolish Livia Cosmo.

I've seen the Hub only in holo-images, but there's no time for sightseeing. Not that you can ignore the place. How they managed to hollow out this much of the Earth is astonishing. The Orphanage wasn't big on science facts and the Academy only built soldiers, but they say over a million people travel through the Hub daily, primarily via tube transporters. There's a steady stream of roaring transporters of all sizes, the traffic directed by a complex system of flashing lights, monitors, and security borders. Once you step into the Hub, your audiofeed, if you're wearing one—and it looks like everyone is—is co-opted to constantly update you with traffic announcements and scheduling advisements. We were never allowed audiofeeds at the Orphanage and only for simulated missions at the Academy, which I prefer. I have too much already going on in my head. Plus this tremendous cavern is a wall of light and sound. You'd think it would be easy to just be a face in the crowd, but I'm sure security cameras are concealed everywhere.

Everyone races to their destinations. I've never seen so many bodies. A continuous swarm of gray and blue uniforms that moves at the same pace, that maneuvers with military-like precision. I welcome the anonymity that joining them grants.

For a second, I imagine Kane's *Book of Indra*, with its jolt of whirling colors.

I feel like I haven't seen color since I've seen him.

I think of Kane painting my laugh.

I think mostly of Kane's lifeless body.

◊ ◊ ◊

I hop a Hub transporter for a transfer transporter before most of Indra is awake, and move on from that to a tunnel transporter. Seems like Hubbers spend half their time getting somewhere and the other half getting back.

At every interval, I hold my breath, worried the DNA reserve on Cassina's synth-print will run out. Each time, the entrance whooshes open.

But will I ever actually *get* anywhere?

Maybe the Upper Levels are a myth. A mass illusion. That would be a cruel trick.

I stare out the window, watching all this newness pass me by. Maybe I'm not going anywhere at all.

The shuttle jolts forward. We stop. More people get on. We stop. People get off. "*Sector Geode,*" says the mechanical speakerfeed.

Sector Magna. Sector Limestone. Sector Granite.

"*Sector Obsidian,*" the speakerfeed finally announces. "*Final stop. All passengers must disembark.*"

The tunnel is just how Cassina described. Hardly big enough for one person. If I extend my arms, I can touch the sides. Rock and sediment encircle me, the hollowed-out path continuing in front of me.

"Only a few people have access," Cassina told me. "I've checked the schedules and they will be otherwise engaged. That passage is only for others like me, those serving in—"

"High-level positions," I interrupted. "I get it. You're important."

Important, but entirely correct about its emptiness.

"You will think it never ending," said Cassina. "But then it will."

I almost smack into the transparent plexi-clear wall. *Thanks for mentioning that.*

It requires my thumbprint. The locking seal lets loose a pressurized burst as the entrance slides open.

The PCF patroller is waiting, as planned.

"Will you know how to fly it?" Cassina asked me.

I answered that one with just a look. If I know one thing, it's how to work a machine. My apprenticeship so far has allowed me access to sim lessons on all SpecOps transporters.

I tug the door open. The hatch releases like an exhale and I pull myself up into the cabin and latch the side closed. I strap myself into the shiny black seat and pop on the pilot's helmet. Then one more use of the thumbprint.

This is how I felt the first time on my air speeder. I had her roaring while the other cadets were still snapping on their riding gear.

The controls aren't too dissimilar, just more . . . complex. A lot more. You don't need flight training if you're assigned to Rock Bottom. Good thing I put in some extra work. I've always set my sights a little higher.

I prime the ignition and the twin engines wake up, one at a time. The power that hums through it also hums through me. I'm careful not to get carried away. This sucker does vertical takeoff and landing. I keep an eye on the gyroscope to make sure the weight is evenly distributed.

I program the coordinates. It charts the flight path to Helix Island.

The enormous ceiling panels above slide open and red lights begin to flash.

I look up. There it is.

Sky.

No booster could ever give you a rush like this.

I lift my visor, just for a second, and it's like my eyeballs catch fire. Real light, bursting off the sides of real buildings as I rise into the open air.

The City of Indra. The tower of the Independent High Council at its center, rising above it all. There are spires equally as beautiful. *This is the world I have always lived under*, I think. Now I can really see it.

No holo-image could prepare me for this. The world's a much bigger place than I could ever have imagined.

I glide the craft forward and up. I control her just like my speeder. I could get used to this. Upping the speed and engaging the turbo gear, I might as well abuse my privileges as much as the rest of the PCF do. I overtake the transporters in my path and cut through a corridor of airscrapers and skytowers. I could get used to this, if I was willing to be corrupt.

I round a corner and accelerate straight for a massive floating rig. I swoop beneath its shadowy mechanical underbelly. The maze of tubing and gears sways, the whole thing threatening to topple at any moment.

A swift upward boost and I merge with the sunlight. Ahead there's a new building under construction. I plunge headfirst, coasting through support frames, and shoot out the other side.

The rig's assignment, I figure. Luckily they haven't finished construction or my shortcut would've turned into a dead end.

I'm higher now, closer to the top of the dome that encases the city. Below me, the City of Indra spreads out like a holomap.

"I grew up in the air," Kane once said. "It's not really that great, not really."

I guess it's time to see for myself.

I point the nose of the patroller upward, check the coordinates, and pull the accelerator back as far as it goes.

My ears pop and I head above everything.

CHAPTER 15

After the Emergence Ball

Livia

From my isolated summit, I watch the world keep going without me. Every transporter that passes, the very few that are allowed in our airspace, is one that passes me by and leaves me stranded here.

In the main quarters, Marius takes tea in the parlor with an Indrithian of Importance, maids posted at corners on high alert to refill saucers and replenish trays of sweet cakes. While the visitor sips, Marius speaks to my outstanding qualities, the likes of which I cannot imagine ever existed.

When forced to address the unfortunate events of my ball, she speaks low, glossing over extraneous details. Clichés, she believes, are best suited for these moments. "The poor thing," she says. "A victim of circumstance. Events beyond reasonable control."

"The surprises life has to offer!" she adds cheerily. "And now we must move forward to discover exciting new horizons."

There are no horizons in the air, of course. But those are pesky details, and she's focused on a much larger task: saving me from complete ruin.

If pressed for specifics, she's evasive. "No, they don't have any information. A disgruntled Young Man with flawed genetics, I suspect.

Yes, an island boy, but with rather unique circumstances. Deceased mother, reclusive father. Terribly unfortunate situation. Perhaps if the signs had been more obvious?"

She shakes her head and sighs at the injustice. Then, with a sip of tea, she diverts the conversation to topics of real importance. My tiny waist, I suppose. My pleasant demeanor.

These are the details she hopes they'll remember.

I know all this because I have listened, ear to the wall of the adjoining pantry. I've been suitably impressed with Marius's gift for strategy.

Unfortunately, like former Earth, even she can't strategize her way out of complete catastrophe.

Between this guest and the last, she sent out inquiry feeds, tracking down cohabitants who have yet, for some inexplicable reason, to hear the specifics of my disastrous debut. She embarks on extended, utterly polite conversations with anyone privy to a Proper Young Man of cohabitable age.

"Perhaps we can arrange a rendezvous? Livia would be pleased to engage in private platform rotation for the suitable gentleman."

So far, gratefully, no one has taken her up on the offer.

Governess has been sent away on retreat. "In need of a rest," Marius said. But I'm not an imbecile; this is no relaxing holiday lounging in Rejuvenation Island's gardens, sipping vitamin cocktails. She began sobbing at first sight of my bloodstained dress; it didn't cease for three days. I held her hand and spoke reassuring words, even going so far as to keep vigil by her sleeper. In the few times she acknowledged me, it was only to ask questions: "Did you finish your pudding, Livia dear? Did you have a lovely time playing in the gardens?"

Once or twice she grew serious, but her eyes remained distant as she reached for me.

"You must be careful not to fall when climbing trees," she said fearfully, grasping my hand tightly with her shaky grip. "We wouldn't want another scrape, my dear."

I wiped tears from her faraway eyes and listened to her mutter of reprogramming the orchards, her sobs reduced to a steady whimper.

"Enough," said Waslo on the fourth day. He was in the doorway, but he refused to meet my eyes, just merely shook his head before exiting as abruptly as he entered.

That was his only word to me since that evening in Veda's stable.

Sunrise Retreat Island. I know that's where they've sequestered Governess. She's in lockdown, undergoing "emotional readjustments" and "electron regulation." Her sleeper pod is under constant surveillance, and so is the rest of her. In her greatest time of need, I can't return the comfort and support she's given me. For all the time spent improving the physical, no science has mastered repairing the mind. I have failed her.

Sunrise Island is rarely mentioned in polite company, though Indrithians know its reputation. A horror no one wishes to visit, even worse than Paradise Holiday, where Hubbies retreat. Lower Levelers will slave away their lifetimes for the honor of being granted a visit to Paradise Island. The best two days of their life, not that they'll remember with the abundance of refreshments. The most powerful of which, Hub suds, are a vision-inducing, mind-altering beverage. It's said you can smell the vomit from several islands away.

At least, according to the rumors.

At this point, I would take either over Helix.

I used to be considered unmanageable; now I'm unmanageable *and* unappealing. Even the synth-trees—fittingly programmed for beautiful fall hues—seem to wilt at my disgrace.

I avoid Marius, fearing the pity in her eyes. "It was not your fault," she told me. "*You* are the victim here."

Victim or not, no Proper Young Man would dare touch me now with the shame I've brought to my name. It's my awful, selfish dream come true. Helix Island is now as tainted as my legacy. I've come to understand I'll be one of those women who never cohabitate. A freethinker, which is a polite way to say *outcast*. They're rarely seen in public, succumbing to a life of seclusion, destined to pay in loneliness for their lack of options.

No one chooses to be a freethinker.

Marius, of course, won't accept my fate so willingly.

"A Young Man with a small estate," she tells me distractedly. "Looks promising. His pastime is fencing. I have been told he has a rather nice disposition."

Nice, I know, means a stutter or chronic odor or an even more serious deficiency. But even those Young Men won't agree to meet, avoiding me like a genetic flaw. Your name and island are all you have, and one doesn't stand without the other.

Below in the City of Indra, Waslo heads up the investigation. Despite his reassurance, Waslo rarely leaves the Council's chambers. The Islands, already predisposed to juicy gossip, are on high alert for strange occurrences.

I'm prohibited from leaving Helix, not that I would be welcomed in any other location.

The maids avoid me. The garden crew hasn't returned since the oaks changed colors. Following the ball, Life Guide resigned abruptly, bags already in hand as he broke the news to Marius.

"Perhaps you shall take a brief hiatus from educational endeavors," Marius informed me.

"He never taught me anything important anyway," I responded. She ignored me.

Master has ceased his visits as well, as is standard of leisure pastime instructors following a debut. Strangely enough, I miss him the most, despite his mysterious advice and bizarre riddles.

Etiquette lessons end with your ball, the ultimate goal being cohabitation. I failed, just as Etiquette Tutor always predicted.

For once, I have lived up to her expectations.

I avoid my father's study and my mother's air harp.

My zinger hangs by my sleeper. Since coming into my possession, it's never been so silent. I take it into the fields with me, but it never leaves its sheath.

I'm alone now, except for Veda.

When I asked Marius about *him*, I was sure to be offhanded, aiming to convey a sense of innocent curiosity.

"He is being detained at Council headquarters," she said sharply. I have never heard Marius speak with such harshness, and knew to avoid all future inquiries about the stranger.

Even if he never strays far from my thoughts.

I could stand here in silence all day, peering into the clouds, and I doubt anyone would notice. Designated edges no longer exist, as there is nothing of value in need of protection.

Perhaps my newly won nonexistence is to blame for my curious turn in thought. There are so many questions I shouldn't want answered, yet still, I do. Moments I should resist contemplating, yet I long to dwell in their details.

I seek distraction. I walk to the edge of Helix every day now, and no one discourages this. The make-believes they told me about the traps and secret hazards are no longer threatening. The world is far more dangerous and frightening than they ever prepared me for. Today I go for a walk without Veda. That way it will keep me away from the main quarters for that much longer. Anything to calm my mind of the incessant whirling. I even go so far as to keep up with Life Guide's favored educational topics.

I ponder Indrithian history, only to find myself pondering the details of *his* face. Were his eyes blue or brown? Was there a twist in his smile?

Indra Evolution and Society becomes a study of his lips on mine; Customs and Rituals the sound of his laugh. *He did laugh, did he not? And was his kiss as soft as I remember?* I am less sure of what I know with each passing day.

He tried to kill you, I chastise myself.

Yet he changed his mind, I reason.

Perhaps this is what happens when you are left to your own devices.

If this continues, they'll send me off to where Governess has gone. Maybe we can do the double mental-meltdown special at Sunrise Island.

Something must happen soon, I think, looking out toward the clouds.

And there it is, flying straight at me.

CHAPTER 16

Lex

It's pretty hard to forget the face of someone you hate.

Recruiter.

Cassina.

Livia Cosmo.

The wind blows at her white dress, making her look like another cloud here at the edge of her island.

She's beautiful. Untouchable, like the rest of us are far beneath her. In a way, I guess we are.

I'll be the first to touch her—and I'll make sure it hurts.

I pinpoint a thicket of trees and I keep my eye on the gyroscope as I take her in for a landing. It's bumpy, but I don't do any permanent damage to the craft or myself.

The Islands are beautiful. That's what they say.

I step out of the craft, but I don't see it. Everything is a chemical green. Too bright and totally fake, like in the Archives. The Archives were built to replicate reality, and now instead reality imitates the Archives. It's as if I could just pull out a chip and this all would melt away.

The air makes me dizzy, and after a few steps, before I'm out of the thicket, I pause for a breath. Why's it so hard to breathe here? My head swims and it feels like my feet are no longer touching the ground.

Remember the task, Lex.

I peel off the PCF uniform, and just the fit of the black skintight silitex underneath calms me.

I'm myself again. I'm still strong, even up here. I just need a few moments. . . .

I adjust my straps and replay my objectives: *Find Kane's location. Rescue Kane. Seek retaliation, then kick her ass.*

Sure, she did damage to Kane, but I'm an army of one. I'll break her.

Someone wanted this airgirl dead. I don't know why, and I don't care. Either way, I'll finish the job.

I'm coming, Kane.

I painted her with my tracker beam on the way in, and checking in on her now, she hasn't moved far.

My blaster has a full charge. I take a deep breath as I emerge from cover.

She's hard to miss. Just standing there, her back turned.

Waiting for me.

Within seconds, I've got her in a stranglehold.

She never saw me coming. Doesn't struggle. Living this high up, she thinks she's above human pain. Nothing can harm you in the air, right?

It could be blood rushing to my head, since there are no fumes up here. Only . . . oxygen. Maybe it's just her stupid face, but for a moment, I forget what I came for.

Focus. Just focus.

Kane, grinning at me on boosters. Painting my laugh.

Kane, unconscious, battered like a busted-up zip ball.

"Tell me where they took him, air bitch," I growl. "Tell me where they took Kane or I'm gonna—"

I don't get to finish. She's reached for something, something on her back.

A sword. Pointed at my neck. She's got a sword and it's *singing.*

"You," she says, "are in desperate need of an etiquette lesson."

CHAPTER 17

Livia

The realization is startling: someone has arrived with the intent to murder me. Again.

I've never witnessed an individual of such unique appearance. This, to be sure, is no Proper Young Woman.

Her garb is a scandalously formfitting shiny black. Stealth is surely not her priority. It's a uniform of some sort, perhaps, though I couldn't begin to imagine her official duties beyond violence.

She's perfect in a way I've never seen, every inch of her wild, from her fierce expression to her untamed hair. I'm rather sure she has never undergone an alteration, though on first glance, I did suspect a chest enhancement.

I've never sensed another so strongly; she pummels me without even touching, her attempt to blindside me spoiled as she began her approach.

She glares and I stare back, curious. My zinger, shiny tip pointed at the softest part of her neck, is no longer silent. It has never touched real flesh. Its faint tune is almost bloodthirsty.

A few seconds pass, yet it seems a lifetime.

Her lifetime. It could be over in a few more seconds, if I wish it.

I feel her confusion and fear and focus, but her loyalty is powerful enough to kill for.

It will kill her. I'm not a killer, but I refuse to be a victim.

There's a sudden change, so quick I almost don't catch it. Within an instant, a frigid void takes over where emotion had just been.

She speaks through clenched teeth, making it almost impossible to understand her. If she even hopes to survive Etiquette, she'll need to pass Elocution first.

"Excuse me," I say calmly. "But might you speak up? I'm having a rather difficult time understanding you."

She narrows her eyes and says, "Put away the sword."

"Absolutely not," I say as my zinger lets out a stream of low notes. "Your first instinct was to strangle me. You should lose your hands for that alone."

"I'm not going to tell you again," she says.

"Perhaps I should start with your tongue."

"Put down the—"

I raise my eyebrows, noting her abilities in Conversational Intercourse are limited as well. "I've fought opponents in the Archives far more dangerous than you," I say. "So you would do well to compose yourself, perhaps take a deep breath first, and then we might have a rational—"

Lex

My pacifiers shut up island girl quick.

I pull them from my belt, one rod in each hand, and as soon as I extend them, they flicker awake and electricity singes the air.

One touch and she'll be out. On the ground, stunned into submission.

Best of all? She won't be able to talk.

I kind of love Rock Bottom Patrol, I think. *For my new weapons alone.*

Startled, she stumbles back. She's never felt anything like the pacifiers before. Her face changes from polite to pissed. Her sword shrieks, like I offended it.

"You won't put it down?" I say. "So guess what? I have to make you."

I rush her. The pacifiers surge, spiraling blue bursts of high voltage.

She draws her arm back, raising her sword. She looks like an idiot *and* I wish her sword would shut up.

The sword arcs down as I reach her and she cuts one of my pacifiers in half. I raise it to fend off another swing, and it's halved again.

I let the stub fall from my hand. It could've really used a reinforced shaft.

Cassina should've mentioned a sword, or at the very least weapons training. Still, she plays her tricks inside of tricks.

Mental note: Kick airgirl's ass first, then Cassina's.

She looks at the other pacifier, still sparking. A smug smile; she's confident in her abilities.

So am I.

The instant before she slices, I hurl my remaining pacifier at her face. It hits her above the eye and she shrieks. Let's see how well she responds to that.

Her body's frozen from the shock. I step into her waist and flip her. She may be tall, but she falls like everyone else.

She's on the ground, eyes wide. Her body's still processing the current: your heart skips a beat after you get stunned, and your muscles contract so tightly and hurt so much you might just burst. This was all part of my apprenticeship. I've felt this pain.

I put my knee to her sword arm. "Don't worry your pretty little head, airgirl," I say, applying pressure inside the elbow.

Her hand pops open, sword falling out of it. "Not singing now, huh?" I say. "That feeling you have lasts for five minutes in an adult

male. You'll have plenty of time to think. Here's something to consider: What I did to your elbow just now? That's a pressure point.
Push my knee a little harder, *snap*. I'd have broken your arm."

I like her much better now that she can't respond.

The convulsions have died down, and now she just spasms every
now and then.

I reach for her sword. The instant I touch the handle, the blade
explodes with noise.

"Shut up!" I yell.

I can't believe I yelled at a sword.

The noise doesn't stop, and my eardrums pound, ready to burst.
I hurl it as far as I can and it lands high up in the branches of a tree.

Silence, finally.

Past the trees, the island keeps going. Back the other way, the
edge becomes endless sky. *Kind of strato*, I think.

"Y'know," I say, unable to pull my eyes away from the view, with
some whole other island orbiting this one very slowly in the distance.
"Right now I could kill you in sixteen different ways."

"Then pick one."

I whip around.

Airgirl is on her feet. *Impossible*, I think. *No one can recover that
quick*. She's not even disoriented. She's already moving. Leaping, actually. For a second, she seems to hover. Her elbow lifted, hand held
rigid.

This time the pose isn't as funny.

Thwack! My neck snaps sideways.

Another strike and my face burns. Then a sharp blow to my gut
knocks me off my feet.

What the hell? This airgirl is full of surprises.

Synth-grass looks soft, but it isn't. Not really. Not enough to cushion my fall. My head aches; I'm dizzy and it was hard enough to
breathe before the air got knocked out of me.

I open my eyes. Airgirl is above me blocking out every piece of sky except the clouds dancing around her head. She smiles.

"I suppose you were correct," she says. "Perhaps I don't need the sword." She narrows her eyes. "My hands and feet are sufficient. In fact, I could kill you in sixteen different ways with them. I need not resort to the aid of sticks."

Her smile fades into something sinister.

Now I know for sure I've been set up. This isn't another uppity cloudcase.

This girl is dangerous and flat-out *crazy*.

Don't forget, I think. *You're PCF's finest.*

She's still looking at me, her head cocked to the side. Nodding, like she hears me thinking.

"Oh," she says, "I see you're anxious for more."

I open my mouth, then answer with my right foot.

It catches across her mouth and splits her bottom lip at the corner.

She puts her thumb to it and it comes away with blood. She seems more interested than upset. Then the interest turns to fury.

Eyes narrowed, nostrils flared, she stares at me, lips pinched and breath quickening. Classic signs of distress. All I see is vulnerability.

She steps back, stands straight, chin lifted: that pose . . . again. *She's tall*, I think. *Like, freakishly tall.* She's ready to strike. The whole thing, mouth kick to strike-ready, takes a split second. But I catch every detail.

I'm on my feet before she launches.

"That was for Kane," I spit, fists raised. "And this is for me."

I throw a closed fist to her belly, going low on purpose to catch her off guard. She never expected that. Airgirls don't lower themselves to anyone.

She lurches forward with a groan, and I'm waiting to meet her.

I head butt her hard enough that I hear her brains scramble.

She grips her forehead and stumbles backward. All those sims she's probably battled through, probably none of them taught her to fight dirty. I've got her now.

Livia

I reach out, wrapping this wild girl in my angry embrace, and we collapse together. *If I fall, then you shall come with me*, I think.

I grip her as we roll across the grass, digging the newly sharpened tips of my nails into her bodysuit. The girl screams in pain.

You were correct, Governess, I think, as we flip over and over, *a pre-debut manicure does fill one with a sense of accomplishment.*

While unique in appearance, her attire hasn't been designed for synth-grass. She slides and skims, trying to find purchase where there is none. Within moments, I've positioned her beneath me, the sharp point of my knee hammering her rib cage, an impromptu variation of a jujitsu mount that would make a true sensei cringe in horror.

True, I'm not following the rules of civilized combat, but I've come to believe she didn't know these rules existed in the first place. She's on my level, but not my equal.

She's forced my hand and now I have no option: regrettably, I must decimate her.

Regrettable for *her*, that is.

She groans in pain, which brings me great satisfaction. She reaches upward for me and I push down her arms. She grasps only air. I reach for her wild mane of hair.

"I believe it's safe to conclude," I say, grabbing two generous fistfuls, "that you don't adhere to the standard social graces."

I yank with all my might.

She bites her bottom lip, a sad attempt to contain the screams.

"I give you permission," I tell her sympathetically, "to express your obvious discomfort and start by begging for forgiveness."

Instead, she narrows her eyes, glaring at me with blatant disgust. In that moment, my zinger moans from a nearby location, uttering a single, lonely note. In that same moment, she begins shrieking.

"Where is he?" she says.

"Who?" I'm thinking she means *Kane*.

"Kane," she says.

"And how exactly would I have such information?"

I feel a small rivulet of blood making its way to the corner of my mouth. I have no idea how this fight started.

An utter breech of etiquette, I decide, *for one to bleed alone*.

A quick strike to her nose and now we bleed together.

She fights through the pain, as if it doesn't pain her as much. Perhaps these ones get their nerves neutered.

"You know where he is," she says. "Tell me now or I'll hurt you even worse."

"I don't believe you're in a position to threaten," I say calmly.

She attempts to wiggle out from beneath me, so I reach for her hair once again. I give it a firm tug, and this time she cannot help but howl. "The pain must be excruciating," I say. "Perhaps I should allow you a moment to recoup?" I ease my grip, offering a brief respite.

The next pull is even harder.

I look down, surprised to be holding a clump in each hand. I dispose of these, immediately reaching for another helping. Master would never condone this kind of fighting, deeming it "Without elegance or strategy. Demeaning to both you and opponent."

Easy for him to say. He has probably never fought for his life.

She rolls backward abruptly, surprising me.

Unexpected indeed, I think, just before the front of her boots slam into my face.

Lex

She smacked me across the face. Held me down and spit insults, not that I understood half of the uppity air talk. But I'm pretty sure it wasn't compliments.

She pulled my hair. Pulled *out* my hair. Even the cadet groomer wouldn't dare go that far.

Now I'll teach her my language. No words required.

We go round and round, circling each other like wolves. I saw them in the Archive once: ragged and starving, growling, teeth bared. Then they ate one another.

"Tell me where he is," I say.

"And supposing I was privy to knowledge of this young man's location—"

"Kane," I bark. "His name is Kane."

I think I see the flicker of a smile. No doubt about it: the girl is evil.

"This *Kane's* elusive whereabouts. Why would I choose to share that information? Especially with *you*."

You sounds like a curse word.

"Because he might die. And *you'll* be a murderer."

"Listen to yourself," she says. "He came to kill *me*, not the other way around."

I charge her, but she sidesteps so quickly I'm grabbing air.

She lives in it. Might be made of it, too.

"He was charming, I'll grant you that. But he tried to poison me with a kiss."

"Did he force that on you like you sicced those PCF bastards on him? You beat him senseless, but you wanted him lifeless, too?"

"What a horrible, horrible lie," she says.

"I saw you!"

I lunge again. She springs away.

Lunge, spring. Like this is a game to her.

"Shall we make a day of this?" she asks.

I stop, frustrated. She's a few feet away now, pacing. Back and forth, eyes never straying from me, always moving. Completely, utterly restless.

"You weren't there," she says sharply.

"I saw everything."

"How?"

"The *Archives*, airgirl! Taken from his memory. I saw *every single second*."

She stops pacing. She questions everything. She would've done well at the Academy. "And from whom did you acquire this memory?"

I don't say anything.

"If you don't want to make this more than a misunderstanding, silence won't do."

Every inch of me is burning. I no longer pump blood, but hatred. I push through the pain. Race for her.

She's too fast. *Where did she go?* I spin around. She's gone. Evaporated into the air.

I hear music. Really crappy music.

Damn. She got the singing sword back. *I got tricks too, airgirl.*

I sprint, ducking behind a tree at the island's edge, then I activate my decoys just in time.

Livia

"I suspect you were looking for me," I say, lifting my zinger.

She dares come to my island? The moment has arrived for her departure. I race for her, zinger first. She doesn't run. She simply watches me.

I slice straight through her . . . yet she's not there. She's dissipated, only faint streaks of electric mist remaining.

A decoy. Clever.

I spin around, my chest hammering. Nothing.

"Here," says a voice. I turn and she's staring at me calmly. I rush toward her with fury, yet my zinger slices empty space.

Another one.

"Not quite," she says. I pivot to find her again, this time grinning. "Wanna give it another go?"

"Or you could try me." There she is again, this time to the left of me.

She's also to the right.

I have to slow down. Three of her bait me with identical smiles on identical faces.

The projections are quite good, not a single glitch to ruin the illusion. I'm left with no other option. I must *feel* the real one. Her anger and will were so overpowering before, but now?

Nothing. Not even the tiniest flicker. Perhaps they're all decoys. There's only one way to find out.

They all come at once.

I stab at one and it dodges my zinger, the second advancing from the left. Blade still pointed at the first, I roundhouse kick the other. That one dissipates on impact.

Fake. Next?

I lift the zinger high and aim for the top of her head.

Perfect form, yet the vertical cut slices through nothing. My blade plunges straight into the ground.

Lex

Finally. *Airgirl is going down.* The decoys really got her.

She reaches for her sword. Just as she pulls it from the dirt, I race from behind the tree. A kick to the arm and a series of punches to the head. One to the liver. Now she'll really pay.

I finish her off with a roundhouse kick to the chest.

She flies backward, lands on the ground, and rolls right over the edge.

Oh no . . .

Livia

I have my zinger in one hand, the rock edge in the other. I'm digging in so hard, one of my nails breaks. The pain helps me focus.

Suspended in space, the longer I hang, the weaker I'll get, and this . . . whatever just happened has worn me out. What would normally be a gentle breeze only makes me dig in harder.

Don't look down, I tell myself. I force myself to look up.

The curling roots of the farthest synth-tree have snaked through the soil and cracked through Helix's rocky foundation. Perhaps I might be able to reach them.

This, unfortunately, will require both of my hands.

Already once today I've lost my zinger. *I'll find it again*, I think, lifting the blade. My grip begins to slip.

Lex

My breathing's ragged. The altitude is making me sick, and now that my adrenaline is crashing, I'm discovering I'm stunningly not okay with heights. So much open space above and below me. I've lived below for far too long.

Then that damn sword comes sailing toward me. It falls short and I know I've underestimated my opponent once again. Good thing she's alive to still question. Bad thing that this fight will continue.

She crawls over the edge of the island. I can't catch my breath. I'll let her come to me. See just who will back down first.

I brace for impact and square up, but she still hits me hard.

We're locked together on the ground, getting ugly.

I've got two fingers on her neck. Right on the artery.

She's trying to choke me. It's working remarkably well.

"I press this spot a little harder, you'll be paralyzed," I say hoarsely. "You'll never walk again, you hear me?"

"You'll run out of air first," she says.

We hold like this, bodies tensed, staring at each other.

That's when I see the symbol.

Tiny as mine. In the same spot on her iris.

We have the same marking. Her eyes are different, just like mine.

That small neon shape, glowing a light greenish. Practically invisible, even if you were looking for it. The imperfection they never caught in the Orphanage. It could've been the end of me, that little squiggle.

And she's got it, too. Something isn't right. Suddenly, my head is vibrating inside. Temples throb like they'll bust my head wide open.

From the darkest part of my brain, a voice explodes from some memory I've never had.

When you find her, you will know who she is . . .

I'm scared. The first time I've ever admitted it, even to myself.

". . . simply by looking her in the eyes," she says to me.

She releases me and I roll away. She looks as confused as I feel.

"How'd you know what I was thinking?" I ask.

"I heard you."

"It was *inside* my head!"

"Still," she says. "The words were already on my tongue. I couldn't keep my mouth shut."

"Huh." I have that problem sometimes, too. "Those words. They weren't mine. It was some other voice. . . ."

"A man's voice." She nods. "Yes. I heard him as well."

It could be another one of her tricks, but one look in her eyes tells me I'm mistaken. She's as freaked out as I am.

"Who is he?" I ask.

We stare at each other. With only his voice, neither of us has much of an answer. For once, I wish she was talking.

"Have you always had that in your eye?"

"Yes," she says, nodding. She looks like a little, frightened girl.

Suddenly, I feel like one.

We stare at each other. Unable to look away. A breeze lifts my hair. Hers, too.

We both look up.

PCF patrollers hover overhead, surrounding us.

"Do not move," booms some mechanical authority. "You are hereby restrained on order of the Independent High Council. Failure to comply will result in the usage of force. Do not move. You are hereby restrained on order of the Independent High Council . . ."

Oh, Cassina, I am truly going to kill you.

CHAPTER 18

Livia

I have lived here my entire life, but it's only recently that soldiers have violated the sanctuary my father established. It seems they drop by every time I have an uninvited guest. I have always been told that trouble could rise from the Lower Levels and no quantity of air would be a great enough barrier without their armed support. But who are these soldiers to warn me, on my own island?

My guest, uninvited or not, demands my hospitality. She growls a name, and I feel her anger is almost endless.

"Who's Cassina?" I ask.

"The reason the PCF are here. She told them where to find me, I know it. That airhead set me up!" She's under the fall trees, crouched low to the earth, looking up at me with fury. "Get down! They'll see us."

I peer at the fleet of patrollers circling directly above us.

"A bit late for that," I say.

"Now!"

I dislike her tone, her strategy even less. The trees will offer us little protection from their scanners. They knew we were here long before they arrived.

"Failure to comply will result in the use of force," blares the speakerfeed. It repeats itself as often as Etiquette Tutor.

"There's too much open field for you to escape on foot," I say.

"You think you're any faster?"

"What I think is that they have certainly not come for *me*."

"I have a craft hidden, not far that way." She points. I can't see it, so it must be farther than we could ever hope to get.

The patrollers draw lower, their dual engines creating violent gusts that sway the trees around us. The leaves blow bare. Soon they'll be no cover at all.

Once again, I sense this girl strongly; her vulnerability is oozing through her silitex. She's growing increasingly frantic, realizing there's little time and too many unanswered questions.

She turns to me, hair whipped into improper stylings, expression ferocious.

"Tell me!" she yells over the mechanical roar. "I need to know *where Kane is!*"

I have reached my limit of tolerance.

"Do all assassins come in pairs?" I yell right back.

We glower in a silent battle of wills.

"You are hereby restrained," blares the speakerfeed.

I won't answer her question, I decide. Not with my blood still wet on her fist. Not with my mark hidden within her eye as well.

Her body tenses. She's going to run for it and they will gun her down. She is my guest. I must show her hospitality.

"This way," I tell her.

For an instant, she doesn't comprehend. Then horror crosses her face. She's used to working alone.

"These crafts above are only the beginning, as you well know," I say rationally. "We're surrounded. As you are also aware, your chances of escaping are nil. You will be obliterated within two feet."

She knows I speak the truth. I am also her only option.

Unfortunately, she is mine as well.

At least I've had Governess and Marius to mold me with proper manners, no matter how resistant I've been. I've learned by being pushed and pushing back. She has only this Kane person. They are curious killers, the both of them.

Marius will succeed in finding me a cohabitant, I know that in my heart of hearts, her charms sealing my fate. Condemning me. I see my future clearly, enslaved to this monotonous system. Death by politeness. By decree of the Independent High Council.

"Listen closely," I tell her, "for your life depends on my every word. . . ."

CHAPTER 19

Lex

I elbow her hard in the belly. She doubles over and I grab the sword by her feet. Then I grab her by the hair and drag her with one arm, the blade against her neck. She moans. If I spill her blood, mine is next.

"Be careful," she says.

"Gotta make it realistic," I delight in saying back.

The sword won't sing for me, not when it means doing her harm.

I'll honor our deal. We both have freedom on our minds. Only rebels consider death freedom. I do not.

We have a plan, and it makes me want to puke.

I have no other option, I tell myself. There are too many PCF. And she still hasn't told me where to find Kane. I can do it without her, I'm pretty sure. But knowing his location would sure make it easier.

Meeting her has only given me more questions. Like the eye thing. What's that about? If I don't take her, I'll never know.

Still, something isn't right. I'm a fighter. I need to stop running. But now is definitely not the time so I have to take her.

I hate her even more now that it's come to this.

I look up toward the patrollers. Indra's finest? I can't believe I bought that. One word from Cassina and they turn on their own. I go from Special Op to enemy of the Indrithian state before most people eat lunch. Surely my record would exonerate me. Surely they would see all I've overcome. Surest of all, I know Indra is an unforgiving bitch that would kick me down to a paroled Hub scrubber.

My fall was planned all along.

Right now, Cassina is reclining somewhere with a pointy-chinned grin.

In SpecOps, you study the PCF training handbook. Then they teach you how to do everything better.

They're hunting me right now. I count six officers in camouflage silitex in the synth-scaping around us. They're fanning out until we're flanked. I hesitate any longer and they'll have us completely surrounded.

I've got a blade to her neck. I've got a half-dozen guys who want my head decorating their holofile.

This can't turn out well.

But why does this airgirl have my symbol?

When you find her, you'll know who she is. That's what the voice in my head said. But who is she?

"What now?" I ask her.

"Your craft."

"No way we can get there with them—"

A shrill, high-pitched whistle cuts me off. It's coming out of airgirl's mouth.

"Are you insane? You really think that's gonna scare PCF?"

Before I can finish my sentence, her gigantic white horse is bounding toward us, tail swinging back and forth. It's . . . astonishing. I've seen one before, but only in an Archive with her.

This is as real as it gets.

"Horses are extinct," I say, mostly to remind myself.

"Then don't get on," she says, lowering the blade from her own neck. I grab her wrist before she leaves me completely exposed.

"I'm staying with you," I say.

"That's up to you." Still I catch the flick of her lower lip. Classic sign of hesitation.

She has no idea how to get off her own island without me. She needs me and she hates it.

I need her and I hate it even more.

I'm fearless on my speeder, cutting air at breakneck speeds. An animal is something else. Speeders and crafts don't breathe beneath you. They don't have minds of their own, unless carefully programmed. You can't initiate turbogear on a horse, but we go so fast it almost feels like flying.

And I might fly off the side at any moment.

"Put your arms around me," she says.

I hold so tight I could squeeze the life out of her. That's one way to kill her, I guess.

"Less than a mile northeast," I say, checking the tracker with a shaky hand. "And the PCF are right on our tail."

Its tail. Whatever. All I know is they're close.

"They won't fire if you stay close to me," airgirl says. "Hold tight."

Not a problem.

"Hurry, Veda," she says. The animal makes a weird noise—a cross between a laugh and moan—then goes faster. She's a different airgirl on this horse. They act almost as one.

Now the trees are tall and dense, and the crafts are unable to follow us through without crashing. Airgirl directs the beast with precision. Her movements are quick, her muscles barely flickering. Veda pounds out pathways that never existed. Branches slap me with every bound.

I'd take dirt and rock any day over all this so-called nature.

A tree comes straight for us.

"Duck," airgirl yells, and I do, just in time. A thick branch brushes the top of my head. A second later, there'd have been no head to duck.

"Duck!" she yells again, and I realize I can die just as easily with her by my side.

I check the tracker. "Just about there," I say. "It's coming up on the right."

We see the smoke before the clearing itself. But it's the fire that spooks the horse. It rises on two legs, making its version of a scream. We're tossed from its back and I crash to the ground.

My shoulder . . . I just did something to my shoulder. It feels loose. I'm on my knees and my left arm just dangles there. I know how to fix it. I just have to clear my mind and . . .

The pain of popping it back in place nearly overwhelms me. Livia holds me steady, and all I'm wondering about is why she hasn't kept running.

You can't miss my patroller. It's right there. Half of it, really. All the pieces are there, just blackened and blown apart. We watch it smolder, and our escape plan with it.

What's left of it just explodes.

I stagger to my feet and I help airgirl up and her horse is circling back, regaining its senses. We hold each other up until the horse comes.

"Hurry up," I say. "I can hear them coming." They knew what direction we were heading. They didn't take us down because we always had nowhere to run to.

"Hurry," I tell her. She's saying good-bye to the beast. You'd think animals had feelings, the way it's looking at her. She ignores my urgency, just stares into the horse's big brown eyes. Whispers something. Of course I can hear.

"Now you have to run. Fast. Find a place to hide until this is over. I'm going away for a while. Don't worry, girl. I'll see you again. I promise."

The horse hangs its head . . . crying?

Creepy, I think. Sometimes I wish I didn't hear so well.

She gives the horse a firm smack and it takes off.

"What are you looking at?" she barks. "Run for your life!"

I think she was almost crying, too.

I follow her into the trees, deferring to her knowledge of this big floating rock. The crafts hover above the tree line, but it's the men on the ground who worry me. I hear their feet behind us. We have a head start, but not much.

"There's only one way off the island," she says, as if reading my mind. She does that a lot. It's starting to freak me out.

We've emerged into glaring spotlights, but she doesn't stop. She moves unnaturally fast and I race to keep up.

"They've probably infiltrated the heliopad, where all visitors land, and that's where we keep the air transporters, so flying away is not an option."

We're moving so fast my silitex sheds my sweat at an unreal rate.

A sharp pain in my shoulder. I've begun to cramp up and I can't get enough oxygen. If I'd planned better, if I hadn't rushed off, I would've taken a ventilator. I was too hotheaded.

Airgirl's barely winded, her face calm, her feet practically skimming the ground. She's chattering on and on, like this is a social occasion or something.

"Audiofeed is in the main quarters. Lamentably, we cannot use it to signal a transporter."

"Speak like a human!" I'm huffing for air now.

"Breathe like one," she says.

"I can't . . . there's something wrong with . . ."

"The altitude is not *wrong*, you are simply unconditioned."

I'd say something mean if I could spare the breath.

"Marius's chauffeur would be an option, yet he's not—"

"Here? I get it, okay!" What's left of my voice is ragged. Defeated. "There's nowhere for us to go!"

I run right into her long arm, stretched out in front of me. She's come to a stop.

"Correct," she says serenely. "Nowhere to go . . ." She lowers her gaze. I follow. "Except down."

We're staring into clouds. There's a massive rig below the island. It's an enormous piece of raging metalwork, its frame an unsightly rust red, yet there's life on it—most important, a large synth-nursery.

"It has been here quite a while," she says.

Kane's rig, I think. Where he spied on her.

"If we aim for the foliage on the outskirts, perhaps that will cushion our fall."

"That's a big perhaps," I say. I've already dislocated my shoulder once today. A fall from this high would dislocate the rest of my body.

"Stop running," booms the speakerfeed, "or we will actively engage. Drop to the ground *now*."

The PCF handbook, chapter 6. "Restraining Enemies of Indra." Right after this comes the penalty of noncompliance.

Death.

"Special Operative Lex, you have abandoned your sworn post," it says next. They know it's me.

"They'll stun us in three seconds," I say.

"Ready?"

"Are you?"

She nods. Closes her eyes. Takes a breath.

"Now," she says.

Together, we take a big leap over the edge.

CHAPTER 20

Livia

For the first second you fall gently. My dress billows out around me. Then it snaps up and I can barely see, the world goes white.

On the island we never had trees with so many branches. I hit every single one, then I hit the ground. The pain lets me know I'm alive. Barely.

When I open my eyes, I tell myself, *I will be somewhere other than Helix Island.*

Instead, I'm staring into the eyes of Lex. She's landed before me. It wasn't a race, but she just had to beat me.

I gasp.

I want to lie here. That's all I want to do.

I move my arms and legs and they feel like they belong to someone else.

"Are you hurt?" I ask, sitting up.

"No," she says. "Are you?"

I shake my head, amazed at our fortune. I start to laugh out loud at the audacity of our escape.

"Never have I seen a vision so beauteous," says a voice. "As women diving from the sky."

A young man stares down at me. He's around my age, yet smiles in a boyish way. He wears a black helmet, his face streaked with dirt and grime. The sleeves are ripped from his uniform, revealing bare arms. We are definitely no longer on Helix.

Proper Young Men maintain discreet attire, their flesh fully concealed, even when engaging in vigorous leisure pastimes.

Then again, they also don't have "RIGGER" stamped across the blue fabric on their chests.

Not surprisingly, the girl—Special Operative Lex, I remind myself—has already risen to her feet, braced to attack. So that's where she received her training, as one of Indra's finest. She wanted to kill me, yet it was also PCF who beat her Kane. Something doesn't match up. And somehow I'm at the middle of it. But why?

The young man smiles at her. "I see no need for that, love. Not until we've had a proper introduction."

"He doesn't intend to harm us," I say, back on my feet.

"Riggers are no better than scavs."

"Except they don't see girls here often. Harm is not what they want to do to us," I tell her in a firm manner, patting down my dress. Reluctantly, she lowers her fists.

"Nothing so vulgar. I'm Hep," he says, then he points to the words engraved across his helmet.

"'Garden Crew,'" I read, finding the actual letters disconcerting. Other than *The Book of Indra*, I have never seen words that were not holo.

He nods at me, his face lit with pride. "Not many scavs can tend an orchard like me."

I try to comprehend, my mind racing. Gardeners, as those of Indra are well aware, serve in a position of utmost importance. "Vital to Indrithian Society, for they are the growers of life itself, caretakers of our very existence," according to *The Book of Indra*. Synthtrees may be birthed in the Aero-Crown, but the gardeners are the ones who nurture them into beautiful specimens. They hold the key to oxygenating our world, literally giving us the air we breathe. A prideful bunch, gardeners. Even cocky. Few would waste their artistry on a rig.

Hep, on the other hand, seems carefree. An artist *and* a ruffian.

"The Islands have so many beautiful women now, they're just throwing them away?" he says, still looking at me. He reaches out his hand to me, Lex wary of it all. She's an oath breaker. She has much to be wary of now. I place my hand in his, diverting my eyes from the filthy fingernails. And yet all I see is that my own are not much better at this point.

"The Islands have a distorted view of all three of us. I'm Livia," I tell him, and he bows graciously.

I send Lex a knowing glance. *These*, I silently tell her, *are referred to as "manners."*

"Great," she says. "Now we're old friends. But our new friends, they're still . . ."

She quiets suddenly. Hep's dropped to his knees and is rooting in the dirt. "Here we go," he says, removing several orange roots still caked in earth. He holds them out to her. "Something to catch your breath?"

"This isn't some tea party."

"Every time you take a breath, you wheeze. She's from the Islands, but you're most definitely not." He takes a bite of the root with a loud snap. "None of us living here are from anywhere even remotely aboveground. So we eat these. They used to grow carrots in the old world, but my own hybrid helps regulate oxygen in the blood." Then he smiles at us, teeth neon green.

"Boosters," Lex says.

"Try one," Hep says. "All natural, plus they'll help you escape from whatever it is you're escaping from."

I take one and Lex does, too. I brush away the dirt, and a few seconds after my first bite, I feel marginally stronger. Lex won't admit it, but I can feel her change in disposition. With her changing moods, she's not a lot of fun to be around.

"Thank you," I say.

He reaches into a pocket and removes a small bottle, which he presses into my hand. It is filled with capsules. "I've dried them and powdered them, too. It's a nice blend. You hold on to these."

I nod in thanks.

"So who is it that's got you on the run?" asks Hep.

"PCF," I tell him.

The change is sudden, Hep's calmness evaporating. He drops the half-eaten root. "This is just the fight we've been waiting for. We won't let the PCF control us on our rig! Come over this way. I have someone for you to meet."

The bulky man is named Durley and his helmet proclaims him "Building Crew." Two patches are ripped from his pants, his knees protruding. He has the same "RIGGER" stamp across his chest, but has added his own sloppily scrawled addition: "I'm a RIGGER. Mine is Bigger."

I focus on his shocked face instead.

"You growing these ladies as well?" he asks Hep.

"Excuse my comrade," says Hep apologetically. "Even down below they could tell he was a brute."

"Unless you count rig gals, which I do not. Rigger diggers, excuse my bluntness, aren't exactly *ladies*. But what's this about, Hep?"

"The PCF are after them."

Durley goes silent, and then he explodes. "I'll kill them!"

I reach for my humming zinger. Lex's fists are up before I draw it from my sheath.

The ground rumbles as if the whole rig is groaning, a PCF craft is now hovering directly overhead. My teeth tremble, every part of me vibrating. I've read of rigs destabilizing. It's rare, but entire crews have been lost. That we seem to be close to its outer perimeter has me even more worried. We all turn to where the thicket of trees part to reveal the sky beyond.

Its engine whirs and sunshine glints off its silver paneling. There is nowhere to hide. I'm sure that this PCF patroller is only the first of many.

"Follow me," Hep tells us. We're in no position to argue.

CHAPTER 21

Lex

The engines swirl up a cyclone of leaves. If we ever were to stop running, every part of me would be shaking. Our island leap has left me off balance. My brain most of all. The air up here clouds my thoughts, boosters or not.

We're racing through the forest that borders the rig and recycles the air and keeps the local atmosphere clean and rich. Hep is ahead, leading us. Durley trails behind us. The big man doesn't quit running his mouth. If this wasn't a rig, he'd be detained for agitating speech. Labeled *instigator* after the first sentence.

"Highfalutin thought enforcers, the sky-high nerve of them! I'll tear apart every last one of 'em, just you wait. Rip out their insides and use 'em for fertilizer. Them softhead PCF. Them crappies, daring to mess with a rigger."

We're fast, but not undetectable. The patrollers circle the rig's perimeter, waiting for us to emerge. They could just blast the whole forest, but they can't risk bringing an entire rig down. No, they'll go by the book. It's never failed them.

"We're not losing them!" I yell.

"We don't want to," says Hep. "We're gonna get those PCF bastards."

"They have my friend Kane," I tell him. "They've hurt him, locked him up."

"We had a Kane here," says Durley from behind me. I slow some to run beside him. "I always thought he was too pretty to rig." He's breathing harder than I am. "Liked the boy. Good with building. But riggers come and go like we got an open door. Make the vow, then jump off the side in two days. If they don't fall off first."

I feel the uncertainty below my very own feet. Rigs are unstable, fitted from Lower Level salvage. These men sacrifice their safety to live up here.

"The rigs serve as havens for the dregs of Indra," Instructor once told us. "Those who cannot function within society. Often recruited from Rock Bottom, for few would take such a job. The surface is unsteady; the minutest of interference might send hundreds plummeting. And yet the true dangers lie aboard: rabble-rousing ruffians, always eager for a fight."

I almost laugh. What would Instructor think if she saw me now? Riggers *do* want to fight, but at least it's for a cause. *Our* cause.

"So where'd they take Kane?" Hep asks.

"The Independent High Council," says Livia.

Shocked—*she knew all along*—I glare at her. Her back, unfortunately. I wouldn't be surprised if she was smiling.

"The Hickie? Riggers aren't even allowed in Indra, let alone the Council building."

"It wasn't his choice," she says.

"Goddamn Idiots Holding Court!" Durley yells.

"Where exactly?" I say to Livia.

"High Security Detainment," she says. "Anything more than that, we'll have to find out from the inside."

"You get the others," Hep tells Durley. We lose the PCF as Hep directs us toward the center of the rig. It won't take them long to find us again, so we can't waste the time we've bought ourselves.

Now we're belly to the dirt in a small clearing. This, I guess, is the rig version of a strategy session. "Tell them the crappies are here, and they'll be coming aboard. Tell them they hurt Kane."

Durley grins at Hep, nodding at every word; then off he goes.

"They'll find us again," I say.

"Sure they will, and I hope they do. I got an engagement for them to attend. It'll take them a while to land. They'll be careful coming into a hostile environment like this."

"So how do we get out of here?" I ask. "Is there a transporter?"

"Sure. A big clunky rattler. Won't get you more than a few feet, though, before it starts losing altitude. Then you go express." He gestures down, down, down some more, then makes the sound of an explosion.

I'm questioning this alliance even more now. *Maybe I'm losing my edge*, I think. *One day in air and my brain is already fuzzy?*

Fuzzy enough to trust an island girl in the first place?

"You knew where Kane was all this time," I say to Livia.

"Of course," she says calmly.

"Then why didn't you tell me?"

"Perhaps because you were trying to kill me."

"What happened to Kane?" asks Hep.

"We had a disagreement, Kane and I," she says, shooting me a look. "Reinforcement was called in, and when the PCF arrived, they wouldn't listen to my objections. A lot of them beat him until there was no hope of him fighting back. He was in no condition to fight in the first place. I attempted to stop them, but they wouldn't listen."

"Bastards!"

"Wait," I say to her, "so you're saying you didn't attack him?"

"Yes, as I previously explained."

The ground shakes. It makes my teeth rattle.

"They're nearby. Probably landing," says Hep, jumping to his feet. "C'mon. We only got one chance of this."

◊ ◊ ◊

Now, surrounded by green bushes, there seems to be no entrance. Seems no way out, either.

I turn to Livia. No need to check for the signs of a liar. Somehow, I just know. Airgirl is telling the truth about Kane.

That memory Archive wasn't real, I suddenly realize. It was tampered with. What I saw wasn't what really happened. Things were cut out or rearranged. I'm not sure how I know this, but I do. I also know who was behind it. Cassina. But my anger has made me core-low dumb.

I wanted to believe it was all true. I wanted to be angry.

Kane being hurt by the PCF, maybe Cassina was the cause of that, too. No matter how much she cares about him, she hates me more. She was willing to hurt him if that's what it took to get me.

Livia is watching me. I feel her stare all over. She didn't hurt Kane, I know that now. *I still don't like her, but maybe I hate her a little less.*

Hep reaches deep into the green thicket. A click. A door swings inward.

"After you, ladies," he says.

The inside of a rig makes the Rock Bottom dirt scavengers look civilized.

This must be the center, the place they make their homes. It ascends high above with levels, platforms, and hoists, then drops to a seemingly bottomless pit. The pit has a series of landings built into the sides. The landings are crammed with riggers and their things. All men, as far as I can tell. They have cots and some have tents for privacy, though there's little they seem to be ashamed of. The ones we can see openly gawk and eyeball us. One more eyeball on their faces and they'd fit in with the mutations.

Each landing is built of scrap: sheet metal, pipes, the hull of a transporter. Metal and plexi. Windowless frames, frameless windows. Disassembled shuttle tracks connect one level to the next. Cranes angled over us, the best way to get from point to point. All welded together. Some of the riggers are welding as we pass them. Constantly repairing and maintaining this space. And it only gets higher and higher. Skylight bleeds in from the imperfect seams. It is like some ancient carcass of former Earth, stubbornly persisting in the modern world.

This is Indra's waste. The leftovers you never see. Collected from abandoned construction sites. The riggers set up and take away the trash and use it to reinforce the rig.

Far above our heads, what must be the top, there's a wide platform. It could be a lookout, or just where they've stopped building, for now.

I can imagine Kane way up there, spying on the whole world from his kingdom of trash. If there's artistry in this assemblage, it's lost on me. It's uncomfortable but functional. Uninviting. But I bet Kane loved it.

Hep leads us under sagging piping. He's nimbler than us. He also hasn't gone twelve rounds with an air-breathing warrior princess. My body's starting to feel awfully pained. I follow nonetheless. Livia's in front of me. Her ridiculous dress is covered in dirt and grime and mud and blood. It looks slightly less ridiculous like that.

We reach a wobbly ridge that juts toward the center.

"Take a seat," Hep says, motioning to a collection of shipping containers under an overhang about thirty feet up. The wing of a patroller angles down and we're cloaked in its darkness. We sit. It feels great to get to do so.

"You'll be safer here, so rest while you can. Now I must see to a few details, so I'll say good-bye for now."

With that he takes Livia's hand, bends his dirty face, and kisses it.

She blushes. They're both enjoying this gross display far more than I am.

"And you," he says, leaning in close to me. No, looks straight *through* me, that's how it feels. "Remember this, Lex. We live for a while, and then we die. Can't stop either when the time comes, so no use worrying about it. That's the same for everyone. Even the outside of the outsiders. People like us."

Then he's gone.

Outsiders? Huh. Guess it's that apparent. I probably smell like one now. Maybe I'm more like a rigger than I thought. I belong to no one, just like them. And just like them, I could fall off an edge at any moment.

Livia and I sit in silence. I've nothing to say to her anymore.

"You believe me now," she says confidently. "About Kane."

"No."

"Yes. You believe I didn't want him harmed. Though I had every right to want that." She nods. "You no longer question I'm telling the truth. Of that I'm certain."

"Don't be certain. About anything."

I turn my back to her.

"I understand a great deal more as well," she says. "Kane had been watching me long enough to know my life. Intimately. Spying on my island from his rig. Perhaps this is why he seemed to understand me."

"You aren't that complicated," I say. "Just another airgirl."

"If that's true, then why would I be his target?"

I have no response. I've been wondering this since Cassina slapped her battery pack of lies in my back and turned me loose. Not Kane, though. She didn't do this to Kane. No, he did it for some other damn reason.

There's something more going on here. I think about that marking in Livia's eye. The one she shares with me.

A tremendous horn breaks the silence. We're out of our seats and peering over the edge of the platform. Hep is looking up at us from the lowest point in the rig's center, the one spot clear of debris.

"PCF close by," we hear Durley say. We look upward. He's standing on a platform many levels above us. "Load of them going to hit any second now. Some landed on the edge and coming by foot. A few headed right here by craft."

"Excellent. Ready?" yells Hep from below.

"Sure thing!" says Durley. The other riggers cheer.

"Then send her off!"

A hiss precedes the trail of smoke shooting over our heads. It whistles sharply past the lookout platform where the rig opens overhead, and flames burst across the sky and rain on the roof.

"Don't worry," shouts Hep. "Harmless little blast. That should get their attention, though. Now they'll know exactly where to find us." Then he looks in our direction. He can't see us, I know. Still, he seems to be staring right at me.

He winks, then disappears behind some scaffolding.

I hear the PCF patrollers faintly and I'm on high alert and ready for whatever. I know their engines by ear now.

The rig starts quivering. The engine sounds bounce around the metal and several craft do a flyby overhead. Landing on a level way above us.

That's when I see Durley jumping up and down. He's right out in the open. Whooping and flapping his arms, his bulky body shaking with fury. He's going to give himself a heart attack.

"He's insane," I say. "They all are."

"I suppose it depends on your definition," Livia says, just as the blasting begins. "Though I supposed you would know."

Durley's faster than I expected. He jumps, dodging one rapid-fire burst, and after one more jump, he disappears.

"He get hit?" asks Livia, intensely worried for his safety.

We hear an ecstatic whoop.

"What do you think?" I say. Only fools rush into battle, but I'm itching under my skin. Here we are cowering under this overhang.

I have no purpose in the shadows.

Except Hep was right. I can see everything from here while remaining undetected. With all the energy a rig consumes, heat signatures must be off the map. Livia's and my body heat won't even ping off their detectors, safe from their launchers and paralytics and all other sorts of hard-core tech.

"Patience is a virtue," says Livia, picking up on my uneasy vibe.

"A virtue that sucks."

I decide I hate her again. Completely.

The PCF land and spill from the crafts. Their blasters hum off safety. There are more soldiers than before. More than I can count.

PCF handbook, chapter 6: "Restraining Enemies of Indra."

"See those camera devices attached to their helmets?" I tell Livia. "It's standard to run videofeed on every op and send it to the IHC, so don't let them see you."

She looks at me like I'm insane. She opens her mouth to contradict me. The clever girl probably has a better option. Hep has other plans.

"Nice of you to visit!" I hear him holler. The PCF all swivel like they share one brain. They're hive-trained, not your standard troopers. Their hand cannons all aim low, in the same direction: the clearing below.

Hep's back in the same spot we saw him last. He's also got a big gap-toothed grin. "You looking for those girls?" he shouts, sounding friendly.

"Tell us where they are." That same mechanical voice from the speakerfeed. Anonymous. Authoritative.

"I saw them. I think the taller one had a thing for me. Gave me a look, sure you guys must know the kind. Strapping PCF like you? Must have your pick of the ladies."

The PCF officers' faces are hidden by their helmets and goggles, but they're anything but amused. "Tell us where they are."

"Well, they were moving pretty fast. Could hardly keep up with those long legs."

"What's he doing?" asks Livia, her voice shaking.

"Hopefully not being an idiot," I say, harsh enough to disguise my own nerves.

"On order of the Independent High Council, you are hereby commanded to reveal all knowledge as it pertains to the whereabouts of known enemies of Indra."

Hep's silent for a moment. He points high above us. The platform at the very top of the structure, hundreds of feet over our heads. The one I know Kane must have loved. "I saw them climb that way," he says, whistling at the dramatic height. He cocks his head to the left. "You fellows are welcome to take the hoist, of course. Quicker that way."

The PCF swarm toward him. Some break off to canvass the area, weaving through the warren of platforms. They move cautiously. I would, too. Too many hiding holes and blind spots to set an ambush.

Hep is all but forgotten. He watches them storm his home level by level, smashing it to bits.

He gets the attention of the lead officer—the one doing all the speaking.

"Hey!" he shouts.

I've seen that look on Hep's face. Made it myself. He's not changing course now, the stubborn fool.

Hep knows exactly what he's doing.

"They're not known enemies, okay? Just girls. You ought to let them be." He marches up to the officer. "You hear me, crappy? Let them be. Let *us* be. You can't control everything. Even if you think you can. We won't be controlled by you." He smiles. "This world is changing, and there's no place—"

The bark of a blaster and Hep falls where he stands.

CHAPTER 22

Livia

His eyes looked directly at me just as the life went out of them. They were alive with anger, yet inside I sensed he was peaceful.

"C'mon," Lex says, though it sounds like it's coming from very far away. She's tugging on me, but I feel as though I'm at a great distance. "I mean it, Livia. We gotta go *now*."

I cannot be moved; my body's turned to stone.

"We have to hurry. They'll kill us, too." Another tug, harder this time, yet just as pointless. Surely it must hurt, but I feel nothing at all.

"I'll leave without you. I swear it." Another pull, the voice agitated. "You think being special will get you out of this?"

Perhaps it's the word *special* that brings me back, but suddenly I'm there, my senses returned. And Lex is right there next to me, yanking my arm violently.

I sense her hopelessness and desperation and, even more, something that surprises me.

She's afraid.

Deep within her—a place she would never admit to having—is a tiny shadow of fear over her heart. She can no longer fathom doing this alone. She needs me, even if she doesn't know it herself.

I'll bear this burden with her. But first, I'll let her beg, if only for a moment.

"Listen to me, okay?" she says, almost dropping to one knee.

I stare off into space, unmoving, collecting my thoughts. "We have to go. Now. You gotta come with me." A sigh, her frustration increasing. "Get up, Livia. I need you to . . . just get up. I need you. *Please.*"

I turn to her sharply. "I hope you know what we're doing."

We move fast and low, crawling through the riggers' sleepers, remaining in the dark. Lex seems to know where she's going. "You always mark the exits," she whispers. "Whenever you enter somewhere unfamiliar, that's the first thing you do."

"But where are we going?"

"This is not the time for questions."

Hep, I think, slipping around a corner. *The gardener. He looked me in the eyes, then nothing at all.*

The PCF pile into the hoister that will lift them to the top platform. They're huddled together, an unmoving mass of black silitex and aggression.

A few stay behind, keeping watch of the ground level. Hep's body lies at their feet.

"Oh," I say, shocked to find us standing over a second dead body, this one much larger. There's no time to think, let alone mourn Durley. I hardly knew him, yet he sacrificed himself for us. What am I to think of that? Were we worth it?

We've climbed all the way to the roof of the rig, where the winds are strong. That booster energy is all Lex is running on, and by now it's wearing thin. I'm not far behind. I can hear the hoister on its way up.

"Hep mentioned a craft, didn't he?" I say. "'Big clunky rattler. Won't get you more than a few feet, though.'"

"Well, won't help us much if it's a dud, will it?"

"It doesn't have to be *that* craft, does it?" I say.

Together we choose the patroller the farthest from the others. The pilot is still inside, watching a live feed of the op on his monitor panel.

"Confirmed," he says. "One boy. Bad attitude. Anti-Indrithian Hate Speech. . . . Copy. Got a heads-up from the dead kid before we took him out. Seems the girls fled topside. One is PCF, but she turned. Team going after them right now."

I draw the zinger. It's already humming.

"Quiet that thing!" Lex whispers harshly. "C'mon . . . what's a sword gonna do against a blaster?"

Plenty, just as it did to you, I want to say, yet stop myself. *Egotistical, pretentious little girl. You still have much to learn of our world.*

I head toward the pilot, Lex's disbelieving fury coming in waves from behind me.

I'm the soldier, she's thinking, already braced to spring. *And now I will be forced to jump in and save you.*

The hoist has risen to the top. The doors are opening. The pilot is still fixated on his monitor.

Now there's a zinger blade to his chest.

"What the—"

I kick him in the gut and use his own weight against him to pull him out of the cabin and throw him to the ground. Two hard strikes and he's not speaking. I lean over, delicately removing his blaster.

I toss it underhand to Lex, having not even broken a sweat. "Well, are you coming or not?"

The hoist gate opens. The PCF spill out and the platform between us is vast and empty, but it won't stay that way.

Lex sits in the pilot's seat and I take the one next to her.

"Get it going!" I say.

One engine hums, then the next. "It takes time," she says.

The PCF move quickly across the platform toward us. We cannot take them all.

Then from out of the nowhere, the riggers mount the sides of the platform. They crawl up through the gaps in the landing zone. They were already there, hiding and hanging underfoot just below the surface, ready and waiting to attack the unsuspecting PCF from every angle. They brandish pipes and tools fitted with spinning metal blades and drills made to crack granite.

Lex has the patroller in the air as the riggers engage, and they whoop loudly as the two groups break against each other. I'm glad we have risen above it. The violence sickens me. I can only hope the riggers have their justice.

Lex works the control panel as though it's an extension of her hands. She's afraid of good-natured Veda, but this machine doesn't faze her. Nor does shooting into the sky at disarming speeds, apparently.

I clutch the arms of my seat, a shriek escaping.

"Strato, huh?" she says with a smile. Next to her is the pilot's backup blaster, which she surprised me by pulling from a compartment under his seat.

"Standard procedure," she'd said, running her hand over the weapon lovingly, as though being reunited with a long-lost friend. Her good humor doesn't last long.

"He planned it," she says. "Hep gave himself up to lead those PCF into the trap." She sighs. "Durley, too."

And they didn't mind dying, I think, *just to make it happen.*

"And now . . . the IHC?" I say.

"I already set the coordinates."

I nod.

"Why would they die for us?" I say.

"I don't know."

I think it probably wasn't for us. That their grudge was older and nastier than either of us can comprehend. Trouble has been festering between PCF and Riggers for a long time, and now it's turned into very real violence.

Lex and I rip through the sky, headed straight for the tallest, most magnificent building in the City of Indra. We don't talk. There's not much to say.

CHAPTER 23

Lex

One is PCF, but she turned.

That's what the officer said. Right before Livia pulled him out of the patroller and left for the riggers to tear him into bloody pieces.

I was a cadet. Rock Bottom Patrol. I lived by my mission. I was never disloyal. The only ones who turned? The PCF. On me.

Now I'm right back where I started. Alone. Outside the outsiders.

Except for Livia, I guess. I got her whether I like it or not.

And I'll get Kane, even if it kills me.

I look at the airgirl next to me. She's clenches her teeth, scared of the ride.

I'll get Kane, I think, *even if it kills both of us.*

I'm pushing this PCF patroller to its limits. Probably doing serious damage to its engine, but it's worth it to see Livia practically hyperventilating.

Less than a day and the City of Indra has already changed. The glossy sheen has grown sinister. Even the light looks wrong now, like it's one spark from igniting. What we just saw, we can't unsee. Who's there left to trust? I can't even trust myself.

I pull up the High Council blueprints on the positioning monitor. The detainment center is just a few levels down from the High

Council halls. Cadets receive placements here. It's not an honor, but there are worse assignments.

"High security's a given," I tell Livia, talking to her, but not really. Thinking my strategy out loud. She nods anyway.

We're about to infiltrate the most secure locale in all of Indra, I think. We're defined by the impossible feats we attempt. Especially if they lead to our deaths.

"We have no other options if we want to find Kane," Livia says.

I hate when she does that. Just full of herself, that's all. No mind reading in that. Girl thinks she's got all the answers.

"There's no *we*," I tell her. "What do you care about Kane?" She doesn't respond. I'm having second thoughts. I could've booted her out at any passing island. "Look, you should back out. Right now. Before it's too late." She won't look at me, but she'll hear me. "Tell them I held you captive. They'll buy it. I'll even hold one of these blasters to your head for the feed. You can make it to your island for evening rations. Be in your fancy sleeper by lights-out."

"No," she says intensely. Just like I knew she would. It's her pretty head, after all. Her right to part with it.

Of course, they'll go for my head first. But still.

"You had your little adventure, okay? But even with that rig chaos, it won't be long. They'll be onto us in—"

A high-pitched beep squeals through the cabin. "Craft 247 cleared for touchdown on IHC landing pad."

"Too late," she says. "Perhaps they don't know—"

"That we hijacked a craft? Of course they do. They've seen the feed by now and they'll be looking for answers."

"Well," she says calmly, "what do you suppose our next action shall be?"

She's gripping her new blaster before I even say the word.

"Give them what they want."

CHAPTER 24

Livia

I've always wanted to see the New Indra Gardens in all their magnificence atop the Independent High Council building. Only I never imagined seeing them quite like this.

We glide toward the landing area, and I can make out a dozen figures on the heliopad hovering beside it. With only a narrow walkway connecting them, the heliopad seems to float in the air.

"They figure we have nowhere else to go," Lex says. "We land and they'll have us surrounded."

We're even closer now. I can make out their blasters; definitely unfriendly.

"What shall we do?" I ask.

"Land, of course." Lex is grossly determined. She takes a beating, literally, and pushes for more. She probably thinks it's her turn to hand one out. "Coming in now. Steady and smooth, just like I taught myself."

"You taught yourself?"

"I know the rules. Far be it for me to break some."

The engine squeals.

My head whips back as we accelerate forward. We slam down on the heliopad with a horrendous metal-on-metal screech, our bodies plastered against our seats.

The PCF scatter. It appears they're not prepared for the unexpected. We may have a shot yet.

We blow by them and keep going. Accelerating right into the New Indra Gardens.

Gardens showcase the utter mastery of nature's true beauty—or as much as we've been able to replicate. The New Indra Gardens are for Indrithians of the Utmost Importance; those select few who make the Great Indra so very great. Waslo, I believe, sees them daily, as my father once did. A trained, high-level garden crew maintains them at all hours. They are like insects—fortunate, because there are none here to aid in growth and pollination, yet at all times the flowers are at the peak of their bloom, fragrant and vibrant and strong. They grow in concentric circles, and if you followed the pathway to the center you'd find an ancient marble fountain, caressed by lush vines, eternally flowing, upon which a winged victory perches as an exemplar of Indra's perfection.

"The gardens," says *The Book of Indra*, "are the epitome of pristine, untouched beauty."

We speed into the expanse of programmed vegetation—uprooting trees, slamming through sculpted bushes, exploding greenery and flowers all around us.

Next to me, Lex wrestles the controls, trying to break our momentum. I know, within moments, we will fly over the edge, plummeting from the very top of the tallest structure in the City of Indra.

This must be the end, I think, just as my body heaves forward. We're caught in a violent roll. The metal hull groans as it's impacted and I fear at any moment we'll be crushed. My insides are shaken and I grip the armrests for some semblance of control in this violent, grinding landing.

I must have blacked out, because when I open my eyes I'm not quite sure how or when we stopped.

I sit there, unmoving, in the disconcerting silence. I look over and

Lex is clutching her seat, eyes wide, and I can feel every bit of her shock. I need not sense her, for these are also my feelings. For once, we're perfectly in synch.

"Did you feel that?" she asks.

"Are you attempting humor? Of course I felt my own death calling."

"No . . . the drops."

I don't answer, for the sudden pounding speaks volumes. We both look up, the sky visible through the newly ripped hole in the roof above us. A cascade of water greets us, the torrent quickly drenching us.

"Out! Now!" screams Lex, and we open our doors and scramble, falling onto the grass. Disoriented, I watch, awestruck, as the water keeps falling.

"The fountain," says Lex next to me. "The fountain is all that stopped us." Her voice is gravely serious, as though this is a great philosophical revelation.

Then she begins to laugh.

She shakes her wet hair, the spray flying everywhere, and laughs hysterically. I can't help joining her. We're being hunted, yet we laugh like truly demented people. *They will take us to Sunrise Retreat*, I think, *and that might well be the correct decision*.

Perhaps we laugh because we just destroyed a legendary fountain and garden, or because we're soaking and only growing wetter.

Perhaps we laugh simply because we're not dead.

A crowd of Indrithians stares at us with the maximum amount of shock they can display without breaking social contracts. I'm sure they would try to capture, restrain, or contain us if they didn't pay numerous PCF to do their dirty work for them. Oh, I'm sure these people loved their gardens, and my eyes scan over our path of wreckage, the laughter dying down.

"That felt good," Lex says, holding up her blaster. She nods, seeing that mine is already in hand. "C'mon then. Let's go get Kane."

CHAPTER 25

Lex

We race through the ruined gardens as high-pitched alarms sound. Man, we—I, I guess—did some bad things. After we pass through the uprooted shrubs and fallen trees, petals and leaves left now to the mercy of Indra's artificial winds, I start to enjoy my first time in a real garden. I'm overwhelmed by its size and beauty, and if I looked back I'd start to feel bad for the devastation. My boots stick in the mud that's everywhere, thanks to the fountain. Beads dribble down my silitex. I have no reason to look back.

"Have you the faintest idea where we are?" Livia asks.

"Through here," I say.

She shakes her head. "You are far too comfortable with this level of destruction. We should take more care. Be more careful once we go inside."

I look at her. Her and her feelings.

This long hallway has dead people watching from holo-images mounted on the wall. I can hear her footsteps right behind me. So, she got over it.

Too comfortable? What does that even mean? I know military operations and strategy. I don't do *feelings*.

She's already slowing me down. Already jeopardizing the mission. She sighs.

"What's your problem?" I say, swinging around.

She's got her humming sword pointed right at me. *Not again*.

"Really? I hurt your feelings that—"

I don't even get to finish before she's leaping toward me, her sword flashing in a silver arc, its melody acidic. There is a PCF soldier behind me. The zinger cleaves his blaster in two. On the upswing it cuts through his chest. His face is on the young side. It is full of shock and disappointment and bears death in no more a dignified way than the rest of us.

Livia

"I killed him because you didn't listen," I say. Lex doesn't respond. "Next time, heed my warning."

This man is no longer living, I think. *And for that, I'm responsible. He wasn't an Archive opponent who will refresh with the next chip insertion. This is a real man made of flesh and blood.*

The blood pools on the floor beneath me. A strange dull ache in the pit of my stomach swells, one word repeating in my head over and over: *killed*.

A strange look passes across Lex's face. She's staring at one of the enormous holo-images now, distracted. I reach for her, gripping her wrist and squeezing hard.

"That could've been me," she says.

"But it wasn't."

"I'm sorry."

She is. She really is, but it's too late for that. We must be merciless if we're going to survive. We can sort out our feelings later.

"Kane," I say firmly. "Kane's still waiting for us."

Her eyes reignite. She catches up and we hurry down the hallway.

The dead man's face lingers in my mind. Both dead men, to be exact. The guard sprawled across the ground, his body rapidly cooling as his life spilled out. And the other dead man, his handsome image on the portrait at which Lex was paused.

"Dr. Armand Cosmo" read the plate beneath it. "Modern Genetic Innovator."

My father.

Lex

I knew that guy. I'd seen him before.

Livia knew him, too. Cosmo—they share a last name. Her . . . father?

Her breath hitched for second, just like mine did. She saved me. She really did.

The glass transporter tube begins to glide down the side of the building after I enter the Detainment code. The tube buzzes. You can see the whole of Indra from here. It's a monument of impossible wonder, and it only reminds me that they have so much more up here. It's hard to be so proud of this city, or act in its favor.

We stop suddenly. The entry panels slide open and we step into a narrow hallway.

I open the tube control panel and punch in numbers. My mind clicks off combinations.

"Do you care to tell me what you're doing?" Livia asks.

"I'm breaking the code. So they can't get in," I say. The alarms have followed us, even all the way down here. The place is on high alert. I punch in another set. "They'll locate us. If they haven't already. I just need to buy us a few minutes."

I pull my hand away for a moment and her sword eviscerates the panel. It sparks and goes black.

"Let us see if they can reprogram that," she says.

I grit my teeth, frustrated. She's getting too quick with that thing. "But then *we* can't either."

Then the room goes black, too.

"Delightful," I say.

"That . . . was not what I intended."

I find her hand in the darkness and place it on my shoulder. "Just follow me."

"And how will that help us any more than it already has?"

"I see in the dark," I say, already moving, "so stop making that pissy face at me and get on the same page."

The door's thirty-six feet ahead, straight shot.

"How's that possible?" she asks.

"It just is, okay? Always been able to do it. Call it a genetic flaw if it makes you feel better."

"No, I wish *I* could do it. Sounds useful."

"You're just saying that. Besides, you got your own tricks. You can't have *everything*. Like, how'd you know that PCF was waiting for us? You read minds or something?"

Nothing.

"What, you didn't see that question coming?"

Livia sighs. "Same as you," she says. "I could always feel people. Not reading minds, exactly. I just get a sense. Intuition, really. Hardly mind reading at all. But people bleed emotions all the time, it can get really gross, and I can pick up the trail."

Fourteen more feet to go. No sound except the alarms, faint, but still there.

"Can you feel me now?" I ask her.

"Yes. That's why I chose to answer your question. Because, for a very brief moment, you felt remorseful for your rudeness."

"Maybe," I say. "But if I did, it was *very* brief."

She stumbles, and I catch her before she falls on her face.

"Careful."

"I can feel him, too," she says. "I think he's . . . dying."

CHAPTER 26

Lex

I press down the synth-print on the security panel. *Beep*. The doors whoosh open.

Then the cold hits me. I've never felt real cold. The Orphanage was temperature controlled. So was the Academy. Every day the same. Temperature control is pretty necessary for human life to continue to exist in the Lower Levels. Next to me, I can hear Livia's teeth chatter

We take a few steps forward. When we turn the corner, I see a light. Livia shudders.

The focused beam cuts from the ceiling down through the pitch black. At its center is a heap. I can't tell of what. I have to turn away, the force of the beam stings my eyes so bad. That's one major drawback of them being so sensitive.

I rush for the control panel, press the synth-print quickly. The light disappears. Spots dance on my eyes. My entire body feels relieved.

What I see next hurts more than any light ever could.

The pile is a person. Their beaten, crumpled-up body. Face pushed to the floor, arms covering head, defenseless, as if that would be enough to block out the light and stave off blindness.

I didn't know skin could be so many shades of purple and black. I can't see the face. Still, I know. I'd know him anywhere.

Kane.

The words just tumble out of my mouth.

"Don't be dead."

Livia

"Dead?" Kane lifts his head steadily and smiles at Lex through his swollen lips, his voice hoarse. He goes to laugh, but it sounds like he's choking. "Don't you know me better than that?" He hasn't seen me yet, I don't think, as I stand in the shadows, watching as Lex kneels before him, finding my sudden shyness overwhelming.

I remember his smile, even through the bloom of bruises. He imparted that same grin, looking up from my arms as I held him. *Livia*, he said, before Waslo arrived and the PCF pulled me off him. I watched as they beat him, screaming my throat raw in Waslo's clutches. I've wondered what happened to him every moment since. I feel responsible.

Now the stark reality hits me.

Blistered and shivering, alone in the blinding light: this is his punishment for desiring to kill me.

"Kane," says Lex, with a tenderness I didn't know her to possess.

"Took you long enough," he says.

She cradles his cheek with one hand, and he recoils at her touch, no matter how tender she tries to be.

"I'm sorry," she says.

"You've gone soft," he says, his laugh causing him to wince. I feel the pain of his raw wounds and know he's hurt much worse in places we can't see. He's very strong to have endured this much without dying already.

"Your chest," I say. Now he sees me.

"Livia . . ."

I feel my insides leap; I can't control myself. *He doesn't care for you*, I remind myself. *It was all part of his strategy.*

"What the PCF did to me," he says, before another burst of pain turns his smile into a grimace, "is still better than if you got your hands on me first." He jokes, but it's not funny.

"Can you move?" asks Lex.

"I don't know. I'm not . . . sure."

"We can carry you, okay?"

He shakes his head, trying to act strong, but pain is all he feels. It will take ages for him to heal.

"He's damaged inside," I say. "Moving him will only make it worse."

This time, Lex doesn't question my feelings.

"Then what do we do?" she asks, her voice wavering despite her carefully guarded control.

I go to Kane, kneeling beside her. Lex forces herself to stand. "I'll keep watch," she says, disappearing with equal swiftness. She wasn't fast enough, though, for me to miss the tears forming.

"Hey," Kane says. In the same instant, the room changes, and the cold gives way to a thick, humid heat. My trembling is replaced by intense perspiration; it forms in places not proper for even a former Proper Young Woman.

"Don't mind that," says Kane, as if it were possible. He sucks in his breath, summoning the energy not to be overwhelmed by his condition. "Climate . . . interrogation," he says, squeezing his eyes tight. "They figure if they just keep changing the temperature, they'll break me. I think . . . I might even be getting used to it."

I keep silent until I feel the agony subside. *We have a few moments*, I think, *until the next wave.*

"Kane," I say. He looks up at me. "I need to touch you."

"Oh yeah?" he says, the grin returning, only this time a little wicked. "Go right ahead."

I gently lift his shirt, trying not to cringe at the sight of his injuries. He watches me, still smiling. "If you wanted to see me with my clothes off, all you had to do was ask."

I gently rest my hands on his rib cage. He's not smiling anymore; it must be draining for him to keep up the good face. His imprisonment is barbaric.

I don't know if they'll be enough, but I have Hep's homemade boosters rattling in my palm. I open the bottle and dump a few in my hand. Too many could kill him. Not enough, and he'll die anyway. I'm no nurse. I have no training.

"Take these," I say, four of them in hand. He eyes the boosters and I put one on the back of his tongue. I coax him into dry swallowing it, and I'm not sure how many more he'll get down. The second one takes even longer, his throat working overtime, his stomach tightening.

Suddenly, his body goes rigid, his eyes rolling back in his head. I keep hold of him so that he doesn't hurt himself further.

"What are you doing?" screams Lex. Kane's body has now come back to life, his limbs and torso shaking.

"Helping him," I say. "I gave him some boosters, but . . ."

The room turns icy again, and Kane's tremor begins to subside, and as much as it pains me to see him like this, knowing even further I am the root of it, I hold steady. His pain is all I can feel; it overwhelms my mind and I imagine that I can take it on, I can take on all of his pain until it stops altogether. It is so raw and vicious I bite my lip until it bleeds.

"If you made him worse, I'll kill you," says Lex. "I swear, Livia, I'll take you by the—"

"Calm down, killer," says Kane. Her eyes widen as he begins to move, carefully pulling himself to lean against me. "I'm okay," he says. "Just a case of the shakes."

He looks at me, our faces close enough to be touching. "You

punch me in the face," he says, "then . . ." He's breathing heavily. Whatever I have done terrifies and intrigues him. "But I must be forgetting something in between . . ."

I don't need to sense him to know that he remembers the kiss as clearly as I do.

"You, Livia Cosmo, are the strangest girl I have ever met." He gives me that curling smile, his eyes glittering with life once again.

No, I tell myself. *You won't allow him to charm you. Not this time.*

"Almost done?" asks Lex.

"Almost," I say. I feel her not quite believing me, but not wanting to argue. She's worried and distracted. "Hurry," she says. "I can hear them coming."

"Perhaps I'm strange," I tell Kane, "but I'm also trustworthy. And if I punched you, it was only because I had good reason."

His grin fades.

"You were sent to kill me," I say.

He nods faintly.

I feel Lex's eyes burning into me. "Give me your injured hand," I tell him. He holds it out to me. I rest my own unblemished hand on his rough, callused palm. The hand of someone who makes things.

"My hand isn't injured."

"I know," I say sharply. "But Lex is watching closely, and I need answers. *Quickly*." I half close my eyes. "First you spied on me, from the rig. Is that correct?"

"Yes," he says.

"You did this for quite a while?"

"Much longer than was required. I couldn't help it. I could have watched you for—"

"No," I say. I won't let him distract me. "You tried to kill me, Kane."

"No. I didn't. I was sent to kill you, but I couldn't go through with it. I had the tablet ready. All I had to do was kiss you—"

"And pass it along?"

"Yes. And then—"

"I kissed you instead," I say firmly, my eyes opening. Kane nods.

"I couldn't have hurt you, Livia. I couldn't hurt anyone, really. But especially not you, not with how I feel about—"

No. He won't escape so easily. This is not another Courting Dance. "Who sent you after me?"

"I have no idea," he says softly. "I wish I knew. I'd go after them myself."

We stare at each other. I sense his pain and confusion. Unfortunately, he's telling the truth.

"I was taking orders," he says.

"For that reason alone, I might never forgive you."

"Hey! C'mon already!" booms Lex, glaring at us. I drop Kane's hand.

"What are you guys doing? Do you *want* them to get us? They're getting closer."

I hear nothing, but she's telling the truth. In that instant, I sense them nearby. They are close enough for me to feel them. There are many of them, and all are burning to punish us.

Yet even more powerful than the approaching danger? Lex right next to me. Her emotion washes over me with powerful intensity.

Kane belongs to her, not me. That is what she is feeling.

Lex

Focus, Lex. You can deal with this later. Right now, they are coming.

I try to help Kane up, but he ignores my outstretched hand.

"Stubborn scrubber," I say, watching him fight to his feet. "Rather get us killed than have me help you." He's standing now, and smiling. He takes a few unsteady steps, but at least he can walk.

"Well?" he says to Livia. "Will you? Let me prove it to you?"

"I might consider the possibility," she says.

Now they're looking at each other and grinning. They already have secrets? What kind of core-low stupidity is going on here? Livia hands him the blaster we swiped from the PCF craft. She pulls out the sword, which is singing like crazy. "That," says Kane, looking at it, "is the most strato thing I have ever seen."

Footsteps bang down the hallway.

"Too late," says Lex.

"There are too many of them," says Livia. "Six, at the very least."

I don't ask how she knows this. At this point, why ask questions? She's a freak, but at least a helpful one.

"We cannot possibly take them all," she adds.

"I don't like this," I say, the air boiling around us. My silitex regulates the heat, but only so much.

Two PCF burst in, weapons at the ready. Livia leaps and slashes the first one before he can even comprehend what he's facing. I blast the other quickly.

I've still got it, I think. There's no time to be proud. More will be coming. We must survive this first.

I hate to be right, but I still have the cadet in me. Another PCF follows through the door, blasting.

I drop to the floor and take aim. As soon as he falls, another is waiting.

So is Livia's blade. She cuts him two times, rating high in efficiency. That's all it takes.

In that time, a wave of four storm us and they've got us dead, if that's what they want. I don't know. I can hope not.

One has his blaster to the back of Livia's head, and he's smirking. Her sword is still raised, and she's thinking about making a move.

"Watch it!" I scream, just as the blast rings out.

The PCF slumps to the floor next to her, and for a second the other goons are just as confused as I am.

One of their own is blasting them from behind. Shooting each one of them in the back. The trooper's blasts sizzle with ferocity. It's only when they've opened their visor that it becomes clear why they've done this.

"Vippy?" Sure enough it's Vippy underneath the helmet. She looks way more threatening than I'd ever imagine she could be. "How'd you get so big?"

"There's lifts in my boots."

I'm not sure if a hug is appropriate.

"Hey, Vip!" Kane says.

She nods at him. "At central command they're monitoring our biorhythms and will see that these three are stunned. Take my access chip, then take my blaster and stun me and go."

"But why would you do this?"

"I'm a rebel," she says. She would be right in assuming my confusion is also disgust. I can't help the way I feel. "Always have been. A team's been dispatched to get you out of here and take you in. Evac point is by the transporter tube on this level. They can help you."

"I'm not going with any rebels."

My saying this hurts her. I almost can't imagine that what she says is true.

"Come with us," Kane says.

"I can't," Vipsinia says. "A placement here is worth too much to our people. I can help them more here than anywhere else."

"I'm not going with a bunch of rebels," I say.

Livia looks at me strangely. Like I'm doing something wrong. "Just what do you think *you are* then?"

Kane looks like he agrees. "After this, you're not going to be welcomed back with some sort of award."

But a *rebel*? I just came to save my friend. I just . . .

I take Vippy's offered blaster and access chip. This girl I showed a kindness to once . . . only once . . . and now she's repaid it more than in full. If she's a rebel, then perhaps I don't know everything there is to know.

"This is going to hurt," I say.

"Of course it—"

I stun her in midsentence and drop the sizzling blaster next to her body. Central command will have questions for her, probably put this entire squad on leave to suss out what exactly happened, but this will help sell the narrative that she's not to blame.

Only I am. Somehow everything I touch goes to hell.

CHAPTER 27

Livia

We race toward the transporter tube in the now-lit hallway.

"Who was that girl?" I ask.

"A cadet who graduated with me and Kane. I like her, but we weren't friends. I don't understand why she would do that for us."

I don't tell Lex that I could sense how much this Vippy admired her and loved her. It would not ease her guilt to know why people do good things for her.

Kane grins as he catches up to us. "We got about five minutes till backup comes."

"And the guys back there?" asks Lex.

"Don't worry about them. They'll have to thaw first."

"Thaw?" I say. Lex is already smiling, as though they speak a language all their own.

"He activated the climate control," she says. "They'll be frozen solid."

"Maybe not solid, but real icy," he says. "Not that they'll be able to open the door with anything less than an arc welder."

We look at each other, all three of us, and smile for just a moment. Even small victories have their rewards.

"Okay," I say. "This is the evac point, right? This is where we meet them."

"But how can we trust them?" Lex asks.

"The rebels didn't do this to us," Kane says.

Lex nods. She's confused. We all are.

Even more so when a team of shock troopers rushes us from behind. PCF. We should've been ready for this.

Around every corner there's always more PCF.

Lex

We're surrounded by PCF. Five of them. I reach for my blaster, Livia her sword.

"Don't even think about it," says the one in front.

I draw anyway.

The blaster jumps from my hand. I didn't even see him move, it was that quick.

"I told you not to, Lex."

He knows my name? Now he's really got my attention.

The PCF uniform fits properly, but it's a bit ragged, especially for Hickie patrol. His long-barreled blaster, while it could still kill us all dead, doesn't look like it's been cleaned or maintained in months.

Rebels.

"Good to see Vipsinia came through. We would've been here quicker, but someone destroyed the garden, which has become a bit of a thing." He lifts his helmet, and he's younger and shaggier than the fine men of rarefied air. His troops follow his lead, and I've never seen anything like them. One has a drawing on his cheek. Another smiles, only to reveal that his top row of teeth is all blistered metal.

"Long way from where you're supposed to be," Kane says.

"Don't appreciate us breathing your air, Islander?" asks the shaggy-haired one.

"I'd rather you weren't breathing any of it," I say.

Him and me, we've come to an impasse. I meant what I said. I don't do overly friendly strangers.

Livia retrieves my blaster for me. "If these . . . rebels are willing to show us the way out," she says, "let's do the logical thing and follow them, for now. A kindness was paid, so now a kindness is done."

Shaggy nods. "It's good to see someone carries the intelligence gene."

I jam my blaster hard in his guts and his men crowd me. "If you're so interested in genetics, I could give you a real good look at your insides."

"Zavier."

The rebels step back, even this unshaven Zavier, all showing deference to the man who spoke. A real man.

That, I think, *is the real leader*.

Livia

"Excuse Zavier's disposition. He's not worked on his social graces as much as his soldiering."

This man's old enough to be any of the rebels' father, but his manner suggests he was born in a different strata than any of them. I suspect he could hold his own in Waslo's presence.

He holds his wiry frame tall, hands clasped in front of him, with not a hint of aggression. He looks relieved to see us. "My ladies and gentleman, I am Roscoe." He bows, as would any Proper Gentleman.

He smiles and his skin crinkles at the corners of his eyes and lips. Wrinkles, I know, though I have never seen them, our science having eliminated all signs of aging long ago in Upper Indra. Yet this man wears his age well, dignified, far from deterioration, his warm eyes glowing as though witnessing something rare and extraordinary.

He catches himself.

"You must forgive my own rudeness. It has been a very long time, Livia," he says, bowing again. Lex scoffs, showing her displeasure with his etiquette, and even her disinterest grants him a gracious chuckle. A true high-born gentleman, masquerading as a scavenger. "And you are Lex, of course," he says to her.

He turns to Kane, his hand extended, when Lex shouts, "Enough with the introductions!"

Roscoe drops the smile, but not his disposition.

"I don't care who you are right now," she continues. "We gotta get out of here. And if you don't plan on shooting your way out, you can join the rest of the bodies that way."

Roscoe draws his blaster. "Well, of course. We're here to escort you, Lexie."

Her eyes go wide and if she isn't about to punch him, then I will cohabitate with a dirty scavenger. Kane must sense the same thing because he grabs her arm.

"He's trying to help us. Let him."

Lex would rather die, I can tell, but Kane she listens to. What they have isn't easy to build between two people. It can't be studied or taught, only forged over the bitterness of time.

Lex picks up the buzzing sound before everyone else and she looks sharply at the rebel from which it comes. He stares back at her, confused, until he hears it too and is embarrassed. He lifts an outdated handheld earfeed up and listens. He goes to tell the older man, but she already knows what he'll say.

"The PCF have locked down our location," Lex says. "We have two minutes in which to leave."

Roscoe isn't surprised at her hearing. Either he is utterly unflappable—quite possible—or he knows more about her than she's comfortable with him knowing. "That is undoubtedly correct. Now, either of these routes you take will lead to a quick capture or fates far worse."

"Your only choice is to come with us," Zavier says. He does it to goad Lex. We must keep our eye on him. He wants to incite people to be as unhappy as he is.

"Why should we trust you?" I say to Roscoe.

Something crosses his face: he doesn't want to hurt us, of this I'm aware. We're terribly important to him, yet I'm unsure as to why.

"Because," he says. "I was a friend to your mother, Livia. And I made her a promise long ago that I would keep you safe. And it has taken me far too long to keep my word."

I'm too shocked to offer a rebuttal.

"Words!" Lex yells. "That's all he has! All you want to do is control us, just like everybody else!"

"He's not lying," I say, taking Lex's hand before she loses control. That she lets me . . . I cannot reason why. The shell has broken. "And yet," I say to him, "you do not tell the full story."

"Our time grows short," he says. "But I know that you must sense the truth I speak."

"You'll keep us safe, on that I'm clear."

Again he nods.

"But if at any time that should change . . ."

"Your meaning is clear."

Lex and Kane wait expectantly. That I've gained their trust is immeasurable. "We have no other choice," I tell them.

"And you *feel* they don't want to hurt us?" asks Lex.

"Yes," I say.

Kane looks at us both as though we're crazy and shrugs. "I'm glad we all agree."

Lex signals our new allies. "Let's get moving, rebel scum."

CHAPTER 28

Lex

"You'll come with me," Zavier says. The one who disarmed me. Who could use some Academy discipline and grooming. His hair almost covers his narrowed blue eyes. If I keep him close, I can take him down if the time comes.

When the time comes.

The rebels become a shield around Livia and me. If it's their intent to disorient us, it's working. They move as we move. They look like PCF, but their disguises won't hold up to much scrutiny. The real ones can't be far behind.

We stop. My human shield loosens their perimeter of protection. I'm standing in front of a hole in the wall. The metal grating has been removed from this vent. The rebels each crawl inside and disappear. When it's my turn, someone shoves me. Zavier. I shoot him a look.

I'm crawling through a tunnel, and Zavier's right on my tail, barking, "Move it!" He gives me another shove and I strike out with my heel, which nails the metal siding by his chin. He's less aggressive after that, and I move even faster.

When the butt of the rebel in front of me clears out, I'm greeted by light and, surprisingly, what feels like fresh air.

I stand up in a small alcove. In front of us is an enormous plexiclear window. Zavier guides me out of his way. He removes a small torch from his belt and its tip ignites into ultra-blue flame. He scorches the panel at its seams, loosening it. It takes all of the rebels to remove it.

The gusts blow violently inward, as if to warn us to keep our distance. So close to freedom, nothing can stop us. All that separates us is the vibrant dusk sky. Night has begun to fall and we'll use its cover to escape. I think on how this all began, in an Archive, waiting for Kane, and since then how I haven't stopped moving.

One by one, each rebel stands in the windowless frame. They cross their arms over their chests, Zavier whispers—a blessing?—then they launch backward and disappear.

I watch, shocked, as they hurl themselves into the air.

"What's going on?" I ask Zavier, but he ignores me.

Livia's next. She's facing me, back to the window. A rebel stands behind her, his arms around the waist of her once white dress, now brutally torn. A large, dirty swath of it blows in the wind and she rips it off and lets it float away. If only all of us could travel so lightly.

I wouldn't admit it, but she looks so strato this way.

I should offer her words of comfort, but I'm not any good at that. Plus I'm . . . uneasy myself.

She drops like a stone. "Hurry," says Zavier in my ear. I'm on the edge of the frame, of a building, my feet leaden. I stare out and watch the others become dwarfed by the vast expanse of Indra below. I'm as high as the clouds themselves. I'm very conflicted on this whole thing.

"No time for sightseeing," says Zavier.

He's all up in my face, doesn't even have the decency to do this like the others. He wants to humiliate me. My silitex body armor can't redistribute my sweat fast enough. He wraps his arms around me, holds me tight enough to hurt. Face to shaggy face. My legs are shaking.

"I thought," he says in my ear, "you were supposed to be the brave one."

I can be. I want to be. But not now.

Livia

The instant before we fall, as I stand in the windowless frame, Lex catches my eyes.

She stares at me, confused, not sure what to believe, and I share her feelings. If only we had stopped to talk much earlier, this mess we're in would not be. We might've changed it all for the better.

"Don't worry now, Livia. We got the parazips to hold us."

My rebel protector refers, I assume, to the thin cord from which we're dangling. The man harnessed behind me releases the round cap from a canister attached to his belt and suctions it to the side of the window frame. He tells me hundreds of feet of microcord are compressed into every canister. These cords could suspend an air speeder from an island without failing.

Then I'm flying backward with zero resistance, unencumbered. I've wondered for so long what this would feel like and it's . . .

Exhilarating.

"They call me Jefferson," says the rebel loudly, rather cheerfully, I believe, especially considering that we're rapidly accelerating toward an uncertain, yet highly feasibly untimely, ending.

The line grows longer and longer above us. One thin line from a canister that, if I'm to believe this man, will continue to hold us aloft as we're falling.

"Just relax and enjoy the fall," he says.

I'm starting to, I really am, when we swing back in toward the Council building. Jefferson bends his knees, makes contact, and launches us into air once again.

Sideways we swing, and rapidly we fall. I swivel my head, hoping to glimpse Kane beneath me, when Jefferson puts his hand on my cheek and gently guides my face toward the sky. "Don't look down. That's the key."

I don't spot Kane, but I think I see Lex above. I can't imagine she's enjoying this as much as I am.

Every few stories, Jefferson halts us, steadying his feet on the side of the building. He's growing tired. For a moment, we rest in midair. He holds the line and takes a deep breath. "Replacement time," he says.

"May I?" I pull a fresh canister from his belt. He's pleasantly surprised by my initiative. "Like this?" I say.

"Exactly."

I've been watching him every drop of the way. I flick the switch and a brand-new string releases and suctions to the surface of the plexi-clear. I pull, checking the grip, then wrap the cord like I observed him doing and attach the canister to his belt. His arms bring me in close once again.

I give him a thumbs-up. "Ready when you are, Jefferson."

Lex

"How many of those . . . are there?" I ask.

"Just enough," Zavier says. "You're not going anywhere."

The rush the parazip creates shocks my system. With a speeder or stolen craft, at least I'm in control. Running from the PCF and now allied with rebels? I've relented all feeling of it, for now. I have to. I'm harnessed to someone I already despise, rappelling off Indra's highest building into the unknown.

He's right in my face the whole time. And this guy—*Zavier*—puts Cassina to shame.

"What makes you so special, huh?" he says. "That's what I want to know. You're not so bad looking, don't get me wrong. Might even find us a place to ourselves and see how that goes. If I didn't know about your rep. If I didn't know the truth."

He lands, feet to the building. Crouches. Pushes off. We soar downward.

"Hardcase cadet. You *like* all those rules and regulations. Bet you can follow orders, can't you? Without question. Kill without remorse. Bet you'd let me boss you around."

"Just try it," I say, my breath halting from the sheer drop. *I'll kill you, without remorse.*

Dangling in space by a thread. He could just drop me, after all. Tell the others it was a horrible accident.

Instead, I bite my tongue. *Later,* I tell myself. *I'll take care of him when my feet are back under me.*

Land. Crouch. Push off. Soar downward.

"I said no when they asked," he continues. He won't ever stop. "Rescue that girl? Not even for all the air in the sky."

Land.

"But Roscoe, he knows more than me. And much more than you."

Crouch.

"'She's the one who will save us.'"

Push off.

"Huh. You can't even save yourself."

Soar downward.

At some point, we break so suddenly my stomach is still dropping. We hover in midair, rocking back and forth. I can feel his breath on my neck. His body hard and tense with anger.

We're immersed in the spires of Indra. A man-made canyon that can even silence this angry rebel. The city's blood, whether we like it or not, beats within all our chests.

What now? I wonder. Did he use the last canister already? We're nowhere near the ground.

"In case you don't understand," he says finally, "you're nothing special. We don't need you, no matter what anyone says."

I fight the urge to kick him. To choke him until he loses consciousness. Right there, hanging in space. He's made this personal. His hate of me runs as deeply as mine for him.

"What now?" I ask.

"Now?" he says. He gives a low, mean laugh. "We go back where you should feel right at home. Give you your crown."

The vibrations bounce off the plexi-clear and I see their shimmering reflections glinting right back at us. Four air speeders whip around the corner, coming straight for us.

"Where are you taking me?"

"What do you cadets call it?" He snorts. "Oh yeah. *Rock Bottom.*"

CHAPTER 29

Livia

When I used to stand at the edge of Helix and look down at the City of Indra, I'd imagine myself visiting one day. I could see myself walking the corridors with Middlers, doing the things that they did in their everyday life. *I would be just another Indrithian citizen*, I imagined wistfully, *not anyone of Importance*.

Truth be told, I had no concept of what *everyday life* entailed. Still do not, in all sincerity. But that was not part of the fantasy. In my imagination, I was no one special, just another body blending into the fabric of Indrithian Society.

I should have known. This is my first time in the city, and the last thing I do is fade into the background. This is unlike anything I could have ever imagined.

I'm on the back of a speeder, my arms wrapped around a disheveled man named Chae. At least, I suppose that's his name, for it was the only word he uttered when he met us in midair.

I have never met someone with hair on their face. Veda does not count.

"My name is Livia," I told him, elated to be on something solid. The man responded by grunting.

"Hold tight," Jefferson said from the speeder next to me, shouting so as to be heard over the roaring engines. "Don't want to go flying right off the back."

The instant Chae took off, though, I knew that could be a problem, and we race through the sky at ferocious velocity, down toward Indra's gleaming streets.

I clutch him as though he is the thread of a forgotten memory that I'm desperate to grasp. We're surrounded by speeders on all sides, Jefferson remaining at our left flank with his arms around a long-haired rebel. A woman, perhaps, though it could well be a man. These rebels have rather unique appearances.

I see another formation of speeders in the distance. Perhaps Lex is among them, I think, or Kane.

Nearing the ground, broad boulevards emerge from the airscraper-created canyons. *Almost there*, I think, believing solid earth has never seemed lovelier.

The only question: Where exactly are we going?

Jefferson breaks into a wide, cheerful grin at my side. He yells something I cannot hear, to which I raise my eyebrows quizzically. He says it again, mouth moving slowly enough to read his lips. He smiles again and this is my last look at him before he goes flying backward, arms and legs splayed at unnatural angles. Blaster fire ionizes the air. Within moments Jefferson will hit the ground, which suddenly seems far from lovely.

He will die instantly, if he's not already dead. Of this I am sure.

His last words were to me:

Enjoy the ride.

Lex

"Man down," Zavier says as he steers the speeder through Indra's canyons. "Left-side enforcement to Cosmo A. Nelson, take up position. We're on Popper radar now, so take the backup route. Rendezvous Drill-Facil, same as before." He accelerates into the turn, and then we're plummeting with the same controlled precision I'm known for. His men follow the best they can. "Be careful," he yells.

He jerks his chin and the whole pack swerves. His hand's choking the accelerator and his piloting is borderline reckless.

I fight the urge to commandeer this speeder. We touch down in some miserable back alley, some stretch where no one walks because it looks like the Lower Levels are seeping into this one. We hover there, his team awaiting his signal.

"Livia?" I say. "Is she—"

"Cosmo A is fine."

"Kane?"

"You don't need to worry about him neither." He gives the go sign. "The only casualty," he says, "was one of our own."

We take off.

At the Academy, you're taught that the city's laid out in a perfect grid with regulated block sizes. There are public recreational spaces at every ten intervals. To promote communal gatherings. The thought being that if you see and communicate with your neighbors, you're less likely to harm one another. But this has never encouraged a feeling of community, since it is felt that it is just another way the IHC can better observe and control your interactions. I bet the good citizens of Indra also don't think about the people living right beneath them, or the feelings that fester there.

Zavier and his men bend tight corners and passages so narrow I can reach out and touch the sides. We careen through a waste dump. Everywhere we go is fit for only Middlers and Hubbers, and they keep their heads down when they hear us coming. We go so fast I have to clutch this man I despise. I make sure to dig my fingernails into him.

The light of the blasts travels faster than their sound. The energy is ricocheting off plexi-steel before it all sounds too close for comfort. I spare a glance behind, and this patrol threatens to overtake us.

"Damn Poppers," Zavier hisses.

Poppers, PCF—whatever you call them—you could illuminate the entire city with the amount of blasting they're doing.

Zavier's doing his best to outrun them, but PCF speeders are far superior. He sets a course for a rigger storage yard to our immediate left. Unorganized and filthy, just what you'd expect from a rigger, but that means space to lie low and duck out of sight. Too bad someone else thought of it first. Those well-maintained, clean-burning PCF engines sound real hungry to me.

Zavier lifts his hand, ready to signal our descent.

"Wait!" I shout. "Not that way. They're already there. I can hear them."

He refuses to acknowledge me. His hand drops and so do we.

We're down in the abandoned heap and I can't get Hep's voice out of my head.

We live for a while, and then we die. Can't stop either when the time comes.

He's wrong. I was born to no one, so no one has claim over my life. And if I don't do anything now, this jackass will get us all killed.

Lying in wait, the PCF grind their teeth. They power up their blasters. Still, they're not quick enough for me.

I start blasting as soon as we round the corner. My shots don't hit anyone, but they distract the PCF long enough for the rebels to draw down. I've evened the odds, but I still wouldn't call it a fair fight.

Every rebel casualty will be pinned on my head, so no one else is dying just yet. We've only just begun striking back.

Zavier steers with one hand, shoots with the other. He curses. I'd curse too if I were that bad a shot. PCF fire hits the speeder on our left flank. A rebel falls off the back. The driver swerves, his arm smoking and enflamed by blaster splash. Still alert, but he's fading quick.

Zavier yells at the driver. "Robertson!"

"Bring me in," I tell Zavier, my feet now on the seat under me.

"Don't you dare!" he yells back.

I can do this on my own. He grabs at me, but no one can stop me if I don't want them to.

I land hard on the seat, straddling the speeder behind the driver. He's completely slumped over by now and the speeder veers wide right. I reach over his body and grab the controls, correcting our course to get out of this dump.

I take his earfeed out and place it in my ear. Zavier's curses hide his wounded pride. Maybe he's not the leader he thought he was, but I just saved someone's life he should've been looking out for.

"If you're really here to protect us," I say to everyone listening, "try to keep up."

The drill-facil location pings red on my nav board. I plot the most direct course.

This time, everyone follows my lead.

CHAPTER 30

Livia

We're waiting at the meet-up location when the dust billows our way. The PCF hunted us and we owe our freedom—and lives—to Chac's quick thinking.

One of the rebels asks how much longer we have to wait. "We're all in this together now," Chae says. No one asks again.

I sit by Kane and we don't talk. I imagine he's thinking about Lex, too. I feel him watching me, and the heat coming off his body is a strange comfort to me.

The three of us, our lives are intertwined now. All my life I've looked for something more than island life and I feel as if I'm on the verge of . . . something. Maybe a nervous breakdown. Maybe I'll soon be recovering alongside Governess on Sunrise Retreat Island.

The dust cloud expands and my eyes sting. I tear away another piece of my dress to cover my mouth before I choke. At its heart I can hear firing engines.

Wild riders blaze out of the cloud with Lex at the lead. I'm relieved, yet far from surprised.

The first rebel we met, the shaggy-haired Zavier, leaps off his speeder as soon as it's touched down. No need to sense his feelings, since he does little to hide his overwhelming fury. It rivals Lex's at her peak. His bright blue eyes shine ice-cold, and he's handsome, even like this, in a way island boys could never be, their natural appeal blunted by endless sculpting procedures. Of course, they're not prone to murder, either.

The focus of his indignation doesn't surprise me. Lex dismounts her speeder, regaining a level of militaristic swagger and . . . calm? How unlikely.

"Who do you think you are?" Zavier bumps right into her. He's a real savage, that one. And her? Placid as a reflecting pool. She refuses to engage with this bully. "You disobeyed my orders, you spoiled little—"

"I think everything worked out remarkably well."

"Just because you went to the godforsaken Academy, you can—"

She grabs Zavier's face with one hand and squeezes his mouth shut. He knocks it away. "Don't you dare take your anger out on me," she says.

Chae inserts himself between them and brushes Zavier back. "Lay off her, Z."

Kane joins Lex's side, but knows not to step up, that she's quite capable of fighting her own battles.

If anything, Chae's interference makes Zavier more furious, and he has no regard for his new target. "Are you taking *her* side?" he yells.

"No sides, Z. Just us."

"Robertson—"

"Got done in by Poppers."

"But if she—"

"—didn't save Luther's life? What? What's your point?"

"One for one? Are you really trying to argue acceptable losses? You already forget what she did to Emil?!"

"I don't know any Emil," Lex says. Zavier whips around, ready to tear her apart, and instinctively I reach for my zinger, ready to intervene.

"Of course you don't," Zavier says. "You're just like the rest of them, aren't you? Score another kill for your holofile, drop another rock on the pile."

"Enough," Roscoe says, not loudly, yet forcefully enough to bring the argument to a standstill. "Remember what we set out to accomplish. We have lost many, but today we have also gained three. Leave your anger for the enemy and be gracious in victory. Indra wasn't erected overnight, and we cannot hope that our dreams, fueled by our blood, will materialize quickly either."

His words have turned half the rebels' eyes on me. The other half are on Lex. Even Zavier's. He swallows his anger, though it isn't far from the surface. But he seems to believe in something much greater than himself, at least some of the time.

I cannot fathom their beliefs, or how we could possibly tie into them. There is much to learn. It's frightening to mean this much to others.

Lex nods knowingly at me; we will go along with this. I nod back. Kane smiles, game for adventure.

"Now," says Roscoe, when they seem to be settling down. "There is still more work to be done. So let us bid farewell to the once and future great City of Indra."

The rebels get to work removing the grate from an enormous drainage pipe. It's already loose, but takes the strength of four to move.

Chae throws a towline down the pipe and secures it to the heavy grate. One by one, the rebels descend, then followed by Kane. Zavier goes last, mounting the pipe slowly. Before he drops, Roscoe puts a hand on his shoulder and Zavier looks up hopefully. He's tired. We all are.

Roscoe smiles. "We will speak, soon." Zavier sighs, his shoulders slumping in relief. He drops, not seeking further affirmation from the three of us.

"I know you have questions," Roscoe says to us, "and all will be answered. On this you have my word. But for now, let us take sanctuary."

"No," I say. "You have the bearing of a Proper Indrithian, so it would be uncustomary to not engage us in conversation when requested, would it not?"

"You are correct."

"Then tell us who you are."

I sense his hesitation; this isn't easy for him, and yet, he desperately wants us to trust him like the rebels do.

"The more appropriate question is not of my identity, but your own," he says.

"You told me that you knew my mother," I say. "That she was your friend. I have never met one who would match that claim. I did not think they existed any longer."

"They do, as long as I live and breathe." He looks to Lex. "I knew your mother as well."

"I do not have a mother," she says, surprising me.

"You do. In fact"—he looks from Lex to me and back again—"you share the same one. In fact, that is not all you share."

Since the discovery of our symbols earlier, it is hard to look at her without seeing it. The flaw in each of our eyes, that shouldn't exist, but somehow does. How we mirror each other, not in exact appearance or attitude, but in our resolves. For almost eighteen years we have fought through life, only to be rewarded with the promise of more fighting to come.

"You share your birthday," he says.

Twins.

Excerpted from The Book of Indra, *Appendix IV:*
"Laws of Indra: The Population Control Acts"

The Law of Twins

As ordered by the Independent High Council of the City of Indra, it is hereby Law:

1. Women are prohibited from giving birth to more than one child.
2. Women are required to take the government-issued EX2 pill to prevent the conception of Twins.
3. Failure to comply in said Law will result in immediate banishment of both parental Cohabitants, as well as prompt seizure of Offspring.
4. Following seizure, the Independent High Council will determine the Twin they deem of Greater Use to Society.
5. The Twin not deemed such will be forfeited immediately to government holding for further tests.

CHAPTER 31

Lex

I look at this uppity girl across from me. She wears gowns and says *perhaps*. She has a singing sword and her own island and a creature that shouldn't exist.

We are nothing alike.

She acts like she's different. From everyone else around her. Like somehow she is special.

Okay, maybe a little alike.

She doesn't say a word. Stares like she knows more than me. Like she sees through me. I hate her for that.

I want to punch her for even existing.

I don't have a chance.

Her arms are around me. And I don't push her off.

It feels good to not be alone for once.

Livia

I hadn't planned on putting my arms around Lex, and yet there they are. She's turned her face away from me, yet she keeps my embrace. I don't know what she's thinking, but the sleeve of my dress is wet with her tears.

I feel her fury: she'd rather not be standing with her arms around me.

And yet, she doesn't wish to let go either.

"I'm crying as well," I tell her. "I'm crying with you. Maybe that's something twins do, I don't know." I pat her back, like Governess would. We will work out what this means together. Of this I am sure.

She pulls back suddenly, her face streaked in tears.

"What is 'twins'?" she asks.

Lex

At this point Roscoe gives us our space and stands lookout. He has nothing left to facilitate between us now, but he can't let us leave his sight.

Livia tells me that one of us should have died. And yet, here we are.

"They would just pick one? To kill?"

"Yes," says Livia. "Though the law is rarely spoken about. It is rather old-fashioned. The EX2 controls the conception of twins, after all."

"Not always, obviously," I say. "And if anyone knew of us, one would die?"

Livia nods. "Though we have done so much wrong, I'm not certain they would spare either of us now."

Now I'm pacing. It doesn't make sense. This is crazy, beyond insane.

"How do they pick?" I ask.

"I don't know. Why focus on things that haven't happened? Our parents refused to make that choice."

That's when I realize she's wrong. Totally, completely wrong.

They picked *me* to get rid of. Yes, I'm still alive, but I didn't get to live on some island like her, to be coddled by a governess, kitchen staff, and garden crew. I most certainly wouldn't have lived there all my life and allowed myself to be so *skinny*. I went to a place where you slept on cots and prayed you weren't the next one to go missing.

I was the twin they killed.

"I was sent to an Orphanage," I tell her. "Did you know that?"

"I didn't even know you existed until today."

"An Orphanage. You understand? Fighting just to eat. I had one uniform. One tiny bed. I was a number, do you get that? Somehow, I survived. Convinced them I was worthy. Without an Etiquette Tutor or Master . . ."

"You know nothing," she says. "Only anger."

We are worlds apart, once again. This is why the Upper and Lower Levels will never coexist.

"They should've picked you!" I say, pushing her against the alley wall. I'm screaming into her spoiled little face. "You got everything! You had an island and people to do every last thing you said and I was just . . . 242!"

I pull back my fist.

Livia

I force Lex off of me, and now *she's* fighting to be free of *me*. Yet at this moment, I'm stronger than her, strong enough that she doesn't have the luxury of ignoring me.

"No one else understands you, Lex, is that to be the correct assumption?" I ask, mimicking her rage too well. "No one else has ever had to suffer, it seems. You were given a number, and for that I apologize. Yet you were trained to do something that matters . . . and I was told to be quiet and look pretty. I was cinched up and spun on a pedestal until I was regarded as having no flaws. So you see, Lex? You are half-right. I did have everything . . . and absolutely nothing."

"And everything I had," she spits right back, "meant absolutely nothing."

"Even Kane?"

I let go and back away, yet she doesn't move.

I stand across from her. Rage, resentment, and regret flowing between us. We're both crying. It's been too long since we've rested. The toll this day has taken overwhelms us both. We blame each other when neither is to blame. It takes a lot of silence for me to come to that conclusion.

There's a long, dark tunnel to travel below. We each grab a line and descend to join the others. Roscoe silently follows.

CHAPTER 32

Lex

The rebels are smart enough to keep ahead of Roscoe, Livia, Kane, and me. I'm stuck with the old man, and Livia isn't helping. She's acting fascinated by everything, asking a million things. She's trying to act as though nothing happened. Doesn't want anyone to see her upset maybe. That is the polite response, I guess.

Polite, I've decided, is a waste of everyone's time.

No one asks the real questions, of course. The ones that matter. *How do twins end up perfect strangers?* I want to ask.

And where are we going?

Instead, we learn about the pipe. How it's part of an abandoned water drilling facility. "Of course, there is no water to be drilled anymore," Roscoe says. "Not from the Lower Levels. We depleted those resources long ago. Which, of course, is the very reason Indra moved upward. All water is now stored in the Aero-Crown."

Shut up, I'm thinking. Or say something that matters. Something I didn't learn in Indrithian History.

"Are you okay?" whispers Kane.

"No," I say. He looks worried. "I'll be fine."

He nods, but I can tell he'll keep asking.

This guy, Roscoe, just turned everything upside down, and now he won't stop talking about pipes.

"These pipes are key to Lower Level survival. They act as transport for scavenged items, though much of the Lower Level is self-sufficient. No one above suspects, of course. The pipes serve no purpose, and therefore do not exist."

Right now, I wish he didn't.

"Others," he continues, "have been appropriated to siphon water from the City of Indra's supply, bringing it to the populace below. Only fair. An eye for an eye."

"Where is that from?" asks Kane.

"It is from a book," Roscoe tells him.

"*The Book of Indra*? I don't think so."

"No," says Roscoe, smiling, "A real book. One of many we keep in our possession."

"There are no real books," I say, annoyed. "There is only *The Book of Indra*."

"'There is more on heaven and earth than are dreamed of in your philosophy.' That is from another book that is not *The Book of Indra*, but what the scribe means is that much has been kept from you."

"No kidding," I say.

I stare at him, waiting for the rest of the story. For him to talk about my birth, my family, my existence.

There's more than the sister part, that's for sure. Though that is plenty already.

Nothing. He just keeps walking.

"Okay," I say. "Tell me something, then. Something kept from me."

Roscoe smiles at me. The kind of smile you give a child. *A child who infiltrated the IHC*, I think. *Who can fly a stolen PCF patroller. Who can outsmart a whole unit of Population Control's finest. So ease back, old man.*

"Then show me these books," I say. "Prove it. In fact, I think it's about time you start proving a lot of things."

"You remind me so much of your mother," he says.

Cheap shot, and it totally works. For a second I lose my words. All of them.

I look at Livia, and she turns away. But I know what she is thinking. Our *mother*.

"Ah," he says, before I can regroup, "we shall continue this later. This, my friends, is our destination."

CHAPTER 33

Livia

I wait patiently for Roscoe to unlock the mysteries of the universe, but we have only reached a small cavern. He and the other rebels have a quick, hushed exchange before they leave us alone. Lex stands by herself, sullen and despondent, barely looking upward when one of them addresses us. Roscoe is tall and sleepy-eyed, and has removed his PCF attire, revealing an ascot and waistcoat. The kind Proper Gentlemen don for formal occasions, only his is rather filthy and fraying.

"I wouldn't worry too much," he says to us all, though his shy smile is directed toward me. "I once heard it's like giving birth. You forget the pain after it's done."

With these words, Lex returns to us, her fierceness stronger than ever.

"Forget the pain after . . . *what*? What are you talking about, Roscoe? You have till ten to tell me what's going on or—"

"Or you'll what?" says Zavier coolly. He's watching her with narrowed eyes and a far from amused expression. "Haven't you realized by now? None of us want you harmed."

Except you, I think, sensing something beneath his collected exterior.

"He's correct," says Roscoe.

"They risked their lives for us, Lex," says Kane. "Vipsinia is still up there."

Lex turns to me, meeting my eyes for the first time since entering the cavern. She glares at me, yet I know this is an excuse; she is searching for an answer in my face. *They are telling the truth*, I say with my eyes.

"Well?" she says, turning back to them. "What do we have to do?"

They don't want us harmed, that much is clear to me. Yet I feel something else that unhinges me: they're worried. Deeply, profoundly worried.

And what will happen in that cavern will be deeply, profoundly unpleasant.

Lex

Livia trusts them. I see it in her face. And I figure I have no other choice.

I turn my back to Zavier. "Well," I say to Roscoe, "what do we have to do?"

"Lexie?" interrupts a voice. I turn. A girl stands at the entrance. "Is that you?"

"Lex," I tell her. She stares at me. She is around my age, I think. And something in her face stops my fury cold. Stops everything cold.

"It *is* you!" she says, breaking into a huge smile. "I knew you'd correct me if I called you the wrong name."

Then she does something completely crazy. She hugs me.

And even crazier? I let her.

I don't exactly hug her back. Just stand there, my arms stiff at my sides. *Second hug in one day*, I think. *This is getting ridiculous. Everyone needs to learn to keep their hands off me.*

Yet I don't push her off either.

She finally steps back. "I know you hated every second of that. But I couldn't help it. It's been so long."

"I don't know you," I tell her softly. I don't want to hurt her feelings. I'm not sure why I even care.

Part of me wishes I did know her. There is something about her that calms me.

"You do," she says. "Look closer."

She is a normal girl, nothing special. Except the glow, maybe. It seems to come from under her skin.

Livia

"Her name is 374," Roscoe says. "She also goes by Samantha. In fact, she has not been 374 since you last saw her."

"I'll always be 374," she responds, smiling at Lex. Lex, if you can believe it, smiles back. It isn't a big smile, but it's genuine. Like a child's.

They both have numbers. They were both in the Orphanage.

"I didn't know the two of you were connected until I was planning your rescue. That's when Samantha told me of a Lex she had known. What a strange, small world!" Roscoe smiles at Lex, who is still in shock. "I'm sure you have a great deal to discuss and there will be ample time to reconnect later. But we thought, for now, perhaps, having Samantha here might make the process easier."

The girl, Samantha, leans over to Lex. The others pretend not to listen. "I will tell you everything later," she says. "For now, you must do as they ask. There isn't much time. But I'll be right here with you. I could even braid your hair."

Lex simply nods, entering the room by her side without question. Kane and I follow, and for a second, I feel almost jealous. This quiet young woman has the power to calm Lex, a gift I had thought not possible.

That, it occurs to me, *is how one would treat a sister.*

Then again, how was I to know? I've had a sister for only a few hours and our history together has mostly consisted of attempts on each other's lives.

But it seems even Samantha's powers have their limits.

"We have a *what* in our *what*?" Lex shrieks.

Samantha holds her hand, and now Lex squeezes back so hard I can almost feel a phantom pressure on my own palm.

"Mandatory temporal lobe implant," says Roscoe. "In layman's terms, a small chip, barely the size of a fingernail."

"In *our brains*?"

"Yes," I say, understanding all too clearly. "Somewhere between the optical nerve and temple, if I were to make an educated guess. The part of the brain that controls memory."

"You," Roscoe says, "are so very much like your father, Livia."

"So you say," I fire back. He peddles memories that are of no use to me right now. They dull my focus. I try to soften my approach. "Perhaps I am right to assume this chip chronicles every moment of our existence. And that information is used to store our history in the Archives."

"Yes," says Roscoe. "Among other uses."

"Other uses?" asks Kane.

"The chip also monitors your whereabouts, your location, at every moment."

For a second, I wonder if I will vomit right here, in front of all of them. The sickness in my stomach is overwhelming. *My whole life has been monitored*, I realize. *I have been watched, just as I felt I had been, only not quite in the way I imagined.*

They have been watching from inside my own head. I have thought millions of terrible things. Have they seen it all?

"That is how the PCF knew where to find us," I say. "But if this proves true, how would we have escaped? Why the lag time in locating us?"

Roscoe nods. He's impressed with my questioning, though flattered is the last thing I feel. Horrified is a more apt description.

"As I'm sure you are aware, you and Lex are of a unique genetic configuration. I assume it took them longer due to the complexity of your psychological makeup and brain functions."

"They did find us, nonetheless."

"Yes, and will again. Even with your curious genetics and the distance we've placed between ourselves and Indra, eventually you will be discovered. And then they will come for you. We cannot risk going any farther toward our headquarters until it is removed. And we are prepared to do just that here."

"And Kane?" I ask, noticing that he has gone silent and rather pale.

"Kane is lucky enough that his was extracted at the Independent High Council."

"Lucky," says Kane quietly, "is not the word I'd use."

"They'll have sent it away for full analysis," Roscoe says. "Standard detainment procedure. In the hopes of understanding the motivation of those who defy Indra and preventing future crime. You were rescued before they could reimplant it, I assume?"

Kane shrugs. "If they did, I don't remember."

"Then he must be reexamined," Zavier says abruptly.

"I bet you're enjoying this," Lex says.

Haunted, I decide, is a perfect way to describe his expression. "The opposite, if you really want to know. I despise this. Everything about it."

"Why is he even here?" Lex asks.

"Because," says Roscoe, "he will be performing the procedure. He is the only one who knows how."

CHAPTER 34

Lex

Samantha hasn't said a word the whole time. Just holds my hand tight. When I try to pull away, she just clutches harder.

Now that I'm stretched out across a makeshift sleeper, she's still holding on. *I'm right here*, she seems to be saying. *I'm not going anywhere.*

I wish I could, though. Go anywhere else but here.

They just shoveled out some dirt and put up a door and called this a room. We had better in the Orphanage. The walls are packed earth, the floor rocky and uneven. In other words, exactly the place you don't want an experimental medical procedure.

Not that we'd been given an option.

Zavier explains that when they found the room it was filled with bones, probably dating back to the Separation—when the colonists extricated themselves from the Lower Levels to build the Upward City of Indra, as it was first known. There were drill rigs stripped for parts and shattered skulls beneath the soil.

Livia's first. She sits on the exam table while Zavier runs a buzzing paddle over her head. The paddle's connected to a weird contraption that I'm surprised even functions. This, I'm told, is her initial scan.

"Strange," says Zavier, checking the monitor. "She's only at twenty percent. I've never seen that before."

Roscoe nods. "I take it you have uncommon sensory abilities, Livia, am I correct? To intuit beyond everyday surface emotions?"

She nods.

Ha, I think. *That's how it feels. When someone can see into your head. Not so great being on the other side, huh?*

"Well, then we are doubly fortunate. The procedure is not necessary in your case. At thirty percent or less, they do not have clear access to your inner workings."

Livia looks relieved. Of course, she got off easy. This is the story of her life.

"Perhaps you will have good news, too," she says in passing.

That is hardly the story of mine. Zavier lifts the paddle and I imagine the worst. The scanning process is slow and torturous, but entirely without pain, so far.

"Seventy four percent," he says.

Roscoe is not so quick to declare anything this time.

"Great," I say. "Let's get to it then. Bust open my brain. Just hurry up before I change my mind."

"Livia and Kane can stay with you," Roscoe tells me. "As can I."

"You don't have to do that." I don't want them to see me like this.

He tells me it will be fine. I want it to be, but I'm not sure. I find no qualities in him that make him better than any other leader. They all use fear as a weapon to control, and right now I fear it's working. I don't want anyone to see me afraid. Having Zavier do this is humiliating enough.

I sit through Kane's scan and he's proven correct that there wasn't sufficient time to reimplant his chip. He holds my hand and I let him do it, but only briefly.

Judging by how everyone is treating me? These could be my

final thoughts. I will be silenced, here where plenty of dead have rested before me. The City of Indra was built on graves.

Livia wants to stay, but she respects my wishes. Samantha doesn't. I won't argue with her. Secretly, I'm pleased. To not be alone.

I know it's almost time. She kneels at my side while I lie back in a cot. She's trying to distract me, I know. Keeping me from watching Zavier prep.

"I always thought I was going to reach twelve," she says. "To be free of the Orphanage, instead of it freeing itself from me. At least I was pretty sure. And the caretakers even hinted good things were just ahead."

"Everyone liked you," I say.

"I know. I worked hard to make that happen."

A hissing noise. I look at Zavier, adjusting a dial on a machine that looks like it lacks an ounce of design or sterility.

"That way," says Samantha, turning my chin toward her, "they never suspected what I was really up to. Remember how I would disappear?"

I nod. "You told me it was a secret."

"It was. I hated that place. The whole thing. The disappearing, the not knowing who was—or if *you* were—next. I wanted to know why it happened. Make sense of this senseless act. We were already in the Orphanage. Our flaws were right there on the surface. We were never wanted in the first place. But complaining? That wouldn't do much except get me bottomed out myself."

"You had no flaws."

She laughs. "Your memories treat me better than I deserve."

I could tell her my memory is practically flawless and that she exists there only exactly as she was, but I want to hear her story so desperately.

"I made everyone like me. The perfect orphan. That way, they never suspected. I started taking the tags when I was just in the Intermediate Dorm. The ones on the new arrivals. I'd go in there, right after the babies had been labeled, with their Gs for 'Genetic Flaw' and Ps for 'Pass.' And I'd snip them right off and drop them in the incinerator. Indra has evaluators throughout the levels who work hard to select out those who will contribute to its continued success. But our lives aren't predetermined. Look at us! Look who *we've* become! And I must admit, I enjoyed the chaos. They'd lock down the unit, trying to decipher which baby was a dud, which did they already agree to approve?"

"I remember!" I say. "It happened all the time! The caretakers would be running around, totally pissed. And it was you!"

"For almost a year. Not that it did much good. Only bought the kids a few extra days. But maybe, maybe one got through. I had to be on the right track if it pissed them off so much."

I can hardly speak. Samantha is just as strato as I remember.

"Of course, they caught me, right before I turned twelve. They tried to guilt me. 'We had big plans for you, Samantha. Placement in Hubber Organization. And now look what you've done!' Hubber Organization. Putting supplies in the right pile. Like I'd given my whole life away."

"And then?"

"They said I was going to Rock Bottom, same place I came from. I mean, it isn't as bad as everyone said. I could remember from where I came. Some memories of my parents before they died. For many, Rock Bottom is horrible, but there're good things there too. Some of us even have families. For so long I believed what they wanted, but now I don't have to."

She glances at Zavier, who is watching us now. Even gives him a smile. He looks away.

"But the stories of the orphans being brought out to the Lower Levels and given over to the mutations—that didn't happen?"

"Not to me. That's a story that instructors tell. I was put on a transporter with some others. We'd pick up more at the other orphanages along the way."

"There are more?"

She nods.

"Once you were gone," I say, "I saw that there were so many orphans who needed someone like you. I tried, but I . . . I tried to help some of them, but it didn't work. I couldn't even help one of them the way that you helped me. And the whole time I thought that it was me that got you bottomed out."

"No," she says, caressing my face, rubbing my tears dry. "I'm truly sorry you had to carry that with you over the years. It was you, little 242, that let me know that my efforts weren't wasted. That change is possible, even if it's one orphan at a time. Even if you did follow me around like a shadow."

I can't help but smile.

"It's time," says Zavier.

He can't look at me. He's not being a jerk, I realize. Even though it's his natural state.

Zavier's nervousness is not a good sign.

"Have you done this before?" I ask.

"Yes," he says.

"A lot?"

"Once."

"How'd it go?"

He doesn't answer.

"Did they die?"

"Distracting me while I'm calibrating only increases your risk."

I have more questions. Mostly about where he got his training. I imagine they don't have high standards for medical care down below.

The machine makes a grinding noise. "I'm sure that's normal," Samantha says, still by my side.

"This procedure should take less than five minutes," he says. "I'll talk you through, even when you're in a state of noncoherence."

He pulls a rubber-gripped tool from the contraption, and contact with the air makes it spark. Its end is a delicate yet nightmare-inducing spike.

"This will go in your ear," he says, waving it gently. The gleaming metal bends slightly, and its malleability doesn't make it more attractive.

I'm suddenly nauseous. *Maybe I'll pass out*, I think hopefully.

Samantha squeezes my hand. I squeeze back and hold it tight. Hold it like I'm holding on for my life.

Another spark. My ears home in on that sharp burst. It overwhelms my eardrums.

"Ready?" he says.

I nod yes, then immediately shake my head no. He's already moving toward me.

"Close your eyes," he says. "Try to relax and take deep breaths."

"I'm sorry about your friend," I tell him. "But I didn't kill him, okay? Whether you believe that or not. So don't kill me."

A look crosses over his face. *Sympathy?*

He feels sorry for me, and that is the worst part of all.

"Do this already," I demand, and close my eyes.

"The only way to remove the chip is by disabling the signal with sound," Zavier says. "A series of high-pitched sonic waves at an accelerated frequency. And to do that, we must get as close to the chip as possible."

That's when I feel the spike easing into my ear. Slow and steady. Cold metal going straight for my brain.

"I will go fast, Lex. Fast as I possibly can. In a second you will feel pain. But that only lasts a few moments."

Instantly, my brain is on fire, like it's going to explode out of my skull. I'm fighting to endure it, fighting not to freak out, and I open my mouth to shriek, when it cuts short and all that comes out, I think, is a whimper.

"There. That's the worst of it."

Now there is just a faint ache, the foreign metal uncomfortably icy against my eardrum.

"Can you hear me, Lex?"

"That sucked," I say in a hollow voice.

"You're doing fine. In a second I'll release the first frequency. That will affect the part of the temporal lobe that controls language skills. We'll use hand gestures to communicate since you won't be able to speak for the rest of the procedure."

Does that include screaming?

"Can you hear me?" Zavier says. "Wiggle your fingers."

It sounds easy, but my hands are dead weights. What has he *really* done to me?

Wiggle, I think. *C'mon. Wiggle.*

"I felt it," Samantha says, then softly whispers in my unspiked ear, "You're doing good. Real good."

"I'm sending the second frequency now," Zavier says. "Then there is only one more to go."

This time, like the last, I can hear the frequency all too well. It's like a speeder racing directly overhead, or an uncomfortably close blaster bolt. Suddenly, I can't feel my body, and I worry that this is permanent. I can no longer hear out of either ear. My body's going into shock. I'm spasming uncontrollably and Samantha holds me down, but I'm only getting worse. I can't fight it. My vision goes hazy. I feel like dying, but Samantha—my lifeline—won't let me.

My eyes are rolling up and someone's pressing something hard in my mouth, and every time my body shakes, I bite down on this thing and I buck hard enough that Zavier has to come hold me down. That's when I lose touch with my body.

It's just a shell now. That I'm trapped in. It has served me well, but I can't hold on anymore. I'm not strong enough.

I'm not strong enough.

I'm not strong.

CHAPTER 35

Livia

"How are you feeling?" I ask. Lex's eyes flicker open and appear a little glazed over, as though she has no idea who I am.

In many ways, she doesn't, but I cannot help but worry. Especially when she tries to stand up and her legs give out. Kane and I catch her and sit her down. Zavier explained she would be light-headed and disoriented, her equilibrium clearly affected, but it will pass as her body adjusts.

"Just lay there for now," I say.

She nods.

Zavier has already called it a success. After disabling the chip, he was able to extract it without risking further damage.

We will stay here until Lex recovers. Roscoe has sent the rest of the rebels ahead. There are many factions down here, and not all are friendly to their cause. Territory changes possession every day, and we must be sure that we'll be granted safe passage as we avoid the Hub and all the heavily trafficked zones.

For now it feels good to rest and sit. To fill the time, Kane and I share stories about the Islands. Afterward, I do not find that I miss them much at all. I tell him he was lucky to have been able to join the Academy. I surprise him with tales of my swordsmanship, and I tell him something I've never told anyone else: how I discovered my mother's sword locked away in a case under their sleeper. I'd been woken by a nightmare and hid under there in the early morning. At first touch the sounds it made startled me, but I refused to let it go and clutched it against my chest, and in my memory it hummed me to sleep. Kane looks shocked. Through his eyes, my adventurous streak makes me blush. It makes me feel . . . silly. Once we start talking, we can't stop. Yet we dance around our first meeting. I err on the side of proper while he . . . perhaps I've scared him.

The day has grown long into night and we lean against each other for support. His touch awakens my body, warming me in the cool eaves of this hollowed Earth, though I know perhaps that his intentions are confusing. I would like to close my eyes and dream awhile. It would be nice.

His eyes close and his bruised body relaxes, and I gather him against me. He's a strange boy. They could all be this way, I think. For all we've talked, I still know little about him. He could still be a danger to me. That, I must never forget.

When Lex is strong enough to sit upright by herself, Samantha breaks bits off a ration bar and feeds them to her. We're all given one bar each to eat.

"I saw things," Lex says. "I only wish I could remember what they were."

"Most certainly your memories returning to you," Roscoe says. "It will take time, but they are there now."

The rebels return and the news isn't great. A clan of mutations has taken over the unfinished transit path that would give us the most direct route back to their base.

"So what's the plan?" Lex says. "If you have another one, that is."

Her voice is combative and angry. In other words, she's herself again. This floods me with relief.

"We'll head for the Old Town Safe Zone," Zavier says. "This clan can't have taken that from us. Just make sure your blasters're charged and stick close to one another, all right?"

There's a snort.

"You got something to say, Marley?" Zavier walks over to a short, scruffy rebel, his head bursting with knotted clumps of hair. He snorts again.

"No one abides by no Safe Zone. Zone's an illusion that ends when the crossfire begins. Can't just dance on through there expecting to get a hero's welcome."

"You got a better idea?"

"Cut through Unifier territory. They'll be too busy counting their supplies to notice."

"With a group this large? They'll think it's a raid."

"Then we split up, half with you, half with me."

"The girls are our only priority," says Zavier.

"Even that one?" Marley asks, pointing at Kane.

The jab doesn't wound Kane. "Even this one," he replies.

Marley chuckles, and some of the other rebels laugh along. "You'll all be dead in under two minutes and then we'll be free to go whichever way we want."

"I give them two seconds," says another.

Lex clenches her jaw, her anger rising; I know the signs. Within a few moments she will combust.

"Silence," Roscoe says. "Zavier is right. The Safe Zone is the most logical choice. We can blend in there long enough to pass through."

Roscoe's word is law. There is no further dissent.

"Let us now, my brothers, have a moment of reflection," says Roscoe, joining hands with those nearest him, "to contemplate a time before our movement found you."

We all come together. I was of the air. My sister, for the briefest moment, must have been, too. We are reunited here below Indra for reasons beyond our comprehension. I suspect the history of our world was broken long before we took our first breaths together. Perhaps this is the start of something else. Something new.

"They'll see you a mile off in that thing," says Chae, handing me a coarse black cloak. He gives one to Lex, and she drops it over her body suit.

Zavier draws figures in the dirt, showing each rebel their placement for when we pass through Old Town. "Stay close to Lex and Livia, but with enough distance so you don't draw undue attention. As for the two of you," he says, motioning my sister and me over, "keep your head down. And for all our sakes, do not engage under any circumstances. Our customs are complex." He smirks, glancing in Lex's direction. "Even though for some, I suspect this will be difficult."

We gather our blasters and gear that we've shed, and it's finally time. Chae rolls the portal open; it slides along its ancient tracks with the sound of stone grinding against stone.

He disappears into the darkness, the others immediately following. One by one, the rebels are gone. Samantha stays by our side, our native guardian. "It's not so bad," she says. "In fact, you might just like it here."

Kane sees my apprehension, catches my eye, and winks.

"Ready?" I ask Lex.

"I was born ready. Same time as you, actually."

"I wonder which of us is older?"

I'm about to enter the most dangerous territory in all the Lower Levels. Yet nothing will surprise me as much as seeing Lex almost smile.

At the door, I take a deep breath and a huge step into the unknown.

CHAPTER 36

Lex

The Hub casts off massive amounts of energy. That energy heats up the Lower Levels, especially when you factor in your proximity to the core. The heat can create a weird haze, almost a fog, and my newly gifted cloak traps it too well. Kane stumbles frequently—perhaps it is the booster wearing off—and our crew's progress is slower than it should be.

"Is this the Safe Zone?" I ask Zavier.

"Not yet," he says. His not-quite-gentle manner during the procedure has reverted to indifference. He's threatened by me, I think.

"Close?"

"You'll know it when you see it."

I lose track of the other rebels in the haze. It's easier to keep my eyes focused on Livia and Kane and try to follow their footsteps. I try not to read into their pairing. They've kissed—I mean, it's not easy to forget, but. It's just easier to try to.

I keep walking. Zavier says I'll know it when I see it, but I start to hear it first.

Voices holler over the thick bass kicks. The music is loud and greasy. I must hear it in advance of the rest because they're wary when the lights dance through the murkiness. In the Lower Levels, it's always night. Harsh beams of white and flashing neon red announce the entry to Old Town, a freakish light show that could make you sick if you stare too long.

"Home sweet home." I whistle. Zavier ignores me.

"Through there," he says, indicating a narrow walkway cutting between scrap plating. Corrugated hovels are built into each other. A man stumbles out of one, howling with laughter or pain, it's hard to decipher, then falls to the ground, stone-still.

"Is he dead?" I ask.

"Maybe. You never know around here."

I know he's messing with my head. I can hear it in his voice. Still . . .

This is the Safe Zone?

Even the Academy sims don't prepare you for the squabble of day-to-day existence down here. Our final sim didn't replicate the stench or the decaying atmosphere. We'd only been given a loose interpretation. They layer their lies with just enough reality. They taught us order with our uniforms and rows of cots. But chaos? How do you prepare for that?

"C'mon," says Zavier.

Act like you've seen it before, I tell myself. *Like this is nothing new.*

I follow him across the main boulevard, a claustrophobic walkway of uneven rocks. The hovels are stacked on top of each other, their tops disappearing into the fog, which disguises the enormity of the Safe Zone. Somewhere, far above, is a domed slab of rock. You'd never know, except for the echo of greasy Rock Bottom rhythms.

The scavs shove past us, some pushing their wares in our faces: expired rations or previously used blades and stunners.

"Getcher emissions right here! Flares, sparkers, particle beamers! Highest voltage in the dirtlands, can't beat the price!"

"Water capsules, honey? You're lookin' a little parched . . ."

"Get you messed up. Two minutes, won't know your own name. Chewers, sniffers, lickers, any way you like it! Best stuff in and out of the Zone."

Zavier puts an arm around me and pulls me in tight. A look

from him to the vendors communicates quite clearly his level of disinterest.

A filthy man pushes something in my face. Half a dried-out wafer held between two black fingernails. He reeks of dead things.

"Yummy?" he says.

"No," Zavier barks. "Get."

I turn my head and a blaster is pointed right in my face.

"I'll give you a good price," says the man-thing holding it. He turns it sideways for a better view. "You're gonna need it, pretty pretty. Gotta protect yourself, y'know? Got us some untrustworthy types round here." He cackles.

I flash the one I'm packing. He scurries off to the next mark.

My head's throbbing. I can't get enough air. I'm starting to wheeze.

Livia, I think. All that rich Upper atmosphere, she can't be better off. These scavs are making me mighty protective.

I spot Kane first. He's pushing through a huddle of half-naked women. They giggle, blow him kisses. "New in town?" says one. "Let me give you a private tour." She reaches out, runs a finger down his cheek.

Marley pushes between them. "Leave the kid alone," he says, shoving Kane forward.

There's Samantha crouched in front of a little girl missing her right arm. The girl babbles excitedly. Glad to have someone listen. Samantha says something, ruffles the girl's hair, and rises. She hasn't lost her touch.

"Don't get distracted," says Zavier gruffly.

"I can't find Livia," I say.

"She's fine. She's got someone watching her. Not much more of this anyway. Now stay focused. I mean it. Stay focused or you'll screw this up for everyone."

I whip my head to face him. He's looking at me like I'm lower than dirt. Lower than Rock Bottom itself. He's almost snarling.

I hate him. Every inch of him.

We're getting muscled by passing scavs. He grabs my arm. "What's got into you?"

I shove him away and lose him in the crowd.

I get grabbed for like the fifth time. They've got no sense of personal space. I try to pull myself away, but I can't. The hand is massive; it's fisted around my biceps. Before I can shout to the others, before I can do anything, another hand covers my mouth and I'm being pulled backward. It happens so quickly I can barely think.

I'm dragged through the door of one of the scrap hovels and thrown on the dirt floor. Before I can draw my blaster, I'm staring down the long barrel of a ventilator. At least, that's what everyone in SpecOps calls it because it leaves such large, nasty holes. Though he's wrapped in a tattered gray cloak, I can see his SpecOps-silitex-enhanced body armor beneath it. His faceplate is a mutated orange skull on a field of chipped black. If this man ever truly served on Rock Bottom Patrol, he looks like he's gone completely core-low native.

"Are you a rebel?" he says. "If you've turned your back that fully on your oath, I will blast you into the stinking mud."

"No," I practically spit.

"Only the unworthy dwell down here." He doesn't take the ventilator off me. "SpecOps Lex, you have been found derelict of your duty. You have stolen PCF craft and made illegal incursions on Helix Island, on a mutinous rig, and in the chambers of the High Council."

"Are you really SpecOps?" I say.

"You do not know me. Know only that your penalty for treason is death."

"I'm not a rebel," I say. "Whatever you think, I'm not that."

The ventilator hums so much, all I can think of is Livia's damn singing sword. Must every weapon cry before it kills?

"You want me to lead you to their base?" I say.

"I will kill you, then find it myself."

I look at him and I cannot believe that this is where my future would have led if I hadn't committed every crime he's accused me of.

"I'm not a rebel—on the oath I swore, I am not. But I believe someone within the High Council has ordered the death of the Helix Island airess, and possibly my own by this point, and the rebels have answers. Answers that I need to know. Will you at least hear me out?"

His breath rasps beneath his faceplate. The ventilator is so close I could kiss it. And it would return my kiss with death.

"Please. Tell me your name."

"Lieutenant Hauser. D Troop."

The name almost shocks me up onto my feet, but I know if I move, the ventilator will bark. "I knew a Hauser. He spoke to me at the Academy. You spoke to us after the rebels attacked the Hub. One hundred and twenty-two dead. If you think that truly I've forgotten those people, or the oath I swore to protect them, then kill me now."

I push my forehead against his ventilator.

If this world is at all worth living in, if not all the PCF are corrupt, then this won't be my end.

Then I remember how off my judgment's been the past few days, and how it's all led me to be in this position, seated in the dirt miles below the surface, closer to the core than I've ever been before, and I'm terribly, terribly scared.

With my eyes closed, all I see is darkness.

CHAPTER 37

Lex

I open my eyes when I can no longer feel the ventilator's touch between them. Hauser holds it by his side. He motions me up.

"I will follow you," he says. "At any moment, if I feel you betray me, I will kill you and everyone who stands by your side. Do you understand?"

I nod.

"You will bring me to the Rebel Base. After that, you will be brought back for judgment before the Court of Honors, but your assistance here could help sway their judgment. Aside from that, your only other option is death. Know that I need no other companion than death, and he is forever by my side."

Standing just feet away from him in this barren hovel that smells of rot and sulfur, I see that his hands are scarred and blistered. He doesn't take his eyes off of me, and I wonder, if this is the same man I met years ago, what he hides beneath his faceplate. Could it be more monstrous than this face he chooses to present?

He opens the door just wide enough for me to slip through, and I'm relieved to be back in the throng of scavs along the boulevard.

I don't know what will come of this bargain. I have saved my own life, but put others in danger. I'm still SpecOps, that remains my sworn allegiance, but this world is more complicated than blind duty affords. I push my way through the pack and try not to look over my shoulder.

It is to my relief that I find Samantha first.

"Have you seen Livia?" I ask.

"She's with Chae. But you really shouldn't be alone. Where's 7?"

"Who cares where that jerk is," I say.

She smiles. "He's stubborn, for sure. Just stay with me, okay?"

Her face is full of kindness. I nod, feeling about six years old. When we get there, I may just take her up on her earlier offer to braid my hair. It for sure could use it. And then I remember that Hauser may consider her a rebel, too. I look behind me but don't see his massive frame. He is too good to be spotted so easily.

Navigating the free-for-all is easier with her. She's comfortable here and doesn't fight against the crowd like I do. She's part of it. "It's not so bad," she says. "It's rough, but there's beautiful places, too. I'll show you. Wouldn't it be nice to have a new start?"

I hang on to her words. I want to believe in what she says. A place to stop running. It feels like a make-believe. It usually is.

I just can't turn that alert side of me off. I can't see the good in these people here. The world is divided, even down here.

I stick my fingers in my ears for just a second. My flaw means I'm hearing everything way too loudly. This massive wall of noise. It masks the danger we're in.

It could even mask blaster fire.

Livia

The crowd's trying to trample me. I don't know if it's the change in oxygen levels down here or just the air quality, but I'm getting light-headed. I make it a priority to draw in deep breathes, but even hugging the side of the marketplace, I keep getting knocked about, the scav's sweaty flesh pressing against me as they fall, the smell intensified by their fear. They don't mean to kill me, but they will if I continue to do nothing.

They're scurrying, trying to get to safety. And I still can't pinpoint what's causing the panic.

Everyone was just fighting for my attention; now they're just fighting.

I lose myself, trying to understand the words jabbering out of all their mouths. There's a hard tug on my elbow.

"C'mon," Marley says. He's not messing about.

Then I hear a sound that no human could make and lose track of what I was doing and only want to flee. Marley is far ahead of me already, his legs carrying him fast in the opposite direction. Will time reveal all these rebels to be such cowards?

The second howl doesn't come as much of a surprise, even more savage and desperate. It hungers. It has hungered before. What sort of creature has been bred down here?

As the scavs thin out, my focus is drawn through the fog to the creature wading through the strangers, a head taller than any of these cave dwellers.

I have never seen a more hideous creature, not in the Archives, not even in my imagination. Perhaps somewhere in the layers of time, its genetics started off as human, but it has mutated into a nightmarish beast. Its face droops and is swollen and bulbous, its hair only stringy patches. Its flesh is riddled with sores from the shoulders down. It opens the cavity of its mouth—a black cave of spittle and rot—and screams again.

The scream is answered by another. And another. Their fractured voices have shattered the Safe Zone with thunder. They're hunting us. Always something is hunting us.

Move, I think, yet my legs won't obey. The first creature spots me, its motions no longer aimless. It holds a rust-eaten harpoon, which it lifts over its shoulder as it aims.

A mutation. That's the word for this thing. That is the name on the scavs' mouths, the same as the name of my death. Blaster fire erupts, and I can only assume it is Zavier and the rebels coming to our defense. But this blaster sounds unlike any I have ever heard, booming through the cavern. Rock blows out from the walls and the surviving mutations roar even louder.

I should draw my zinger. I should. I really should.

The harpoon goes flying, quicker than I can grab my next breath. It will spear me, then drag me back to its feet for . . . feeding?

My legs give out as someone shoves me down from behind. Woozy, I pull myself to my feet. The harpoon has missed me and plunged deep into the chest of another. The mutation drags its victim toward it, leaving a trail of blood behind. The creature roars. The body bumps across the rocky terrain.

I dash toward the harpoon line. I grab the line in front of the body and pull it with all my might.

The mutation howls at me defiantly, the other end of the line held in its grasp. The cord burns my palms as we struggle for control.

I pull the zinger from under my cloak and strike the taut line.

The creature falls backward, landing with an impact I feel under my feet. It moans and tosses itself from side to side, a writhing mass struggling to get back on the disfigured stumps it uses for feet. It will get there if I let it. It has survived this long in the toxic wastelands; it will always find a way.

I sprint at the fallen creature. The zinger plays furiously, my first full melody, a moment for which I should feel accomplished, as the mutation's monstrous head separates from its body.

Lex, I think, as it rolls over toward my feet, *what have I done?*

CHAPTER 38

Lex

Hauser's ventilator nearly deafens me. I see him light up a mutation, and it explodes along an upper ridge. I quickly draw my blaster and get him in my sights. Hauser, you can't miss him, is drawing down on another mutation, marching along the same boulevard that we entered from. It's long and lean and its face is all exposed bone. I could take it out, but this might be my only chance at Hauser. I've got him right in my sights.

I pull the trigger.

My blaster doesn't fire. I keep pulling the trigger and nothing's happening. My blaster's got no charge left. In fact, it doesn't even have an energy clip. Someone must have . . .

Hauser . . .

He's already blasted the second mutation when I hear the third's death cry. It distracts me, and Hauser sees that I intended to gun him down and he's in the wind. I made my choice, and now, someone has paid for it. I wasn't there to protect her.

The scav cowards crawl out of their hiding holes. They all want to get a good look. The harpoon is still lodged firmly in her back, and I can't remove it until I'm sure how badly she's hurt. The rocky soil collects the blood leaking from the wound, and the puddle keeps growing larger.

Samantha.

The best I can do is roll her onto her side. I take her pulse and it's weak, but I swear I can feel something.

"You're fine," I say. "We'll get you patched up and . . ."

Her eyes start to close.

I yell Livia's name. She's knocking past the gawkers and fighting her way to me.

She kneels beside me and lays her hands on Samantha's body. I hold Samantha's head in my lap. Blood leaks from her mouth to my hand. She's growing colder. Livia's hands won't stay still and I know something's not right. She takes the harpoon out slowly and . . . I can see Samantha's life leaking out. Livia gets her hands right in and she's trying to help, tears of frustration working up, but, "She's dead."

I push her out of the way and lay my hands over the wound. There must be something I can do, some way to pull her back together. The only warmth I feel is her blood

Then I'm crying. Out there for all to see. I don't care. I'm crying and I don't try to stop.

Livia wraps her arms around me from behind. "I am so sorry, Lex," she whispers into my ear.

"No!"

"Yes," she says. "You have to let her go now."

Samantha believed there was beauty here. She was wrong. There is only death. There is nothing worth saving.

I bury my face in Livia's cloak, sobbing like a child. She rocks me.

"We need . . . to take the . . . body," I blubber. I can feel the scavs approaching. I won't let them take more from her than they've already got.

"We will," she says. "We will do it together."

Through my tears I see one, a small one, stroking Samantha's hair. It's the little girl with one arm. She pushes 374's hair back with her one hand. She cleans the blood from Samantha's lifeless face with a rag.

There are others who gather around her body, seeing to her appearance. Children, all of them. One takes the cloak from his back and wraps it around her. These disfigured children see to her dignity in a way I didn't think possible.

They all have genetic flaws. One is missing an eye. A ruby scar winds across the bridge of another's nose to the side of her neck. There are misshapen teeth in their cracked mouths and one has a cleft palate. Freckles and birthmarks, more than I can count.

In the Islands, this is all cosmetic work. But these guys never had access to that tech. They wouldn't have lasted a day in the Orphanage. In fact, they probably didn't. Maybe they were sent back here, just like Samantha. Maybe they never got to leave in the first place.

The adults stay away, but the children keep coming to pay their respects. How many has she helped?

The one with one arm takes my hand and strokes it with her soft little thumb.

"Don't worry," she tells me. "We'll take her somewhere she liked. A pretty place. She'll rest there forever and ever." She stares at me and her eyes are very clear and blue.

"Don't cry anymore. She wouldn't have wanted that, Lex."

I look down, shocked. "How did you know my name?"

"Samantha told us you were coming. That you'd be able to help us more than she could even hope to."

CHAPTER 39

Livia

The Safe Zone is deserted now, which makes our escape faster. It's still horribly unwelcoming, and we must watch out for more mutations.

At the far border, the neon dies and the dark caverns hide evidence of old settlements and the old battles fought over them. There are still residents, but they don't emerge as we pass through. They live alone for reasons we don't need to question, and it should be left that way.

Zavier moves quickly. I race to keep up, grabbing Lex and pulling hard, afraid we might lose him for good.

Lex doesn't argue. She's gone somewhere else.

And I know, if I don't distract him, Zavier could leave us as well. He's taking Samantha's death about as well as Lex. We cannot keep running. We have already lost Kane and Roscoe and the rest in our flight. We're left to hope for the best, but already I prepare for the worst.

"How did it become that way?" I ask.

"Chemical contamination. Toxic waste. Where do you think Indra sends it? Every day more are corrupted and babies are born with defects. That mutation was probably just born that way, their broken genetics damaged long ago in their lineage. The way they fight, I almost feel they were here first. I can take you to see them if you're so concerned. But even Samantha didn't have the heart for that."

"Indra has clean-burning fuel. Radioactive materials have been banned since the Great Catastrophe," I say.

"You can eat up all that make-believe you like. Your air may be clean, but the core is getting hotter. The Earth's just dying from the inside now. That way, you can't see it as good from up in the air. It's time for you to stop thinking about yourself for once."

"I wasn't aware."

"So let me make you be more aware. Anything undesirable goes here. And the people who live here? They matter even less. And that, citizen of the great and honorable Indra, is the gift you've given us." His hate tires him out. "Does that answer your question?"

Before I know it, Lex snatches Zavier up by his collar. "What do you know, you arrogant, pompous ass? What do you know about *my* people? Or me, for that matter?"

I have never seen her this furious, and Lex, as I have come to realize, does not save her fury for special occasions.

"I know what you're capable of," he says, screaming right back. "I know that you kill without batting an eyelash!"

"In cold blood, yes, exactly as we were taught. We kill Emils and Alicias and Samanthas without regard."

"Exactly!" he bellows. "Finally! You admit it! You'd already blown his craft to pieces, but it wasn't enough. So you landed right there—"

"You're a maniac."

"In fact, *stole* one of our crafts, after you'd already broken treaty in *our* territory."

"Your territory?!"

"He's protecting the only territory we have and you and your rebel-hating compatriots take him out. By the time you land, he's trapped in his own craft, and what do you do? Someone gives the orders to blast him right in his scav head!"

They stare at each other.

"Hey," I say, seeing my chance, "perhaps it would be wise to take a moment and—"

"I wasn't there," she says, ignoring me. "I didn't give any orders. I was an apprentice on monitor. I saw the ship lying in wait and told them where it was. Before *they* got blasted. I didn't pull the trigger! End of story."

He glares at her, and I sense him wanting to believe what she's saying. But there are old wounds rising to the surface; he cannot trust her, even if he wants to.

I realize she's forcing herself to remain calm and reasonable. "An enemy craft? Look. An apprentice doesn't plan missions. I didn't even know who the enemies even were yet."

"You should always know your enemy."

"I would've done things differently, okay? If I'd planned that mission."

"Exactly," he says. "*That* mission. There's been more since. They're probably planning one right now. To come down here and do away with anyone who crosses their path. Guilty or not. That's the mission, isn't it? *Your* mission." He shakes his head. "You have a lot to be proud of, Lex. You can kill without remorse."

So much for being reasonable.

"Do you think you're the only one who's ever lost someone?" She pummels his chest, but he's stronger, gripping her wrists and holding them to her sides.

I feel her pain course through me, watch her fight against restraints she cannot break. I want to run over, jump between them.

I use every bit of strength I have not to.

I have battles I don't want her to fight for me, and she doesn't want me in this one.

This had to happen, I tell myself, *and now you must allow it to run its course.*

"Samantha," she says, breaking down. "I had her, after all those years. I had her back. And now she's gone."

"I lost her too, okay?" says Zavier. "I lost her too. . . ."

Lex stops fighting, and he eases up his grip, but doesn't let go. "Lex," he says. She turns her head away. He chases her gaze until she has nowhere else to look. I can see where there should be a bond deepening between them, to be filled with grief that they can share. But they are too hardheaded to acknowledge that neither's pain is greater, that each is dealing with the same thing.

"She was my friend," Lex says.

"She was my sister," says Zavier softly. "Once we found each other, I always looked out for her down here, and now she is gone, gone forever."

CHAPTER 40

Lex

She was my sister.

"How's that possible?" I say, pulling away from Zavier. "Siblings are illegal."

"This is Rock Bottom," he says. "Nothing's illegal. There's no EX2 pill. Some siblings even have different fathers or mothers. And some are just left on their own. There's no *Book of Indra* telling us what to do. We already know what to do. Survive." He shakes his head, his face hard. "You are so naive," he tells me.

I can't think of anything to say. I hate that he's right.

After that, he doesn't speak. Neither do I. Livia starts to say something, but one look from me shuts her up quick.

The tunnel we travel on eventually becomes a street, just like I saw in the Final Sim, except no church, and the residents are right out in the open. It looks safe, but I hold my blaster like a club just in case. Hauser's out there, I know it.

We follow Zavier, past places with signs like "Old Town Electrodes" and "Bargain Rations and Blasters." We catch the curiosity of everyone we pass.

"Ignore them," Zavier says. *You had a sister*, I think. "They won't bother us. They're sympathetic to our fight." *You had a sister, just like me.*

He stops outside the Red Dog Saloon. "This is the place you were brought here to see."

◊　◊　◊

There's a long table along one wall. Behind it, a woman pours thick liquid from a bottle. A sign hangs above her head: "Dirt Fuel by the Glass."

He brought us all this way for a drink?

On the other side of the table, every stool is occupied, almost shoulder to shoulder. A half-dressed woman sprawls across an old man's lap. His beard reaches the floor and she twirls it with her fingers, laughing. Two men hold cards. One slaps down a handful and the other groans.

A little man at the far end notices us and his eyes widen. "They're here!" he yells.

The lady stops twirling the old man's beard. The men look up from their game.

"C'mon," says Zavier, ignoring the new attention the loudmouth got us as we pass. Zavier smacks the tar wall with his fist. Two taps of his elbow to the left, a swift kick to the right.

The wall relaxes. A door swings open a half inch and he pushes it open the rest of the way.

Better than a sim, I think, though I'd never tell him. In fact, the idea of speaking to Zavier is just too much for me.

We head down a rocky tunnel, and I start hearing footsteps that aren't ours. I glance over my shoulder and see that they're following us. All of them. Some still clutching their glasses of green brew. We've become curiosities to them. Don't they realize following us could get them killed? It's not up to me to change their minds. Maybe, just maybe, we owe them something more.

We continue to descend and at the end we reach another wall. *Smack, tap-tap, kick.*

Just like that, we are on the inside of the Rebel Base. Now we get to see what the fuss is all about.

◊   ◊   ◊

Hundreds of feet above our heads, the cavern finally crests. At intervals, there are levels cut into the rock, which signify the progress of their forebearers in the long, long ago. The surfaces are worn and smoothed by age. There is a warren of passageways that disguise the true inner workings of this place. We are wound through one and another; perhaps they're trying to disorient us, I'm not sure. Trust must extend both ways, I understand. No matter where we pass, I get peeks into these rebels' lives. They are not all warriors. They're just people. They're a community.

Some stock and organize their supplies. Nearby there are those that prepare food, food that looks nothing like rations, that has color. There are those that mend clothing and patch uniforms and repair blasters. Some of the young train together and practice combat exercises. Their classmates sit on the sidelines and observe. In rooms we can't see, I'm sure some sleep and dream in this place that has no days or nights, just like how I grew up. But there is the greater hope that here children have room to play and be happy.

Then I hear a note, and thankfully it isn't from a singing sword.

A man holds an instrument. He runs his hands across the strings and its face, and the melody soothes me in a way I have never experienced. He sings and people gather to listen to him in an intimate dining area. I want to sit down before him.

Next to me, Livia is breathing faster. She's as stunned as I am.

"Lex! Livia!" Kane flags us down and leaves the area to join us. "I was worried."

"I'm fine," Livia says. "We're both okay."

"I lost you. And then I heard there were mutations and I didn't know if—"

"Look at me," she says, holding her hands up for him to see. "In one piece."

His panic turns to relief. Then something else. An expression I've never seen, not even for me. He takes her hand and she squeezes his back.

Fury is bubbling up inside me. My face is hot with it. *He's mine*, I think. *Kane belongs to me. Who are you to just come in and snatch him?*

I break them apart by hugging him so hard he's forced to drop her hand to keep his balance. He doesn't need her, not as much as he needs me.

Not as much as I need him.

She's had everything she wanted her whole damn life. But the airgirl can't have . . .

"It's okay, Lex," Kane says, and I can feel all my emotions colliding so hard I can't even tell what I'm reacting to anymore, and I hide my face in his shoulder. "We've made it. We're finally here."

When I look up, I'm looking right at Zavier—and he's looking back.

Instantly, every hair on my arms rises. My face goes from hot to burning. I don't have control anymore. Not over my words or my own body.

Now Livia is staring at me. I wish everyone would just stop. I turn away so no one can see my face. I turn toward the cavern.

That's when I notice they're watching me. Us. They're staring at Livia and me.

All of them. Every face in the core-low cavern. They've emptied into the hall and watch us and whisper. The whispers are rising.

"I think that will do," Roscoe booms. "This is a momentous occasion, I know, but our visitors have had a long and difficult journey. Let us allow them time to adjust." They murmur in agreement and go back to pretending to ignore us.

I still feel their glances, shot from the corners of their eyes. They talk, just as before, but I'm pretty sure the discussions have taken a new direction.

"Enough!" I say. My outburst surprises them. "No more of this. No more talking like I'm not here. Like I'm not right in front of you." I look at Livia. "Like *we* aren't right in front of you."

"You must understand—"

"I *must* do nothing, Roscoe. I've already taken enough of your orders. Let you put a spike in my head, gone through your so-called *Safe* Zone and watched my friend die. Now I want answers. And someone better give them to me, or *we'll* be out of here before you have time to argue."

I look at Livia. She nods. "Yes," she says calmly. "We have proven our strength and survived, both with and without you. So perhaps now you will fulfill your end of the agreement."

"So," I say, tearing the cloak from my shoulders and tossing it aside. "Where do we start? Because my sister and I have some *serious questions*."

I hadn't planned to say it. It just fell out of my mouth.

Sister.

CHAPTER 41

Livia

My sister.

I have never known anyone who has a sister, or a brother. How these relationships are managed have never been illustrated for me. The depth of the bond and what our obligations to each other are cannot be anticipated. However, now I can see that protectiveness is one of them.

I understand that, while how she feels about me at any given moment will change, we will forever share something that no one else does.

We are bonded, whether we like it or not.

Kane is Lex's friend, I know that. And yet I reached for him because that is exactly what I wanted to do. I held his hand, and if she were not there, I would've done more.

She's my sister, but she won't dictate my actions. I have spent a lifetime having others tell me how to live, and now that lifetime is over. I feel Kane's eyes on me. I'm not shy about looking at him, either.

However, it's hard to ignore Lex at this very moment. She's standing there with her hands on her hips. "Are you ready, then? Are you ready to answer our questions?"

Roscoe gives a deep sigh, then nods. "Yes. That is only fair. But we should conduct ourselves in private. Follow me. I'm sorry," he says to Kane, "but it's best if you wait here for now. Zavier, show him where he can get something to eat. We've all had a long journey."

Kane grabs my hand. "I'll be all right," I tell him. "After all, you are the only one here who's tried to kill me." I don't bother to mention my altercation with Lex earlier.

He's ashamed, I can tell. He should be.

Yet at this moment I want him to surprise me with a kiss. As soon as I'm sure he won't try to poison me again, he wouldn't dare, I would kiss him back and hold it until I'm satisfied. Perhaps if I made the first move?

Lex glares at me. Let her do that all she wants. It won't change a thing about how I feel or what I want.

I follow Lex and Roscoe, though I allow myself one last look at Kane. His lip curls into a smile.

Improper. Most Improper.

Some things *are* better down here.

It's constantly warm here. We no longer need cloaks. There's a ventilation system that circulates the air and keeps the electrical systems from overheating, but it's a far cry from the climate-controlled islands.

Roscoe leads us through a tunnel that glows with fluorescent lichen and moss. It has been cultivated into long strips and circular patches that provide constant illumination. "We try to avoid excessive energy use," Roscoe explains. "Our mechanical systems are severely outdated, and a dampened heat signature prevents our detection, especially this far into the planet's heat wells."

The meeting room is circular, its floor a collection of area rugs. At the center are comfortable-looking reposers. They're upholstered with fabrics I have never seen. I run my fingers along one covered with the softest deep blue material, and I feel a wave of exhaustion. I imagine, for just a moment, spreading out across the softness and closing my eyes and escaping everything—mutations and blasters and parazips and rebels. I have never felt exhaustion like this before.

Of course, this is not possible. I know they would still be there in my dreams, overtaking me. The faces of the fallen on both sides: Hep, Durley, Jefferson. The dead PCF, zinger cutting through his chest, sprawled beneath the holo-image of my father.

Samantha.

I'm reminded of their sacrifices.

I turn to Lex for comfort, and that's when I see what she sees: books.

Entire shelves of them, arranged so neatly, in every size and color imaginable. Some are dusty and ancient-looking, others as though they have never been opened. Books that have never even been touched! I have a feeling *The Book of Indra* is not among them.

"My study," says Roscoe, smiling at me. "And please, my dears, make yourselves feel at home."

"Roscoe," I say. "Lex and Livia are more appropriate."

"Of course."

"Can we start already?" Lex says.

"By all means," Roscoe replies.

"Since you took that thing out of my head, something's different."

"As is normal. By placing a chip in that certain location of your cortex, the IHC believes they can control certain emotions, like joy, and can then release the amount they deem fitting."

"They really control how much *joy* I feel?"

"Yes," he says. "Too much, they believe, is dangerous. Though they feel the same about too little."

I feel the horror rising up inside me.

"They control pain in the same manner. Now, Livia has already felt those emotions. And so have you, Lex. Just to a slightly lesser degree."

"And now I'm normal? Is that what you're saying?" Lex asks.

"Those last few blocks have been removed, along with your chip. Now you will feel more depth of emotion. Your happiness more extrome, your sadness more intense. Removing the chip has made you who you truly are. At the core. As for normal, here is my assessment: you will never be that. And neither will you, Livia. Normal is not in your genetic makeup. You were both unique from the moment you were conceived."

"That's what I wish to know," I say, my voice shaking. "About being born. About my mother and father. Our mother and father. How it came to pass—"

"That you were sentenced to an island prison?" he asks. "And Lex to the darkness below?"

"Exactly," I say. Now my hands are shaking as well. Every part of me, especially my insides, jangling with energy.

"I have been waiting to answer those questions," he says, reaching into his sleeve, "for longer than you could possibly know."

He holds something in his open palm.

"Archive access chips," Lex says softly.

"The only ones, I believe, in the entirety of Rock Bottom. They are my most valuable possessions. Ones for which I would give my life."

"What are they?" asks Lex.

"Memories," says Roscoe. "I have kept them all these years. Kept them for the two of you. To be presented upon your arrival."

"You knew we would come?" I ask.

"It was in your natures to seek the truth. And I have been here to make sure you found it. Here," he says, holding up chips, "let me just show you."

I'm spread out across the reposer. It's as comfortable as I imagined.

Sleeping, though, is the last thing on my mind.

Roscoe sits to my left, Lex in a chair across from me. Her body is rigid, her face tense with worry. We have each built up stories in our heads on how this is supposed to go. Who we are supposed to be. Who our parents were. Answers we've searched for our entire lives—even if we didn't know it consciously—are here and it worries us both. The truth isn't always welcomed.

Each of us holds an access chip in our cupped hands. Roscoe has violated another of Indra's rules and duplicated a citizen's memories.

"Shall we?" he asks.

"Yes," says Lex.

Perhaps I nod, but I cannot be sure, for the room is spinning with my excitement, my head and body throbbing with anticipation.

"Then let us enter," he says, "into your father's memory. It is time you met him."

Lean back. Two quick taps. Thumb to wrist.

The last thing I see is Lex. We are there for each other, at this moment when we need it most.

Ready?

Yes. You?

Yes.

Now?

Now.

Then we close our eyes.

CHAPTER 42

Lex

A bright room, a woman sitting alone, back turned toward us. Her hands flutter through the air, releasing waves of color and music. The colors are dark, the song sad.

I move toward her.

"Stop," says Roscoe. "Any closer and we will be flung."

"Is she . . ." I can barely say the word.

"Our mother," says Livia. "At her air harp."

A man enters. Armand Cosmo, our father. Handsome as his portrait. He moves to our mother and puts a hand on her shoulder. At his touch, she slumps. The music stops and the colors dissipate. As he begins speaking, she stares into the colorless void.

"Why can't we hear them?" I ask.

"Perhaps your father extracted the voices," says Roscoe. "Perhaps this memory is too painful and he blocked out some of the details to preserve its integrity. The science is tricky."

"But how will we know what they are saying? How will we know when they—"

I stop suddenly. The woman looks up, and I see her face for the first time.

Even through the tears, she is beautiful.

"You have her eyes," says Livia.

"I was about to say the same about you."

Then everything fades.

Darkness.

We are somewhere new, and our mother is gone.

I had her for a few seconds, but now she has disappeared once more. There is a hollow ache in my chest, an empty spot, and I realize it has been there as long as I can remember.

I have never allowed myself to feel it before now. I do not have to look at Livia to know she feels something similar.

We are in some sort of lab, though it's small and a bit cramped. The place is cluttered with machines and monitors, a table of glass tubes swirling with liquid. Holocharts line the walls and a pair of men's shoes are carelessly left in the middle of the floor.

"Our hideout," says Roscoe, his voice sweet with nostalgia. "We built this when we were children."

"You knew each other as children?" I ask.

"Our whole life," he says. "From neighboring islands. This is where we did our early experiments. Armand's parents, your grandparents, encouraged us, when they weren't perturbed by our occasionally explosive results." He chuckles to himself. "We both ended up geneticists, but Armand was always the brilliant one. And this is where he escaped to do his most important work. A lab we built beneath the ground, with their permission. After the EX2, the High Council would've funded his every whim, a new lab with a view of the gardens was only the beginning, but he was cautious not to become indebted to them."

"And you?" asks Livia.

"I found minor success in enhancements to keep my skills relevant, pictograms and the like."

"Designer birthmarks?" Livia asks. "That was you?"

"'Express your Individuality,'" he recites bitterly. "'The only genetic flaw you will actually want!' Until they were outlawed, of course."

"Fascinating," I say dryly, circling the room for the fifteenth time.

"Your father evolved the field and pushed the boundaries beyond what anyone thought possible. But still he had time for me and a few others, to discuss our endeavors and help us, of course. It was only luck that granted me such a genius for a best friend and mentor."

"And where is he now, exactly?" she says.

"Look," says Roscoe calmly, "and you will see for yourself."

Our father has entered with long, confident strides.

"This is much earlier," says Roscoe, "before your mother and the air harp."

"How can you tell?" asks Livia.

Roscoe laughs. "His hair. He wore it like that when he was young. One of his proudest possessions. He could've grown rich just by enhancing the heads of others, myself included."

As though my father has heard, he runs his hand through the strands distractedly. He does have nice hair. Thick and shiny and dark, just like Livia and me. Only his is wild and untamed like mine.

Livia

Our father moves about like the ruler of a kingdom, like a man with answers. He checks a chart and adds a few notations. His penmanship is horrid. He catches his reflection in a beaker and quickly runs a hand through his shiny mop, smiling.

"I speak the truth," says Roscoe. "The women loved it, too. In fact, they loved everything about him." Father removes a test tube from a rack and sets it in a machine that, when powered on, spins wildly. When it stops, the liquid in the tube has been separated into two distinct colors. "He was invited to every Emergence Ball in Upper Indra. He teased the girls. Flirted. Made them fall in love. Yet ultimately, they bored him."

He carefully pours the top layer into a funnel, where it flows through piping into a small analyzer. It beeps and he checks the monitor. Unsatisfied with what he has seen, he bites his bottom lip and paces the room.

"Until, of course, he met Delphia. Your mother."

Father looks up with gleaming eyes and races to a chart and crosses out his newest notations. He scribbles around their edges and, upon observing his work, grants himself a self-satisfied smile.

"One look at Delphia and he was finished. The other Proper Young Women became as interesting to your father as the air his island floated upon."

Darkness.

We are in a dressing parlor, our mother clicking a device. The soft surface beneath our feet goes from red to gold. Another click and we are standing on intricate tiles.

This is an important night, I can tell, and everything must be *just right*.

She strokes a blue garment, and it shimmers beneath her hand. Now she's at her floating vanity, running a colorizer across her lips. They turn bright blue and she wrinkles her nose at the reflection. Changes them back to their natural rosy hue.

"Never one for fads, Delphia," says Roscoe. "Not even minor enhancements."

Another face appears in the reflection, startling her.

Our father, a devilish grin across his face. She swats him hard, laughing, and takes the colorizer to his lips. Instantly, they are a neon orange. He swipes the instrument from her and turns them back, though he's also laughing.

She pins up her hair and he watches, mesmerized.

"He adored her," says Roscoe, a longing just under his words. Armand was probably not the only one.

Our mother turns her face to our father and waits to be kissed.

Darkness.

A massive ballroom, and we are at the center of its polished dance floor. "Their New Cohabitation Gala," says Roscoe. He is staring at someone and I follow his gaze.

Young Roscoe, captivated by the presence in the room, perhaps more than everyone else. We are momentarily blinded by a swirl of enchanting blue. Our father has whirled our mother past us.

They are what everyone is watching, and the reason is obvious: they are beautiful together.

Her head is thrown back in pleasure, her gown swirling around them like an aqua cloud.

I want to look at her forever.

Darkness.

"Slow it down!" I say frantically.

"I wish I could," says Roscoe.

Mother and Father sit in a garden, framed by blooming lemon trees. They have been newly programmed by the gardeners, I can tell, the fruit plentiful, their fragrance sharp and sweet.

I know their location, a spot deep within the orchards, a place where I spent many hours hiding from the demands of Governess.

Mother and Father have aged quickly, or perhaps it is just the dimness in their eyes.

Mother is crying. Father holds her hands, but she won't listen. She turns from his touch with a violent shake of her head.

"Please, Armand!" she says.

Lex and I look at each other, stunned. Her voice enhances and defies her delicacy. Lilting and powerful at the very same moment. It's mannered like mine, with all the anger of Lex's.

"Armand. Listen to me. I do not ask for much, and this is the only thing I want in the entire world. Nothing else matters."

"If they find out—"

"They will not find out," she says firmly

"We will lose everything," he finishes. My mother has tears in her eyes, but she is too strong to release them. My father holds her in his arms.

"I would do anything for you, Delphia. You know that. But you must know the consequences."

She removes herself from his touch. "I do not care about *consequences*! Everything in Indra has consequences. The IHC would punish you for breathing incorrectly if they 'Deemed It Inappropriate'!"

"They will take the things you love most if they find out," he says. "Helix. Veda. They will take *me*, Delphia. Everything."

"They will not find out. We will make sure of it."

"The highest crime is blatant disobedience against the IHC."

"The highest crime will be if I cannot have a child."

She draws farther away, the space between them growing larger.

"You blame me," he says quietly. "You blame me for creating the EX2. You believe I did this to you. That it made you unable to conceive. But that is not the cause of this. I promise you. I would never create anything that did harm. This happened . . . for some other reason. A reason I have yet to understand. Please do not blame me. I only want to make you happy."

"It does not matter who I blame," she says. "The only thing that matters is who fixes it."

She takes his hands, and I see that she has the power to make the smartest man in Indra doubt his judgment.

"Please say yes, Armand. Please, my love."

Darkness.

Wait, I want to say. *I don't understand!*

No time to speak, for we are back in the lab, only it has changed. The charts are illegible, overrun with his scrawl. The water baths are overflowing with contaminated beakers and plates with half-eaten rations or aborted experiments, it's too hard to determine which.

Our father circles the room. He's changed as well: attire wrinkled, hair growing on his face, his smug smile replaced with defeat.

"What happened?" I ask. Roscoe doesn't answer. Lex watches our father with deep concentration.

"He is doing this for her," she says.

"But why?"

"A child," Roscoe says. "That was all she ever dreamed of. And somehow, it would not happen. A genetic flaw, perhaps."

Father sits in his chair and rolls up his left sleeve. He ties a length of rubber tubing around his biceps and punctures a vein with a needle. Bloods flows through some piping into one vial, then another. All the while he puzzles over formulae on his tablet. Another vial fills and another. That is where he hopes to find his answer. Within himself.

"He will not stop," says Roscoe, "until he finds a solution. A genetic enhancement that will allow her to conceive."

Darkness.

A dim room, our mother sitting motionless, eyes screwed tight with concentration. To her left, our father holds a syringe full of thick liquid.

She is not concentrating, I think. *She is praying.*

He injects her.

Darkness.

Everything is moving too quickly. The memories are hurtling straight for us, becoming more agitated and frantic by the second. Melting into each other so fast there is no darkness or light, just a faint grayish overcast.

Our mother, face glowing, with a hand on her belly. The hand belongs to our father, and he smiles as wide as she does.

Darkness.

Our father at his monitor, projections of the two fetuses growing within her womb.

Darkness.

Our mother at her air harp, belly enormous on her slender frame. The melody soft and lovely, her hands releasing crystalline shades of rose, the pinks punctuated by sudden bursts of crimson. Her eyes are closed, her smile blissful.

Darkness.

CHAPTER 43

Lex

A curtain divides the lab. My father pours water on a white towel. He hurries behind the curtain where our mother, I strongly suspect, breathes sharply. It's punctuated by cries of pain.

The cries become screams. Livia and I are causing her pain. This is our birth.

Darkness.

We're still in the lab. Young Roscoe stands patiently on the other side of the curtain.

Roscoe observes his younger self, their expressions equally pained. Men who have no reason to celebrate.

Our father slips through the curtains, removing his wrinkled and stained gown. His skin is colorless, his eyes ringed with exhaustion. Our father doesn't look like a man who has achieved the impossible.

"Are they healthy?" Roscoe asks.

He nods. "And beautiful."

Darkness.

A baby cries, woken from its sleep.

"She knows it's time," he tells Roscoe. "The imprint and then you must go."

Father pulls back the curtain. Mother is huddled on a sleeper, a baby clutched in each arm. It can only have been days, their flesh still pink. They've only had days as a family.

Father bends down and takes a baby, which my mother kisses

before she lets go of it forever. "We have to hurry," he says, "or it will be too late."

Father passes the child to Roscoe. *That's me. Little Lex.* I gurgle in Roscoe's arms. This was the end of our only time together. Mother clutches the other baby tighter. She rests her chin against the small head, tears falling on tufts of brown hair.

My father unwraps her arm and carefully takes Livia as well. Now her arms are empty. My mother buries her face in the sleeper to muffle her heartbreak. Father closes the curtain, leaving her to her privacy.

He holds Livia in outstretched arms. Looks at her. She smiles, all warmth. She reaches for him. He allows her to grab his finger, but his eyes are cold and hard. His jaw trembles faintly.

Notations are swept aside. Livia and I are laid side by side on his workstation. I watch, mesmerized, as he holds my chin still and lifts a laser to my eye. "You will find each other again," he says.

The laser flashes and baby me opens her mouth to scream. I close my mouth and stare at him defiantly.

Little Livia is next. She cocks her head to the left and gives him a curious look.

"You will find each other and know. Just by looking each other in the eyes."

Livia wails at the flash. My father chokes back his emotions and pauses as if making a decision. "Put her in the cradle pod," he whispers. Roscoe places Livia in the tiny capsule. She's asleep instantly.

As Roscoe turns back, Father holds me tight. He kisses my forehead. "Go with her," he says. Roscoe takes me. Father turns away from him, unable to bear the sight. When he looks back, Roscoe is gone. So am I.

I turn to the Roscoe still in the room. The old one who shows me horrible Archives. "Where did you take me?" I ask.

"The Lower Levels," he says quietly. "The Orphanage."

Livia

"I am ready," my mother says as she emerges from behind the curtain to join our father, her face tearless and hard as stone. She lifts me from the cradle pod, and I remain asleep. My eyes move fast beneath the fragile skin of my eyelids. *Hopefully I am dreaming of something pretty.*

"It did not have to be this way," says my father.

"Of course it did. I could not live . . . if they had not." She pulls me close to her chest. "Besides, I should have left long ago. I hate this place. *Indra*. You can ignore the truth for only so long. We were never meant to be up here. The Founders did us all a disservice."

"It's not safe out there," he says.

"Not yet. Because we've stopped trying to make it so. Imagine if you'd turned your mind to making that possible?"

"Then our daughters would not exist. You cannot have everything."

Her face softens. "That doesn't mean we shouldn't stop trying. We owe the world to them. We must try to ensure that it welcomes them when the time comes."

"If only we could do that together."

She stares down at baby me, then up at the ceiling. Anywhere but his face.

"Where will you go?" he asks.

"I'm not sure. My mother has told me all my life that we're descendants of the Founders. That the blood of Atros is also mine and my children's. But now I know his mistakes are ours as well. I will survive, do not fear." She takes a deep breath. "I wish I was that certain about you."

My father moves toward her, his gaze unwavering, until they are very close. The baby me gives a small sigh from between them.

"Look at me, Delphia."

"I cannot."

"Please," he says.

Their eyes lock. Suddenly, she reaches for him, grasps him tightly, and pulls him toward her. She kisses him with ferocious abandon.

A good-bye kiss.

She pulls away and then she's gone.

CHAPTER 44

Lex

We are returned to Roscoe's study. *In a cavern*, I remind myself. *In Rock Bottom.*

No one speaks as we remove our Archive chips. There is no more to see. That is all that remains of our parents.

I can't look at Livia or Roscoe. I can barely tolerate my own racing mind.

"Where did she take me?" Livia asks, her voice smaller than I expect.

"Her music studio," Roscoe says. "She left you sleeping at the base of her air harp. She couldn't take either of you, she knew that. If she was found out, one of you wouldn't have survived. That was not an acceptable risk."

"And the imprint our father gave us both," I say, "why did he do that?"

"Only he and your mother have that answer."

"Great," Livia says. "So we'll never know."

"Did you never receive your father's research?"

Livia shakes her head. "Marius told me it no longer existed."

"Marius?"

"My guardian."

"Yes, yes, I remember Marius, but . . . Waslo had orders." His face boils with anger. "Your father's work is rightfully yours! You should have been given that long ago. You must retrieve it at all costs."

"What about our father's lab?" Livia asks. "Would it help if we went there?"

"I should think, if it's still hidden beneath your grandparents' island," answers Roscoe.

I ask, "The Island, does it have a name?"

"Orona. I haven't been there since you were born . . . The PCF raided it when they came after your father. They even instituted a no-fly zone over its airspace for the shame he brought upon Indra. I even heard rumors that riggers tried to demolish it, but it was booby-trapped, and they fled."

"That wouldn't have stopped a rigger, no way," I say. "What about that law? The one you told me about."

"The Law of Twins," replies Livia.

"Yes," says Roscoe.

"I never heard of it in the Academy. Even in Indrithian Customs."

"It is not something spoken of even in Proper circles. An older law, though still viable. Not mentioned because it is so rarely needed. The EX2 pill, after all, was your father's greatest creation."

"Not us?"

"Yes, of course." He barely smiles. "I am sure you take dosages yourselves." Livia and I look at each other.

Of course we do, I think. *Popping your daily EX2 is like getting up in the morning. You do it without even thinking. All thanks to one man. Our father.* "As you know, Indra must protect its limited resources. With the creation of EX2, multiple births would never be a problem. A single-child limit could be easily enforced." I can hear the bitterness creeping into his voice. "Want a child? Just trade the EX2 for the 2.2 Supplement. Conceive said child, birth the infant, and live pleasantly ever after." He sighs. "As long as you resume your daily EX2 dosage, you will be obeying Indrithian guidelines to the letter."

"Is it used down here?"

"Of course not."

He sounds so clinical. The geneticist side, I know, but I'm uneasy. He's talking about children, after all. He's talking about *us*.

It's been days since I've had my last dose. Livia, as well. I guess we will see what happens without our father's invention.

"But why did he create it?" I ask.

"To preserve Indra that is."

"Then he was a fool."

"Your father realized his mistake."

"Too late for him, and too late for us."

"Your father," Roscoe intones, "paid for his *foolishness*. We have all made mistakes that haunt us, do not think that gives you the right to . . ." His anger overcomes him.

"But our mother," Livia interjects. "It didn't work on her?"

"No. She could not conceive at all. Could not have what she wanted most in the world: a child."

"So our father created something new to help her. Reason to say it would probably help any woman with a similar condition."

"Yes, but his lab was destroyed, and Indra had no need of more children. There are some flaws it does not wish to fix."

Livia looks at me in the firelight. The imprint in her eye is shining. "The people of Upper Indra are wrong to fear us," I say, "and not to hope that we can show them a better future."

Livia

"There was no other option," says Roscoe. "Since your mother refused to abort the embryos and insisted upon bringing the babies to term, she and your father only had one choice. She was a wise woman, Delphia. I miss her every day."

Lex and I exchange knowing looks. She gives me a sad smile.

There is no reason to ask Roscoe, for we already know the answer. We heard it in his words: *I miss her every day.*

Truth be told, we probably knew long before that. Our mother is dead. And she has been dead for a very long time.

"What about our father?" I say. "What happened to him? After you took Lex to the Orphanage and Mother left me at her air harp?"

A strange look crosses Roscoe's face. Pain?

"I do not know," he says. "I never saw him again."

From the tone of his voice, I know Armand Cosmo's fate as well. Father's outcome was most likely the same as mother's.

I am an orphan, just as I always knew I was.

We are orphans.

"You are special, Lex and Livia," Roscoe says. "And even before you were born, Delphia already had a sense."

"A sense of what?" asks Lex. She's trying to keep strong, I know, yet I hear the faint shaking in her voice.

"That you would be special. *Very* special. And for that fact, your mother was eternally thankful."

For the first time in my life, I do not mind that word.

"The injections changed us," Lex says.

"I do not know if that is what he intended, but I suspect you are correct. He knew you would have to survive on your own."

"Then he chose for us to be different," I say.

"The drive to be different, to separate from the pack, is what motivated the Founders. Our history may show us to be slow to accept new ideas and ways of thinking, but we desperately need them. We can always be better. Though Indra believes itself to exist in a perpetual state of perfection, you must show them what they cannot see.

"Perhaps the injections were an influence, but they are only part of what makes you two so special. There is far more to your uniqueness than a twist in your genetics."

"More?" says Lex. "How much *more* can there be?" She's reached her limit, and soon she will explode. *Stay calm*, I want to tell her, but I would be a hypocrite, as my own heart is racing, my mind searching for answers.

"I get it, okay?" she continues. "Livia and I are *against the law*. We have these weird capabilities—"

"Gifts," says Roscoe.

"Maybe because of injections. Or maybe not. It doesn't matter either way." Her voice is growing strained. "But what more could there be? We are freaks, *end of story*."

"There is also the matter of destiny," says Roscoe. "Your destinies, to be exact."

"Destiny?" Lex is incredulous. "To the core with your destiny. *Destined* to be outcasts, perhaps, and you are *destined* to search for another set of saviors. Let's go," she says to me, "before he fills us with more nonsense and half-truths."

I stare up at her face. She is an angry stranger, yet she is also my sister.

I rise, standing next to my twin. But I cannot move with her. "I think Roscoe misspoke. Destiny is written in stone. It is the stuff of make-believe."

"An old man who still places his trust in make-believe is a danger to both of us."

"Make-believe, perhaps," he says, "but let an old man believe in something. In the days after former Earth but before New Indra, it is said that a pair of twins shaped the world into what it was to be. Andru and Atros, two of the Founders were twins, your ancestors. So some were taught, and yes, I am one who believes them, that twins will come again to unite our two worlds, the way they're supposed to be. Since the Lower Levels came into existence, every child on the day they are born is told that one day twins will arrive below in their seventeenth year."

"And do *what*?" asks Lex.

Roscoe takes us both by the hand. "Lead us all out of Indra."

Lex

Livia looks like she might pass out. I put my arm around her, and she's amenable to my touch.

"Leave Indra? We'll burn to a crisp," I say. "Everyone knows that. Burn up the second we step outside. The Earth is uninhabitable. That's why we came here in the first place."

"Not the entire Earth," says Roscoe. "Just the area bordering Indra. That is the only place that still burns, but only because Indra wills it. The radiation is a by-product of its own overworked ecosystem. But beyond that . . . an inhabitable world exists. Some have already escaped to the Outlands."

"How come more do not flee?"

"The journey is hard. The supplies, even harder to come by. It's not meant for all."

"How would they get past?" I ask.

"There is a tunnel. It comes up right past the irradiated area. It is long and dangerous, but two such as you, you have already faced much worse. All hope that you will go yourselves, and seek out others who you will find living in the Outlands. Bring them back to the Lower Levels. Unite their forces with the ones already gathered."

Sure, I think. *Just that easy.*

"With your help, Lex and Livia, we will take back all of Indra. Upper and Lower."

"I don't want to rule Indra," I say.

"Me either," Livia agrees.

"Then return it to its people," Roscoe says.

"That," I say, "is core-low crazy. Its people are what have gotten us here in the first place."

I don't believe it's possible, what he suggests. I don't think he misleads us, but I'm far from a dreamer.

Then I hear something. Livia, softly whispering in my ear. "We can do it," she says. "I feel it."

Together we have experienced most of what this world has to offer, and found it sorely lacking. I have followed orders, and she has conformed to Indra's highest social standards, and yet, here we are apart from it all. Unwanted. Roscoe may be crazy, but he is right, too. This world needs improving.

A shudder runs through my body. *Is it possible?* It sounds like a make-believe. Not something that could actually happen.

And yet, part of me feels it's possible. More than possible.

It's then that I think we're experiencing a groundquake. This close to the core, the results could be devastating. The books fall from the shelves and Roscoe huddles us under the doorway, where the structure is most stable. A low, slow horn whines.

"What's happening?" Livia asks.

A group of four rebels charges right past us.

Roscoe steps us back. "We're under attack. . . ."

It's my fault, I think. *Hauser . . . he's already here?*

"Girls," Roscoe says, "your time to make a choice has run out."

"If what you're saying is true," I say, uncertain, "if all that's true—and I'm not saying it is—then there is just one issue. What if we don't want to?"

"What my sister wants to know," says Livia, "is simply this: What if we choose *not* to be chosen?"

"I do not think you will," says Roscoe. The alarm's still whining, and we experience another groundquake, which I now realize is an explosion.

"Why not?"

"For the simple fact that your mother is out there. And she is waiting for you."

EPILOGUE

Livia

There are no crowds or well-wishers. They are fighting for their lives. They're fighting for us.

Just on the other side of the secret Rebel Base entrance, a squadron of PCF—Rock Bottom Patrol, Lex can hear, even from this distance, battling with rebels that have saved our lives, and changed them forever.

Zavier's men have packed enough supplies for the four of us. There is little time to discuss plans; we must trust what has been drawn up in advance. I accept this easier than Lex does. Her guilt weighs heavy upon her. She was one of them once. Now? It's too early to say.

We're as prepared as is humanly possible. Still, my body throbs with giddy unease.

"Just pretend we're going to Paradise Island," says Kane. Lex is already ahead of us, leading the way to the hidden tunnel. She doesn't like the sight of us together.

Our group is only four now. She will have to get used to it.

This resistance won't stand forever. The PCF won't stop hunting us. But I will try and do as Kane says, as hard as that will be, even if I know there is no peace to be found there either. Another make-believe.

"On our way to party with the Hubbies, that's all. Drink too much and lie in the sun. If you think that, then it will be easy."

His smile is for my comfort. I feel something join the uneasy excitement. Something that, in all the planning, I have not felt until this moment, in the face of despair.

Hope.

Lex

I check my wrist monitor. Eighty feet to the entryway.

"Promise me you won't make rash decisions. You'll work with the team," Zavier says. "Promise me, Lex. That you won't do anything crazy."

He's asking for promises I can't keep. He has none of his sister's charm or understanding. He's a blunt force . . . with the hands of a surgeon, I guess. There are complexities within us all. This journey to the Outlands will be a learning experience to us all.

"I can try, Zavier. That's all I can do."

He stares at me. Then, just for second, he does something I don't think I've seen him do.

He smiles.

I smile back. No promises I won't kill him.

Livia

"Forty-two more feet," she tells us. Her voice seems to travel past us and keep going, perhaps to the very end of the tunnel.

There are some things that cannot be planned, I think. *Some things for which you can never prepare.*

I have a sister now. She angers easily and is stubborn, possessive and reckless. She is my only family for now. She will grow to like me.

Lex. Kane. Zavier. Before I met them, I thought I was doomed to be a Proper Young Failure. Now?

I feel ready to be what I'm meant to be.

Lex

"Twenty-five more feet," I announce. We're almost there.

I turn to look back at Livia. She's already watching me like she's my protector, instead of the other way around. My sister. In the two days since we've met, she has tried to steal my only friend, because she is beautiful and arrogant.

She is also a killer.

"There!" says Zavier.

Livia

A blazing beam of light now illuminates our path. We stop for a moment to gaze at it.

The entrance to the hidden tunnel, I think, *is this where our ancestors first tried to forge out of Lower Indra?*

And it is now the beginning of everything else.

Lex & *Livia* Cosmo

"Ready?"

"Yes. Are you?"

"I hope."

We reach out in the dark and grasp hands.

Together, we move toward the light.

. . . to be continued.

ACKNOWLEDGMENTS

Kendall & Kylie's Acknowledgments

We want to thank our entire BIG family for always being so supportive. Especially our Mom, the most amazing Momager EVER! You make all of our dreams come true! To our Dad, for always being so encouraging. You always believe in us and taught us that with hard work anything is possible! We love you! To Liz, we never get tired of hearing your stories—we can't believe we created one together! Thank you for always being there for us and for all of the guidance you've given us over the years. You are the best!

Elizabeth Killmond-Roman's Acknowledgments

I first want to thank Kendall and Kylie for going on this incredible literary journey with me—it's been a blast! Working with you is never ever boring and I love it! To my fantastic husband, Mark, and wonderful son, Ethan, for your never-ending love, patience, and support! I am so blessed you are "my guys"! To my inspiring mentor and fabulous friend Kris Jenner, my appreciation for your trust and belief in me is truly incalculable. Thank you from the bottom of my heart! To my fantastic cheerleading section led by my mom, Mary Killmond, and in-laws, Hal and Jan Roman, followed by my whole family, and my incredible friends. I would be lost without all of you! Thank you all for always being there to encourage me along!

Everyone's Acknowledgments

To our cowriter, Maya Sloan, for taking the leap of faith on this story-telling adventure with us. Your tenacious and creative spirit truly helped make our story come to life. You are so talented and we are so grateful you shared your gift with us. To Karen Hunter and Charles Suitt from Karen Hunter Publishing, for your patience, cheering us along with enthusiasm and always having the faith that we'd make it to the finish line. To Louise Burke, Brigitte Smith, Jen Robinson, and Hilary Mau from Simon & Schuster, for believing in "Lex & Livia" and letting the story be told so it could be shared with our fans. To our editor Sean Mackiewicz, your insight and contribution were so vital to the fine-tuning of the story. Sorry about the endless nitpicking e-mails. To our super agents, Mel Berger and Lance Klein, and the whole team at WME. Mel, your guidance has been so invaluable. To our tireless support team: Jennifer Stith, Katherine Ellena, Matthew Ryan, Thomas Warming, Samantha Weil, Todd Wilson, Esq., Boulevard Management, Matthew Wallerstein, Esq., the always amazing Jill Fritzo and Michael Geiser from PMK*BNC, and our teacher Tiffany Pou. Thank you for always listening at every stage of this story and for your dedication to helping us with "Lex & Livia." We couldn't have done this without ALL of you!

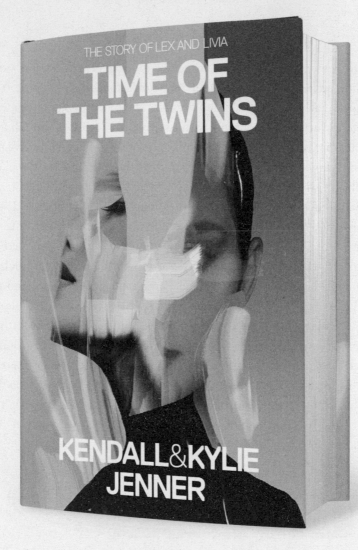

NOVEMBER 15, 2016

LEXANDLIVIA.COM

Regan Arts.